THE CASE OF

THE CROSSEYED STRANGLER

Anthony Celano

This book is dedicated with great love to the memory of
Enrico Celano   Grace Celano   Edward A. Celano

And

The heroic men and women of law enforcement, who continue
to serve and keep our communities safe under conditions few
can withstand.

1

The One That Got Away

Circa 1998

"It's the damn Bride of Frankenstein!"

-Jeanette Pergamint

THE TEENAGER NUDGED HIS FRIEND. "Take a look over there," he said, pointing to a person walking along the street

His friend rolled his eyes. "See if you can get her telephone number."

The first teenager pulled his head back, making a face. "Yeah, right," he replied as they continued on their way.

The stranger they noticed was a high school science teacher with a propensity to cross-dress. Usually the muscular educator could be seen presenting himself as a ruggedly handsome man attired in a suit and tie. Several inches over six feet, the fifty-one year old Everett Skidmore had broad shoulders, powerful hands, and a perpetual five o'clock shadow that contributed to his masculine appearance. These physical characteristics did much to undermine his attempt to achieve feminine credibility. Nevertheless, such drawbacks did not deter Everett from taking to the streets of Manhattan's West Village in drag.

As he neared the subway station at West 4th Street, Everett's attention was suddenly drawn to the screech of brakes. Turning toward where the sound was emanating from, he saw a frightened woman in her mid-thirties crouched in front of an oncoming taxi. The pedestrian froze as she braced herself for an impact that never materialized. After the cab came to a halt the attractive brunette gathered herself. Going on the offensive, she lashed out at the cabdriver.

"WHERE ARE YOU RACING TO?" she screamed.

"Get out of the way," said the cabbie, waving his hand dismissively. His gesture only served to further inflame the already agitated pedestrian.

"WHAT THE HELL ARE YOU TRYING TO DO...KILL SOMEONE?"

The bearded cabbie stuck his neck out of the driver's side window. He responded using the same tone. "ME? YOU'RE THE ONE WHO CROSSED AGAINST THE LIGHT! NOW GET OUT OF THE WAY, BITCH!"

The pedestrian stormed up to the driver's side window. "WHAT?" she shouted, "YOU HAVE THE NERVE TO CALL ME A BITCH AFTER ALMOST RUNNING ME OVER?"

The cabdriver sized up his adversary. Her white athletic footwear, charcoal track pants and workout jacket made her appear formidable. "Ahhh, go on," the cabbie said, deciding it best not to get into it with her.

"Let me have your number. I'm reporting you to the Taxi and Limousine Commission. Now c'mon, give me your license number," demanded the pedestrian.

The request for his hack number changed the complexion of their argument, influencing the cabbie. As the woman fished around her bag for a pen, the driver sped off with a sneer, using his middle finger as a means to convey adios. His parting gesture caused the perturbed citizen to detonate. Filling the air with angry expletives, she shook her fist menacingly at the departing vehicle.

The sight of the shaking fist unearthed a dark side in the cross-dressing science teacher. The vexed pedestrian morphed into an entirely different person in his eyes: she transformed into the wizard-like Granny Trapani, the elderly neighbor who traumatized Everett as a child many years prior. The illusion triggered a rare ocular malfunction, causing Everett's eyes to grossly cross. The teacher reached into his purse for the dark sunglasses he came to rely on when cloaking his secret affliction. Seeing or hearing Granny were the sole stimulants capable of causing Everett's eyes to deviate.

To the reality challenged Everett Skidmore, the pedestrian and the long dead Granny Trapani were now one and the same. Hearing the old woman's voice in his head was nothing new. Everett had been jousting with Granny's mental invasions since childhood. However, these materializations in human form were a new phenomenon that began after the recent death of Everett's mother. To date, the West Village pedestrian was the fifth female body that Granny assumed. In terms of extermination, Everett learned that doing away with Granny's human hijackings were much more difficult than disposing of her past fly and cat transformations.

"Eh, cafone," said the intrusive evil voice of Granny, telepathically calling Everett an uncouth peasant.

"Ignore her, dear—she always hated you," rang in the good voice of Everett's late mother, Adele. "I know now that she never did want you around her granddaughter."

"I know," Everett answered, stunned that his mother reached out to him when he was garbed in the clothing of a woman. As a rule she shunned him whenever he acted upon his inclination to cross-dress.

"Look-a-you…how you dress!" It was the evil voice, once again ringing in.

Everett absorbed the barbs stoically. He viewed Granny's ridicule as validation of his belief that she was of limited capacity when it came to understanding the life choices of others.

"Why you-no-go someplace?" asked the evil voice.

"Ignore her, dear," advised the good voice of his mother.

Caught between the two voices in his head, Everett shoes to ignore both, opting to concentrate on his latest assassination target. Unbeknown to the young woman almost struck by the cab, she was about to become the focus of a very disturbed man.

STILL MIFFED OVR HER run in with the taxi driver, Jeanette Pergamint replayed the incident in her mind as she continued home. As she did this she came to realize what caused her to walk against the light in the first place. Mounting financial obligations had begun to take their toll. She and her husband Forrest owned the Pergamint Bakery, a struggling small business located on MacDougal Street. In recent years sustaining the entity had become increasingly more challenging. The couple reached a point where they were compelled to take up residence in the rear of their store to make ends meet. A thick velvet curtain was installed to separate their living quarters from their storefront business. The barrier served as a grim reminder of their limited success.

Out of habit Jeanette regularly looked behind her when navigating the streets. It was a precaution she began taking when she first relocated to New York City. After traveling several blocks, she noticed the ominous presence of a large woman with red hair walking behind her. Feeling uncomfortable, Jeanette picked up her pace in an effort to establish a respectable distance from the stranger. Her elbows briskly pumped back and forth as she counted off the steps she took. Had she not accelerated, she might have overheard Everett talking to himself.

"Oh no, it's not going to be that simple," Everett said. "You can go ahead and speed it up all you like."

After taking one-hundred additional steps Jeanette was confident that she created a comfortable separation. She slowed to a normal pace before glancing over her shoulder. She was appalled to see that her efforts achieved nothing.

"Damn!" she said, sounding frustrated. More intent than ever to shake Everett loose, Jeanette ramped up her pace. She was sweating at the conclusion of the three-hundred additional steps she took. Unable to any walk faster, she turned around apprehensively, not being sure what to expect. What she saw confounded her: the stretch between the two had actually shortened.

"For God's sake, what the hell is this?" Jeanette asked loudly. Her voice traveled far enough for Everett to hear.

Jeanette began to wonder what was behind all of this oddness. Was it some feeble attempt at a pickup? Jeanette dismissed the thought: no one could be that socially awkward. Could her husband Forrest have learned about the banker? Could he have possibly retained this character to shadow her? Of course not, Forrest had no clue. Besides, even if he had suspicions, he lacked the funds to retain someone. Could it be Forrest's mother perhaps? No, never. She'd never spend the money. Old moneybags could squeeze a buffalo nickel until the buffalo dropped a load.

Jeanette decided to confront her provocation head on. But first, she needed to be certain that she was in fact being targeted. Once convinced, she'd apply the war paint. The bakery owner quickly devised a method of verification.

"Let me see what this big bastard does," said Jeanette to herself. Biting down on her lower lip, she turned onto MacDougal Street.

After taking a few steps down the block Jeanette crossed over to the other side of the street. Stepping onto the sidewalk she looked over her shoulder. To her dismay, her suspicions were now confirmed: her stalker also crossed over. Jeanette took up a position in front of a restaurant. Standing into the front window, she cupped her hand over an eye, giving the impression that she was looking for someone inside. In actuality, she was taking advantage of the glass reflection. All doubts were eliminated once Jeanette observed the woman halt underneath a no parking sign at the curb directly behind her.

"Oh, my God!" she said, now knowing for sure that she really did have a problem.

The reflection in the glass made facial recognition difficult. However, the dark sunglasses, handbag and red hair were clearly distinguishable. Taking in a deep breath, Jeanette spun around to face her antagonist. She was prepared to go toe to toe.

"LOOK, YOU..." said Jeanette, before she abruptly stopped talking mid-sentence. Her silence came after getting a *good* look at who she was up against.

Jeanette was in awe of the person towering over her. With confrontation no longer an option, the frightened business owner prudently backed off. How could she not?

"It's the damn Bride of Frankenstein!" Jeanette whispered under her breath, after turning away from her pursuer.

Pressing her bag tightly to her chest, she lowered her chin and quickly scooted down MacDougal Street in the direction of her home. Since she was so close to her destination, Jeanette was hesitant to dial 911. What would she tell the police? After all, what actually had been done to her? Left to her own devices, Jeanette began looking for pedestrians on the street for assistance. To her misfortune, there was no one in close proximity of where she was stationed.

"Where the hell is everybody?" she asked aloud as panic began to set in. Feeling vulnerable, she telephoned her husband Forrest. Jeanette felt some relief when he answered the phone on the first ring.

"Forrest, listen to me. I'm at the far end of the block. Are you home?"

"Yes, of course I'm home. I'm in the bakery, where else would I be?"

"Shhhhh...be quiet and just listen! I need you to come outside and meet me right now. I'm—" Their conversation was abruptly interrupted.

On the other end of the line, Forrest heard his wife scream. As Everett was manhandling his wife, Forrest could overhear sounds of a scuffle. "What's going on? What's happening?" yelled Forrest into the phone frantically. Realizing that he was not going to get a response, he rushed onto the street in search of his wife.

It was a very strong grip that tugged at Jeanette's hair from the rear. It came with enough pull to spin her entire body around, causing her to stumble to the ground. The clothes she wore provided little insulation from the hand that brushed her below the waist. Fearing a sexual assault, Jeanette began to swing wildly with punches that were enthusiastic, but pathetically inaccurate. The skirmish was brief, coming to an abrupt halt when the victim received a hard punch to her solar plexus. The blow knocked the wind out of Jeanette, incapacitating her. As she went down, Everett clamped his hands around her throat.

"*Not here, dear...NOT HERE!*" bellowed the good voice.

Hearing the imagined voice of his mother brought Everett to his senses. Quickly looking around, he realized that this was not the right time or place. The science teacher made a pell-mell dash for the subway, fleeing in the direction he came from.

"*What-a-you-do?*" asked the evil voice that entered Everett's head.

"This is just a taste," responded Everett, with a trace of satisfaction. "Now that I *know* your hiding place, I'll find you."

By the time Forrest arrived Jeanette was in a sitting position on the sidewalk. After a few minutes she was again breathing normally. Using the heel of both hands she rubbed her eyes energetically in an effort to clear her fogginess. Forrest helped his wife rise to her feet. He then immediately began peppering Jeanette with questions. As he awaited her response bystanders began to gather around them.

By the time the police and an ambulance arrived, Everett was long in the wind. While Jeanette's bruising was substantial, nothing was broken. The crime victim declined the offer to be taken to a hospital. While she agreed to file a police report, she informed the officers that she wouldn't be able to positively identify anyone. Truth be told, she wanted no part of pursuing the matter. The description she provided to the authorities was limited, describing her attacker as someone she believed to be a woman or possibly a man who dressed as a woman. Refusing to drive around in search of the suspect, Jeanette maintained that she couldn't make a positive identification. She told the officers that it was pointless for her to meet with detectives or view photos. Desperate to get home, Jeanette asked to leave. Efforts to convince her otherwise proved ineffective. All that the crime victim wanted to do at this point was to go home, lick her wounds, and put the matter behind her. Police involvement ended after their taking a report that reflected Jeanette being attacked by a big woman. The authorities then escorted Jeanette and her husband to their residence. As a result of Jeanette's lack of cooperation, the case was closed at the patrol level, never reaching the desk of a precinct detective for a follow up investigation. The incident became just another statistic.

BY THE TIME JEANETTE arrived home, she was physically drained. Her only desire was to shower and go to bed. Forrest stood outside the shower once again peppering his wife with a series of questions. The assault victim labored through his inquiry while washing. After drying off she was through being accommodating.

"Look Forrest, I'm going to bed," she announced. She fell onto their queen-sized mattress and closed her eyes. She felt a degree of protection underneath the thin sheet that covered her body. It provided all the security she needed to fall sleep.

Jeanette awoke to find her husband's arm around her. Feeling smothered, she managed to free herself without waking him. She rested quietly on her back reflecting on her life. As the daughter of an army major, she grew up privileged by military standards—but even so, she'd found life on the base too restrictive. She glanced over at her husband next to her, wondering if she should have regrets. Relocating to the Big Apple after marrying Forrest had seemed like the right thing to do. After all, New York City was an exciting place that came with few rules, lots of fun things to do and tons of opportunity. Their first apartment was on the top floor of an Alphabet City tenement, where the joys of baby oil, bathtub sex, and recreational drug use reigned as a priority. Sighing, she now viewed things in harsher terms, admitting to herself that they lived shabbily. Her initial attraction to Forrest stemmed from his having faith in her ambitions, unlike her father, who rejected her business plan with swiftness and certainty. His caustic remarks still embittered her. The major's dismissive words that called for her to "smarten up" continued to fuel her rebellion.

Jeanette found reassurance by snuggling closer to her husband, taking solace in the comfort of pressing her body against his. Her thoughts turned to how great things were after receiving the seed money from Forrest's late father. It was all so perfect then; it seemed they were on the way to building a successful enterprise. She was going to make her father eat his words. But that dream never materialized. Jeanette consoled herself by transferring blame for their lack of funds on her husband's inability to raise capital. The justification came with a cooling effect, causing her to move to the far end of the mattress, away from the man her father once called a Yankee milquetoast. Little did she realize that soon money would cease being at the forefront of her problems.

2

If At First You Don't
Succeed...

"And for goodness sake, stick to wearing suits!'

-Adele Skidmore

EVERETT READ ABOUT HIS ATTACK of Jeanette Pergamint in a neighborhood newspaper. The story contained enough information to make finding her easy. He was now aware that his demon was masquerading as the owner of the Pergamint Bakery on MacDougal Street.

"Be careful, dear," counseled the good voice of his mother. "And for goodness sake, stick to wearing suits!"

"Alright, alright," he replied, tired of Adele's harping.

The next day Everett rose long before dawn. He left his Tenth Avenue apartment wearing a conservative blue suit and a red tie. The teacher rode the downtown local to the West Village. The early morning hour saw few passengers riding the trains. Never shy around females, Everett attempted to strike up a conversation with a woman seated nearby.

"This is what it must feel like to ride a mechanical bull," commented Everett, casually addressing the forty-something-year-old passenger.

The commuter remained expressionless. After a few seconds she responded will coolness. "Excuse me?" she asked, her tone making it clear she didn't appreciate his overture.

Everett took the hint. "I'm sorry, no offense meant. I'm just saying that the train ride is bumpy." His reassuring voice came with a smile.

The teacher looked away from her as he bounced from side to side in his seat. Before he could come up with something clever to say, the evil voice of Granny Trapani rang in.

"You-no-see? She-no-like-a-you!"

Everett placed his fingers to his throbbing temple. Choosing not to respond to the evil voice in a public setting, he closed his eyes to avoid anyone from seeing his eyes cross. He then removed a pair of dark sunglasses from the breast pocket of his suit jacket, putting them on. Everett had long given up trying to solve the mystery of where his demon got her power to do the things she did.

"Don't be baited, Everett," were the maternal words of guidance he received from the good voice. It was advice that he heeded.

There was an hour of darkness remaining when Everett arrived at the bakery. The only activity on the block was an occasional vehicle passing through. As Everett expected, all of the businesses were still closed with the exception of the bakery. Looking into the front glass of the store he saw Jeanette, who was visible from the chest up.

"There you are," he said in a low voice, observing his target behind the counter. His delusional mind continued to see the bakery owner as Granny.

Everett watched his prey as she engaged in conversation with a man of around the same age and size as she. He had no choice other than to wait patiently for his chance. Instead of standing idly by, Everett circled the block, hoping one of them would leave the store before daylight approached. If this was not to be, he'd have no other choice but to return the following morning to try again.

❖

FORREST WAS EATING A BROWNIE that he lifted from the tray on the counter. "I should be back before lunch, Jeanette," he advised his wife, taking another brownie for the road.

"Why are you leaving so early?" asked Jeanette, who wasn't exactly thrilled at seeing her profit being gobbled up by her husband. "Look at the time."

"You know how my mother is, she's planning on our having breakfast before I take her to her appointment," he replied. "She simply insists on not rushing through meals."

"How silly of me, I forgot how she needs two hours to eat her grits. It gives her the time she needs to give *you* the third degree."

"Now stop it, Jeanette," protested Forrest. "I doubt she even knows what grits look like." His wife's reference to his being questioned by his mother went unaddressed.

"Don't forget to ask her for the money, and be sure to emphasize that it's *only* a loan."

"If that's what you want, I will."

"It's what *we* want. Make it clear that we intend to pay her back," she reminded.

"You know Jeanette, I'm not very optimistic that this will fly with her. You remember what she said last time about lending us money."

"I remember," she answered, with an edge to her voice. "Look Forrest, let's face facts. Mother dearest never liked me. That woman always considered me a negative influence that prevented you from being another Flash Gordon."

Forrest got defensive. "That's very unfair, Jeanette. She just doesn't see the sense in throwing her money into a business that she views as a losing proposition."

"Well *she* has to start thinking about prying open one of those bankbooks of hers to help out her only son!"

"Okay, okay, let me get going. I don't want to start the day off with an argument."

Forrest, as was usually the case, contained his inner resentment. It irked him that Jeanette's criticism was always directed at his mother, while her father never entered into the equation when the topic of borrowing money arose. When it came to being cheap, few could out-stingy the major.

Jeanette let out a deep breath, taking things down a notch. "You're right, let's not argue. Just do me a favor and *please*, see what you can pry out of your mother."

"Alright," Forrest answered unenthusiastically. "I'll try my best."

"Take whatever time you need, then—this is important to us. Don't feel bad about asking for the money…remember, she is not going to be able to take it with her."

"No, she can't take it with her," echoed Forrest.

As Forrest was exiting the store, he ran into Carson Wallace, the landlord's handyman.

"Hey Carson, pretty early for you to come by, isn't it?"

"I came now because I know you folks are the first to open up."

"Go right inside to the back. The pipe behind the toilet is leaking," advised Forrest over his shoulder as he left the bakery.

"No problem." Carson said, entering the store. "Good morning, Mrs. Pergamint."

"Good morning Carson, do you want anything?"

"No thanks, I'm fine. I got my music to listen to while I work," he said holding up a small orange transistor radio.

"Okay, then. Just keep the bathroom door closed if you play the radio."

UPON EVERETT'S RETURN TO the bakery, he cautiously peered into the front glass from the opposite side of the street. This time he was able to see that his quarry was alone. Jeanette stood in clear view behind the store counter. With darkness on his side, Everett made his move. The bakery owner was happy to hear the bell on the door jingle, signaling the first customer of the day. Turning to the front door, Jeanette took a hard look at the well-dressed man who resembled the person who previously attacked her on the street. After envisioning him wearing a red wig, she began to feel uneasy.

"It has to be," she thought. "He's about the right size, his nose is the same, the jaw and those sunglasses…it must be the same sicko!" But how could she be sure?

Knowing that Carson was in the back provided some degree of comfort. Jeanette watched warily as her customer looked over the freshly made blueberry muffins. Intending to appear nonchalant, Jeanette attempted to front a happy face. Failing miserably, she projected the image of someone on the verge of panic.

"How may I help you, sir?" she uttered slowly, struggling not to fracture her words.

"Give me a blueberry muffin and a large coffee to go," he directed. "Be sure the coffee is hot, black and without sugar." He spoke with authority, as if issuing orders.

His manner reminded Jeanette of her father, who addressed everyone as if they were an underling. Everett pointed to the blueberry muffins, indicating specifically which muffin in the tray he wanted. This dictatorial behavior was also reminiscent of the major. He too communicated in a way that left a person feeling subservient. Jeanette turned to face the street glass. Her back was now to her customer as she placed the muffin in a small take out bag. As she held the plastic lid over the coffee cup, she was still trying to decide what to do. Part of her felt that an attack from the rear might be imminent.

"You did say black, right?' she asked slowly, without turning around. She peered out the window hoping to see someone walk by. She was stalling in order to discreetly reach for the knife on the counter in front of her.

"I said black, with no sugar."

Jeanette slipped the knife between the lower two buttons of her blouse. Feeling the coldness of the blade against her flesh provided a small degree of comfort. Even though she was now armed, she knew that she was still vulnerable. Jeanette turned around just in time to see Everett slip on a pair of rubber gloves. She watched him walk over to the front door, lock it and pull down the door shade. Her worst fear was now realized. With a resolve that even surprised her, Jeanette held up the knife to her face. She stared Everett down on his return to his original position in front of the counter.

"You better leave now, or I swear, I'll kill you," she threatened. "CARSON! CARSON!" she yelled. With the bathroom door closed the handyman couldn't hear her call above the music.

Neither displaying the knife or her calls for help influenced the insane teacher. "You revealed yourself with that cabdriver, Granny," said Everett. "No disguise you assume will ever fool me."

"*I no-afraid-a-you!*" came the defiant evil voice that entered Everett's brain.

"And I'll not ever fear you again!" replied Everett, speaking aloud to his demon.

Jeanette tried to decipher the perplexing words of the deranged man. It was a mistake. Her plan to stab him went awry the moment the athletic teacher hurdled the service counter. Being caught by surprise, Jeanette had no chance. Everett smothered her body with his, using his weight to pin down the hand that held the knife. Now, on the floor and out of view from the street, her hope of rescue seemed non-existent. She tried in vain to mount a one-handed counterattack. From her disadvantaged position there was little she could do. The ensuing scuffle, while brief, gave her ample opportunity to look into her antagonist's face. After the sunglasses slipped off Everett's nose, Jeanette freaked out at the sight of his blue eyes being so grossly crossed. The look of her assailant was maniacal, and yet goofy at the same time. With Everett atop her, the bakery owner attempted to raise her knees against his torso in an effort to separate their bodies. Without considering the harm to herself, she desperately reached upward with her free hand to grasp the handle of the coffee pot, hoping to pour the hot liquid down on her attacker's head. But he was too strong, easily pulling Jeanette's hand away before it got close to the handle of the pot. With both her arms now pinned beneath his knees, Jeanette was helpless. Everett removed the red tie from his neck and

17

wrapped it around her throat. Her teeth began to grind as she felt the coarseness of the material ripping into her flesh.

"What do you want, you bastard?" she hissed, just before losing consciousness. Her final thought was of the major's shocked reaction to the news of her death.

The noise emanating from the front of the store finally penetrated the bathroom door. The handyman stepped out from behind the curtain singing along to *Hey Jude* with the Beatles. With a small wrench in his hand, he stepped to the front of the bakery where he witnessed the head of a middle aged, gray-haired man behind the store counter. A closer inspection revealed the man kneeling atop the bakery owner.

"What the hell!" Carson raised the wrench with every intention of braining Everett. But this ambition was short lived after making eye contact with the assailant. Carson halted his rescue effort, taken aback at the sight of the severely cross-eyed teacher.

Everett was now fully focused on Carson. Carson's hesitation was all it took to give Everett enough time to draw the handgun he had secreted in his waistband. The display of the firearm put an end to any heroics the handyman might have intended.

"I advise you to remain back," ordered Everett as he drew down on Carson. "This affair is between me and Granny Trapani."

Carson immediately dropped the wrench and raised his hands in surrender. "I hear you dude, I'm no hero." The streetwise handyman knew when it was time to back off.

"Let's walk back to where you came from...*now!*" Carson slowly did as instructed.

"Look man, I got me a wife and some kids home. Whatever goes down here ain't no business of mine." Thinking he might have interrupted a robbery, the handyman thought to add, "I got forty bucks on me, you could have that too."

"Keep moving," said the man with the gun.

Carson threw it in first gear, hastily making his way back behind the curtain. "Ok boss, whatever you say, man. You can count on me being blind, I don't see anything!" Carson was no fool—he knew there would be no pass for him. Using talk as a diversion tactic, he was just waiting for an opportunity to make his move.

"Put your hands on top of your head and face the mattress," ordered Everett.

"Sure thing boss . . . I hear you . . . anything you say, we're cool." The handyman felt certain that he was about to buy it.

"Step closer to the mattress."

Pretending to comply, Carson took his best shot. He sharply turned and made a desperate lunge for Everett's gun. The physical exchange caused an accidental discharge which resulted in Carson taking a bullet to his groin area. Pulling free from Carson's grip, Everett raised the weapon and fired one round into the handyman's chest. The impact caused Carson's body to jerk upward and then down onto the mattress that rested on the floor. Everett answered Carson's groaning with a round into his forehead. The science teacher paused for a few seconds to look with fascination at the blood flowing out of the holes in Carson. He stood mesmerized at the sight of the handyman's pink shirt as it turned red. The leakage slowly penetrated the fabric, gobbling up the dry patches of pink until the shirt transformed into a soggy crimson. Returning to the front of the store, the killer grabbed the bag containing the muffin and coffee he ordered. He then went behind the counter to retrieve his tie and sunglasses off the floor. Glancing down he saw Jeanette lying on her side. He felt the uncontrollable urge to administer more punishment. Acutely aware that he was running out of time, he took a chance. Everett unzipped his fly and began watering down the fallen body of Jeanette with his urine.

Once bled dry, he peeked outside to determine if the time was conducive for a getaway. Seeing the street clear, he unlocked the door and made his departure. On his way to the subway he took off his gloves and looked at his watch. There was plenty of time for him to find a sewer to toss the gun into and then get to work. After doing so Everett went on about his business believing that he successfully committed his fifth and sixth killing. His calculation was off by one.

3

Showtime Sally

"The poor bastard is among the great majority now."

-Rudy "The Hunch" Catlett

POLICE OFFICER NORMAN REESE, realizing he was out of condition, paced himself as he ascended the stairs. The five flights were challenging, even for a non-smoker like himself. Being weighted down with a gun, handcuffs, radio, bulletproof vest and other equipment didn't make it easier. Reese and his partner, Della Lincoln, were responding to the apartment of a chronic 911 caller who the cops nicknamed Showtime Sally. The job was always the same, with the police finding Sally naked on the floor aside her bed. They routinely rectified matters by lifting her back onto the mattress she supposedly fell off. Since Sally never spoke, the assumption was that she was partially paralyzed. Preferring to keep things uncomplicated, the cops left it at that.

"Are you alright, Della?" Reese asked, after realizing that his partner was a lagging behind—apparently, she was having a harder time negotiating the steps than he was.

"I'm fine Norm...just catching my breath," said Lincoln. The eighteen-year veteran of the force was fighting off a flu bug that was taxing her stamina.

"Take your time, there's no rush. If you want, stay where you are, I can go check it out."

There was no way Lincoln was going along with that suggestion. "Wait up a minute, I'm coming," she responded, wishing that the two Advil she took would begin to kick in.

Reese, a worrier, wouldn't let it go. "You sure you're okay? Did you take the Advil?"

"No problem, Norm. I'm *all better*...so stop with the questions."

"Hey, go scratch your ass," Reese said snippily. He found her lack of appreciation for his concern bothersome. The two partners often bickered like an old married couple.

As always, the officers found the front door to the apartment open. They proceeded directly to the bedroom. The wedding picture on top of the dresser featured a smiling bride, standing alongside a groom with an eyebrow mustache. The groom had the look of a man on his way to the electric chair. Although no longer smiling, the nude woman splayed out on the floor retained much of the youth displayed in the photo.

Sally was about fifty, give or take a few years. She was of average proportions and blessed with clear skin and few facial lines. Her short rust colored hair was wet, shining and combed back. There was a certain sparkle to her, even though her expression suggested sadness. Her nudity revealed a body that was clearly deficient of sunshine. Her face was doctored with lipstick and just the right amount of make-up. These enhancements could have been construed as being intentionally seductive. Her green melancholy eyes conveyed, to someone of experience, a starved look of want.

"How are you feeling, Sally?" asked Lincoln cheerily. As usual, the aided just blankly stared at the officer. "Take her legs, Norm, I'll take the other end."

"I can take the heavy side," he offered–mainly to avoid facing the downed woman.

"No, I got it, Norm."

While some might have seen benefit in taking in a free flesh show, Reese was not so inclined. Reluctantly, he took a position facing the aided while trying to avoid looking at

22

her private parts. He couldn't help but wonder how the motionless body got gussied up. Did she have intentions of going someplace? The prone woman's burning desire was beyond the scope of the officer's insightfulness. Reese was startled when his grip slipped after grasping the legs of Sally. Surprised to find that her lower limbs were lubricated, Reese wiped his hands dry against his uniform pants. Now looking, he could see that her moistened legs were shaved smooth. It was apparent that either someone was dolling her up or she possessed more mobility than people were being led to believe. It was an enigma that he had no interest in figuring out. Reese's unease intensified when the naked woman began telegraphing her thoughts through the medium of her eyes. At the speed of a ticking clock, Sally's bulging eyeballs played ping pong, darting from his face to the section below his gun belt and then back up again.

"You ready yet, Della?" Norm asked, finding Sally's message more creepy than alluring.

"Yeah, let's lift her up," instructed Lincoln. "Swing her at the count of three." On cue, Sally was airborne. After being swung up high on the third swing, she came down onto the center of her bed bouncing off the mattress.

When the partners returned to their vehicle, Lincoln advised the dispatcher that the condition was corrected and that they were again available for assignment.

"Poor Sally is pathetic. You never know what can happen to you in life, Norm."

Reese didn't share what occurred at his end of Sally. "They should think about tying her down in bed."

"That's a thought. Let's head into the house, it's almost time to call it the end of tour."

As they proceeded into the precinct, the sector received another call from the dispatcher. "Six-David…"

"David, standing by," advised Lincoln.

"Why are you answering? We're going off duty. Let them hold the job for the day tour."

"It may be important," answered Lincoln, who was feeling much better.

"Investigate shots fired at the Pergamint Bakery on MacDougal Street."

"On the way, central," said Lincoln, turning to her partner. "See, what did I tell you?"

"Hey, go scratch. When you end up sick in bed, don't cry to me," replied Reese tartly.

"Stop with the worry," Lincoln replied, activating the emergency lights.

NEARING THE BAKERY, THE officers saw a thin older man in the street waving them down. Wearing a blue long sleeve shirt, the man sported a Darwin-like snow white beard. "It's murder!" he shouted excitedly, rushing over to the open window of the police car. "My worker has been murdered and my tenant strangled!"

Officer Lincoln exited the passenger side door. "Alright sir, calm down."

"Come quickly, please!"

"Where are they?" asked Lincoln, stepping onto the sidewalk.

"They're inside the bakery. C'mon, hurry! The poor woman was left for dead."

"Who are you, sir?" asked Lincoln, after noticing that the man had a crooked back.

"My name is Rudolph Catlett, I'm the landlord here. This is my property," he said pointing to his building. "I called 911. Now come inside, please...hurry!"

Rudy Catlett was a hunchback. His condition, along with his profuse whiskers, made him a readily identifiable figure. To the people living in the West Village he was Rudy the Hunch. Rudy led the police to a dazed Jeanette Pergamint, who was sitting on the floor behind the store counter with her head resting lazily against the counter wall. Lincoln immediately requested that an ambulance and the patrol sergeant respond to the scene. "Central, put a rush on that bus," ordered the officer.

As Lincoln did her best to comfort Jeanette, Rudy led Officer Reese to the back of the store where the body of Carson Wallace had fallen across the mattress. The Officer began checking the handyman's vital signs. He didn't need to. The bullet holes, the blood-soaked clothing and Carson's stillness made it obvious that he was dead.

"Forget it, he's a goner," advised Rudy with disgust. "The poor bastard is among the great majority now," he said sadly. Rudy began to caress his white beard.

Reese nodded in agreement. The officer updated the dispatcher, advising of the homicide. He requested that the precinct detective squad respond to the location.

Detective Gary DeCesare, who was newly assigned to the precinct squad from the narcotics division, was the first investigator to arrive at the scene. By the time he got there, Jeanette was on her feet, wanting to change into dry clothes. Appearing worse than she actually was, Jeanette was tended to by the responding emergency medical technicians. For the second time within days, she refused to go to the hospital.

DeCesare recovered the victim's soiled garments for safeguarding and later analysis. Unfamiliar with the proper handling of non-narcotic related evidence, DeCesare made the mistake of sealing Jeanette's clothing inside a plastic bag. The detective then had a uniformed police officer voucher the bag as evidence. He later learned that it would have been best to let the urine dry out naturally in the open air, with each soiled article of clothing later individually wrapped to prevent cross contamination.

When the forensic team arrived, they processed the bakery as two crime scenes. The results were limited. In Jeanette's case the only physical evidence consisted of her soiled clothing. The marks on her neck made it clear that someone tried to strangle her. Considering there was a struggle, it was surprising that no skin, hair or clothing evidence was gathered from underneath Jeanette's fingernails. The bullets that killed Carson were later removed by the medical examiner and sent to the ballistics unit for analysis.

DeCesare was later joined at the bakery by his partner, Detective Sheridan. Sheridan rushed to the scene from a car wash where he was having the squad's vehicle cleaned.

"Did you make any notifications, kid?" asked the burley veteran detective.

"Not yet," answered DeCesare.

"I'll take care of it for you," said Sheridan. After taking a closer look at Jeanette, he asked, "Isn't this woman going to the hospital?"

"The bus was here. The EMT's checked her out and left. She refused medical aid."

Sheridan was taken aback at hearing this. "What's her name?" he asked.

"Jeanette Pergamint."

Sheridan approached the crime victim. Leaning in close, he spoke to Jeanette in a relaxed voice.

"Do you know the person who did this to you, Ms. Pergamint?"

"No," she replied in a scratchy voice. The strangulation had damaged her vocal cords.

"Can you describe the person for us?"

"He was goofy...he looked like Jerry Lewis." She strained to get the words out.

Sheridan could see that she needed time. Her raspy words were painful to listen to. He raised his hand, signaling her to stop talking. "Jeanette, listen to me, you *have* to go to the hospital before we talk."

"No, I'm alright."

"You don't understand. You *have* to go," the detective insisted. "There is no choice here. Besides, they'll give you something to make you feel better."

After some doing, Sheridan managed to convince the crime victim that it was in her interest to go to the hospital. He then turned to his partner. "Have a radio car take her. You should go along with them and I'll tie up the loose ends here. I'll round up everybody we need to talk to and we can sort this shit out when we regroup back at the squad later."

"Okay," replied DeCesare. "You know we have another body in the back."

Sheridan looked at his partner with surprise, "Another body?" Sheridan was directed to the second victim. He returned to DeCesare after a few minutes. "The DOA took one close to his nuts. You saw that, right?" Sheridan asked.

"I did."

Sheridan, with a suspicious expression on his face, raised his eyebrows "Is this woman supposed to be married?"

"Yeah, I think so."

"So where was the husband?"

"I don't really know."

"Take note of where this guy was dropped, and of the time," Sheridan advised. "So I ask you again, where was the husband?"

DeCesare shrugged his shoulders. He had no answer.

"Interesting . . . ain't it, kid?"

4

Duke Or Mook

"How we ever retired John Wayne as a role model is something I'll never understand."

-Detective Oliver Von Hess

DETECTIVE SERGEANT AL MARKIE and Detective Oliver Von Hess, both newly assigned to the Strangler Task Force (STF), chatted casually as they drove over the Brooklyn Bridge. Their orders were to report to Inspector Harry McCoy at his office in headquarters.

"So Ollie, what's the story with McCoy?"

"They say he's a gentleman. He's been in the Major Case Squad for years."

"Is he an old timer?"

"Oh yeah, he's a dinosaur like me. He may have even come on the job before I did."

"You guys had to rap your nightstick on the sidewalk for help back then," teased Markie.

"Very funny," said Von Hess. "McCoy is tight with the chief of detectives. Word is their joined at the hip. They were in the same academy class."

"That should be good for us. He'll get whatever he asks for," observed Markie.

HEADQUARTERS, A PROTECTED FIEFDOM, is home to the movers and shakers of the department. To anyone on the outside looking in, everything appeared to be nice and orderly. Those assigned to the building dutifully wear their identification card affixed to their outermost garment. Most feel that it's a great place to be for someone looking for advancement. It was where Inspector McCoy wanted to be. While many officers looked ahead to retirement, McCoy dreaded it. Aside from the financial reward that accompanied his elevated status, he had another reason for remaining on the job. Lots of people could boast of big wages and fancy titles. But how many could claim to have thousands of gun toting valets at their disposal?

At sixty-one-years-old, McCoy was nearing the end of his career. In a couple of years he'd be aging out. In good health and still ambitious, the inspector couldn't envision himself relegated to sitting in a yard listening to a ballgame with a baseball cap on his head. *That* fate was for some other old fart...not him. Worse yet was the notion of hoisting a few at a local bar every afternoon, telling war stories that began with, "Back in my day . . ."

An Air Force veteran, the soft-spoken inspector with the crew cut sported a manicured mustache that ended exactly at the corners of his mouth. When he rolled up his sleeves a tattooed green shamrock could be seen adorning one forearm and a bald eagle draped in a flag visible on the other. Affixed to the belt that held up his pants was a leather ammo pouch that was cracked due to aging. The long barrel Smith & Wesson .38 caliber revolver he packed dominated the right side of his body.

McCoy made it a lifetime practice to stand erect. His entry into the department met with a complication that took the form of a height requirement. He spent the week prior to his physical exam sleeping on a wooden board in the hope of extending himself. The tactic paid off because he managed to squeak through by a sixteenth of an inch. It helped that a detective from Sligo did the measuring.

The inspector was waiting patiently for the arrival of his new task force members. "Hey, Silvie," called out the inspector from his office to one of the detectives assigned to his unit. "Put them in the conference room when they get here."

Detective Silverlake, whose duties included greeting visitors to the office, was sitting at his desk when Markie and Von Hess arrived. "Sergeant Markie?" he asked, looking at Von Hess.

"I'm Ollie Von Hess, this is Sergeant Markie."

Silverlake nodded. "Stand by a minute, while I call the inspector."

Inspector McCoy picked up his office phone on the first ring. "McCoy," he answered.

"They're here boss." After hanging up the phone Silverlake rose from his seat. "The inspector wants you in the conference room. He's been waiting."

"There was a problem on the bridge, advised Von Hess, making up an excuse for their tardiness.

"Don't worry about it, he's not upset."

Markie and Von Hess were escorted to the empty conference room in silence. Looking around, Markie was curious as to where the other members assigned to the task force were. "Where's everybody else?" questioned the sergeant.

"You're it," answered Silverlake.

"It's just us? What happened?"

Silverlake shrugged his shoulders. "It got cut back I suppose, but don't go by me, I'm just another one of the grunts around here."

Markie and Von Hess exchanged bewildered looks. Judging by his appearance, they could see Silverlake had been around for years. "Have you been working here long?"

"Yeah, I've been here forever. I got thirty years on the job and I've been here close to twenty-five of them."

"That's a pretty good run," commented Markie.

"Yeah...and I'm still a third grader!" pointed out Silverlake.

"Why is that?"

"Because we got a chief who thinks a house-mouse shouldn't get grade. He forgot that I didn't get here because I was a house mouse."

"How did you get here?"

It was a tale Silverlake enjoyed telling. "I'm a cop doing a late tour, in the bag, with my partner," he began. "It's about three in the morning when we spot two mutts in a car parked in a desolate area. So, being young and full of piss and vinegar, we give it a look see. We come up with a gun in the car. Turns out, one guy killed two cops in Corpus Christie, Texas, two years earlier. Everybody and their sister wanted this mother."

"That was a good collar," commented Markie.

"They threw up the confetti with that pinch. Next thing I know it's like...*presto*, we both get the gold shield and land here. How's that for good fortune?"

"Where was that, I think I remember reading about it," said Von Hess. "That happened in the Bronx, right?"

"Yep, in Hunts Point," acknowledged Silverlake.

"Your partner is still here too?"

"Nah, he retired a few weeks ago. He went down to Arizona to open a car dealership with his brother. That empty desk in the corner over there was his. It's just waiting for the next contract to transfer in and assume ownership."

When Inspector McCoy walked in on their conversation Silverlake immediately left the conference room. After he was gone the inspector got right down to business.

"Gentlemen," began McCoy, "welcome. This task force was formed to address a disturbing pattern of strangulation homicides in Manhattan. Luckily, so far these killings have garnered little attention from the press. But they can't be expected to go unnoticed forever. Eventually people are going to wise up. When that happens we'll be facing the heat that comes with a serial killer. Needless to say, there's an urgency to get ahead of this thing."

The two newly minted task force members sat somberly. It was Markie who was the first to speak up. "How many bodies do we have assigned to the task force inspector?"

"You're it. Chief of Detectives Randolph feels a sizable task force would draw attention to the problem," advised McCoy. "If we need support, I've been assured that we'll get it."

Markie nodded. "There's been nothing in the media about these killings, then?"

"Nothing came out that created any buzz. As it stands, our pattern remains under the radar."

"How could it go this far undetected?"

McCoy was tart in his response. "Let's stay focused on what we need to do moving ahead, sergeant. You men were handpicked for your ability, not on the basis of *who* you know. You'll report directly to me and are not to discuss these cases with anyone else." Markie and Von Hess nodded their understanding. "You'll be working hours and days that will vary depending on the needs of your investigation. That'll be entirely your call."

"What about today?"

"Today you men are working a day tour. You've been on the clock since 8:00 A.M. If you make headway at any point, of course you'll remain on duty to continue working the case. Are there any questions?"

"Where are we turning out of, inspector?"

"Right here," McCoy answered. "This is your new home. To save time you can call in from the field when you go on and off duty. Make your own hours as you see fit. All reports, overtime slips, lost time requests and so on will be submitted to Detective Silverlake. He'll take care of the processing. Anymore questions?" There were none. "Good. Inside this envelope you'll find folders," said the inspector, producing a brown manila envelope. "The folders contain some of the particulars concerning each strangulation case."

The inspector advised that earlier that morning the strangler struck again, this time victimizing a woman and a man in the West Village. The information he received thus far indicated that the incident involved the killer using a firearm for the first time. It was also the murderer's first attack on someone other than a woman. The inspector stated that the female victim survived thanks to the intervention of a handyman, who subsequently became a homicide victim himself.

"I'd like you to get down to the West Village as soon as you can to get started."

"No problem, inspector," said Markie, passing the envelope to Von Hess.

After concluding the meeting, the inspector pulled Markie outside of the conference room for a private conversation. "Call me anytime, sarge...night or day. If things are breaking or if you run into a problem, I want to know about it. Otherwise, post me once a day so I can remain up to date. There's a lot riding on this for me."

"No problem, inspector."

"You'll find that you have a long leash with me. I'm giving you the tools and the leeway to get it the job done. Trust me, success in this will be well rewarded, *that* you can take to the bank. I'm talking promotion...lieutenant's money for you."

"Got it boss, thank you, I'll do my best."

"Okay, then. Just to reiterate, crack this and good things will come to me," said the inspector with a wink. "And *that* could mean better for *you* down the road."

"I hear you boss."

Markie returned to the conference room so that he and Von Hess could go through the information provided by the inspector. While doing this, Markie received a call on his cell phone from his ex-wife.

"Flo, I gotta call you back. I'm in a meeting," the sergeant advised, brushing her off. She'd have to wait.

Their review was completed in fifteen minutes. "Ollie, let's go see where things stand with this last one in the West Village. After that we'll figure out what to do next."

"Very good, boss," acknowledged Von Hess.

"I don't want us to come off as if we are out to critique the work being performed by the squad detectives. There's no sense in alienating anyone, so let's make sure they understand that we're there to support their efforts in solving *their* case."

"Understood," answered Von Hess.

"Ollie, do me a favor. Talk to Silverlake and get us a department car to use. I gotta make a quick personal call. I'll see you downstairs in a few minutes."

Once alone Markie dialed up his former wife. As the phone rang, he wondered what Flo wanted. He remembered how pleasant her voice used to sound when they got along. The fond memory quickly faded once their conversation was underway.

"Hello," she answered.

"It's me, everything okay?"

"Where are you?" she demanded to know. "I've been trying to reach you at home, are you away or something?"

"No, I've been around. Just a little busy that's all."

"I left you a message on your answering machine. Don't you ever listen to it?"

"I guess I must have forgotten to check. Why didn't you just call my cell phone?"

"If I remember right, you said to call you *only* in an emergency," she said with a bite.

That was a rule from when they were married. Markie didn't want to go there so he let it go.

"Alright, I stand corrected. Now that you got me, what's up? Is it anything important?"

"That depends whether or not you consider the well-being of your child important."

He took the intentional poke knowing that whatever was eating at Flo couldn't be anything too serious. If it were, there'd be no time for beating around the bush.

"Which one Flo, I have two sons and a daughter. Who are we talking about, Matthew, Karen or the little guy?"

"I'm talking about the little guy, our nine-year-old lover boy!"

Matthew was a senior in high school who played on the football team and Karen was a sophomore who swam for her school. Because they were athletes, the sergeant was confident they could take care of themselves. The little guy however was another story.

"What happened?"

"I received a call from the principal to go to the school because Richard got in trouble," she said. Flo remained quiet, waiting for his reaction.

Markie always held the suspicion that whenever his wife procrastinated she did so with the intent of getting under his skin.

"*And?*" he asked impatiently.

Once Florence heard his exasperated response, she continued. "So, I had to leave work to truck all the way over to the school to see the principal. That left only Rose to hold down the dental office. We had two emergency appointments scheduled."

"Look Florence, can we just get to the point? I have enough things to do over here. I don't need a song and dance about somebody's impacted wisdom tooth."

"Don't get testy with me! Those days are over!" she responded sharply.

Markie caught himself before things could escalate. Taking a deep breath, he continued their dialogue in a more respectful fashion. "You're right, Flo," he lied. "I didn't mean to get testy. Now *please*, just tell me what happened." His change of tune worked.

"The principal said that Richard passed a love poem to a girl in class. Can you imagine?"

"Richard passed a love poem? What kind of a love poem can a nine-year-old write?"

"This kind," she answered. Florence then cited a stanza from their son's poem. "Your lips are like a porterhouse steak, thick and juicy!"

"You've got to be kidding me...you aren't serious."

"No joke Al, I'm dead serious. The principal wanted to know where he got such things in his head. He's worried that the girl's parents might make a big deal over this and say their daughter was traumatized, so that they can then sue the city."

"Traumatized? This is incredible...so what's the wind up here?"

"Just this, the principal is recommending that Richard go for a psychological evaluation."

"What? Did somebody drop that tub of lard on his head?"

"This is no joke Al," stated Flo.

"You aren't going along with that bullshit, are you?"

"It was just a suggestion; I don't think we *have* to do anything."

Markie was pissed off. "Richard's going to the Catholic school if they push this. I don't care if I have to work three jobs!"

"I don't think it will come to that."

"How is the boy doing?"

"Crazy as it seems, this fiasco made him the most popular kid in the school. All of a sudden everybody is his friend. Go figure!"

"Do you need me to talk to Richard or anything? Go up to the school maybe?"

"No, I took care of everything *myself* as usual, so you don't need to do anything. I just thought *you* should know."

"Alright, now I know. Post me if anything more comes of this," he said. Markie hung up wondering if there was anything he should do. He came up dry when it came to ideas.

The sun was shining when Markie exited One Police Plaza. He got in the passenger side of the waiting unmarked car. As Von Hess drove the sergeant noticed a young family walking on the street. A man, who was wearing a backpack, was pushing a child in a stroller with one hand while holding a baby bottle in the other. Walking alongside him was a woman, likely his wife, sipping coffee. Although his thought were on his young son, the sight of this registered somewhere in the sergeant's head, unearthing sentiments that were buried in his subconscious.

"Your two kids are big now, right Ollie? Things are going well with them, right?"

Von Hess turned to look at Markie, thinking the question odd. "Yeah, my two girls are fine. One's an accountant and the other one is a nurse who is engaged to a doctor. Why do you ask?"

"No particular reason."

"You have one daughter, right sarge?"

"Yeah, I got one girl and two boys."

"I would have liked a boy to round things out," confessed Von Hess. "My wife didn't want any more kids though so that idea was out."

"Yeah, I guess wives do pull the strings in that department. Were you involved a lot with the girls when they were growing up?"

"Nah, not so much, you know how things are with the job. I was working most of the time. My wife handled everything, even the money."

"You didn't go to their games and stuff?"

"Me? Not a one. My wife was the one who represented the fan club."

"Because they were girls, you didn't go?"

"Oh no, not at all," Von Hess replied. "I was always working. You know I was a pretty good football player as a kid, a quarterback. My old man came to just one game."

"You wanted him there, right?" Markie was curious to hear his driver's response.

"Not really. I was having a great game; I threw two touchdown passes by halftime. He paced up and down the sidelines like he had money on the game."

"He must have been really proud of you."

Von Hess laughed. *"Proud? Do* you want to know what he said at the half?"

Markie took a guess. "What did he say, you could do better?"

"He said I should sit my ass down and give somebody else a chance!"

The sergeant was puzzled. "Why would he say a thing like that?"

"He was afraid I'd get hurt. Funny thing though, to me, it showed he cared. That was better than his coming to a hundred games," reflected Von Hess. "Besides, how many fathers went to games back then?"

"I don't know," answered Markie, who grew up without a father.

"Not too many. If daddy started showing up every place you were at, he'd be doing you no favors. There was no babying back then."

"I hear you—those were the days of only one winner," observed Markie.

"Hey, don't get me started. How we ever retired John Wayne as a role model is something I'll never understand."

The statement made by Von Hess impacted Markie. Returning to his mind was the image of the stranger with the backpack, pushing the stroller. The sergeant cringed at the very thought of presenting such an image in public. In the macho world of cops and robbers that Markie traveled in, any perception of weakness would inevitably lead to being tested...and on the street that could get you killed. When it came to *his* son, the scales weighed heavily in favor of The Duke. It was Rooster Cogburn and Ethan Edwards all the way. A sit down with some shrink for writing a silly poem? Not on Markie's watch. The little guy was going to grow up strong, and that process was going to start with his learning how to stand up like a man. There would be no hand-wringing coming from the budding poet. That decided, all Markie had to do now was get on his knees and beg his ex-wife to see it his way.

5

For Better Or For Worse

"That's right, dear. Let them know where the power lies."

-Adele Skidmore

UNAWARE THAT JEANETTE PERGAMINT SURVIVED, Everett was able to return to work at his East Harlem high school with a clear head. While his victim was still dealing with the aftermath of the attack, the science teacher was preparing for his first class. He meticulously lined up desks and raised the window shades to let daylight into the classroom. After erasing the blackboard, he centered his own desk at the front of the room. He preferred the old school positioning of the furniture. The teacher felt that being front and center enhanced his image as an authority figure. He equated restricting himself to a corner to being an afterthought. By the time the bell sounded Everett was satisfied that everything was righted. Sitting high in his chair he awaited the students.

Rambunctious voices echoed throughout the halls as teenagers made their way to class. The boisterousness gradually subsided at the sound of the final bell. Once the students settled into their seats Everett shocked everyone by announcing a surprise quiz. As he passed out the exam papers he took pleasure in listening to the groans of the students. The ability to manipulate the climate was the ultimate power trip for Everett. As a child no one listened to his woes. But now, in this environment, people were compelled to listen to him.

"That's right, dear. Let them know where the power lies." said the good voice of Everett's late mother. *"Remember to be firm, but fair. No one can expect any more than that."*

At some point Everett would alleviate the concerns of his students. His strategy was to play the role of the good doctor who provides the salve that calms the sting of the lash wounds he inflicted. In effect, he secured fidelity by creating dependency.

"Take it easy people and relax. It's a multiple-choice open-book test. Between your textbook and class notes, you should have no problem passing," assured Everett.

Several in class were without a textbook, causing Everett to instruct the ill-prepared to partner with those who had books. As the teens fleshed out answers, their teacher slipped outside the room. Everett stood with his back to the corridor monitoring those inside the room by staring into a small pane of glass that was imbedded into the open classroom door. The reflection provided an ample view of half the students. Since it was an open-book test, doing this served no legitimate purpose. The true benefit of such sneakiness was in catching cheaters during non-open book exams. It was just one of the many tricks the educator employed to stay one step ahead of his charges.

JEANETTE LEFT THE HOSPITAL feeling dirty and damaged. Self-conscious, she insisted that Detective DeCesare return her home so that she could shower and find something to hide the ligature marks on her throat. When they arrived at the bakery she was disheartened to see that the forensic teams were still hard at work. Most bothersome was Carson's bloodied body spread across her mattress. Unable to shower, the crime victim settled for a white chiffon scarf that she placed around her neck. With the unsightly marks now concealed, Jeanette felt comfortable enough to go the precinct. The crime victim and DeCesare arrived at the squad ahead of Markie and Von Hess by less than an hour.

Once at the squad Jeanette was asked to look through old arrest photos of white men between forty and sixty years of age. As she did this, DeCesare made sure there was an ample supply of green tea. By the time Jeanette finished, several mugs of the beverage had been consumed. Although unsuccessful in identifying anyone, Jeanette remained undiscouraged.

"Any luck?" asked DeCesare.

"He wasn't in any of those photos," she answered in a scratchy voice. The trauma she sustained caused damage to her vocal cords. It would take awhile before Jeanette would be able to speak normally.

"Are you feeling okay?"

"I'll be fine, thank you."

"I'll be with you in a few minutes. Can I get you ore tea?" asked the former narcotics officer.

"No," answered Jeanette, curtly. The crime victim was in no mood for pampering, more tea or procrastination. "What's next on the agenda?"

"We'll be interviewing you shortly. Your husband is here; I'll send him in to see you."

When Forrest first entered the room Jeanette was glad to see him. The joy in their reuniting soon deteriorated. She resented his second-guessing her, as if what occurred at the bakery was attributable to her own negligence. "Why didn't you call the authorities when he first came in?" and "How could you not call for Carson?" were received as blistering critiques. She answered his questions with just a few words, then only gestures. Eventually she ceased to respond at all.

"Your mother..." she finally said, "did she give you the money?" Forrest lowered his head as if he were caught looking at dirty pictures. "So you didn't get a check?"

When Forrest shrugged, Jeanette looked away in disgust. They sat stiffly in their chairs, each consumed with thoughts of revenge. Jeanette fixated on her being urinated on, an act so vile that it warranted a bloody payback. Forrest viewed revenge in more epic proportions. Who entered his mind was Francois Rabelais, whose writings told of Gargantua, the fictional giant who took a whopping piss that felled masses of people. Forrest pictured himself drowning his wife's attacker in his own flood of yellow fluid.

40

MARKIE AND VON HESS entered the squad soon learning that their presence was no surprise to the detectives assigned to the precinct.

"I'm Detective Sheridan. We received word that you were coming to help out," said the squad detective. "Welcome, we're glad to have you as part of the team."

"That goes for me as well, sarge. I'm Detective DeCesare."

Markie had been around long enough not to be swayed by such blatant ass-kissing. "Is your squad commander working?" asked the sergeant.

"Our lieutenant's out sick," advised Sheridan. "He's got mononucleosis."

"That's the kissing disease," said Markie. "It takes a long time to get over that. What about a whip?" he asked, looking for a second in command.

"Gone," answered Sheridan. "He put in his papers last week. We've been told a replacement will be coming...but not to hold our breath."

"They didn't assign you guys a temporary boss?"

"No," answered Sheridan. "By the way, Manhattan homicide called, sarge, —they advised that they won't be responding because you guys from the special task force were going to be here."

"I guess news travels fast," commented Markie, thinking that there was a nose or two out of joint over their presence. "What have you got here?"

"This was almost a double. The DOA is a handyman for the building. He's a gunshot victim. The female store owner was strangled and left for dead. She survived."

"How did you guys make out with interviews?"

"We didn't get that far, sarge. We were just about to start them when you walked in. The victim is waiting in another room to be spoken to," apprised Sheridan.

"Who is catching this case?"

DeCesare answered up. "It'll be my case, sarge."

"Did the victim look at photos?"

"Yeah, she just finished. We got negative results."

"Okay, how about we do this. You and Ollie interview the victim," said Markie, pointing his thumb to Von Hess. Once that's done, get a sketch made up of the perp."

"Right boss," responded DeCesare, taking a quick look at Sheridan to see his reaction.

Looking wounded, Sheridan remained silent. He didn't like the idea of orders being given by the visiting sergeant. His displeasure was evident by his expression. That touch of expressiveness was going to cost him. Picking up on the look, Markie promptly responded.

"Sheridan, you prepare a case folder, do the unusual report for the borough and notify the family of the victims."

"Check," answered Sheridan, who wrote his instructions down on a pad.

As the detective was writing, the sergeant gave him more jobs to do. "After that, figure on conducting a canvass," directed Markie. "Oh yeah...before the canvass, do a criminal history check on the two victims and make sure we have elimination prints taken of everybody."

Sheridan knew he was getting the business. "No problem," he answered calmly, without looking at the sergeant.

❖

AVERAGED IN SIZE, DECESARE was a man with a full head of black wavy hair. In his early 30s with less than six months in the bureau, the detective was still acclimating himself to working in the squad. He had no problem following Markie's directions, especially after seeing Sheridan fall in line. This being his first homicide, DeCesare was amenable to soaking up knowledge from the senior investigators. He earned his gold shield while working in the narcotics division as an undercover. His true forte was purchasing drugs from targeted dealers. Those were long-term investigations, unlike the variety of cases assumed in a precinct squad. With the exception of homicide, squad cases were truncated undertakings—they had to be, in order to keep up with the continual influx of new work.

"Do we have a private room to interview her in?" Von Hess asked.

"Yeah, she's in a room down the hall that we use," replied DeCesare.

"Is she with anyone?"

"Her husband is with her."

"Ok, let's not keep her waiting any longer."

DeCesare had a puzzled look. "No problem, but one question. Why is everyone getting printed?"

"Elimination prints," relied Von Hess. "We need to separate the prints of people with legitimate access to the crime scene from those unauthorized."

"I see."

Von Hess's first impression of DeCesare was favorable. "Before we go talk to her, let me ask you something. Were you in the service?"

"Yeah, I was in the army...why?"

"R.A.?"

"That's right, Ollie, regular army. Why?"

"No particular reason. I just figured you for regular army."

"Were you in the service, Ollie?"

42

"I was in the Marines Corps. How about I start off questioning the victim and you jump in whenever you want, does that work for you?"

"No problem." The two proceeded to where Jeanette and her husband were waiting.

"Hello, I'm Detective Von Hess," he began, "I think you already met Detective DeCesare."

"Yes," she answered.

"You are Mr. Pergamint, correct?" Von Hess asked, addressing Jeanette's husband.

"Yes, I'm Mr. Pergamint," answered Forrest.

"Would you mind waiting in the squad room, Mr. Pergamint, while we interview your wife? We need to talk to her privately."

Forrest was startled by the request. "Why privately?"

"Nothing personal, we conduct all our interviews in private. Doing it that way works best for us—no outside comments, distractions or barriers," explained Von Hess.

"Look here, my wife has just been through—"

"Forrest please," interrupted the exasperated Jeanette. "If I need you, I'll find you." Her words came out scratchy, yet unmistakably dismissive. "Now please go!" Forrest complied with his wife's wishes without offering resistance.

The detectives did a double take. They paused, waiting for a reaction from Forrest that never came. It was clear to all who the dominant force was in their relationship. Once alone, the investigators began their questioning gently.

"Would you mind telling us what happened, Ms. Pergamint? Start from the beginning."

Jeanette nodded, prepared to begin her narrative in a direct fashion. "You want me to start from this morning...right?" she asked Von Hess.

"Yes."

The crime victim went on to describe the events of the morning to the detectives. After she concluded her narrative, the follow up questions commenced.

"Do you think you can identify the person who attacked you?" DeCesare asked.

"Yes! Definitely," said Jeanette with emphasis.

"Can you describe him for us? Be sure to include anything unusual you may remember about him."

"There were four things," she said decisively. "One, he wore sunglasses. Two, gloves," she said pointing to her hand. "Three, he was cross-eyed."

The detectives were taken aback by Jeanette's directness "How did you know he was cross-eyed if he was wearing sunglasses?" asked Von Hess.

"They came off...I tried to scratch his eyes out," she explained, with some exaggeration.

"I see. Was there a fourth thing?" asked DeCesare, who was somewhat taken aback by the crime victim's directness.

Jeanette's mouth tightened after hearing the question. "He *urinated* on me!" she said. Her words came with an edge sharp enough to cut a throat.

"I'm sorry to hear that you had to go through that. You said he was cross-eyed. Did you mean to say one of his eyes turned in?"

"No...he was *totally* cross-eyed! Both eyes," she clarified adamantly. "He was goofy looking...like Jerry Lewis!" she explained, referring to the zany comedian.

Von Hess looked at Jeanette very seriously, while DeCesare simply looked down at his brown bucks.

"Please continue with your description," said Von Hess. "Include the color of his eyes, his height and his approximate weight."

Jeanette stopped to drink some water. After several sips, she continued. "He was built big and at least six-two. He was a blue-eyed, cross-eyed bastard!"

"Okay," acknowledged Von Hess, showing no emotion. "What about his hair and physique?"

"He was broad shouldered, had short gray hair and he was crazy."

"Do you mean insane? In what way did he seem unstable?" asked Von Hess.

Jeanette threw up her hand in frustration because her throat was now giving her trouble. She asked for a pen and paper to write some of her answers out. After writing her response she handed the paper to Von Hess who read her answer aloud.

"His whole face was twitching—every muscle quivering. He must have been insane, right?" After hearing her words read back, she looked at the detective for confirmation.

Von Hess shook his head, in a neutral way. "I suppose he might be. About how old would you say he was?" he asked, passing back the paper to her.

"Late forties to early fifties," she wrote.

"What was he wearing?"

"He had a dark suit on and a white collared shirt. I don't remember if he was wearing the tie when he came in."

"He definitely did use a tie though, right?" asked DeCesare.

Jeanette responded to the question dramatically. "Did he use a tie?" she wrote using a bold question mark. Jeanette rose to her feet and tore the scarf from around her neck, revealing her injury. "I've been at death's door!" she declared with a rasp.

"Did you ever see him prior to this morning?" asked Von Hess calmly, not reacting to her emotional outburst He had seen such theatrics on other occasions.

"Yes and no," she wrote, going back to the pen and paper. Her response surprised the Detectives.

Von Hess looked puzzled. "Yes and no? I'm confused."

"So am I!"

"Please explain what you mean."

44

"Last week I was followed while walking home..." Jeanette went on to write the story of how she was accosted on the street.

"What about the eyes *that* day on the street?"

"I'm not sure," she wrote. "She or he...or whatever, had sunglasses on."

"Were there any physical similarities between the two attackers? Built around the same size, or, perhaps there was some other common identifier, like a scar or tattoo?"

"They had the same glasses and were the same size. It had to be the same person."

"What about the voice? Did it sound the same?"

Nodding, Jeanette wrote quickly. "Yes, exactly alike. He had perfect diction and spoke authoritatively and with confidence."

"So the man and the woman sounded the same?"

"They should sound the same...they *are* the same person!" she answered, loudly as possible. She looked at Von Hess with dead seriousness, nodding in the affirmative.

"Do you have any idea of who might have wanted to hurt you Ms. Pergamint?" The crime victim shook her head no.

"Have you had problems, arguments or disputes of any kind?" Again, she shook her head no.

"Have you had any *personal* interactions that might have resulted in a problem?"

Jeanette studied Von Hess carefully. After evaluating him, she sensed that he was just doing his job. She had thought he might be alluding to her tryst with the banker. "No," she replied.

"Have there been money issues? Did you owe anyone?" She shook her head no.

"Have you had any dealings with people who use drugs?"

"No."

"Can you describe the gun?"

"I never saw any gun," she uttered.

"You never saw a gun?" Jeanette shook her head no.

"Did you hear a gunshot?"

Jeanette took the pen to write her reply. "I thought I heard something coming from the back. It sounded like a firecracker, but I can't be sure...I was out of it."

"Are you up to meet with our sketch artist? We would like to put out a wanted poster."

Jeanette picked up the pen to write her final reply. "Let's do it." After passing the paper to Von Hess she added verbally, "You got no idea how bad I want this bastard!"

"I think we do," commented Von Hess.

"Give me your gun and I'll go out looking for him myself!"

"We hear you Ms. Pergamint, but that won't be necessary," assured DeCesare.

After concluding the interview with Jeanette, the detectives updated Markie concerning the facts they gathered. "We got a credible witness here boss. She's certain that she can make an I.D." Von Hess advised.

"Well, that's something. Mrs. Wallace and her sons are here."

"Is that the handyman's wife?"

"Yeah," advised Markie. "Sheridan is talking to her."

"We're going to take Jeanette over to headquarters to see if we can get that sketch made. Okay?"

"Hold up on that, Ollie," Markie said. "This woman has been put through hell. Let me see if I can get out of us jockeying her all over town. While I make a call, you guys go join Sheridan. See how things are working out with the handyman's wife."

Markie dialed McCoy, who was glad to hear that a witness could make an I.D.

"Terrific! What do you need from this end?" asked the inspector.

"Can you get a sketch artist over here?" Markie asked. "I'd like to accommodate our only witness. She's on board with us so I'd like to try and keep her that way."

"No problem, I'll have someone there ASAP."

"Thanks boss, I'll keep you posted. By the way, the victim was groped on the street a day or two earlier so we'll check with sex crimes. There can't be that many towering red headed cross-dressers with broad shoulders waltzing around town unnoticed."

"Red headed cross-dresser? I hope this wasn't a sexual attack as well?"

"Not exactly, but who the hell really knows what gets inside a person's mind. We're still trying to piece this mess together. I'll fill you in once we get more."

"Keep me in the loop," instructed McCoy before he hung up.

Markie walked over to Sheridan's desk where Von Hess and DeCesare were. The sergeant apprised the three detectives that a sketch artist would be responding to the precinct. He then directed his attention to Sheridan. "So how did you make out?"

Sheridan, a man with a full head of bushy white hair, was many years north of fifty. The squad detective doubled as a union delegate. Having spent his entire investigative career attached to the West Village precinct, he knew the neighborhood like the back of his hand. Something of a glib conniver, he was well versed at working things to his advantage. He knew how to take short cuts and was adept at disposing of cases that didn't warrant wasting man hours on. A more than competent investigator when he chose to be, he also knew how to make friends in the street.

"I took care of preparing the borough report, boss. I also put together a case folder. Neither victim has an arrest history," informed Sheridan, adding, "Ms. Pergamint was accosted last week on the street. Somebody grabbed her by the seat of the pants."

"Was there anyone in the squad assigned to follow up on that?" Markie asked.

"She said she couldn't make any identification, so the complaint never made it to the squad. It was closed at the patrol level," explained Sheridan. "It took her almost getting killed to motivate her."

"You made the notification to the Wallace family?"

"I didn't have to, it was already done, sarge. They were notified by Rudy the Hunch."

"Who is he?"

"Rudy Catlett, the landlord of the building where the bakery is. Rudy was the 911 caller. He owns lots of properties in the precinct. Wallace worked for Rudy."

"Is he here now?"

"I have him downstairs waiting to be interviewed."

"And *what* do they call him?"

"Rudy the Hunch," advised Sheridan. "You'll know why when you see him."

"You already interviewed Mrs. Wallace?"

"Not yet, she's downstairs too. I was going to talk to her before I head out on the canvass."

"Let us take care of the interviews. You go do the canvass, and after that, reach out to somebody over at sex and find out if they know of any broad shouldered, gray haired psycho with screwed-up eyes. And see if they have anything on a female giantess with red hair."

Sheridan looked down his long nose at Markie. Having learned his lesson, he exhibited no overt enthusiasm or resistance. "Ok, I'll take care of it," responded the detective, wondering where Markie hid his whip.

"Want to take someone along with you for the canvass?"

"No sarge, I'm good. It's only a canvass. After that, I'll take care of sex crimes. I shouldn't be too long."

Markie was satisfied that Sheridan got the message. He always held a certain suspicion when it came to union representatives. Meanwhile, the wife of Carson Wallace waited patiently on the first floor of the precinct with the two youngest of her four sons. After being alerted by Rudy, the family showed up unannounced to speak to the detectives. A fistful of dampened tissues could be seen held tightly in the hand of the crime victim's widow. After what seemed like forever, Mrs. Wallace and her boys were finally received by the detectives.

The family of the deceased was taken to an office where introductions were made. DeCesare offered the handyman's wife something to drink. Declining the offer, she listened to Von Hess intently as he conveyed the little information he had. She said that Carson was a good man who had no enemies or personal problems. She described him as having been a God-fearing individual throughout their marriage, adding that Carson was a hard worker who kept the Wallace family debt-free. After a while it became evident to all that the handyman had the misfortune of being in the wrong place at the wrong time.

6

Rent Or Consent

"Look at the way this handyman was found, flat on his back, on the love raft. And...one of the slugs lands close to his one-eyed snake."

-Detective Gary DeCesare

EVERETT LEAFED THROUGH THE TEST PAPERS while walking to his next class. After a few steps he came to an abrupt halt, mortified at seeing all the incorrect answers. "This is inexplicable! It was an open book test, for God's sake!" thought the baffled teacher.

"*This is no reflection on you, dear,*" said the good voice of his mother. "You can only do so much with dullards."

"But still, an open book test?" he answered, momentarily forgetting that conversing publicly with Adele wasn't a prudent thing to do.

Dispirited, Everett carelessly stuffed the exams inside his briefcase. He decided to forego all further testing until he figured out what he was doing wrong. When he addressed his next class, he did so with a watchful eye to see if he was reaching his pupils. The course, earth science, was considered to be relatively simple material.

"Geology, oceanography, meteorology are all branches of science," said Everett, pausing to scan the classroom. Satisfied that all eyes were on him, he continued. "They each have something to do with the physical constitution of the earth and its atmosphere."

It didn't take Everett long to realize that the only students engaged were those sitting directly in front of him. He chastised himself for previously being so unperceptive. A student seated up front with her textbook open gave him an idea. He'd begin with the basics. Everett called on the conscientious student.

"Ms. Figueroa, if you were stumped on an earth science question, explain to the class *exactly* the steps you would take to research the answer in your textbook." By the time the period ended, the class at least learned how to go about passing an open book test.

MARKIE LISTENED CLOSELY AS Von Hess and DeCesare brainstormed among themselves. Keying into the insights of his detectives helped protect his own credibility. At all costs the sergeant wanted to avoid saying something that didn't come across as logical. In the sphere of law enforcement, sound judgment fostered a respected reputation.

"There may be more to Jeanette's story," said DeCesare.

"How do you figure?" asked Von Hess.

"Look at the way this handyman was found...flat on his back on the love raft. *And,* one of the slugs lands close to his one-eyed snake."

"So what does that tell us?" Von Hess asked, playing the devil's advocate.

"It tells us that maybe the husband interrupted a romantic interlude."

"Perhaps," replied Von Hess, "but I doubt it."

"Why?"

Von Hess welcomed the question. "Assume that Jeanette *is* being truthful," replied the senior detective. "The bad guy, believing he killed Jeanette in front of a witness, now has to take out the handyman. So he clips him. Maybe they scuffled. Couldn't that account for an accidental discharge, with a wayward bullet striking the handyman low?"

DeCesare countered. "Since we're assuming, let's assume Jeanette is full of it. Or, maybe the handyman was the target and Jeanette has to go because *she's* the witness."

Von Hess digested what DeCesare said before responding. "If the handyman was the intended target, why would the dirty work occur where it did? The venue would make it complicated. I see it as a stretch."

"Do you also see it as a stretch that an irate husband goes off after walking in on a boyfriend doing his old lady?"

"I do at that time of the morning," answered Von Hess. "Look, the husband's here in the squad now, how about we interview him and see what he's got to say."

"Good idea, you guys do that," injected Markie. "I'll interview the landlord."

"No problem," said Von Hess, as Markie left the room.

With Markie gone, DeCesare sought a clarification from Von Hess. "Ollie...let's get back to the husband. You really think we should rule this guy out as a suspect?"

"I'm not ruling him out," said Von Hess. "But think about it. If the husband whacked the handyman, then Jeanette has to be protecting him. To pull that off she has to be pretty fast on her feet in coming up with such a detailed story...minutes after he almost strangles her to death. Who could be that creative under those circumstances? And why would she protect him?"

"But how do you explain the low bullet?"

"Like I said, my *guess* is that maybe there was a struggle."

"I didn't see any defense wounds, did you?"

"Sometimes there aren't any. You usually see that when cutting is involved."

DeCesare realized Von Hess was making sense so he switched course. "That's the way I figure it. Sherry saw it differently," he said with a straight face, followed by a smile.

Von Hess nodded. "Gary, do me a favor. Go and get the husband while I go to the head."

WHEN DECESARE FETCHED FORREST he found him reading *Inferno* by Dante Alighieri. The slightly built, round shouldered man wore thin circular eyeglasses. His crossed leg revealed a black sock that was crunched down close to the ankle. Forrest presented the contented image of a bibliophile at peace with his favorite book. Jeanette's husband was so engrossed in his reading, that he never heard the detective approaching him.

"That's interesting reading," commented DeCesare, giving the impression that he was familiar with the book.

Forrest didn't engage the detective, preferring to just nod his head. Jeanette's husband was then escorted to an office where Von Hess sat waiting.

"Are you through with my wife?" asked Forrest, who was upset because he'd only been able to spend a short time with Jeannette after arriving at the precinct.

"She is doing fine," advised Von Hess. "Please try and be patient a little longer."

"I've been patient. After what Jeanette's been through, she needs me at her side."

Von Hess sized up the situation to be more likely the other way around. "We understand your concern Mr. Pergamint, but I'm afraid you'll just have to hang in there."

"Don't worry, you'll be with your wife shortly," assured DeCesare.

"I hope so," Forrest said, exhaling deeply.

"How did you meet your wife Mr. Pergamint?" asked Von Hess.

"We met in college."

"What made you go into the bakery business?"

"It was Jeanette's dream to own a business."

"Not yours?"

"My sights were initially set on working at NASA. But, things change in life."

"I suppose they do." Von Hess sensed some resentment. "Are you regretful that you changed direction?"

"Sometimes I am."

"Is it an expensive proposition to start a business in Manhattan?"

"It can be. We were fortunate to receive help at the beginning."

"What kind of help—financial?"

"Yes. After graduation we eloped. My parents live here so my father generously gave us the seed money. He wanted me close to home."

"What's your father's business?"

"He was an actuary. He passed on a few years ago."

"I see," said Von Hess.

The veteran detective soon put together a mental profile of the couple. He surmised that after meeting Jeanette, Forrest's interest shifted from outer space to things more earthly. In considering Jeanette's perspective, he felt Forrest likely represented a fluid path to owning a business.

"Where were you, Mr. Pergamint, at the time this thing went down this morning?"

"I was running an errand with my mother."

"With your mother," echoed DeCesare. "What time was that?"

"I left about six this morning, or perhaps earlier I suppose."

"Where did you go at that hour?"

"First we had breakfast."

"Where was that?"

"We ate at my mother's house in Forest Hills."

"You drove to Forrest Hills?"

"No, we have no car. I took the train to Queens."

"So breakfast was the errand?"

"No, of course not," replied Forrest. "What's the point of all this" Why do you care?"

"You don't care to tell us what the errand was?" asked Von Hess.

"I didn't say that, I just want to know why you need to ask me such questions.

Von Hess gave Forrest a straight answer. "So we can verify or disprove what you say."

"Are you suggesting that I'm a suspect in this?" asked the offended husband.

"No. On the contrary, these questions are being posed to eliminate you as a suspect."

"I took her to see her financial advisor," answered Forrest, accepting the explanation.

"At such an early hour?" asked DeCesare, a trace of suspicion in his voice.

"As I said to you earlier, we had breakfast first."

"Where does the financial planner work?"

"She works for Brown-Gatewell-Loring. The advisor's name is Sabrina Loring."

"Very good," commented the satisfied Von Hess. "When you left for Queens this morning, you left Mrs. Pergamint alone in the store?"

"Yes." Getting defensive over leaving his wife alone, Forrest added, "It isn't unusual for one of us to remain at work when the other has something to tend to. We're a small business, not yet at the point of taking on employees."

"Were you aware that the handyman was coming by this morning?"

"Yes, that's right. I forgot about him; Carson was there when I left the bakery. We knew the poor man was coming, but we didn't know what time to expect him."

"Were there ever any problems with Carson?"

"No, never...he was a good guy. Wasn't he?"

"No reason to think differently," replied Von Hess.

The questioning continued without raising any suspicions concerning Forrest. Once the session was ended, Jeanette's husband was thanked and reunited with his wife.

The two detectives next spoke with the first officers who responded to the scene. These conversations produced nothing to further the investigation. Afterward they posted Markie, who was with the landlord in the squad commander's office. After the update, Von Hess was directed to make arrangements to meet with the squad detectives assigned to the other strangulation cases. While he took care of that, Markie and DeCesare interviewed the landlord that everyone called Rudy the Hunch.

THE DETECTIVES SAT DIRECTLY across the desk from Rudy Catlett. The landlord's hands were of average size, with the fingers on his right hand stained a gross yellowish-orange.

"Are you a smoker?" asked DeCesare. "If so, you can light up if you want to."

"I gave it up years ago," answered the landlord. "It's a nasty habit."

To the former narcotics undercover, Rudy's fingers made it obvious that he was a heavy pot smoker. "That it is," said DeCesare.

"Mr. Catlett, let's start from the beginning again," said Markie. "You own the building where the bakery is, correct?"

Catlett allowed his attention to be distracted by an outdated photo board hanging off a wall in the office. On display were old pictures of prisoners with numbers across their chest. These men represented the precinct KG's, known gamblers, who in days past operated within the confines of the West Village.

"Mr. Catlett?"

"I'm sorry, what's that you said, sergeant?"

"You own the building that houses the bakery, right?"

"Sure I do, I told you that already. I own a lot of properties in the area." Rudy pushed out his chest and began tapping his stained fingers against his breast as he spoke.

"Jesus, look at those fingers! How did they get so discolored?" asked Markie bluntly.

"These?" the landlord asked, as he wiggled his fingers in the air. "Let me tell you sergeant, this coloring is from when I used to smoke cigarettes...Chesterfields." It was the best explanation the pot-smoking property owner could come up.

"Ok, whatever you say, Mr. Catlett," answered Markie.

"You see that board you have on the wall sergeant? I bought my first property off that guy there," he said, pointing to one of the dated black-and-white mug shots. The landlord stood to put his finger on the photo he was referring to. "I still got the building, it's on Sullivan Street."

"Who is he?"

"Lefty Piccolo was his name. They called him Lefty Little in the street. He was married to my cousin. Poor Lefty dropped dead of a heart attack walking on Carmine Street about ten years ago. He was a big smoker. When he went, it was enough to make me quit."

"That's interesting. But let's concentrate on today," said Markie.

"Certainly, sergeant, whatever you say."

"Start from this morning, after leaving your house."

"Well, this morning I went by my building to collect the rent as usual. I always go to the bakery first thing because I can grab a muffin and coffee there."

"That's your regular routine?"

"Sure, the first of the month like clockwork. I know the bakery opens up early, so I kill two birds with one stone. I collect my money and get something for breakfast," he said.

"But make no mistake. I *always* pay for what I get at the bakery. There is nothing for nothing in this world—that, my friend, has always been my motto."

"What time was this?"

"It was maybe close to seven in the morning, or thereabouts."

"Go ahead, continue—so what did you do next?"

"Well, the door to the bakery was open, so I went in. I recognized the smell inside right off the bat, and I'm not talking jelly donuts. There was shooting in the air!"

"How did you know that?"

"I knew because I was in the army. So don't worry, I know the smell. I was on the guns"

"You were assigned to artillery?"

"Sure, I worked on the big guns. In the army they called me Gunner Rudolph."

"I see. So go on, Mr. Catlett, you convinced me."

"Thank you. Anyway, I heard moaning from behind the counter, so I go and take a look. There I find poor Jeanette on the floor, half dead."

"What did you do?"

"I tried to find out what happened, but she couldn't talk." He shook his head as he recollected the sight. "I only wish I'd have arrived there a little earlier so I could have gotten my hands on the bastard. She's such a beautiful girl."

The detectives nodded as if they believed the old man's bravado.

DeCesare focused on Catlett's back, wondering to himself how long he had the hunch. He couldn't see how the landlord got into the service with such an affliction.

"You saw her neck...terrible!" said the landlord.

"Yeah, I did. Please go on."

"She lifted her arm real slow. I remember her doing that, because she couldn't talk. Jeanette pointed to the back of the bakery. She was telling me that I should go back there. That's where she and her husband live you know."

"We know."

"So I go and find poor Carson all shot up! This is a terrible, terrible thing."

"Tell me, what's Carson's exact relationship to you again?"

The landlord waved his hand dismissively, he needed time. Once he regained control of his emotions, he continued the conversation. "Call me Rudy. Carson Wallace is, or I should say was, my handyman. I've been using him to maintain all my buildings for years. I just spoke to Carson's wife a little while ago. You know, just to let her know what happened. I told her she should come down here right away."

"What occurred next, Rudy?" asked Markie.

"I dialed 911. The cops and ambulance got there in minutes."

"Have there been suspicious people milling around, or have you received complaints of any kind concerning the bakery, Jeanette, or Carson?"

"Nothing, not a complaint made by anyone. No strangers come around here causing trouble. This is a safe neighborhood, very rarely a problem in this area. Even the cash register, which I checked, still had money in it. Believe me, *this* was no robbery. This was *intentional* murder!"

"Do you know if the Pergamint family was having any problems like owing money, drugs, fighting with each other, things of that nature?"

"Ahhh, money is always an issue in any family," said Rudy, dismissively. "They are honest, hardworking people. Maybe, once in a while, a little slow to make the rent because sales are down, but that's expected in any business. I know they're good for the money, so I wait sometimes."

"Does Mr. Pergamint have a temper? You know, is he the excitable type?"

"Forrest is a man without a temper. A mellower person you would be hard pressed to find, a real lamb. She was the one who could be a tough cookie. Between you and me, she rules that roost."

"Let's get back to Carson, what kind of guy was he?"

"Carson was just a beautiful man, a hard-working slob from Avenue D...a family man."

"Did you ever have any problems with him? Did he drink, use drugs, a womanizer maybe?" asked DeCesare.

"No! None of that existed with Carson. Look, don't get me wrong, he started out as a street kid, but he came from a decent family. He's leaving a nice wife and good kids."

"So he was no Romeo," said Markie, looking to clarify that point.

"Oh, no...he was nothing like that."

"As far as Jeanette, could she be, let's say...out there?" Markie asked.

Rudy didn't understand the question. "Out where?"

"You know, was she the *flirtatious* type."

Catlett snickered as he shook his head in the negative. "Let me tell you, that woman is all business, very determined to be somebody."

"Go on."

"She's very strong, very ambitious and a real work-horse No question about that. But when it comes to fooling around, she's the greenest apple in the barrel."

"So she's not, you know, a gal who *gets around*?"

"What does Jeanette know about getting around? She's a good girl all the way, you know what I mean?"

"I think so, Rudy," acknowledged Markie.

The landlord leaned toward the investigators. "Look, I've been in this neighborhood forever. I've gotten to know a lot of tenants over the years with different types of problems. Some know how to help themselves and some don't. With the smart ones, we get to work things out. You know...a little quid pro quo...consent for rent."

"I see."

"So I get what you're driving at. Believe me when I tell you, there was no romance involved in this terrible murder thing. Jeanette's not that type of woman."

"You seem pretty sure of that," commented DeCesare.

"I *seem* pretty sure?" asked Rudy, snickering. "Let me tell you something, she knows that her obligation could be negotiated, maybe even overlooked once in awhile, *if* she were...let's say, a little *friendlier*. Know what I mean?"

"I think so," replied the detective.

Rudy nodded his head knowingly. Raising a finger, he pointed to his ear. The besotted landlord whispered his next words. "Although I heard different, I know she's a virtuous girl. She's the type that would rather struggle!" he said, shaking his head. "For that I have to respect her. A good girl, yes...but not a very bright one."

"So who was it that said she wasn't virtuous?" asked Markie.

"Ahhh, forget I said that."

"That's not the way it works, Rudy."

"What do you mean, sergeant?"

"You can't say something and then not want to talk about it."

"In all due respect sergeant, I can say or not say what I want in this country."

"Can I ask you a question Rudy?" asked Markie, now knowing he had to apply some pressure.

"Ask all you want," replied Rudy confidently.

"Those apartments you rent...are there bars on all the upper floor windows to protect kids from falling out? What about smoke alarms? How about those rents, do you take some of the cabbage in cash? You know what's really interesting about owning property..."

"It looks like I underestimated you sergeant," said Catlett, with a silly grin. He now looked at Markie quite differently.

"A lot of people make that mistake, my friend. So who said Jeanette wasn't virtuous?"

"It was some banker, but he's a dog," answered Rudy dismissively. "You can't believe what he says. He's always bragging. That guy keeps a scorecard."

"Can you describe the banker?"

"He's a pretty boy. Well dressed, short hair, early forties, average height..."

"Thank you, Rudy," said Markie, cutting him off once he knew the description didn't fit. That's all I needed to find out."

"That's it?"

"Yeah, that's it. I think we got enough. They fingerprinted you right?"

"Yes...the other detective did when I first got here."

"If you think of anything later that may be important, please give us a call."

"Of course I'll let you know, sergeant. I think the world of Jeanette."

"I can see that," commented Markie, with a slight trace of sarcasm, as he watched the property owner leave. When it came to sleazy, Markie put him right up there.

7

Pitching Wu

"We do postmortem reconstructions, skull reconstructions, age progressions, stuff like that."

-Detective Howin Wu

THE YOUNG WOMAN ENTERING THE SECOND FLOOR squad room was dressed conservatively in a black suit, black shoes and white collared shirt.

"I'm Detective Howin Wu," she announced. "I'm here to do the sketch."

Markie was the first to greet the detective. "I'm Sergeant Markie, thanks for the quick response. Our complainant had a rough go of it, that's why we requested you to respond to the squad," he explained.

"Oh...I figured it was something like that," she replied.

"Let me get the detectives working the case. Sit tight and help yourself to the coffee."

Markie informed DeCesare and Von Hess that the department artist had arrived. He advised that the sketch, when completed, should be distributed throughout the department. He specifically wanted copies immediately posted for public viewing in all of the Manhattan precincts.

"What about putting one up in central booking, sarge?" Von Hess suggested.

"Definitely, I want every cop and prisoner passing through the system to see it."

"No problem, boss."

"Ollie, let me have the car keys, I have to run an errand. Call me on my cell if anything comes up." Taking the keys, Markie then turned to DeCesare. "You have a vehicle assigned to the squad that you guys can use, right?"

"Yeah," confirmed DeCesare. "We have two cars assigned to our squad."

"Good. Get Jeanette set up with the artist, and remember, try to keep your mind on the job. Don't get sidetracked," warned Markie, giving the detective a knowing look.

"What do you mean, sarge?" asked the puzzled detective.

"Remember what happened to that giant ape who took a cement swan dive sixty-five years ago," Markie warned, clouding matters further.

After the sergeant left, a baffled DeCesare sought council from Von Hess. "What giant ape? Sixty-five years ago was 1933, what the hell is he talking about?"

Von Hess thought about it for a few seconds. "My guess is that this Detective Wu is a honey."

"I still don't get it."

"What kind of detective *are* you? You must have seen King Kong, the original movie in black and white."

"Of course I did. What's the point?"

"That was made in 1933. Remember the scene when the ape falls off the building?"

"Yeah, the planes shot him down."

"Correct. Do you remember the impresario saying it was beauty that killed the beast?"

"Oh, now I get it," replied DeCesare, finally making the connection. He couldn't help but think that that Markie and Von Hess were two strange people.

"Get used to it, the sergeant's an old movie buff. He'd probably give a payday to thump the chest of a dead man just to be able to shout, 'IT'S ALIVE!' after bringing him back."

"That was from Frankenstein right?"

"No you got it," confirmed Von Hess.

Wu was looking out the windows when DeCesare entered the room. When she turned to face him their eyes locked. The physical attraction between the two was mutual. After introducing himself, DeCesare led Wu to the room where Von Hess, Jeanette and Forrest were waiting. Their few minutes together was all it took for the positive vibes to begin percolating. Von Hess was quick to pick up on the *gosh-golly-gee* grins the two detectives were sharing. He had to admit that the clairvoyant Markie had correctly forecasted the possibility of a love connection.

Wu assumed a position at a desk with Jeanette seated alongside her. The artist began by securing a description from the complainant. She then drew two ovals. From the first oval she created the head, lips, nose and chin based on Jeanette's recollection of what her attacker looked like. There were some complications when it came to the eyes.

"How does it look now?" asked Wu, adjusting the eyes for the third time.

"No good, they need to be *closer* toward the nose."

"How is it now?" asked Wu, after making the change.

"No...still no good. Make it *like Jerry Lewis!*" insisted the crime victim.

After numerous failed efforts, the artist grew frustrated. Wu finally drew the eyes as far inward as possible. "Now how is it?" she asked skeptically.

"Perfect," announced Jeanette, satisfied that the artist captured the proper image.

The end product surprised everyone. Doubt clearly existed as to the accuracy of the sketch. The composite seemed far too weird to be plausible. This pessimism was only enhanced when the eyes were reproduced in the form of a cross-eyed, masculine-looking woman. Regardless, the crime victim stood by the accuracy of the composites.

When finished with Wu, Von Hess arranged for a radio car to return Mr. and Mrs. Pergamint to their MacDougal Street home. He then went about arranging for copies of the sketches to be immediately posted throughout Manhattan South. Detective Wu readily accepted DeCesare's offer of a lift back to her office at headquarters. Not in any rush to drop Wu off, DeCesare made it his business to drive slowly.

The detective purposely remained quiet, waiting to see if Wu would initiate a conversation. It was his way of testing her interest. After a period of quiet, Wu finally broke the silence. "So, how long have you worked in the West Village?" she asked.

"Under a year," answered DeCesare. "Before that I was in narcotics. I got my detective shield after doing a hand to hand with Speedo Reed in Washington Square Park."

"Oh, wow," said Wu, "you were an undercover?" she asked, not letting on that she never heard of Speedo Reed, a major narcotics trafficker.

"Yeah, I worked undercover for five years. How much time have you got on the job?"

"Three years," she replied.

"How long were you in the bag?"

"I was in uniform for about a year or so, I suppose."

"You must have had a good hook to get where you are with only a year in uniform."

"I had the artistic talent they needed. I was really lucky getting in *when* I did though."

"How so?" asked DeCesare. "I'm sorry, what was your first name again?"

"My name is Howin."

"How-in? So tell me, *how-in* the world was you so lucky?" Wu ignored his little joke.

"We're a tiny unit. Right before I got there one of the detective's retired, creating an opening for a gold shield to be given out. Since I was the only white shield in the unit, I got it," she explained.

"I bet you getting the gold shield that fast must have pissed off a few people," commented DeCesare. "It took me years," he noted, with a slight trace of bitterness.

"You should have gone to art school," she answered, making light of his comment.

DeCesare let it drop. He found her too appealing to jeopardize the progress he was trying to make. "So what else do you do over there in addition to sketching?"

"We do postmortem reconstructions, skull reconstructions, age progressions, stuff like that," she answered.

"I guess there's a substantial amount of sketching to do."

"Not really. With so many cameras out there now, there are fewer calls for sketches."

"Did you enjoy art school?"

"Yes, of course. Are you surprised?"

"No, I'm not surprised. You know, I'm taking an acting class," he pointed out with pride.

"You are?"

"Yeah, it's something I always wanted to try."

"Is it expensive?"

"Not too bad, but let me ask you something. What's your favorite painting?" The detective weighed in with a question that was designed to impress her.

Wu was more amused than impressed. She could tell that DeCesare was working to win points. "*Mona Lisa* by Leonardo da Vinci," she replied. Wu figured he'd have at least heard of it.

"Old Mona was alright, if you like them without eyebrows," he answered. His comment suggested some knowledge, leaving Wu pleasantly surprised.

"So do *you* have a favorite painting?" she asked.

"The one that really impressed me was *The Scream*."

The reply gained Wu's attention. "I'm quite familiar with that work. Who was the artist again?" she asked, testing him.

"Edvard Munch, not Edward...*Ed-vard*. It was an expressionist painting, done way back."

She responded with enthusiasm after seeing that he knew his stuff. "Very good, I'm impressed! The backdrop for that painting was in Norway in the 1890's, I think."

64

"Oslo. I'll never forget how struck I was at how eerie looking Munch made the guy in that painting," he recalled. "That gaping mouth...I found it spooky as hell!"

Wu's eyes brightened. He was talking her language. "You are so right! I found it chilling as well!" Wu was now sincerely interested in DeCesare. She found it wonderful that he seemed not to be typical.

"I never heard of the name Howin before, is that a common name?" DeCesare asked.

"It's about average."

"Does it have any special meaning?"

"It means loyal swallow."

"Loyal swallow," repeated DeCesare, tilting his head and scrunching his lips. He looked out the window of the car and inhaled deeply. His exhale was released in a slow controlled fashion. The detective wasn't sure if Wu was sending him a message or not. All he could think to say was, "That's a very nice name."

❖

EVERETT WAS TAKING HIS LUNCH in the school cafeteria. He chose a table adjacent to where students were in line to buy their food. The location was ideal for him to listen in as they talked among themselves. He viewed this not as snooping, but rather, as research.

"Do your homework when it comes to the students, dear," advised the good voice.

Everett was drawn to the guffaws of two boys on line. Their tone had a familiar cruelty to it, alerting him that someone was being picked on. The bullies were boys Everett occasionally played basketball with. They were having fun at the expense of a teenage girl wearing dental braces. Sitting up to his highest capacity, the science teacher began loudly clearing his voice. This, coupled with a stern look of displeasure, was sufficient to put a halt to the insensitivity. Thanks to basketball, Everett garnered a reputation as a teacher not to be trifled with. Those who played against him understood that it would be unwise to run afoul of someone who wouldn't hesitate to administer an elbow smash when coming down with a rebound. When the bell signifying the end of the period sounded, Everett decided to have a word with the youths. He intercepted them at the double doors leading out of the cafeteria into the corroder. The boys listened respectfully.

"Angel, do you know what your name means?" The larger boy didn't respond so Everett helped him out. "It means God's messenger."

Angel nodded in silence. He would have had the right answer had he spoken up.

65

"Messengers of God should not mistreat others. You're the leader here," said the teacher. Then, turning to the second youth he added, "And you follow him. I realize you were just kidding around, I get that. *But,* can't you see how you're *hurting* that girl's feelings? Why would you want to do that?" No answer came from the boys.

Everett continued, this time speaking in a firmer tone that was reminiscent of the way Adele spoke to him. "How would you like it if I made fun of those two flappers you use for ears?" he asked, pointing his finger at Angel. "Or," addressing the second youth, "I began calling you pimple puss? Would you like that?"

The boys remained silent, as Everett accentuated their imperfections. After seeing that his words had the youths smarting, Everett provided the remedy for their aches. "Look guys, you already know what you did was wrong, so let's make it right. All you need to do is to find her, say you are sorry and promise not to do it again. It's as simple as that."

"No problem Mr. Skidmore, we'll do it," agreed Angel, speaking for both boys.

Everett made it a point to personally follow up with the teenage girl the following afternoon. "I saw those boys upsetting you yesterday over your braces. I spoke to them about their behavior, it won't happen again. If it does, let me know."

"Thank you Mr. Skidmore. They said this morning that they were sorry. What they think doesn't bother me anyway," she lied.

"I'm glad," Everett said in a friendly tone. "You know, my cousin had imperfect teeth. She wore braces for awhile and today, nobody has more beautiful teeth. Hang in there."

"Thank you, Mr. Skidmore," the girl replied, feeling a little better. Everett, who had no relatives, was satisfied that the white lie he told did some good.

8

Opening A Can Of Worms

"Cross-eyed guy? What cross-eyed guy?"

-Greasy Jake

SHERIDAN STOOD IN FRONT OF THE PERGAMINT BAKERY wondering about the chocolate frosted donuts. With the store closed, he had no way of determining first hand if they were good. When anxious to know something the detective lacked patience. Seeing a corpulent man walking his dog, Sheridan felt that he might be a resource that could provide the answer.

"Pardon me, sir. Do you know if the chocolate donuts in this bakery are any good?" asked the detective.

The middle aged man tugged on the leash to hold back his white poodle. At first he wasn't sure if the stranger was being a wise guy. Once he realized that Sheridan was being sincere, he laughed at the question. "What makes you think that I'd know?"

Sheridan rubbed his own ample belly. "Hey man, we're members of the same club."

"You're getting there," replied the amused stranger. "Their stuff is way overpriced."

"How do you rate the chocolate donuts?"

"They are dark chocolate, sort of small and hard. I'm not crazy for them. You'd do a lot better for the money at Momo's Munch on West 13rd Street."

Sheridan nodded his thanks. Cost was of no concern—he was figuring on Jeanette not charging him for the donuts anyway. "I'll check it out. Have a good day, my friend."

As he stood alone on MacDougal Street, Sheridan looked at his surroundings before deciding where to commence his canvass. He began by questioning the businesses on the block. When that netted no results he switched to ringing residential bells and knocking on doors. Things remained uneventful until he entered a weathered four-story walk up.

"Probably full of leftovers," the detective thought, conjecturing that the apartments were home to long time residents of the neighborhood.

The entry door to the building was unlocked, making it simple for him to gain access. The detective placed his ear to the door of the first floor apartment. Hearing nothing, he stepped to the side of the door frame before knocking. It was a standard precautionary measure taught in the police academy. In the event Sheridan was interrupting something questionable, at least he would be out of the line of direct fire. The detective knocked twice. When there was no response, he took the stairs to the next floor where he repeated his routine, again getting the same results. Continuing upward, he heard voices coming from the third-floor apartment. Sheridan rapped on the door announcing, "POLICE!" A sudden dead silence preceded the unlocking of the door. Sheridan was greeted by a well groomed man in his mid-thirties. He was clean cut and wore jeans, dark brown desert boots and a blue short-sleeved polo shirt.

"I'm Detective Sheridan," announced the investigator. He produced his gold shield and ID card, allowing the man standing in the doorway to examine his credentials.

"Whudda-ya need?" The voice was very old-school New York.

"There was an incident on the block…" Sheridan paused mid-sentence after noticing the activity going on inside the apartment. Looking over the shoulder of the man at the door, the detective could see into the living room. An elderly man was seated in a rocking chair staring down at the ground. At his feet was a white cat that was toying with a small mouse. Each dash for freedom the mouse made was foiled by a paw that pulled the rodent back to its starting point. Sheridan's assessment was that the people occupying the apartment weren't all there. Nevertheless, he went through the motions of explaining the purpose of his presence. Nodding understandingly, the man at the door identified himself first, and then the cat-and-mouse-watcher as his father.

"So you haven't seen anyone in the area fitting the description I gave you?"

"Uh-uh…I never saw anybody around here looking like that."

"What about your father? Does he ever go outside?"

"Yeah, he goes out to see his friends when the weather ain't bad."

"Do me a favor and ask him to keep an eye out. If you guys ever spot this big cross-eyed bozo around, give me a call. I'll owe you one. Here, take my business card."

"I can do that." The son stepped outside the apartment to have a word in private with Sheridan. "Do you think maybe you can do something for *me*, detective?"

"Depends, what do you need?"

"I got a situation over here," said the son, speaking in a low whisper. "I need advice."

"No problem. What's the story?"

"My friend Wadim comes around and my old man don't want him here."

"He must have a reason," said the detective. "What is it?"

"He thinks Wadim is controlling me."

"How is he doing that?"

"Nah, c'mon, it's all bullshit. Wadim's alright, my old man just got it in for him."

"What is Wadim, the bossy type?"

"Yeah, sometimes he is. But the old man's real knock against Wadim is that he thinks he's some kind of a gypsy that comes and goes."

"If he's got a hard-on for gypsies, that's his prerogative. Nothing you can you do about *that*."

"You don't get it. My old man said he wants Wadim…*gone*."

"He's gone now isn't he? Just don't let him in again," suggested the detective.

"I mean *gone-gone,* like…in *dead*."

Sheridan turned very serious. "You think your father's capable of something like that?"

"You don't know him. If he said it…he means it."

"Sometimes people say things they don't really mean. Where's this Wadim now?"

The next words coming from the son were spoken in a new voice, one with a hardened edge. "He's not going to believe you, Robert. I already told you that." The sudden switch in personalities caught Sheridan off guard.

"Say what?" blurted the startled detective. Sheridan wasn't sure of what exactly was happening. The next sentence came in the Robert's normal speaking voice.

"Wadim is here now."

"Don't waste your time," Robert said, again speaking as Wadim.

"C'mon Wadim, met me handle this," Robert voiced, interrupting himself using his normal speaking voice.

The exchange spooked Sheridan, who was squeamish when it came to dissociative identity disorders. "I'm afraid I have to leave you two, I'll come back later after you straighten things out." Sheridan couldn't exit the building quick enough.

Once outside the detective lit up a cigarette. After calming himself with several long drags, he resumed his canvass. He entered an apartment house just east of Avenue of the Americas. Going from floor to floor he came upon a foul smelling apartment. His knock was answered by a man who opened the door just wide enough to reveal one eye and partial chin, nose, and mouth. He looked to be in his forties, tall, brown haired and clean shaven. The crack in the door freed a hot stench that blew out from inside the apartment. The odor was awful, causing Sheridan to back away from the revolting reek.

"Are you Mr. Wadim?" asked Sheridan, using the first name that popped into his head.

"No," the man answered in a low growl. All that was lacking was the organ music.

"My error," said the detective, rushing to exit the building.

Once outside Sheridan savored the fresh air. Convinced that this was not his day for conducting a canvass, he aborted his mission. He dialed the precinct desk officer.

"Hello, this is Sheridan from the squad."

"What's up?" asked the desk lieutenant.

"I stumbled on something while doing a canvas, boss. You may want to check it out," he advised, providing the lieutenant with the address.

"What's the condition?"

"I almost fell on my ass from the stench coming from inside an apartment on the third floor. There's gotta be something dead inside."

"Who lives there?"

"Some pasty-faced Zacherle-like psycho opened the door. The stink is putrid, something is definitely ripe inside. You may want to send a radio car to check it out."

"You'll be there?"

"I can't stay because I'm working on a homicide, but if it turns out to be anything for the squad, just have them call me and I'll double back to the apartment forthwith, okay?"

"I'll send a car over."

This last experience convinced Sheridan that the time had come for him to eat. But before he did he called up a friend who worked in sex crimes.

"Is this the great Fogel?"

"Yes, this is Detective Frank E. Fogel. Who is this?"

"It's me Sherry, how in the hell are you!"

"Hey, it's the last of the big spenders! Are you still in the West Village?"

"Yeah, I'm still here."

"I can't believe that you still do those turnaround tours. I hated them! Do yourself a favor and get civilized, get into a detail with steady days off and regular hours."

"That's not for me, I like working the chart. It gets me out of the house at night."

"I can get you a soft spot here in this unit. We do squat over here."

"No thanks Frankie, I don't mind working. I'm fine. So what can I do for you? I know this isn't just a social call."

"Here's the thing. We're working on a homicide where the perp is believed to be cross-eyed. We're looking for a big bugger who sometimes wears women's clothes. You got anything over there that fits this?"

"Nah, someone cross-eyed I would remember hearing about. But hang on, I'll check."

"Okay, thanks Frank."

After a few minutes Fogel returned to the phone. "We got nothing like that over here."

"If you hear of anything that even smells like a possibility, will you give me call?"

"You bet. So when are we meeting for a drink or are you on the wagon?"

"Are you working Friday? It's my last day tour," suggested Sheridan.

"You got a date, it works perfect."

"Okay, good. How about we meet at The Kangaroo's Pocket?"

"I'll put it in the book."

"Wait a minute Frankie, before you go, you said Frank E. Fogel. I never heard you use that initial before, what does the E stand for?"

"It stands for excellence."

"Of course, see you at the Pocket, Frank."

Talk about The Kangaroo's Pocket brought to Sheridan's mind the bar's tasty sliders. The thought prompted him to head over to Greasy Jake's sidewalk lunch counter.

The seventy-six year old Jake always dressed for work in a clean white apron and a white v-neck undershirt. An engaging conversationalist, the business owner always seemed to be in need of a shave. He smiled as Sheridan approached him.

"Detective Sheridan, ya got me! What did I do this time?" asked Jake throwing up his hands jovially, as if surrendering.

"Hello Jake, how you been? I don't see your wife. You finally gave her a day off?"

"What day off? She only works three days a week as it is. While she's off...I'm the guy busting my ass in here all the time," he explained. "What are you having?"

"Let me have a couple of hot dogs with relish and mustard."

"You want a seltzer with it?"

"Yeah, that's great," replied Sheridan.

Jake placed a cone shaped paper cup into a metal holder and poured the seltzer. He then began to turn the hot dogs on the grill for the detective.

"Hey Jake, let me ask you something. You know of a crossed-eyed guy around here?"

"I don't know any cross-eyed guy. What cross-eyed guy?"

"He's a big bugger with gray hair. He might even go around in drag wearing a red wig."

"You must be pulling my leg."

"No, it's square business."

"I never saw anyone like that around here. What did he do?"

"Murder," related the detective. "If you spot anyone with screwed up eyes, be sure to give me a call, will ya?"

"Certainly, I'll call," assured Jake. "Do you have that detective card for me?"

"You bet, and I got something else for you." Sheridan handed Jake a Detective Endowment Association card *and* a miniature gold detective shield."

"What's this?"

"Keep it in your wallet. If you're pulled over show it and tell the cop we're related."

"Thank you."

"Do me a favor. Let the other businesses know about the guy I'm looking for."

"No problem. I'll take care of it," promised Jake.

Knowing that Jake was an old-time fight fan, Sheridan decided to tickle his interest by going down memory lane. "Hey Jake, did I ever tell you how I met Ruby Goldstein?"

The mention of the name instantly perked Jake up. "Ruby Goldstein...you met Ruby Goldstein the referee?"

"None other," said Sheridan.

Jake was clearly impressed. "My family knew him from the lower east side when he was a fighter. They called Ruby the *Jewel of the Ghetto*. How'd you meet him?"

"He lived in Florida, in the building where my uncle lived. I am going back, they're both long gone now," advised Sheridan. "Wasn't he related to Charley Goldstein, the trainer?"

Jake grimaced at Sheridan's question. "Who Charley Goldstein? You mean Charley *Goldman*. Goldman made a champ out of Marciano. No relation to Ruby."

"I stand corrected. You know your sport my friend. What do I owe you for these dogs?"

Jake had to laugh at what he heard. "Now, all of sudden you owe me something." He said, knowing Sheridan had no intention of paying.

"Thanks, Jake."

"Next time you come by ask me to tell you about the Benny Leonard and Lew Tendler fight."

"You got it Jake. Remember, let me know if you get a line on anyone with ass-way eyes, about fifty years old, real big, man or woman.

"No problem. By the way, Willie the mechanic said he's waiting for you to come by.

"Tell him, I'll see him soon. I'll have the knives for him then.

"What knives?"

"Willie's a collector. I got about fifty knives in my locker that I took off people over the years. I promised to give them to him," explained Sheridan. "I'm just waiting for when the time comes to take my car in for servicing."

Detective Sheridan returned to the building where the putrid odor was coming from. As he got close he saw two police cars parked outside, one of which belonged to the patrol sergeant. The cars were vacant with the exception of the sergeant's driver, who sat comfortably behind the wheel smoking a cigarette.

"Hey, how's it going? What does it look like inside?"

"The guy inside is a psycho," said the cop. "He's been living in there with three dead Dobermans. That's where the stink is coming from."

"Let me go in and show my face."

"I wouldn't do that, they're pissed off at you," cautioned the driver.

"Why?"

"You opened up a can of worms with this job."

Sheridan nodded. "I suppose I did. Do me a favor, let the boss know I swung by." The detective headed back to the precinct, wondering what kind of additional work Markie had in store for him.

9

Unpleasant Dreams

"Ma, it's her. She's talking to me right now."

-Everett Skidmore

MULTITASKING, EVERETT WAS SQUEEZING a hand grip in one hand while grading papers with the other. Frequently glancing at the clock on the office wall, he was anxious for the time to pass. He was scheduled to play basketball with the seniors after school. Arriving at the schoolyard early, he warmed up without having to share the court with the other players. Everett associated being there first with ownership of the court. It was something he viewed as a hometown advantage. When the other players arrived they were limited to just a few warm-up shots before forming an I-formation at the foul line. In hit-or-miss fashion, the first two who sunk a basket played on Everett's team. Everett played to win. When he was on, he'd rack up points with his jump shot. When he cooled, he relied on his strong body to see him through, scoring often under the basket after taking down rebounds. As a precaution against Granny drop-ins he played with his sunglasses hanging from his neck. It turned out to be a fine afternoon, one that came without unwelcomed interferences

The after-game praise Everett received over sodas hindered his departure. After soaking up accolades, he headed for home a happy man. When he finally arrived at his apartment, he watched some television before turning in. His final thought before closing his eyes was to imagine what it would be like to be Michael Jordan. The notion of his being able to dunk from the free throw line simply blew his mind. It would have been one of his three wishes if he were to happen upon a genie.

Unable to fall asleep, Everett sat up in bed to read a magazine article about the possibilities of colonizing Mars. He was well into the story when he was pestered by the evil voice. *"Up inna-space...ats-a-the right place for you."*

"Flake off," Everett answered in a low, cold voice as he felt his eyes crossing.

"You gonna-like-a-Mars."

Everett sighed mightily. "GO SCREW YOURSELF!" he cried out in frustration, as he reached to turn off the bedside lamp.

The school teacher rolled onto his stomach, placing the pillow over the back of his head in an effort to suppress any further unwelcomed conversation. This technique had worked occasionally in the past. However, such was not to be the case this night. The teacher was in store for an evening of nightmares, as he relived the childhood trauma that warped his mind.

Shortly after falling asleep Everett entered into an overnight cinema that returned him to his early years. The opening scene was set in the kitchen of a top floor cold-water flat on Yarrow Street, where the presence of a black cast iron stove dominated the room. A small radio sat atop the white General Motors Frigidaire. Everett's mother Adele could be heard warbling the then-hit tune *Wheel of Fortune* along with Kay Starr, as she fed clothes through the wringer of a washing machine. It was all so real, so accurate, with Everett re-living his life as a small boy. Each reenactment came complete with the same emotional intensity. He was at play as the Lone Ranger, jumping off the stringy mop that he pretended was Silver, his horse. Taking cover under the kitchen table he exchanged fire with the murderous outlaw, Butch Cavendish. He followed the trajectory of the white plastic bullets as they flew from his toy six-shooter. The next scene saw little Everett at the kitchen table poking his spoon into a bowl of oatmeal. His mother Adele stood nearby imparting her wisdom.

"Remember dear, always speak up for yourself. Never let others get away with telling you."

Things got dicey for the sleeping teacher when the locale shifted to the front of his little friend Leslie's house. It was also the home of Leslie's grandmother, the root cause of all his problems. The mental image of Granny Trapani caused the sleeping Everett to twist and turn. The memory playing in his mind reignited within him that long ago sensation of a terrified little boy. He once again cowered on the sidewalk in cuffed jeans torn at the knee. The dream seemed so real that it caused Everett to shudder as he faced his evil nemesis with her high cheekbones and chiseled face. Granny stood behind her front gate pretending to be the warm neighbor she wasn't. She didn't fool the youngster any more than her sneaky cat agents who passed themselves off as harmless house pets. Everett was wary of the cats as he watched them slink around on all fours. When stationary, Granny's minions could be seen rubbing themselves against the black stockings that covered the old devil's stick-like lower limbs. Adele's presence alongside her son offered no reassurance for the boy. His mother never realized that the old woman possessed such mysterious powers. As Granny gestured for Everett to come closer, Adele innocently urged him to go to her.

"You don't understand," Everett muttered in his sleep, frustrated that Adele didn't comprehend the spell the old woman cast on him.

"Go on Everett, go say hello," prodded Adele.

"You-come-a here, you-no-be-afraid," Granny cooed, as she leaned over the waist-high black iron gate smiling warmly.

Every time the old woman spoke, her brownish, wood-like teeth could be seen. Little Everett cupped his small hands over his squinting eyes, making it appear as if he were shielding himself from the rays of the summer sun. Nothing could have been further from the truth. He was hiding his eyes.

The next dream sequence flashed back to the apartment, with the boy trying to explain to Adele how he'd lose control of his eyes whenever he was in contact with Granny.

"But it's true," he insisted.

"Don't be ridiculous, dear," answered Adele, totally dismissing her son's claims.

"She changes my eyes!" The sleeping Everett felt the anguish as he relived his pleading.

"Alright, let me take a look, dear." Adele went through the motions of examining his eyes to appease the boy. She saw no indication of anything abnormal. "It's time to stop this foolishness, Everett."

Another apartment scene saw Adele losing it after her boy began speaking about hearing Granny's voice in his head. At this juncture she shut her son down pronto.

"Cut the crap," she hollered. "Are you afraid of a little old lady? Really now, enough is enough!"

"But..."

"I'll get you to stop this damn ridiculousness!" shouted Adele. "Let me see, open those eyes wide for me," she ordered. Peering deeply into the boy's blue eyes, she once again saw nothing out of the ordinary. "Your eyes are perfectly fine!"

"But my eyes are messed up...and I do hear things!" Everett insisted through tears.

The whimpers of the adult Everett could be heard emanating from his bedroom. The mental movie now shifted to the office of an eye doctor. Seeing nothing wrong with Everett's eyes, the optometrist attributed the problem to the boy's vivid imagination and too much idle time on his hands.

Everett's sleeping mind next swung back to the apartment where he once again complained of his condition. Things turned ugly, with Adele dragging him by the neck into the bathroom. She pushed Everett's nose up against the medicine cabinet mirror, forcing him to look into his own, now bulging, baby blues.

"There isn't a thing wrong with your eyes!" Adele shouted. In the deepness of his sleep Everett felt the coolness of the mirror glass against his nose. He also felt his mother's grip on his neck. Her strong hold on him felt so real that he reached out into the air above his bed in an attempt to neutralize the power of his mother.

"You-no-wanna-listen to mama?" taunted the evil voice in the little boy's head.

"Ma...it's her. She's talking to me right now," cried out Everett.

Adele blew her stack. She unloaded a series of stinging slaps to her son's face, hoping that this would put an end to it all. Her brutality proved effective in silencing Everett. From that moment on he never again spoke of his eyes or hearing voices...to anyone.

"Ahhhhhhh," groaned Everett as he raised his arms to ward off the imaginary blows. The shock to his system caused him to jump up in bed, temporarily rescuing him from his nightmare. The teacher's skin had become clammy, leaving him reposing on a sheet dampened with sweat. Finding the experience exhausting, he soon fell back down into bed. He reached across the bed feeling for a cool spot. Finding one he shifted his body in that direction. He returned to his sleep after assuming a new position on the cool side of the mattress. He hugged the extra pillow tightly to his chest for soothing support. Act two in the drama, took him further back in time...to that fateful day in Granny's backyard.

"C'MON EVERETT, LET'S TAKE Ducky in Granny's backyard for a swim in the pond," suggested the little girl with the ponytail.

Along the cement in front of her grandmother's house, Leslie was pulling on a long white cord affixed to a wooden yellow duck on wheels. Everett turned to look at his mother who was standing nearby talking to her friend, the little girl's mother. After receiving permission, Everett innocently followed Leslie into the house.

Inside Everett noticed, off to his right, the living room where Leslie's grandfather sat stiffly in a high back cushioned chair. A Methuselah-like figure, he seemed to be mummified. His hands were tightly gripping the rounded curvature where the wooden arms of the chair ended. In defiance of the season, the old man was attired in a long sleeve gray v-neck sweater, worn over a flannel red and black shirt that was buttoned at the top. His white mustache was substantial, covering most of his mouth. Everett looked at him curiously, wondering how food penetrated the jungle brush. The boy extended no greeting, nor did he receive one. Traveling along a narrow hall, the children proceeded to the back of the house toward the yard. Just before reaching their destination, they passed the kitchen, where they were met by Leslie's grandmother. The old woman stood open mouthed, as Leslie and Everett walked by her. She suspiciously watched the two children, following them into the yard. Little Everett sensed an unfriendly vibe. Playing with Leslie now ceased being fun. The boy wanted out of the yard. As Leslie watched the duck floating in the circular pond at the back of the yard, Everett was sneaking peeks over his shoulder to see what her grandmother was up to. He broke into a panic when the old woman stationed herself at the yard door with her arms firmly folded across her chest. After their eyes met, Everett and the old woman both knew that he was in the wrong place. Granny, sensing the little boy's fear, mustered up her meanest look possible. She balled her right hand into a fist and slowly raised it up to her chin. She then shook it menacingly at Everett. Petrified, the young boy came close to soiling his pants. But weighing down his trousers was the least of his worries. He had just been the recipient of the fright of a lifetime. It was an assault on his fragile psyche that left him both mentally and physically scarred for life. The shock to his nervous system was substantial enough to cause his eyes to cross. It was destined to be a lifelong condition that would come and go based on triggering stimulation. When his eyes crossed, Everett was able to fuse the images of double vision, allowing him to still see clearly even though his eyes appeared to be severely altered. With an out of control trepidation, Everett feverishly began to look for an opportunity to escape from the yard. Anticipating an attack, the boy's now crossed eyes remained glued on his adversary.

The first time the old woman stepped away from the back door, he bolted from the yard, through the house, and into the safety of the street.

"MAMA!" Everett screamed out, violently arching himself upward in his bed. His legs had been cycling in his sleep, as if running. Groggy, he slowly sunk back down onto his back, now fully awake.

❖

EVERETT GREW UP ON a block comprised of factories, a few houses, and including himself, just two children. With his ties to Leslie severed, the future teacher was compelled to become self sufficient in terms of amusement. This, along with being saddled with his occasional eye affliction and the evil voice of Granny entering his head, made the next few years difficult. He was forced into being a loner, a boy who played by himself for hours with a rubber ball. He'd fire the ball against the steps of a stoop, throw it upward against the tallest buildings and practice catching one-handed on its return. These activities, in conjunction with going over iron fences, sliding down banisters, jumping down stoop steps and climbing up to the top of lampposts, developed his strength, coordination and confidence.

Everett was about eight or nine when Adele announced that Leslie's grandmother dropped dead while bending to pick up a can of tomatoes. The youngster was overjoyed. As people came and went into the old lady's house to pay their respects, Everett sat quietly on his stoop devouring a cupcake. It was at this moment that Everett first came to learn that Granny was able to reincarnate herself.

"I'm-a-no-go-way, I'm-a-still-here," said the newly departed after taking the form of a fly that began buzzing about Everett's cupcake. This was a first. The old woman had never before assumed the body of an insect, or of anything else.

Feeling his head begin to throb, Everett donned the cheap plastic sunglasses he had taken to carrying. He tried to swat his tormenter away without success, the fly being too quick. He fared no better when he began throwing his ball at his target. After giving it some thought Everett devised a method to catch his winged antagonist unaware. He stationed himself on the sidewalk over ground he salted with a piece of his cupcake. He then waited patiently until the flying pest landed on the enticement.

"This-a-for-me?" asked the voice in his head.

Not responding, Everett slowly extended his arm to his shoulder once the fly landed on the candy. Holding the rubber ball several feet directly over the fly, his target was now a sitting duck. He gently released his grip on the ball, without jerking or moving his arm, allowing it to free fall. The winged version of Granny Trapani never saw the ball approaching. The crash landing of the ball stunned the insect. Everett then placed his prisoner inside a coffee tin he retrieved from a garbage pail. Covering the tin with a piece of cardboard, he then ran upstairs to the apartment to fetch several wooden matches. Upon his return to the incapacitated fly he began poking the insect with his mini torches, eventually lighting up the wings. Everett relished watching the suffering he caused before putting an end to his demon. Not long after this incident, Everett came to realize that Granny had many lives. In terms of sheer enjoyment, killing Granny in fly form was something only surpassed by eliminating her when she took on the body of a cat.

By the time he was old enough to venture off the block, the Granny hallucinations greatly diminished, although her voice continued to weigh in regularly. When Everett started playing basketball at a local court, he began to make new friends in addition to those he knew from school. A natural athlete, he took to the game easily. Soon he was accepted by the better players. They nicknamed him Shades, due to his tendency to always have a pair of sunglasses hanging from his neck when playing. Entering his teens, he grew bigger and stronger than most, gaining him a certain respect among peers. He came to understand one of the basic realities of the street...snitches get stitches. Regardless of how distasteful the behavior, there was simply no acceptable justification for informing on another. This protective umbrella masked one of Everett's worst eccentricities: the slaughtering of a cat now and then.

Everett developed a reputation for volatility after a winter snowstorm. He, along with another fourteen-year-old, happened to be passing through a street where a group of boys were congregated. The two were accosted by the group, who were a year or so older. The bullies threatened Everett and his friend with snowballs. Being given three seconds to run, Everett stood his ground. This resulted in one bully dropping a pile of snow down his back. Everett, without the aid of any voice in his head, snapped. As the chilly snow made its way down Everett's back, he lunged at his assailant throwing a flurry of punches that dropped the snowball bully, bloodying his nose. Completely out of his mind with rage, Everett straddled his antagonist, burying his head under a pile of snow. He began caking the teens mouth and plugging up his nostrils with snow. Several boys, including his friend, jumped on Everett to pull him off. This singular incident established Everett's reputation as a bona fide head-case.

Everett went on to live a relatively productive life. Being bright, he took nicely to the world of academia. To defray the cost of his college education, he took to selling marijuana with a diminutive, but highly intelligent, classmate who saw value in his new partner's physical prowess. This combination of brains and brawn made enough money for the two to seriously consider selling marijuana for a living. To the amazement of those who were aware of Everett's explosive side, he went on to become a high school teacher of science at a public school in East Harlem. The work suited him well. Now, with enough money coming in, he was able to move himself and his mother to a nicer neighborhood. He took a two bedroom on Tenth Avenue in Manhattan, two stories above a liquor store. It was considered a step up.

The adult Everett was a handsome man who was afforded more than his share of relationship opportunities. Married co-workers were forever playing matchmaker. Their introductions were always welcomed by Everett, even though he knew that amorous seas were never guaranteed. Granny Trapani's vocal visits often stepped in to effectively undermine Everett's romantic opportunities.

The science teacher stayed in shape by participating in rigorous physical activities. His primary outlet was to play schoolyard basketball. Still known on the courts as Shades, Everett engaged in games at various public venues in Manhattan. He played primarily with his students. This joint interest enabled the teacher to bond with the teenagers he taught. There was one particular incident at the school that perpetuated as a whispering secret year after year. Everett came upon several youths huddled at a corner locker between classes. Stepping in to see for himself what was so interesting, he saw one of the youths return a .357 Magnum to his inside jacket pocket. Taking the gun from the youth, Everett had the boys worried...and at his mercy.

"Where did you *find* this again?" There was no response to his question..

After looking around to make sure no one was watching, the teacher examined the loaded weapon. Unflustered, he announced to the boys that he would take charge of the firearm. "I *know* you just *found* this piece on the street," he announced, providing them with an excuse for having the gun. All of the teenagers were grateful for the play they knew they were receiving. Once back in his office, Everett mulled over what to do with the gun. He decided that it would be easiest to simply get rid of the weapon, rather than concoct a story as to how he came upon it. It was something he never got around to doing.

10

Going, Going...Gone

"Please, please don't hit me anymore. I've had enough..."

-Doctor Harriett Culbrenner

THINGS BEGAN TO DANGEROUSLY UNRAVEL for Everett a month prior to the attacks in the West Village bakery. His downward spiral came after a visit to the bedside of his hospitalized mother. Poor circulation was responsible for the cardio problem that led to her open heart surgery. Immediately after the operation, the prognosis was that the patient would fully recover. Since Adele had been such a robust woman throughout her life, there was little reason to doubt this projection. Her unanticipated health reversal came as a total surprise to everyone, including Doctor Harriett Culbrenner.

The doctor was making her rounds at the hospital the afternoon Everett decided to leave work early to visit Adele. He arrived just as the physician was reviewing his mother's chart. Everett detected *some* decline in Adele's condition by her labored breathing. Each breath sounded deep, coming at a slow pace and loudly. He turned to the physician for answers.

"How is she today, doctor?" Everett asked.

"Your mother is a very sick woman Mr. Skidmore," said the medico grimly.

"She'll be alright, won't she?"

The physician cleared her throat. "You must realize that recovery can be very unpredictable." Her tone suggested that things were not going well.

Everett had never considered that Adele might be down to her final out. "I guess she's just having a bad day," he said, hoping his optimism would be shared.

The physician's countenance remained sober. "Mr. Skidmore, I'm sorry to inform you of this, but in her present condition, it is unlikely she'll be able to go on much longer."

The doctor's update was served dispassionately— her words had the warmth of a calculus test. Staring down disbelievingly at his bed-ridden mother, Everett began to process the news. The greatest bedside manner could not have sufficiently cushioned the devastating effect the distressing news had on him. Adding to his grief was the merciless voice of evil crashing the gate leading to his brain.

"You gonna cry?" asked the evil voice, tauntingly.

Everett looked away from the doctor, mechanically reaching for his sunglasses. After concealing his eyes with the dark shades, he turned to address the physician.

"Doctor, you said she was going to be alright. What happened? She was sitting up reading a magazine yesterday."

"Her kidneys ceased functioning properly. It's acute renal failure, Mr. Skidmore. Let's be grateful your mother isn't in too much discomfort. She lived a good long life. Reaching eighty-five-years without any prior illness is a gift. It's something to be thankful for."

"How many months has she left?" Everett asked curtly, ignoring her added comments.

Doctor Culbrenner's eyes widened. "Months?" she asked, shifting her head back. The doctor displayed a puzzled look. "We're facing a much, much shorter window."

Everett received the news as if he were blindsided. "How could you wait to the last minute to spring something like this on me?" he asked. There was a cool edge to his voice.

Just as the doctor was about to respond, she all of a sudden realized that the room had gotten quiet. The rhythmic sound of Adele's labored breathing had abruptly ended. The halting of the gasping cadence could mean only one thing, that the grim reaper had entered the room. Doctor Culbrenner moved in quickly to check her patient's vital signs. The results were as expected, causing her to lower her head for a few seconds. The doctor lifted her arm, using the palm of her hand to stroke the side of her hair. Then, after slowly forming a fist, the physician began slightly shaking her clenched hand. It was her reaction to having the misfortune of being present in the room with a family member when a patient expired. Her personal preference was for death to arrive in the middle of the night, when no one was around other than a nurse to break the news to a loved one...telephonically.

"She's gone," declared the doctor in a low voice, after turning to face Everett.

The shaking fist of Doctor Culbrenner did not escape Everett's attention. This gesture, coupled with the reality of Adele's death, caused the teacher to snap. A long dormant homicidal side was now unleashed. Everett turned away from the doctor to put on his sunglasses as the transformation process into Granny Trapani began. Acutely aware of Everett's peculiar behavior, the doctor extended her condolences.

"Mr. Skidmore, please accept my *deepest* sympathy." The only thing audible that Everett heard came from within the confines of his head.

"*Poor you!*" needled the evil voice.

In Everett's warped mind, Granny Trapani for the first time materializing into the form of another human being. The science teacher swore revenge for what he deemed to be a nefarious collusion between Granny and the physician.

"*Don't you fret now, dear, I'll always be with you.*" Everett was filled with joy at hearing the voice of his mother reaching out to him...the good voice! He immediately left the room.

"How can you come back like this?" he asked in a whisper. "Where are you?"

"*Never mind that for now, it's something you will understand when it's your turn, dear. Remember your surroundings, you need to be careful. There are people around.*"

❖

WITH NO FAMILY TO CONSIDER, there was no need for an extended viewing at the funeral parlor. Adele's wake was attended by a few of Everett's co-workers from the school, his landlady Frieda, and a surprisingly large number of students. While on bereavement leave, he spent time strategizing on how he was going to assassinate Granny Trapani in her guise as Doctor Culbrenner. With his plan formulated, Everett prepared himself a tuna salad sandwich and a glass of milk. He then took a seat in what had been his mother's favorite chair. It was the closest he could come to feeling as though he was in her embrace. He remained in the chair until it was time to enact his murderous plot.

Pulling out all the stops, Everett seized the opportunity to kill two birds with one stone. He intended to spend the evening hunting his quarry, and also satisfy a long suppressed desire to experiment with cross-dressing. This was to be his maiden voyage wearing the clothes of the opposite sex. With Adele now in a better place, this item on his bucket list no longer needed to be shelved for a later date.

"*Everett! What are you thinking?*" asked the good voice.

"This is something I've been meaning to do," replied Everett. "Please understand..."

"What's to understand? *You'll never be hearing from me during this silliness!*"

"Alright, let's talk later," answered Everett, not surprised at Adele's reaction. She always gave him the silent treatment when displeased. He was confident she'd get over it with the passage of time.

Everett laid out his mother's clothes on the bed in her room. He selected garments that were large enough for him to squeeze into. Everett decided to wear the dark blue stretch pants with a loose-fitting, matching top. After stuffing Adele's bra with his socks, he slipped into a pair of her panties, surprised to find they stretched wide enough for him to fit into. Everett wore his own white Nike sneakers and the khaki-colored woman's raincoat he purchased specifically for the occasion. Looking in a mirror, he applied a thick foundation to cover any telltale facial shadow. This was followed by a generous application of rouge. After putting on red lipstick, he was finished altering his appearance. He spent time studying himself in the mirror, unable to arrive at an objective assessment as to how he looked. Finally he shrugged and placed a red wig atop his head. Thinking that it made a difference, he managed to convince himself that he'd draw no more attention than any other free spirit. Everett pulled one of his red silk ties out of the closet and placed it in the large handbag he intended to take along on his lethal outing. He then went to the storage area under the kitchen sink to retrieve a pair of rubber gloves and a small plastic container filled with a mace-like preparation of his own creation. He pointed the plastic container into the sink and pressed the dispenser cap to make sure the spray was functioning. Once satisfied, he placed both items into the bag. He then debated whether or not to take the gun. Opting to do so, he removed the loaded gun from a locked attaché case in his closet. It was the same weapon he had taken from a student many years prior. Aware that Doctor Culbrenner had evening office hours on Thursdays, Everett set out on his deadly mission.

"*Where you go?*" questioned the evil voice.

"You'll find out," Everett answered, putting on his sunglasses.

THE CONSENSUS AMONG HER peers was that Doctor Culbrenner was an excellent physician. While her husband was off delivering twins, Doctor Culbrenner stayed beyond office hours to go through mail and pay bills. Their shared office was on the first floor of the three-story townhouse they owned.

"You can leave now Lois, go on home. I'll close up when I'm through," the physician said to her office manager. "I have some things I need to do before I go upstairs."

"Thank you doctor," Lois answered cheerily. "You don't have to say that twice!"

Everett had been to the doctor's office with Adele on many occasions. He stood at a bus stop watching the townhouse from afar. Unaware that Culbrenner lived in the upper duplex, the teacher waited for the physician to leave for the evening. Everett saw the office manager's departure from work, noting that she left the office lights on behind her. The lights, visible from the street, made it likely that the doctor was still inside. As Lois passed the bus stop on her way to the train, she never took notice of Everett. Being overlooked caused the teacher to feel that his altered appearance was effective in camouflaging his true identity, even from someone who knew him. Everett pushed his sunglasses closer to his eyes as he made his way to the townhouse. He peered through the wooden shutter slats that were slightly separated. The space offered enough of an opening to provide a clear view of the waiting room. Everett could see that there were no patients waiting to be seen. His target was standing behind the reception desk going through her mail. Spotting an empty cardboard box on top of one of the trash cans, he retrieved it. Everett then locked the four flaps into each other, turned it upside down and placed the box at the foot of the door before ringing the doorbell. He then assumed a position on the stoop so that he would remain out of view. At the sound of the gate opening, he stepped off the stoop, rushed to the front entrance and pushed his way into the building. The force of his entry knocked Culbrenner to the ground. As she rose he landed a blow to her forehead, immediately producing an egg shaped lump. After securing the front door, he returned to the grounded doctor. Saved from a knock out thanks to the blow landing high, the physician remained alert as she stared up at her attacker. Her face turned ashen with fright at the sight of who was looking down at her. The doctor's mind raced even more frantically after noticing the rubber gloves worn by the assailant. Not knowing what to do, she remained down, preparing herself to absorb possible further punishment.

Everett looked sternly down at Culbrenner, who he saw as Granny. "The day for us to settle the account with my mother has finally come," he said.

The doctor now realized that it was Everett Skidmore in drag standing over her. As odd as it would seem, the assault victim found some underlying comfort in her assailant being someone known to her. This strange feeling of familiarity provided her with the added confidence that would allow her to speak.

"Mr. Skidmore...is that you?"

"So now it's *Mr. Skidmore*, is it?" Everett asked.

"What's this all about?" asked the felled physician.

"I've grown up, Granny! I'm no longer your granddaughter's helpless little friend."

"What granddaughter? I don't have a granddaughter."

"So now you don't know your own grandchild? Don't make me laugh! I can *see* who you really are under that false façade you've taken on. Where are those little meowing beasts of yours?" he inquired, referring to Granny Trapani's beloved cats.

"*You gonna do...then do*," injected the evil voice with bravado.

"I'll *do* alright," Everett answered though tightened teeth.

Listening to Everett talk to himself convinced the doctor that she was up against a deranged lunatic. She tried reasoning with him by using a soft low voice.

"Can't I do something to make things right?" asked the shaken doctor, as she slowly inched upward, venturing to get to her feet. "If this is about your mother, *please* realize that she was a *very* sick woman. If it's my fee, I can certainly..."

Everett's left jab came with the speed of a lizard's tongue. It packed enough of a wallop to floor the physician. Dazed, her mouth was now bloodied. As the cobwebs slowly cleared, she began to lift herself onto her elbows. Unsuccessful in fully rising, she shifted her body onto her side. On the alert for additional blows, she desperately attempted to negotiate.

"Please, please don't hit me anymore," she begged. "I've had enough."

Fverett scoffed at the doctor's appeal. "So *you've* had enough?"

"Yes...I can give you money," offered the doctor in desperation, "ten-thousand-dollars."

"You want to give *me* ten-thousand-dollars?"

Sensing skepticism in Everett's voice, the doctor sweetened the pot. "I can give you even more. I can call someone who can come right over with cash...how much?"

Looking into her terror-filled face, all Everett could see was the image of Leslie's grandmother as she'd appeared to him in his childhood. The doctor's efforts to buy him off only aggravated the situation. The crazed teacher reacted by administering a beating that left Culbrenner unconscious. Everett stared at the physician's bruises, surprised to see how her right eye quickly sprouted into a bubble. The swelling filled up the socket, leaving a closed slit. Removing the red silk tie from his bag, he strangled the unconscious physician. When he was done he gazed down at the doctor. The madman hoped that with the destruction of the demon's shell, his misery with Granny would be over. It was wishful thinking. Before he left the scene he returned the cardboard box he used as a ruse to the outside trash.

DUE TO THE LACK OF LEADS gathered in the days following the Doctor Culbrenner homicide, the police were pessimistic about the case being solved anytime soon. With no indication of a motive or evidence, the squad detectives were stymied. There were no tool marks, impressions or chipping on any of the windows or doors, so a break-in was ruled out. Since all of the access points were secured, the assumption was that the perpetrator was either invited into the office or pushed his way in. Investigators unearthed no work-related arguments, no information pointing to revenge, and no hint of substance abuse. There was no property missing. When they began to delve into the physician's personal life, their probing eliminated blackmail, unpaid loans, and infidelity as possible motives. The detectives checked to see if there was an insurance policy substantial enough for a beneficiary to commit murder. There wasn't: the doctor's husband came from money and had plenty of his own. As far as anyone could see, things seemed wholesome in the household of the slain doctor. The husband's delivery of twins was an airtight alibi. The interviews conducted turned out to be fruitless. Since the detectives were stumped, the Culbrenner investigation ultimately found its way onto the back burner, where it would remain until new information surfaced. As far as could be seen, Everett's first homicide was a successfully executed undertaking.

11

"Give Me One Without The Thumb"

"I'm gonna put Edna in a pan of oil, fry her up and feed her to you for dinner one night!"

-Thelma Curcio

WITH THE DOCTOR CULBRENNER HOMICIDE BEHIND HIM, Everett reverted back to his usual routine without giving the murder a second thought. He took the same uptown train to work each morning dressed in a suit and tie. During one morning commute he was engrossed in a newspaper article about a New Jersey man who received the first hand transplant. Everett was so fascinated by what he was reading that he never noticed the attention he was receiving from the woman seated opposite him. The woman in the black leather skirt had been studying him since he first got on the train. Seeing Everett as her type, she endeavored to gain his notice by crossing and uncrossing her legs. When this failed she repositioned herself, spacing her legs apart. Everett was too immersed in his reading to be distracted. He not only failed to pick up on her overtures, he also missed her look of annoyance when she exited the train.

When Everett arrived at his school, he ran into one of his students standing near the front entrance. "Are you prepared for the rematch?" asked the teacher.

"All set, Mr. Skidmore. I hear those Portuguese dudes have been practicing," said the lanky teenager. "You think we'll be able to beat them again?"

"I can't see us *not* taking two out of three."

"You gonna stuff one? They fell apart after seeing you do that last time."

The remark puffed Everett up. "If the opportunity presents itself, rest assured that Shades *will* jam one. But remember, on a team there is no room for showboating."

The teenager laughed at his teacher referring to himself by his nickname. "I got it, Mr. Skidmore. We'll play right after school next week in the same schoolyard, right?"

"That's correct. Did you work on that move I showed you?"

"Yeah, I got that down."

"Remember to use it anytime you're under that basket."

"I will. So how about we play them for ten bucks a man?" suggested the teen.

"No, no, no...no gambling. We never play for money, just bragging rights."

The student felt disappointed, he could've used the ten dollars. "You got it Mr. Skidmore, see you later."

Later that day, Everett stepped outside of the school building to get some air. He looked up at the blue sky, admiring its heavenly loveliness. Having time before his next class, Everett walked to a nearby candy store that was a long time fixture in East Harlem. The mom and pop business occupied the ground floor of a four story corner building. A green metal sign, running the width of the storefront, was prominently displayed above the front. The logo of an ice cream concern occupied the left hand corner of the sign, while the rest of the space advertised cigarettes, cigars, soda and candy. Alongside the property was a fenced lot that was rented out monthly to neighborhood residents willing to pay for a safe place to park their cars. Entering the store, Everett passed an elderly, but still robust man. It was Gussie, the owner. Next to Gussie's station, atop a stand, sat a large bird cage. Behind the bars was Edna, a chatty

African Grey who the candy store owner had named after an old flame. Gussie's affection for Edna was equaled by his sixty-one-year-old daughter's hatred for the bird.

Despite being ninety, Gussie maintained an eighteen-inch neck and a bushy head of thick white hair. He had a barrel chest, with the only obvious sign of sagging coming from his breasts. Sitting ramrod straight on a high chair with his arms folded, Gussie Curcio gave the appearance of a monitor overseeing test takers. Aware that he looked much younger than his years, he liked to tell people that he discovered the Fountain of Youth in Marcus Garvey Park.

Everett stood by waiting his turn while Gussie's daughter was busy preparing a black and white ice cream cone for a boy in his early teens. Somewhat disheveled, Thelma was of average height with shoulder-length jet black hair that she wore parted in the center. Gray roots sprang up along both sides of the line in her part. She was dressed in dark pants, white orthopedic shoes and a long sleeve burgundy sweatshirt that helped hide her thick upper arms. Preferring to go without make-up, her only indulgence consisted of an Omega watch that came with a thick gold band. It was a present she received from her father after turning twenty-one. "Remember Thelma, the money is in the band," he would frequently mention to remind her.

After scooping out the chocolate from the large tub in the freezer underneath the counter, Thelma packed the ice cream down tightly into the cone. Glancing up at Gussie, she could see that her father was watching her. Long accustomed to being under his microscope, she labored on, now scooping out the vanilla to cap off the cone. When finished, she licked the excess ice cream off her thumb. Thelma then wrapped a second fresh napkin around the base of the cone and handed it over the counter to the youth. The boy balked, issuing a dismissive wave with the back of his hand.

"Did you want sprinkles?" she asked innocently. The boy shook his head no. "What's the matter then?" questioned Thelma.

"How about you give me one *without* the thumb?" asked the smirking boy,

Thelma's face became flushed at hearing the remark. She held her temper and spoke calmly. "Look, do you want the cone, or not?"

"I'm not eating *that crap*, you put your thumb in it," protested the boy.

"Then get your little ass out of here!" she shouted, incensed at his impertinence.

The young man responded by placing his thumb to his nose and wiggling his four free fingers vigorously at Thelma. That did it. Gussie's daughter, when angered, was known to do unpredictable things. The explosive reaction the boy sparked came without warning. The highly agitated Thelma began by pointing the cone at her customer. Looking directly at the youth, she unloaded.

"You want one without the thumb you half-pint, spoiled son-of-a-bitch...okay," she growled, "I'll give you one without the thumb!" The youth stood in awe, surprised at the fire he lit. "*Here you go*, take one without the thumb you little shit!" Thelma roared, throwing the ice cream cone at the youth. After dodging the cone, the boy made a hasty retreat.

After launching the cone, Thelma ran from behind the counter with surprising speed. Holding a foot long piece of pipe in one hand, she began to shake her upraised fist violently at the youth with the other. The store owner's daughter began to chase after the boy. Realizing that she could never hope to catch up with the disrespectful adolescent, Thelma aborted the pursuit a few steps beyond the front door.

"You *better* run, you little turd!" she hollered from the sidewalk. Her last act before going back into the store took the form of a vulgar arrivederci. Raising the pipe in her left hand, she bid good riddance to her customer by slapping her right hand into the crook of her upraised arm, conveying what the boy could do with himself.

Gussie, now off his stool, confronted his daughter upon her return to the store. "Jesus! Thelma, what the hell are you doing? You can't start chasing down every punk kid that comes in here busting chops?"

"I'm not about to start taking crap from some pimple-faced asshole, daddy. Not at this point in my life!" she declared adamantly.

"Thelma, you're getting too fat," cracked the caged bird out of the blue. *"Give me one without the thumb,"* were the next words that came from the African Grey, repeating what was said moments earlier.

Thelma heard enough from her father's pet. "And YOU shut the hell up, Edna!"

Gussie shook his head, finding things amusing. "Be nice," the old man said calmly.

"I'm gonna put Edna in a pan of oil, fry her up and feed her to you for dinner one night!"

The old man turned serious. He disliked hearing such talk. "Don't get any ideas daughter of mine. Because, if you do, there's gonna be two in that oil," he bluffed.

"You forgetting Little Blue Bird?" asked Thelma, referencing Gussie's dead parakeet.

Gussie held his tongue after that. The old man still ached over the unfortunate demise of the parakeet that he kept in the apartment. After playing cards in the yard with some of his cronies, Gussie retired to his digs only to find Little Blue Bird croaked, lying face down at the bottom of the birdcage. Thelma told her father that she let the parakeet out of the cage to fly about for exercise while she took a shower. After finishing, she didn't see the bird around, so she decided to watch television. After turning on the TV, Thelma claimed that she plopped herself onto the recliner in front of the set without looking into the seat where the bird had been resting. The human avalanche snuffed the life out of Little Blue Bird. As a result of this long ago mishap, Gussie never fully trusted his daughter again...particularly when it came to Edna, the costly African Grey who replaced the ill-fated Little Blue Bird.

Thelma got down on one knee to clean up the mess made from the cone she threw. As she was picking up the broken pieces of cone and wiping the ice cream off the floor, she noticed a pair of legs in dark suit pants standing alongside her. Her eyes followed the suit up until she saw the face of a tall grayed haired man wearing sunglasses. It was Everett, who was in the store still waiting for his turn. Thelma's fury still had not fully subsided. She glared upward as she addressed her customer.

"Well?" she asked, in not the friendliest of tones.

The science teacher was looking down at Thelma Curcio but seeing Granny. *"So you find-a-me again!"* said the evil voice in his mind.

The sight of a shaking fist had once again activated Everett's dark side. Realizing that killing Doctor Culbrenner hadn't disposed of Granny permanently, he arrived at the sad conclusion that he would have to continue to kill. Everett had the presence of mind to realize that he couldn't take care of his nemeses with Gussie around.

"That's the only thing these little bastards know around here mister," voiced Thelma, explaining herself. "They got no respect for anyone! Fifty-one years I'm working in this store, since I'm ten years old. TEN YEARS OLD!" she bellowed loudly, wanting her father to hear. Thelma then looked over at Gussie for a second before returning her attention to Everett. "Ahhh...what the hell is the use in my complaining, nobody listens. So what do you need, mister?"

"Basketball Stories Illustrated and six packs of Spearmint gum. I have the exact change," Everett replied, adding in a whisper, "I'll be seeing you soon."

Thelma didn't catch the last part. "Alright, take what you want then and leave the money on the counter," she instructed. "I only wish we still had the dog!" Thelma was referring to an attack dog she and her father once kept in the store for protection.

Everett placed his money on the counter. "I'll see you again, very *soon*," he said ominously. The science teacher then exited the store, breezing by Thelma's father.

Thelma remained on her knees as she continued to clean up the floor. As Gussie looked down at his daughter he grew sad. Perhaps it was guilt. His paternal juices awakened, he waited until Thelma further calmed down before speaking to her.

"Thelma, talk to me," said the old man.

"Ahhh, I'm disgusted!" she answered with a dismissive wave of her hand.

"C'mon, forget it. You looking to get yourself sick over here?" he asked. Receiving no response, Gussie tried to get to her another way, "How about we go out to eat Sunday at Turco's? We haven't had the pork in the Sunday gravy in awhile. I know how you love that."

Thelma thought about the meal she so thoroughly enjoyed. "Alright," she replied. "It has been a long time."

"Okay then, it's a date." A minute later Thelma again heard the African Grey weigh in. *"Thelma, you're getting too fat,"* uttered the chatterbox bird.

"Give me one without the thumb."

"Thelma, you're getting too fat."

Thelma just glared at the bird. As she picked up the money Everett left on the counter she noticed that he overpaid. "That man left too much money. He's got change coming to him," she said to Gussie.

"Don't worry about it. We'll return what we owe the next time he comes in."

"Sure, I'll make a note of it," she commented.

12

Too-Da-Loo Thelma

"Poor, poor Mrs. Trapani."

-Edna, The African Grey

EVERETT ROSE EARLY TO RETURN TO EAST HARLEM before daylight. His purpose was to carry out his mission to murder Thelma Curcio. For this dubious occasion he chose to wear a recently purchased rose colored ruffled shirt, black skirt and spider leg pantyhose. These items of feminine apparel were kept in the bedroom closet of his late mother, whose room remained the same as if she were still among the living. Adele's belongings could be found neatly stored in drawers and closets in her room. Everett left her toothbrush in the bathroom, using it every so often to maintain a connection. On top of Adele's dresser was a framed photo of Everett as a young boy. He smiled fondly as he reflected sitting atop the brown and white pony that day many years ago. "Remember this?" he asked Adele, without expecting an answer. He knew that his mother's displeasure with his cross-dressing was certain to result in a temporary shunning.

As the coffee was brewing, Everett turned on the radio he kept in the bathroom. He always liked to listen to the news as he brushed his teeth, shaved, and showered. Hearing that thousands were dead due to Hurricane Mitch in Central America gave him pause. He wondered why those poor souls had to die while the demon Granny continued to live on. After having his coffee the teacher dressed, prettied himself with some makeup, donned the red wig and stocked his handbag with his tools of mayhem.

It was well before the morning rush hour when Everett boarded the uptown train. The few passengers in the car had the look of people not getting enough sleep. Some riders willingly dozed during their bumpy ride, while others attempted to ward off the urge to nap. One alert man proved to be the exception. He sat at the far end of the car exhibiting an apparent interest in Everett. The teacher soon became aware that the passenger had him under observation. Since this was the first time Everett was showing his legs publicly, the attention of the stranger stimulated his curiosities. The fact that he was being checked out, favorably or otherwise, was a turn on for Everett. The streets of East Harlem were still dark when the wig wearing science teacher in the dark sunglasses came to his stop. Lack of daylight was a good thing. The brightness might have drawn attention to the awakening under his skirt.

GUSSIE CURSIO NEVER PLANNED for Thelma to lead such a limited life. It was just the way things played out. If his wife could've beaten the cancer, things might have been different. But that wasn't the case. With her mother's death came the anchoring of the ten-year-old Thelma to her father's candy store. Over the years Gussie drummed into Thelma's head that the key to financial security came from hard work, saving money, owning property, and most importantly, living modestly. The Curcio formula, which included remaining debt free, was not without merit. The father and daughter lived in a two-bedroom located directly above the candy store. A spiral interior staircase connected the store to the apartment, creating easy access for coming and going. The apartments in the building were rented out at the going rate. Aside from the East Harlem building Gussie also owned commercial property in lower Manhattan and Saratoga. The enclosed lot he owned alongside the candy store added to his cash flow. He numbered seven parking spaces in white paint for neighbors to park their cars for a monthly fee. These were strictly cash transactions in which Gussie's only responsibility was to provide renters with a key to the lock on the gate. He didn't even have to assume responsibility for clearing the winter snow. Thelma was always there to provide renters with a shovel when there was need to dig their car out.

By his way of thinking, Gussie fulfilled his paternal obligation by assuring that Thelma would never be left to eat cat food in her old age. He socked away a small fortune in cash inside tin cans that he buried in his backyard. These underground treasures were never a secret to Thelma. Gussie made sure that his will reflected that his daughter inherit all of his assets once he passed on. The pending inheritance gave her something to be optimistic about. However, with each passing decade it seemed to Thelma that Gussie might never die. Now, even if he did suddenly ride off into the sunset, where was she going? Thelma recognized that she was probably too old to *really* enjoy the money. Even the thought of digging up the yard lost its shine.

THE MORNING AFTER THE INCIDENT with the ice cream Thelma rose early, as was her custom. She opened up the store as usual, purposely making lots of noise in doing so. Thelma took pleasure in disrupting the feathered Edna. Passing the bird's cage she scratched the bars with her keys as a means to roust her confined nemesis. The bird responded to the provocation by speaking her peace. *"Thelma, you're getting too fat,"* was the first irritating chant uttered.

"Shut the hell up!" hissed Thelma, before giving the cage a fierce shake.

Gussie's daughter vowed that Edna would pay a severe price once her father transitioned to the next world. Aside from the inheritance, killing the bird was the most important thing that Thelma had to look forward to. She conjured up a number of appropriate send offs for her father's pet. Her most diabolical plan called for her to clip off one of Edna's wings and then embed one of her feet in a large glue trap. After doing this, she intended to salt the helpless bird's body, before leaving Edna in the yard for the visiting mice, rats and squirrels to feast on.

"*Thelma, you're getting too fat,*" repeated Edna.

"*Give me one without the thumb.*"

Thelma sneered as she looked over at Edna. She kept a black water pistol, fully loaded, in a drawer behind the counter. After hearing the irritating words of the African Grey, she approached the bird cage armed with the water gun in her hand. Thelma gave the antagonistic Edna a few quick squirts. It was pure enjoyment for her to see the bird's head abruptly jerk back, and then shake her wings violently after each pull of the trigger.

"Feeling refreshed my little Tweetie Pie?" Thelma asked in a whisper, as she watched the tormented bird flap wildly. The five-squirt morning left Edna looking like she had gone fifteen rounds with a harpy eagle.

Thelma always felt a little better after hosing down Edna. She was careful to dry off the bird cage and change the paper before it Gussie came down to the store. Thelma's spirits remained high until the arrival of Everett. She stared in awe at who she believed to be a big redheaded woman wearing sunglasses.

"*What-a-you-do?*" asked the evil voice in Everett's head as he moved toward Thelma.

Remembering that the shopkeeper kept a pipe behind the counter, Everett advanced swiftly without saying a word. The open mouthed Thelma didn't know what to make of what was happening. She could do little other than watch the stranger come toward her. The teacher displayed a cruel smile when he finally replied to the evil voice.

"You may have many lives, but I'll hunt you down and kill you at every sighting!"

The spray Everett removed from his handbag contained a specially prepared solution he created. The bursts of the liquid entered Thelma's eyes and mouth. Thelma leaned back coughing, unable to scream. Blinded, she began to rub her eyes fiercely. She frantically reached for the bible on the shelf behind the counter. Everett's face expressed contempt as he watched her stretch for the good book.

"Hah! So it's religion you now seek," he said mockingly, slapping her hand away.

"Take the money, the register is open," Thelma pleaded, between coughing jags.

"Poor, poor Mrs. Trapani," mocked the insane man.

"Leave me alone," she begged, "I'm not Trapani. You got the wrong party. Who the hell are you, lady?"

"So now you don't recognize me?"

Thelma began to whimper pathetically. "I'm an old woman living here all my life..."

Everett removed the red tie from his purse. He dragged Thelma from behind the counter to the rear of the store where they would be further out of view from the street.

"Isn't payback a bitch?" Everett asked coldly.

"But I didn't do anything," Thelma sobbed. These were to be her last pathetic words.

When Everett was through with his strangulation, he took a newspaper to read during his subway travel home. After picking the spray off the counter, he returned it to his handbag. He then closed the store door behind him when exiting. The teacher removed his rubber gloves as he walked, placing them in his handbag alongside the spray and red tie. Had he stayed a little longer he would've heard Edna's babblings.

"Thelma, you're getting too fat."

"Give me one without the thumb."

"Poor, poor, Mrs. Trapani."

13

<u>Lights Out</u>

"Have a seat on the couch. I'll only be a minute."

-Laura Johnson

EVERETT TORE AROUND THE COURT like a man on fire. He ended the game with a long hook shot, this time scoring from well behind the foul line. The final basket represented the second win in a row for the Dominican students over their Portuguese rivals.

"Way to go Shades!" shouted the elated Dominicans, as they began giving man-hugs to their science teacher.

Losing two straight games hit the Portuguese players hard. "Damn...why didn't you stay on him, man?" criticized a losing player to his teammate.

"I *was* on him! What am I supposed to do? He was just sizzling, man" came the reply.

"*Sizzling Shades*," proclaimed one of the players. It was a name that stuck.

Victory was sweet for the teacher. Surprisingly, the strenuous competition didn't exhaust him. In fact, he could've played yet another game. After the usual refreshments with the teenagers, Everett headed home. Once there he found himself restless. The victory left him far too high-octane to stay home. He cleaned up and put on a crisp white shirt, red tie and recently pressed suit. He decided to visit a bar restaurant that he had wanted to experience. As always, he slipped a pair of sunglasses into the breast pocket of his suit jacket. It was a precaution he never failed to take.

LAURA JOHNSON WAS A TRUE ROMANTIC. Within the privacy of her bedroom, she leaned into the full length mirror for an up-close check of herself. Without age lines and blemish free, what she saw met with her approval. She took several steps back to examine her figure from afar. Turning to one side, she sucked in the little stomach that existed. Could there be more here or there? No, she was satisfied that things were fine as they were. Not one to undervalue herself, her self-rating was just shy of a ten.

It being her birthday, Laura headed out for a big night with her new love interest. It was also an anniversary of sorts. Exactly two weeks ago to the day she met Aubin, a beret wearing Frenchman in his late thirties. The two became acquainted at Danny Dimes, a restaurant lounge located just a few blocks from her home. The incredible chemistry they shared surfaced almost immediately. Laura thought Aubin summed it up best when they stood together looking into a store glass, "We look good together." It was precisely what she wanted to hear, but more to the point, it was what she wanted to believe.

A handsome man with a slight graying at his temples, Aubin cut an impressive figure. His smooth demeanor and impeccable appearance led most people to assume he was an affluent man of breeding. Laura was convinced Aubin was for real, a gentleman advanced enough to *listen* to what she had to say. Enveloped by infatuation, the real estate broker saw a future with Aubin.

On the walk over to Danny's, Laura reflected on a conversation she'd had with a girlfriend. Laura resented the well-intentioned advice she was given. What nerve *she* had to talk about relationships! With her track record no one in their right mind would permit themselves to be influenced by *that* woman's wisdom? Where was *her* keeper?

"Hello," Laura said happily, greeting the beefy bartender as she sauntered cheerily to the center of the mahogany bar at Danny Dimes.

"Hello Laura, the usual?" The bartender watched her slide onto a stool facing the mirrored glass behind him.

"No, I'll just have white wine for now. I'm going easy this evening," she answered with a smile that suggested mischief. "Do me a favor and make it Pinot Grigio."

"No problem." The bartender knew Laura as a good natured customer he could kid around with. "What are you looking to do, gaff a big tuna tonight?" he asked, as he placed the drink before her.

"What do you mean?"

"You know what I mean," he replied with a knowing look. "You gave yourself away by looking *extra* sensational this evening."

"Oh," she answered with a smile, "no, no gaffing tonight. But thank you for the compliment." She returned to her lofty thoughts of Aubin.

As a rule, Laura's strategy with an appropriate suitor called for moderation when it came to intimacy. Her feeling was that if a serious relationship was the goal, she needed to remain a bit unattainable at first. This translated into no lovemaking without a commitment. As it turned out, on that very first night she met Aubin, her blueprint for love went out the window. The Frenchman proved *so* exceedingly special that Laura's defenses were negated. The whirlwind of passion that followed so overwhelmed her that she became blind to the imperfections that others could see.

Truth be told, Aubin was a conniving hustler who passed himself off as a European dealmaker. He would boast of his ability to identify opportunities abroad that would generate a healthy return on investments. In reality, his true expertise was in finding financially secure marks that were susceptible to his brand of larceny. His methodology was relatively basic. In Laura's case he began by furnishing compliments regarding her engaging smile, her intelligence and whatever else he thought she'd find plausible. Her non-questioning acceptance of his honeyed words signaled that she was buying into his con. Aubin filled her head with bunkum about a motherless beginning and his yearning for a family. Sizing Laura up as a do-gooder, he customized his pitch to present a fictionalized passion for supporting good causes. It wasn't surprising that she found the seed money he spoke of to be perfectly understandable when launching a charitable foundation.

Now, alone at the bar, Laura reflected on how confident Aubin was. She found impressive his taking the initiative at dinner by ordering her food and wine. His talk of a joint venture, a French-American charity to benefit disabled children, was appealing. The Frenchman ran into little opposition when he suggested that she match his twenty-five-thousand-dollar cash investment. The Laura-Aubin Gift Foundation was a delightful idea! What could be finer than a charity for special children of low income families on both sides of the pond? Her head was so turned that she failed to recognize his slipperiness when it came time for the bill. Her polite offer to pay was met by a shrugging of his shoulders. Rather than viewing this as poor form, she convinced herself that this was probably the way they did things over in France. Laura broke into a toothy grin as she reflected on the bunko artist's seductive ability. She had to close her mouth to hide her teeth as she recalled how he smoothly enticed her into visiting his hotel room. She stayed for days, covering her absence from work by calling in sick.

Laura's demeanor began to turn somber as she grew tired of waiting. Forty-five minutes had elapsed without any sign of Aubin. Since the Frenchman had no phone, another oddity that she chose to overlook, she called the hotel he was staying at. "How could there be no one there by that name?" she demanded to know. After hanging up, Laura called for a car. Before leaving she signaled the bartender, "If a man comes in looking for me, tell him I'll be back."

A sympathetic desk clerk at the hotel informed Laura that the man she described checked out the prior day after settling up his bill in cash. She felt as if someone twisted the knife that was stuck in her back. The hotel doorman contributed to her misery by recalling that the "French guy" instructed his cabdriver to take him to Kennedy Airport. His recollection was vivid because of the twenty-dollar tip he received for opening the taxi door. With Aubin in the wind, Laura knew the police would have little chance of recovering her money. She tried not to think of the trimming she took. With no better place to go, she returned to Danny Dimes. It was as good a place as any to lick her wounds.

"Let me have a dry martini," she ordered grimly, once back at the bar.

The bartender could see that things had taken a bad turn. After fixing the drink he laid the filled martini glass in front of Laura. He then tapped the top of the bar with his knuckles to indicate that there was no charge for the drink.

"Thank you. Can I ask you a question?"

"Certainly, ask me whatever you want."

"Why do I attract the wrong men?" It was a question the bartender often fielded.

"Sometimes it's best not to expect too much from people. If you figure on the worst, you'll never be disappointed If things work out, then you'll be pleasantly surprised."

Laura nodded. "That's good advice." As she drank Laura's spirits gradually began to lift.

"What the hell, it's only money," she eventually said, accepting her situation.

Around the time Laura was about to confide in the bartender about how Aubin swindled her, a tall gray haired man in a blue single breasted suit and red tie stepped up to the bar. The new arrival took a position standing alongside the seated Laura. He casually nodded to the bartender, indicating that he was seeking service. The stranger peered into the bar glass he faced. Seeing the woman seated next to him in the mirror, he took an interest. When their eyes met, Everett nodded and smiled politely as if to say hello. Laura hesitated a bit before reacting to his gesture. It took her a couple of seconds to arrive at a verdict. Throwing caution to the wind on the theory that things weren't likely to get any worse, Laura returned the greeting reflected in the glass.

"Let me have a Jameson on the rocks," ordered Everett, placing a one hundred dollar bill on the bar. It was his habit to display a large denomination on such excursions. He felt that it always improved his odds by creating the illusion that he was prosperous—somebody to be taken seriously.

"*She's quite pretty, dear. Offer to buy her a drink,*" suggested his mother. Everett nodded, saying nothing to the voice in his head.

"May I buy you a drink?" Everett asked, turning to face Laura.

Laura studied him closely. While a bit long in the tooth perhaps, he seemed safe. Her evaluation completed, she gave him a passing grade. After all, it *was* her birthday she reasoned. "You can buy me a drink if you want," Laura answered.

Upon receiving their drinks Everett held up his glass, wishing his new acquaintance luck. Removing the olive from her drink, Laura reciprocated the sentiment, tapping glasses.

"Excuse me, I forgot to introduce myself. I'm Everett, and you are?"

"I'm Laura. Are you from around here?"

"Not very far from here, I live on the west side."

"Do you work in the city?"

"I teach high school in East Harlem," he replied confidently.

"Let me guess, you teach physical education, right?"

"No, I teach science. How about yourself, what do you do?

It was a relief to hear that he had a regular job. Not big money perhaps, but at least he was legitimately employed. "I'm a real estate broker...and it's my birthday!" she said with enthusiasm. "So what the hell, how about we have another round?" Her spurt of energy came with an air of optimism.

"Well, happy birthday, Laura." Everett said, broadly smiling himself. He then signaled the bartender, indicating that another round was called for.

"You should be a gym teacher with those broad shoulders," she commented.

"And you look like you should be...a model," he answered.

Laura was used to hearing that line. "Thank you. Tell me about teaching science."

Everett laughed. "The most complex aspects of science I've always grasped easily. As for the students, well, it can be challenging for them."

"Are the students difficult?"

"Oh no, I do fine with them. Actually, I played basketball with some of them this afternoon. They probably learned more from me on the court than in the classroom."

"You play basketball with your students?" she asked with genuine interest. Since Everett taught science, she assumed he was smart. The nice guy factor, along with his having all his hair *and* muscles made him attractive in spite of his age.

"I play ball with them to keep in shape, but it also gives me a good feeling inside."

Laura's eyes widened. "I think I can understand that." She was beginning to display obvious signs of warming up to Everett.

"Being a role model, I could never disappoint them and be anything other than exemplary. If I say something, I mean it. If I promise something, I make good on my word." Without realizing it, he was saying things Laura respected.

"That's wonderful," she said, looking up at the standing Everett with admiration.

"Where kids are concerned, I never judge them. I just try to set the right example."

"That's wonderful," she again answered, finishing her drink. "Are you married?" she asked. "Do you have children of your own?"

"No, I've never been fortunate enough to marry. I always thought I'd want to have a family one day, but I'm afraid the chances of that happening are quite remote."

The words he spoke were something Laura could relate to. "Why would you say that? You're a very charming man. You could easily find someone."

"I'm sure you probably have a long line of suitors outside your door."

"No, I'm actually quite unattached," she conveyed boldly, looking at him directly.

At Everett's suggestion their conversation was continued over a bite to eat. Once seated at a table it became her time to tell all. Everett proved himself to be a good listener. Laura spoke of being raised in Connecticut, having a sister, and all about the world of commercial real estate. When Everett insisted on paying the bill, it made an impression on Laura. Happy to have found each other, leaving as a couple seemed natural.

Laura lived in a secure, multi-family high rise. The man assigned to the lobby desk was well accustomed to seeing tenants taking home company. Laura and Everett looked straight ahead as they strolled by the seated man. Arms locked, they entered the elevator. When the door opened on Laura's floor it interrupted the passionate meeting of their tongues. Once inside her apartment, Laura put on some mood music while she prepared for a romantic release. Sammi Smith could be heard vocalizing *"Help Me Make It Through The Night,"* in the background. Laura dimmed the apartment, leaving the only illumination coming from three blue candles.

"Have a seat on the couch. I'll only be a minute," she said in a soft, sensuous voice. She then retreated to the rear area of her apartment. She removed her clothing, brushed her teeth and went under the shower. After several minutes she returned to the living room attired in a loose fitting t-shirt and jogging shorts. Taking a seat next to Everett on the couch, he was surprised to see that she had an ashtray and two joints in her hand.

"Are you okay with smoking weed?" she asked, her legs now folded underneath her.

"Why certainly." By now, he'd do whatever it took to be permitted to jump her bones.

Laura lifted the candle off the coffee table in front of the couch and lit the reefer. Looking directly at her, Everett could see the flickering light of the candle dancing across her face. After taking a long toke she passed the weed to Everett. It had been many years since Everett last smoked the product he spent his college years selling. For him, it was like riding a bicycle, something you don't forget how to do. The two proceeded to chat as they got high. The mood darkened when Laura got on the topic of Aubin.

"How could anyone do a thing like that?" Even the mellowing effect of the weed couldn't suppress Laura's anger at having her affections tampered with and money stolen.

"Console her, dear," advised the good voice.

"I'm so sorry Laura, that was such totally reprehensible behavior," said Everett tenderly.

Everett sucked a long drag of smoke into his lungs. Fighting to hold the smoke down deep, he turned to look into Laura's eyes. The flickering light continued to brighten and dim her appearance. Following the advice mentally conveyed by the good voice, he gently lifted his hand to affectionately touch the side of Laura's face.

"Oh, how I wish I could catch up with that bastard!" Laura blurted, as she raised her hand and began shaking her fist in the air for emphasis.

Everett reacted the way a vampire does when faced with a cross. He now found himself sharing the couch with someone who converted into Granny Trapani. "You-wanna-kiss-a me?" asked the evil voice that entered his mind.

Everett, whose head was now turned away, felt the crossing of his eyes. Laura noticed the sudden change. She didn't understand why her guest was looking away from her while fishing for something in his jacket pocket.

"Is something wrong, Everett?"

Everett realized there was no need to put on sunglasses. He turned back to look at the face of the demon that was now alternating between light and dark at the pace set by the flickering candle. Laura was aghast at his appearance. The science teacher was the first to speak. "Won't you ever learn to leave me alone?"

"What?"

"You heard me, Granny."

His eerie words flipped Laura out. It was clear that the man she took home was disturbed. Thinking fast, she tried to get Everett to willingly leave her apartment. "It's getting late now, so it may be best for you to go. I really have to get up early."

"Not quite, Granny." His response was terse, with the words traveling through lips that now seemed cruel.

"Everett, I'm asking you nicely to leave. If you don't go, I'm calling downstairs."

Everett's response was a cold stare. Sensing imminent danger, Laura made a dash for the front door. Everett grabbed a handful of Laura's hair from the rear. She tried in vain to defend herself against his attack by reaching over her shoulder to get at him. Her poor positioning made it impossible to prevent Everett from wrapping his tie around her neck. Incoherent gurgles were her final utterances before losing consciousness.

At the end of this dastardly strangulation Everett folded his tie and placed it in his jacket pocket. He removed a damp dishcloth from the kitchen and then carefully wiped down everything he touched in the apartment. He flushed the remains of the joints down the toilet. Everett took his final look at the dead body. The sight didn't faze him in the least. He blew out the candles and left the apartment dark. Once in the hall he put the dishcloth in the rear pocket of his pants for later disposal. The teacher passed through the lobby and entered the street without incident. On his way home, he had to admit that this time the demon took the form of a decent looking woman.

14

The Final Curtain

"Now what's wrong with *that* fish-eyed bozo?"

-Martha O'Sullivan

EVERETT SAT ALONE IN HIS APARTMENT WONDERING IF there would ever come a time when Granny would finally die once and for all. It was a recurring question he had. Since the school teacher felt justified in performing the liquidations, he had absolutely no remorse for his actions. However, he did find doing the same thing over and over to be tedious. Seeking relief from the monotony Everett turned to the theater as a diversion. Alone in his apartment he read the reviews of the shows playing on Broadway. A play called *Abstraction At Large,* currently playing at the Bigelow Theater, gained his attention.

"Brimwell's review was lukewarm, so that cinches it," he said, speaking into the paper.

"You know what that means, dear," said Adele, *"it must be good."*

The good voice of Everett's mother didn't have to elaborate. He knew his mother well. She wanted him to stick to their tradition, which was to take in all the plays panned by the critic. Adele always possessed an acute dislike for the critic, often describing him as a self impressed bore. In protest of his reviews, mother and son made it their business to see every play Brimwell disliked. Everett always went along with his mother without argument. He checked the time, not wanting to be late for the show. It would mark the first time he'd be going go to a theater without Adele.

MARTHA O'SULLIVAN WAS A SLIM, gray-haired woman who used lots of hairspray. Originally from County Cork, she had been living on Eleventh Avenue in Manhattan's Hell Kitchen for most of her adult life. She lived contently in her rent controlled apartment four stories above McAvoy's Tavern. The seventy-five year old widow was the independent sort. Not one prone to dwell on gray skies, she could often be heard humming Maude Nugent's popular old favorite, *Sweet Rosie O'Grady,* as she went about her business. Ever the optimist, she faced her advanced years confident that she'd continue to give the undertaker a good chase for his money. Part of her longevity strategy called for her making the journey up and down the stairs three times a day. She viewed the flights not as a hardship, but rather, as a means of preventing her body from atrophying.

Martha rose early to attend Mass at Sacred Heart on West 51st Street. The first thing she did after rising was to check the mousetrap she set. The droppings had become an annoying reminder of the nocturnal visitors. Disappointed that the trap was undisturbed, she put on a pot of tea while she prepared herself for Mass.

After the service Martha walked to a nearby park, where she met up with other elderly residents of Hell's Kitchen. The long-time neighbors sat on a park bench, where they drank coffee from thermoses and shared neighborhood gossip. Once Martha was up to speed on the doings she headed home. Her only stop was to pick up a newspaper. When she arrived back in her apartment she tidied her bed and did some light housecleaning. Her second trip downstairs came when it was time to pick up the mail. When Martha returned to her apartment, she sat at the table to sort through her correspondence and read the *paper* over a cup of green tea. The brew went well in washing down the scones she baked earlier in the week. By the time she completed the crossword puzzle in the newspaper it was time to watch *Follow Your Love,* the first of her favorite afternoon soap operas. Friends and family alike knew not to disturb Martha when her shows were airing. Taking a seat in the cushioned chair in front of the television, she slipped off her white moccasins before resting her legs on the round leather foot stool in front of her. Checking the Timex on her wrist, she saw that the program was still five minutes away from commencing. Just as Martha raised a glass of pineapple juice to her mouth, her tranquility was suddenly disrupted by the sound of loud music blasting from the street.

Being many stories up didn't prevent the disruptive noise from finding its way into her apartment. Martha went to the kitchen window to investigate the source of the noise. Looking down at the sidewalk below, she saw a group of teenage boys sitting on the steps beneath her window. They were all smoking cigarettes and moving their bodies to the pace set by the music. One lanky teen stood on the sidewalk holding a blasting stereophonic radio atop his shoulder with one arm. Martha watched in disbelief at his exaggerated gyrations as he rocked to the music emanating from the boom box.

"For cripes sake, now would you look at this big string bean," she said aloud. "Now how ridiculous can you get?"

Martha finally shouted down from her window, quite annoyed at being distracted from her television time. "Go on home and stop making that racket down there!" None of the boys even looked up at Martha; the music had completely drowned her voice out.

"I said move out of there and go someplace else!" she yelled, raising her voice to maximum capacity. Again the boys took no notice, hearing nothing but the music.

It was a mystery to Martha why the landlord, who also owned the owner on record of the downstairs tavern, would allow the youths to congregate out front. With one eye on the television, she telephoned the bar to register a complaint. Martha soon grew frustrated. She couldn't pay attention to the television, shut out the noise below *and* patiently wait for the phone to be picked up, all at the same time. She hung up to address the matter herself. "I'll get them moving," she said, staring down at the youths from her perch high above.

Martha rushed to the faucet and turned on the cold water. Reaching into the storage area under the sink she removed the large metal pot she used to boil her potatoes in. Thinking that a nice cold shock would disperse those gathering below, she filled the pot to full capacity. Reappearing at the window with the filled pot, Martha poured the water onto the youths. She then quickly pulled down the window and back-stepped away out of view. Upon receiving their liquid awakening, the startled boys jumped from their positions screaming profanities at the top of their lungs. As the boys shook their clothes dry they looked up in search of the source of the drenching. All that was visible to them were closed windows. Having no way of knowing for sure where the water emanated from, the boys were stymied. Martha's eyes twinkled as she listened to their chorus of curses. The boys were now playing the kind of music *she* wanted to hear...a symphony of lament. She had no fear of retaliation because her building was protected by some very dangerous people.

Martha returned to her shows without further interruption. Once they were over it was time for her to prepare dinner. She was disciplined when it came to her food, sticking to a menu that hadn't changed since her husband died. Her daily intake consisted of boiled chicken, a green veggie and a boiled potato. Her menu served her well, leaving the senior citizen with a flattering figure to carry into her old age.

McAVOY'S TAVERN WAS CONSIDERED a bucket of blood saloon. Those who frequented the establishment were not all hoods. Legitimate working men with varied vices in need of satisfaction were also drawn there. "They come like moths to a flame," as Knucks liked to say.

It was no secret that Knucks McAvoy, a onetime iron worker, was in cahoots with The Seven Studs, a Westside street gang. He served as the front in the gang's ownership of the property and the bar that bore his name. Knucks, who stood about five-five, was a solidly built man with gorilla-like arms that hung almost to his knees. This unusual characteristic caused him to be referred to by gang members as a knuckle-dragger. The description eventually evolved into the nickname Knucks.

The leader of the Seven Studs was Martha's nephew, Archie "Two-Fingers" O'Sullivan, so called because of his propensity to poke two fingers into the eyes of those who ran afoul of his interests. Two Fingers used the backroom of the bar as his headquarters. This sacred area, known as Stud Court, was a venue in which disputes were resolved and verdicts rendered in return for court fees levied by the gang leader.

Martha's blood relationship to Two-Fingers came with benefits. The senior citizen never had to fret over a rent increase or a lack of heat in the winter. It was through her nephew's influence that she was hired as an evening usherette at the nearby Bigelow Theater, a longtime extortion victim of the gang. The playhouse was within walking distance of Martha's apartment. The work gave her a purpose, an opportunity to see shows and a chance to get to know the cast. It also earned her an income that supplemented her social security and the small city pension her husband left behind.

As was her custom, Martha stopped at the bar for a single quaff before reporting to work at the theater. Her favorite libation was a Cameron's Kick. "Easy on the lemon juice," was her favorite line when ordering the potent Scotch and Irish Whisky mixture. It was destined to be a day that exceeded her usual alcohol consumption. After assuming her regular seat at the bar, she took the opportunity to fill In Knucks about the earlier disruption.

"So what was that they did, Martha?" asked McAvoy.

"They were using the front steps as a hangout. The music was so loud they couldn't even hear me calling down to them. It just isn't fair to the poor people who work nights and have to sleep in the day."

Martha went on to describe the boys to McAvoy, who listened attentively. When she was done he assured the tenant that she would not be bothered again. "Don't worry about a thing, I know who it is you're talking about. I'll have a word with them."

"Now please, Knucks...don't be telling my nephew Archie about this. You know how excitable he can be," she warned. "I don't want him to go around poking people in the eyes over this."

"No need to bother Archie about this. I'll handle it quietly."

When Martha was through talking to Knucks, a wiry man leaning on an old wooden cane, approached her from behind. Of average height, his long nose looked like a bent red pepper. Feeling her shoulder being tapped, Martha turned to see who it was. It was an old family friend, a crony of her late husband.

"Martha! How are you?" greeted the man jauntily, removing his tweed cap. What was left of his hair was arranged oddly. The thin white strands stretched upward from both ears, as well as from the rear, with all points aimed toward at the center of his head.

"Michael Cahill! I didn't know ya at first. Since when have you been using a stick?"

"For a long time now," he answered, "you haven't seen me in awhile. So, how are you?"

"I'm grand, thank you. So tell me, is your own health alright, Michael?"

"Good as can be expected. Getting a little old of course, but putting the lumbago and my trick knee aside, I manage to get by."

"Did you say lumbago? Good God, Michael, nobody says that anymore! Sure, people wouldn't know you're talking about a lower back pain."

Cahill smiled at her frankness. "Aye, I suppose that's the truth."

"Lumbago!" she scoffed, displaying a crooked smile.

"What can I say, other than we lose a step in the late innings, eh Martha?"

"That's a fact...for some," she clarified. "What do the golfers say we're in?"

"They call it the back nine."

"That's right, the back nine. Well, I intend to stop off at the clubhouse for awhile, at the end of my game...*before* going home."

Cahill laughed aloud. Then, after a few seconds of silence he turned serious. "Too bad about poor Joe, I saw his name listed in the church bulletin. It was his lungs, wasn't it?"

Gripping her chest, she paused at the thought of her late husband. "Yes, he was riddled with cancer. It was the smoking of those damn cigarettes of course," she said bitterly.

"I know he used to favor the brands with no filter."

"He did. I told him a thousand times to switch to a cigar or pipe but he never listened. Joe had a mind of his own."

"I'm sorry we couldn't pay our respects properly. My Rose with her bum hip and me with my back giving me trouble, we were prisoners in the house for a couple of weeks."

"Sure Michael, I understand, I received the card," she replied softly. "How is Rose?"

"The old girl is hanging in, thank the Lord. She has her bad days of course, you know how that goes. But, look...we need to get together, the three of us while we still can. What do you say to that?"

"That would be a fine idea, Michael."

"And you can still manage those stairs every day?"

"I do," she replied with definiteness. "I make those steps three times a day...*every* day. If I don't, I'm afraid my legs will weaken and I won't be able to."

"That's the right attitude. How about we figure on a Saturday or Sunday? We can meet here, the three of us, and then after a taste we'll go for a bite at Edmund's Restaurant n Broadway."

"Why that's great Michael, how about six o'clock, on the second Sunday of next month. I never work on Sundays...so we'll meet right here then?"

"Perfect, Martha, just perfect. It'll be like old times again."

"That it will," agreed Martha. "Only the cart will have just three wheels I'm afraid."

Cahill nodded understandingly. "That's true." Then, with a burst of energy he added, "Let's have one in honor of Joe. What's that you're drinking?"

"No, I can't Michael, thank you. I've had my limit. I have to go to work soon."

"Bah, you can't travel on one leg," he said, dismissing her resistance. "Mr. McAvoy, would you do the honors of pouring out another round for this fine woman?"

"Alright with you, Martha?" asked Knucks, who was not overjoyed at the prospect of juicing up the aunt of Archie Two-Fingers.

"No. No more for me! I have a job to go to you know," she reminded.

Cahill was insistent. "C'mon now, I know your ability." Realizing that resistance was going to be a futile, she agreed to accept the drink

"Now don't forget to go easy on the lemon juice," Martha instructed, as she settled back awaiting her round with a naughty smile on her face.

"Did you hear about the fire at the Gilhooley home in Hoboken?" the old man asked.

"Which Gilhooley do you mean?"

"Clara. Poor Morgana died a couple of months back. She suffered from Alzheimer's, you know, didn't even know her own sister, and them being so close all these years."

"I wasn't aware of that. What a shame," Martha said, taking the newly poured drink to her lips. She then changed the subject. "Now listen here, Mike, I have to get myself off to work in a little while so we can't be making this no marathon party."

Martha, who was trying her best to behave responsibly, was thoroughly enjoying herself. The attention she was receiving made her feel like a young girl at a dance.

EVERETT SECURED A TICKET to the show at the box office. Before making his way to his seat, he ordered a whiskey on the rocks from the bar inside the theater. With his drink in hand the teacher proceeded toward the center aisle of the theater. He was surprised to see the large number of patrons taking in the show. It seemed that he and Adele weren't the only ones who paid little attention to the reviews penned by Brimwell.

MARTHA O'SULLIVAN HANDED OUT copies of *Playbill* as she helped the incoming theater goers find their seats. She looked like someone out of a '30s musical in her black double-breasted, gold-buttoned usherette jacket and matching cap. Her fair skin went well with the tinted spectacles that rested on her nose.

A taut faced man of about forty, wearing beige pants and a collared shirt approached her. A perfect straight-line part on the left side of his slicked down hair gave him a certain rigid appearance. After noticing how his belt buckle was perfectly aligned with his zipper and the buttons on his shirt, Martha presumed him to be a military man. She leaned back when he got close, trying to avoid his smelling the alcohol that might be lingering on her breath.

"I need your assistance, ma'am. There is a young man seated behind me who keeps kicking the back of my seat."

Martha responded by speaking slowly and as clearly as she could. The last thing she wanted to do was get caught garbling her words. "Where are you sitting, sir?"

"Over there, in front of the young man in the aisle seat," he said, pointing to a boy twenty rows away in the direction of the stage. "He's wearing the green striped shirt."

"I see him."

"I certainly don't want him doing that during the performance."

Martha could tell he wasn't from New York. "Did you ask him to stop it, sir?"

The man looked at her oddly, as if puzzled by her question. "Why no, I assumed you would be the appropriate one to speak to him."

"You can do it as well as I can, sir. The next time it happens just ask him to please stop kicking your chair. If he continues, *then* by all means, let me know."

The man wasn't buying it. "I am asking *you,* ma'am, to speak to him *before* the curtain goes up. I paid good money for my seat and I don't intend to have my entertainment disrupted during the performance. Now are you going to speak to him or not?"

Martha pegged him as the type that wasn't going away easy. She replied just prior to hiccupping. "Alright sir, have it your own way."

She followed the man down the aisle to where a boy in his early teens was slouched down in his seat. Seeing that the youth was with his family, Martha made her approach discreetly. Casually leaning down she whispered in the boy's ear.

"Excuse me, young man. I have to ask you to please sit still. The gentleman sitting in front of you complained, so try and be careful not to kick the back of his chair."

The youth looked up at Martha as if astonished. Shifting his position to sit erect, he took an indignant posture. "Well, I'm glad you're here," he replied. "I was about to look for you. This man in front of me sits in his chair as high as a cat's back. I'll need a ladder if *I'm* to see anything," countered the boy, who proved adept at turning tables on adults.

The usherette continued to keep her voice down to a whisper. "Now look here, I'm sure it's not you causing trouble young man, but please try and keep your feet on the floor. I don't want to have to take this up with your people."

The boy protested. "How about taking up *my* complaint with the man sitting in front of me? What are you going to do about him?"

His response put Martha over the edge. "Now you be still and keep those gunboats planted on the floor, sonny," she directed. Then, turning to the adult who lodged the complaint, she warned, "And you sit lower in your seat! Anymore nonsense and I'll have the whole kit and caboodle of you put out of here," she growled, before releasing a surprise hiccup. "Have a little human decency for heaven's sake and show some consideration."

Both complainers sheepishly nodded, each being caught unprepared for the old-fashioned tongue lashing they received.

"Good Jesus, what wimps!" Martha muttered under her breath as she proceeded back up the aisle to resume her duties of pleasantly greeting people.

Everett never saw the usherette making her way up the aisle. His eyes were focused on the seats off to his right. The accidental collision caused him to spill his drink on Martha, with a couple of drops splashing onto her face. The surprise feel of the cool liquid caused the startled usherette to react by raising a hand to the side of her face in a defensive gesture. Martha's hand trembled as she balled it into a fist. All Everett could see was a shaking fist...and the evil Granny Trapani. Head down, Everett donned the dark sunglasses and scurried toward the exit.

"Now what's wrong with *that* fish-eyed bozo?" asked Martha, as Everett stormed off.

"What happened?" asked Martha's friend and co-worker, who was standing nearby.

Martha shook her head as she responded. "Can't hold his drink I imagine."

❖

EVERETT WAITED OUTSIDE FOR the show to end. His intention was to pounce on his unsuspecting target at the first opportune moment. Seeing Martha exit, the teacher carefully followed her from a safe distance. Martha didn't walk very fast, so shadowing her wasn't difficult. Shoulders back, the septuagenarian's steps were taken with a disciplined concentration that enabled her to maintain a straight line. She placed one foot down firmly after the other, as if marching to a slow cadence. Everett was glad to see that his intended victim bypassed the subway entrances. This meant that the woman he saw as Granny probably resided nearby.

A block from Martha's home, on a dark street between Ninth and Tenth Avenues, a trio of men had pitched an urban campsite in front of a factory that had closed hours earlier. It was their habit to remain there until it was time to break camp when the factory reopened in the morning. Highly intoxicated, they sat on the ground with their backs up against the brick wall of the commercial building. Martha was used to seeing the men on her way home, so she walked by them without concern for her safety.

Wary of the street people, Everett passed by them cautiously. His fears were put to rest once realizing that the inebriated men were too far gone to pay him any attention. Seeing that the road to the next avenue was without lighting, the demented science teacher picked up his pace. He closed in on Martha before she reached the end of the block. In a cross-eyed frenzy, he attacked the old woman from the rear. With his powerful right forearm pressing against Martha's windpipe, he cupped her mouth with his free hand and dragged her into an open lot. Everett threw Martha to the ground behind a large green dumpster inside the lot. Slipping off his tie, he quickly strangled her. He then put her lifeless body into the dumpster. When he exited the lot he saw his victim's purse on the sidewalk. Since there was no one around, he casually picked it up, returned to the dumpster and threw it in.

"Pleasant dreams, Mrs. Trapani," he hissed, as he headed home after completing his fourth murder.

15

All In The Family

"I did all that could be done, it's a loser at this point. So what's wrong with my shoes?"

-Detective Cynthia Billings

ALLEY HAD MIXED EMOTIONS regarding Markie. Her feelings were torn between hurt and unreasonable expectations. The fact that she hadn't heard from the sergeant in awhile was distressing to her. When he finally did call she picked up the bar phone with saying anything.

"Hey, babe...it's me," repeated Markie after receiving no acknowledgment. "Alley, are you there?"

"I'm here," answered Alley, in a tone sounding less than thrilled.

"How is it going?"

"It's going," she replied curtly.

"Is something wrong?" he asked.

"No, nothing is wrong. I'm working."

By her responses it was evident to Markie that something was eating at her. "C'mon, clue me in, what's bothering you? Did I do something?"

"Look, Al, I really can't talk now. I'm working."

"Do what you have to do, I could hang on."

"I have to take care of customers."

"Alright, do me a favor then before you hang up. Can you at least let me know what's eating you?"

"Alright," she said, "where have you been all this time?"

"I've been working my ass off, you know how it goes."

"No, I don't know."

"C'mon, I didn't think you needed hourly bulletins."

Alley felt Markie could have found the time to pick up the phone or stop by to see here. Not being married to the sergeant left her in a gray zone as to the rules of their relationship.

"No, I never expected hourly bulletins but it would have been nice to know you were still alive and kicking."

"Okay, now I know how you want it. To tell you the truth, I didn't think you cared."

"Well now you know."

"Yes, I do."

In the end she Alley let it go. "So do you want to get together tonight after I finish work?" she asked.

"No, tonight all I want to do is go home and get some sleep."

His declining her offer cut deep. "Whatever," she said icily. Having thought she won a minor victory, she viewed this rejection as a setback.

Picking up on her disappointment, he offered a compromise. "How about I stop by the bar for a little while to see you? I'd like to at least check in."

"Oh...okay," she answered, sounding surprised. At least this was something. "What time?"

"Soon, I gotta just make one stop to get something in my stomach first, I haven't eaten."

"Want me to order from Mario's?"

"Yeah, that's a good idea. Get me something."

Markie's phone indicated to him that he was receiving an incoming call from his ex-wife Flo. "I'll see you later, I gotta pickup this call," he said, hanging up abruptly. "Yeah Flo, what's up?"

Flo spoke into the phone excitedly. "The toilet bowl in the upstairs bathroom is spilling over onto the floor, and there is water coming through the light fixture downstairs!"

"Okay, okay, relax. Where exactly is the water coming from?"

"From underneath the toilet bowl...can you come over?" Markie couldn't bring himself to refuse.

EVERETT THREW THE COMMUNITY newspaper down on the table in anger. He couldn't understand how Jeanette Pergamint was still alive. Of all his Granny eradications, the bakery owner was by far the most challenging.

"You can't go back now, dear," advised the good voice.

"I know," replied Everett. "I have to wait until things die down over there."

Everett put the radio on. He needed something to take his mind off the botched strangulation of Jeanette Pergamint. Turning the dial, he stopped when he came upon an acid-tongued radio personality. He was shocked by the rudeness exhibited by the host toward listeners who called into the show. "Why would these people even call this guy?"

"Some people are gluttons for punishment, dear." answered Adele.

"He eats them alive every time they voice an opposing opinion."

"It's his show, dear. What have I always said? Give some people a little authority and soon they'll think who the hell they are," reminded the good voice.

Everett's mental conversation with his mother ended when the doorbell rang. He turned down the volume on the radio and answered the door. It was Stan Addington, a teacher in the science department at Everett's school. Stan, who was seven years younger than Everett, was a clean-shaven man of average size. His most unique feature was a head of brown bushy hair that seemed to stand straight up on his head.

"Stan, what brings you here? Is everything alright?"

"Everything is good. I'm meeting my wife later for dinner. I'm early, so I thought I'd stop by to ask for a favor."

"No problem, want a drink?" asked Everett, letting his co-worker into his apartment.
"No thanks, Everett."

"Take a seat." Stan complied, sitting on the living room couch. "What do you need?"

"Well, it's like this. As it turns out, the get-together we're having over my house is going to be all couples."

"I intended to bring someone anyway."

"Did you invite anyone to come with you yet?"

"No, I haven't. But don't worry, I'll dig someone up."

"That's great," said Stan, seeming relieved. "You may not have to find someone. Here's the situation. My wife's cousin is in from California, so as it stands now—"

Cutting his friend off mid-sentence Everett said, "No problem Stan, if you need me to round out the couples, I'm there for you. What can I bring?"

"Terrific! All you need to do is bring yourself."

"So tell me, do I need to know anything about this woman?"

"She's from the west coast. You know how it is, she's divorced awhile and now she's looking for someone."

"Has she got all her teeth?" Everett asked jokingly.

"She's got more than that. Trust me on this one. Doris is forty-one year old beauty, a real looker."

"Did you say hooker?" asked Everett, pretending to have heard his friend wrong.
"You only wish!"

After Stan left Everett returned to his radio. He'd lost interest in listening to confrontational bickering and searched for an alternative. He turned up the volume when he came upon a station featuring music from the sixties. As Percy Sledge sang *When a Man Loves a Woman,* Everett's mind became occupied with thoughts of Doris.

DETECTIVE VON HESS DROPPED off Markie in front of the post office so that he could buy stamps. The detective sat waiting behind the wheel of the unmarked car. To pass the time he started looking at the people walking by. They were a mixed bag comprised of all sizes, colors, and genders. Some walked fast, some slow. A few looked in shape, some didn't. Then suddenly it dawned on Von Hess...where *were the* people like himself? The reality of a changing population was unpleasant for him to think about. Were these vanishings attributable to people relocating to a pension friendly state? Was everyone housebound? Or even worse, were they tucked in tight someplace on the wrong side of the grass? These were the thoughts running through the mind of the detective when Markie arrived back at the car.

"Let's head over to the First Precinct and talk to Detective Billings about the Doctor Culbrenner homicide," said the sergeant.

"You know sarge, I was just wondering something...where are we going?"

"We're going to see Billings regarding the doctor strangulation."

"I know that. I'm talking the big picture. You know...here today, gone tomorrow."

Markie gazed out the passenger side window. He didn't like this topic. After a short silence, he answered. "I never dwell on tomorrow; I'll worry about the end of the line when I get there."

"I hear you, sarge. Life is strange though, when you think about it. Some people fall into clover right out of the chute, while others land in cow pies. Kind of makes you wonder."

The conversation was beginning to depress Markie. "What's the difference? The windup is still the same for everybody when we cash in our chips."

"It might be nice to have your remains scattered over the ocean or..."

"Tell you what Ollie," Markie interrupted. "You can stick my ashes in an urn and put it on a shelf next to the condoms in Sugar Sadie's whorehouse for all I care. When the ballgame is over, it's over. Why are you so worried about this crap all of a sudden? It could be a moot point anyway—on this job there could be a bullet with your name on it anytime."

"Thanks sarge, that's a comforting thought." Von Hess changed the topic. "So what do you make of our chances in cracking this thing?"

"We'll crack it," the sergeant answered without hesitation. "I'd just like to know the reason *why* this sicko is strangling people." The two investigators thought it over in silence as they made their way over to the First Precinct.

DETECTIVE CYNTHIA BILLINGS WAS drinking water at her desk while awaiting the arrival of the task force investigators. The thirtyish detective was irked that her work was being placed under what she perceived as a microscope. She was a serious-minded woman from a police family. Her father was a lieutenant and two older brothers were police officers. When it came to the job, her family usually banded together to dilute her opinion during discussions. The domestic solidarity of the men served as an incentive for the detective to strive for perfection at work in order to reduce the chance of criticism.

When the task force members entered the squad room a frown could be seen on the face of Billings. The mere physical appearance of Markie and Von Hess reminded her of her father and brothers. With her squad commander out of the office, Billings was left without supervisory support. With the situation being perceived as two against one, this left the detective feeling vulnerable to being overruled in the event there was a difference in opinion. Billings rose from her desk, threw her shoulders back, and faced the task-force members. With her head held high, she extended herself to her full height of five-feet-eleven-inches in flats. Before she could say anything, the telephone on her desk rang. Picking up the phone, she raised a finger, indicating to her visitors that they should standby. Von Hess listened as Billings explained to the caller the availability of several social service programs being offered by the city. He was impressed by the time she afforded the caller in answering questions. Most detectives would have just provided the number to an appropriate agency. Von Hess also found it unusual how the pixie-haired blond spoke out of the side of her mouth while maintaining a stiff upper lip. She reminded him of a stroke victim. Markie likewise used the wait time to study Billings. He noted her tan pants suit, white collared top and the fact that she wore no make-up. What made an impression on both men were the black referee type shoes she wore. Her selection in footwear, while hardly stylish, was a practical choice in the event running after someone became necessary. Billings had her cases neatly arranged on her desk, suggesting to the sergeant that the precinct detective was organized.

"Detective Billings?" called out Markie, after the detective hung up the telephone.

"I'll be with you in a minute."

"I'm Sergeant Markie and this is Detective Von Hess."

Billings responded with a slight nod of her head as she looked through papers on her desk. Markie sensed that something wasn't right. Before he could say anything the phone rang again.

"Detective Billings, how may I help you?" As the detective listened to the caller she began jotting down notes. "Okay, see you in a few." The detective then turned to Markie. "So what is it that you need from me?" she asked, sounding as if she had no time for him.

"We came to talk about the Doctor Culbrenner homicide you caught," said Markie.

"Sorry, but you're going to have to wait. My two partners are in Staten Island on a case and there is a DOA that just came in that I have to go out on. Make yourself comfortable, I shouldn't be *too* long." The precinct detective didn't realize that by putting the sergeant second, she had thrown down the gauntlet.

Billings raised her head, lifted a water glass to her lips and casually sipped slowly. Markie saw her throat jiggle as the water made its way down. After swallowing the liquid she dabbed her lips with a napkin as she prepared to leave. Markie took these actions as intentional provocations after noticing a faint gloat cross the face of Billings. Markie just smiled...for now. His long memory would remind him to square the account with Billings at some point down the road. In matters such as this, the sergeant had *Alzheimer ala Markie*...a condition in which he could forget everything but a grudge.

"Let's do this *detective*," proposed Markie in a calm voice, while reminding her of her lower rank. "I'll stick here to read through the Culbrenner case while Detective Von Hess goes out with you on the DOA. You can fill him in on the way over there and back. I hope *that* works for you."

The detective's antennas went up immediately. "It works," replied Billings. She knew that she had made an enemy.

Rising from her desk, Billings walked to a nearby file cabinet and removed the homicide case folder pertaining to Doctor Culbrenner. She intentionally placed it on a desk far away from where Markie was standing.

"Here you go, sarge," she said, pointing to the out of reach folder. Having the sergeant walk over and get the folder was her way of pushing his buttons.

After Billings and Von Hess left the squad, the sergeant got comfortable, settling in behind a desk. Going through the case folder, he dug for indications of ineptitude. Finding none, he had to begrudgingly admit the detective had done a decent job on her investigation. He took notice of the date that the last follow up report was submitted: it told him that the case was currently on the back burner and being treated as a loser.

THEY WERE A BLOCK AWAY from the precinct before Von Hess thought to ask Billings where they were going.

"It's just a few blocks from here. We can drive, *if*...you're not up to walking it."

"You can drive if you want, I'll just trot alongside the car," replied Von Hess.

Billings couldn't conceal that she was amused. "That's okay, we'll both walk."

"Are you comfortable in those shoes?" Von Hess asked, messing with her head.

"They're fine, why do you ask?"

Von Hess left her guessing. "Have you made any headway on the case?"

"I did all that could be done, it's a loser at this point. So what's wrong with my shoes?"

"Nothing is wrong with them. Why is this case a loser?"

"Look, the doctor was beaten and strangled. There was no forced entry, no robbery. She either let the perp in, he hid himself or it was a push in. Without prints or a motive, we have nothing. The victim had no issues with anyone and we have no leads."

"It sounds like a loser," agreed Von Hess, looking not to lock horns.

132

His concurrence loosened Billings up a bit. "It's a total loser. There is just no place to go with this case, it's a dead end. I don't know what they think you guys are going to find."

"Well..."

"All we can do at this point is interview prisoners coming through the precinct, and that's exactly what I've been doing. Eventually someone might give us something."

Von Hess thought that was a good idea and said so. He then quietly began to think of ways to give the case a transfusion. A thought came to him. "You know maybe..."

"Anyway, I wouldn't be holding my breath," interrupted Billings, before Von Hess could finish his sentence.

"What about the doctor's personal life?"

"What about it? She lived with her husband, another doctor. They get along just fine."

"Where was the husband at the time of the crime?"

"He was working. I checked on him right at the onset of the investigation. I was able to confirm that he was busy delivering twins at the time of the murder," advised Billings.

"I see."

"Like I said, this case is a loser. There's nothing more that can be done on it."

"Definitely no robbery involved here, correct?"

"Everything was left untouched, nothing taken from the scene, no medicine...not a thing out of place, nada," answered Billings. "Even the doctor's purse wasn't disturbed, and she had a few hundred in cash inside it."

The question and answer session continued until they arrived in front of a three-story limestone located among a small pocket of two-family homes.

"I never even knew these houses were here," commented Von Hess. "They must be worth a fortune."

"These houses were always a fortune," advised Billings. "You could never touch one of these, even years ago." Billings stopped to address Von Hess before they went inside.

"What's the story with that sergeant you're working with?"

Von Hess looked directly at Billings. "No story," he said, hunching his shoulders. It was clear that he wouldn't go there.

The detectives were met at the door to the house by a uniformed police officer. He led them to a second floor bathroom where a man, fully dressed, died while apparently shaving. A moist shaving brush and cup sat on top of the porcelain sink. A razor was on the floor next to the body. Detective Billings, based upon her preliminary investigation, concluded that the death appeared to be from natural causes, probably a heart attack. Supporting her contention was the heart disease medication that she found in the medicine cabinet. Pointing to the pills she turned to Von Hess.

"Looks like nothing suspicious here."

"It's amazing how many people die in the bathroom," noted Von Hess solemnly.

Billings nodded. "Do we know who this man is?" she asked the uniformed officer.

"Yeah, he's been identified by the housekeeper downstairs. She's the one who called the job in," replied the officer. "He's seventy-five-years old and owns the house. He's got a daughter who occupies the apartment upstairs on the top floor."

"Anybody in the family notified?"

"Yeah, we contacted the daughter living upstairs. She's supposedly on the way home and should be here shortly," explained the officer. "The DOA's got two other daughters, both of them live local."

Detective Billings nodded her head approvingly. "Good. Did anyone say anything about his health?"

"The daughter mentioned that the deceased was under a doctor's care for a slew of health issues," advised the officer.

A loud wail was suddenly heard coming from downstairs. Looking down the flight of steps they observed a grief-stricken woman in a highly agitated state. She was flailing her arms above her head as she proceeded to the staircase.

"PAPA! PAPA!" came her emotionally charged bellow, as she hustled up the stairs.

Although large, she managed to negotiate the steps to the upper floor with surprising swiftness. It took time to calm down the grief stricken fifty-two-year-old. The uniformed officer guided her to the first floor couch, where she mourned quietly in the living room. The quiet was short lived. Within minutes another daughter, a forty-seven-year-old, came barreling through the front door shouting through tears.

"PAPA! PAPA!"

As the sisters embraced tightly, the older woman's grief was reignited. Wailing in unison, the two sisters hurried up the stairs to their father's body. Their duet of sobbing took some doing to quell. When a semblance of order was restored, the police were able to coax both women into reconvening downstairs. They comforted each other on the living room couch, awaiting the arrival of the third sister.

Von Hess turned to address Detective Billings. "Are we about ready to call this a wrap?"

"Almost, let me just have a word with the doctor." After a phone conversation with the deceased's physician she turned to Von Hess. "It's all good, let's go."

As Billings was about to inform the officer that they were leaving, the third sibling arrived in whirlwind fashion. The fifty-year-old flung open the door, crying loudly, "PAPA! PAPA!" Now there was a tearful trio rushing up the steps. Once the sisters got control of their emotions, they made their way downstairs, where they engaged in a serious discussion among themselves. Their conversation was destined to take an ugly turn when the talk focused on the estate.

"But Papa said he was leaving the piano to me..."

Billings looked over to Von Hess, tossing her head in the direction of the front door.

Arriving back at the precinct, Von Hess saw Markie sitting in the passenger side of their unmarked car. Von Hess got behind the wheel after thanking Billings for her cooperation. Billings simply nodded. She then looked into the car to address Markie.

"So did you solve the case, sarge?" she asked, flashing a crooked smile.

"Not yet, but I think we might," he answered, giving her something to think about.

"You didn't take the case folder or anything out of it, did you?" she asked."

"Everything remains safely in the file, just as you left it *long ago*." Markie gave Von Hess the signal to drive off.

16

The Sheridan Stroke

"You can rest assured that there will be a price to pay. Do you always leap before you look officer?

-J. Hanley Delmont

EVERETT RENTED A CAR TO DRIVE to the Long Island home of the Addington family. Pulling into the long driveway he gazed at the impressive home of his friend. Stan, who happened to spot his fellow teacher from the window, hurried to the front door. "Hey Everett, welcome to Addington Manor," Stan joked, as he swung his arm expansively.

"Jesus, Stan...this place is magnificent."

"*Don't show you are so impressed, Everett. After all, Stan didn't earn all these things himself,*" reminded the good voice. Everett discreetly nodded his agreement.

Before answering, Stan made sure to look around, as if wanting to be certain no one was listening. "Yeah, her father really did alright for himself," he whispered. "I guess there was a lot of money for a judge to make in Queens back in the day."

"I suppose there was. You know, I've been here before but you never really showed me around."

"I didn't? Let me tell you, this place is like a museum. If you like to shoot pool, we have a nine-foot Brunswick Pfister that goes back to the eighteen-nineties It's made of African ribbon mahogany with exterior leather pockets. It has to be worth a small fortune. Her old man knew how to live. This house has a full bar, a movie room...the works."

"The taxes out here must be murder."

"We manage. Her father died a widower and Iris was his only child. She inherited everything, so at the end of the day, I'm lord of the manor instead of the gardener."

"Nice," Everett said.

"Yeah, I guess I really stepped in it."

"You sure did, and I don't mean the house. Iris is a wonderful woman."

"Yeah, I'd have loved her poor or rich," said Stan, taking liberties with the truth.

"C'mon in, I'll introduce you to Doris."

Stan introduced Everett to his guests. Everyone seemed to be mingling cordially as they drank cocktails. After being introduced to the shapely Doris, Everett was *very* glad he accepted the invitation. He discreetly gave Stan that special "guy look" of approval. Judging by the smiling face of Doris, it appeared to Stan that the attraction was mutual.

The newly matched couple spent a good part of their time isolated from the rest of the company. They were dismayed when the rhythm of their privacy was interrupted by guests who integrated themselves into their conversation. Doris and Everett were engaged with a flower shop owner named Dexter when they were joined by a gruff, roundish man in his early fifties. The newest addition to the conversation sported a double chin and a collared long sleeve pink shirt. His head was quite large, sitting atop a squat frame. His rapid-fire fashion of speaking was the sort that soon became irritating.

"Stan mentioned you attended West Point, Dexter. My kid is interested in going there. His grades are excellent," said the motor mouth. "I got all the letters of recommendation lined up...politicians, schools, everybody that matters. You went there, right?"

"I attended West Point for two years," answered Dexter, an impeccably dressed soft spoken man. His demeanor led some to characterize him as a snobbish dandy.

"Two years...did you skip grades?"

"No, I didn't skip grades. Their routine was simply not to my liking."

"I see," said the man, not knowing what to make of his comment. He pulled his head back, then down and up, sizing up Dexter. "What's life like at West Point anyway?"

"Life at West Point is all about having the highest integrity."

"That goes without saying."

Dexter wanted to be clear as to what he meant. "I'll give you an example. At West Point, a classmate violated the honor code in my presence. I was asked to identify him by an upper classman. I did so and he was asked to leave West Point."

Everett looked on in disbelief. Admitting to being a snitch was something that made no sense to him.

"Well you had no choice," commented the man with an interest in West Point. "What else could you do? If you lied for him you would've been kicked out, right?"

Dexter's reply came smugly. "No, I could have lied. They'd have never known the difference. But as I said previously, West Point is all about integrity."

Everett was so appalled that he needed to remove himself from the discussion and Dexter, who he now considered a snitch.. He asked Doris if she was ready for another drink. Being amenable to the suggestion she followed him to the bar area with thoughts having nothing to do with West Point or integrity.

The Addington party was going smoothly for Everett. There came a point where he found himself sitting on a couch between Doris and Stan's wife. They were in a small sitting room, just off from where the other guests were congregated. The second time Doris leaned over him to say something to her cousin, Everett knew for certain that the presence of her breasts pushing into him was intentional. After Doris straightened herself up, he discreetly began to gently stroke the highlights that ran liberally through the back of her long hair. After a few minutes of this without her flinching, Everett became emboldened. He anxiously waited for her next pass over his lap. When it came, Everett dropped his hand down, palm up, onto the couch where her butt had been. Returning to her normal position, she found herself touching down on Everett's open hand. The thin, black slacks Doris wore gave the science teacher more of a feel than he expected. Since there was no recoil, Everett took the next step by wiggling his fingers. He allowed his hand to be pinned down as Doris settled her full weight on top of his palm. It became a party with many possibilities now that he knew the cousin of the hostess had the same needs.

"I'll be back in a bit," Doris announced coyly, excusing herself. "I need to go to the little girl's room...*upstairs*."

"Alright," answered Everett, getting her drift.

"I'll talk to you both later, I'm going to mingle," advised Iris, leaving the couch at the same time.

Before extricating herself from an unfulfilling marriage, Doris relied upon provocative novels to meet her needs. She found these risqué romances to be arousing, taking her to heights where a husband who kissed suspiciously with his eyes open was incapable of reaching. She lived vicariously through the characters, finding their detailed escapades fascinating. The novels acquainted Doris with romantic aberrations that one never spoke of in polite company. Those few reckless minutes spent on the couch with Everett identified him, in her mind, as just beast enough to partake in her most forbidden naughty desires. Thoroughly turned on, Doris was prepared to go the limit. Fortunately, she had just what it took to get Everett to follow her upstairs.

The cousin from California slipped away from the party not for a bathroom visit, but rather to retreat to her assigned bedroom in the east wing of the house. She stood in front of a mirror freshening up as she waited for Everett. Doris was touching up her lipstick when she noticed through the corner of her eye someone standing by the door that she'd left ajar. Her lips parted as he approached, her heart pounding with a fierceness that bordered on being medically dangerous. She dropped her hands to her side as she looked up into his face. She was his for the taking. The teacher didn't disappoint as he took her with the ferocity she desired. It was a welcomed subjugation received and digested as those she relished reading about in the pages of her spiciest novels.

JEANETTE'S ASSAULT BECAME HOT news in the neighborhood. The buzz turned out to be an economic blessing for her business. Everyone suddenly developed a sweet tooth: the line of busybodies went out the door. The customers wanted to hear a firsthand account of the details. The questions were never ending.

"Oh my God, you fought him off?"

"He tried to kill you?"

"Did he try to force himself on you first?"

"Did he expose himself?"

"Did you have to...you know...?"

Jeanette was only too glad to rehash the incident as long as she got to ring up purchases. Seeing each inquiry as a dollar sign, she milked her victimization for all it was worth. Her customers listened closely to every embellished detail. The thicker she laid it on, the thicker their waistlines were going to get as they kept ordering more pastry. Customers were so fascinated that they never noticed the price increases.

The attack had a profound effect on Jeanette psychologically. Even with an influx of money, she remained obsessed with avenging her assault. Until closure was attained, her husband Forrest was destined to deal with her highs and lows. It didn't help that Forrest lacked the wisdom to know when to give his wife space. He persisted in trying to soothe Jeanette. Forrest's good intentions were seen as annoyances—more evidence of his timidity. Jeanette was not the sort of woman to be coddled or shelved in a safe space with a cupcake. When it finally became evident that he was gaining no traction, Forrest began to silently monitor his wife's every movement. It was behavior that Jeanette found irritating, causing her to lash out.

"Must you keep watching me?" she asked angrily. "I feel your eyes on me all the time!"

"But Jeanette, I'm worried about you," replied Forrest.

"Look, I know you worry about me, but do me a favor, just worry about the business."

"Of course I will, but before I do that, would you please just entertain one question?"

"What is it?" she asked, sighing heavily.

"What do you intend to do with that carving knife?"

Jeanette became defensive. "What carving knife?"

"Jeanette, I *saw* you put it in your shoulder bag. Is it for protection?"

Jeanette was brutally direct in her reply. "Do you really want to know? I'm doing what *you* should be doing. I'm going out looking for this bastard who used me for a toilet!"

"*Something I should be doing*? We don't live in Tombstone!" This is a job for the cops."

"Don't sweat it, Forrest—I'm well aware that I'm not living with Wyatt Earp!"

Forrest thought that the remark was a low blow. Can't you even try to be reasonable?"

"Okay, let's be reasonable...you take care of the store while I'm gone. Now stop bothering me with your bullshit," she said, storming out of the bakery.

Forrest stepped behind the counter to rotate the glazed donuts. After doing so, he decided to call up his mother. He needed advice on how to deal with his wife.

JEANETTE SCOURED THE WEST VILLAGE in search of her attacker, fully intending to plunge the knife into his/her back. It was a mission that was only partly based on revenge. She was mostly out to ensure her own survival. The bakery owner felt certain that the sicko would return to take a third crack at taking her out. She pounded the pavement for hours, speaking to mail carriers, cab drivers, and delivery men. She looked inside businesses, checked the bars, and hung around the subway entrance at West 4th Street . . . all to no avail. Before giving up, she swallowed her pride and turned to the one person in the neighborhood that she thought could be of help: Rudy the Hunch. She walked over to Rudy's house on Mercer Street. Sitting out front on a beach chair was the aging custodian she knew only by the initials R.E. The landlord paid the worker to take in barrels, shovel snow and field tenant complaints in connection with all of his properties. Jeanette always wondered what the initials stood for but never dared ask. R.E. hardly ever spoke to her when he came to her building. She knew why. It was her failure to take care of him during the holidays, as was the custom of most tenants.

"Excuse me R.E., do you know if Rudy is home?" she asked politely.

"Not here."

"Do you know when he usually comes home?"

"Could be anytime," he answered, shrugging.

"Well, could you tell me where he might be?"

"Try Maxie's on East Houston Street."

Jeanette walked away. At first she thought to call the deli but then decided to just go there. When she arrived she saw Rudy seated alone at a table eating a sandwich. She took a breath and approached her landlord. Rudy's mouth dropped when he saw her.

"Look who it is! How is my favorite tenant feeling? Are you getting all better?"

"I'm doing better."

"So what brings you here, baby doll?"

"I came to see you, Rudy."

The landlord's eyes lit up. "You came all the way over here to see me, how wonderful." He was hoping that she was finally coming around to his way of thinking.

"Well, I need some help—"

Rudy, who immediately assumed she was seeking financial relief, cut her off. "Of course, I told you we can have an understanding. We—"

It was now Jeanette's turn to cut him off and quickly put an end to his fantasy. "No arrangements, Rudy. I told you long ago, I'm a married woman. But I do need a favor."

Rudy was disappointed, but not bitter. "Sure baby doll, I know. I can dream, can't I?"

"Yes, Rudy you can dream all you like. So, how about doing that favor?"

"Okay, as long as it has nothing to do with money. What is it?"

"I want you to find out who is trying to kill me. I know you know people."

Rudy let out a one-syllable, scornful laugh. "Baby doll, baby doll, baby doll," he sighed.

"What you must think of me. Don't you know I've already been making inquiries so I could get my hands on this bum?"

"You have?" asked Jeanette, sincerely surprised.

"Of course I have. Can I afford to let someone get away with abusing my tenants? Especially someone I like as much as my baby doll?"

Jeanette felt a little embarrassed. "So how are you making out?"

"No luck...this bastard must be invisible!"

"Well, thank you for trying; I really appreciate it, Rudy."

"You need anything else?"

"No, I'm alright," she said dejectedly. Then, suddenly brightening, she asked, "One thing...about R.E. What do his initials stand for?"

"Don't you see his ear?"

"What about his ear?"

"It's made of rubber. So, he's a rubber ear...R.E."

Jeanette headed home with a mind more conflicted than ever. Of all people, Rudy had impressed her in a way that Forrest had failed to do. Thinking of Rudy brought back memories of the banker and the financial pressure that made her succumb to his romantic extortion. It was her lowest point. But, the banker did come through on his part of the bargain, as would Rudy if given the opportunity. Only Forrest was anemic in delivering results. There was no question that she married Forrest out of love. The fact that he came from an affluent New York family only sweetened the pot. However, at the end of the day, she had to admit that Forrest fell short when the chips were down.

WHEN MARKIE AND VON HESS entered the precinct in the Village, the desk officer signaled them over. "This just arrived in the department mail for you," advised the lieutenant, handing the sergeant an envelope.

Markie went upstairs to the squad where he opened the envelope. He removed a copy of a wanted poster with a fly drawn in black ink on the nose of the cross-eyed suspect. The sergeant passed the poster for Von Hess to see, while he looked at the attached note that read, "Chief Randolph had a fit over this. This is no time for fun and games. Get serious." It was signed McCoy.

"Do you believe this?" Markie asked, doing nothing to veil his anger. "Some jerk thinks this is pretty funny. Now I got the inspector up my ass."

"What does he expect us to do?" asked Von Hess. "Every precinct has a few assholes, sarge."

"Ollie, I never mentioned it but I found one just like this myself. It was posted downstairs, under our own very noses. It was in the lobby of *this* precinct!"

143

The silence in the room was only broken when Markie spoke again. "Okay, so maybe this sketch does appear to be too ridiculous to be taken seriously. Maybe nobody can look like this and still be walking around unidentified. But, it's *not* ridiculous to Jeanette Pergamint who came close to being killed by this character."

"You are preaching to the choir boss," commented Von Hess.

"I know, Ollie. But so help me, I'm going to get to the bottom of this. I'm going to have DeCesare reach out to outside agencies asking them to send a photo of *anyone* they may have arrested, of either sex, with eye abnormalities. And I'm going to have them debrief anybody in cuffs who comes through the door of this precinct."

"Good idea, boss."

"Ollie, we're going up to visit the Two-Three to see about the old woman who got clipped in the candy store. That was the second strangulation. Let's see where that can take us."

"Okay, boss."

"I hope that there *is* a cross eyed killer out there—our reputation depends on it."

"We *all* had our doubts about that sketch, but don't worry, we'll get him. He can't hide forever."

"You go get the car and I'll check in with McCoy." After Markie's conversation with the inspector he joined up with Von Hess. "The old man was pretty steamed up about that sketch," said the sergeant. "He gave me an earful."

"I figured he would."

"He said that the chief of detectives flipped out when he saw the sketch with a fly on the perp's nose. According to McCoy, the chief wanted to know if we've all gone crazy in the West Village."

"Shit travels downhill."

"For sure," replied Markie.

DECESARE AND SHERIDAN SLIPPED BACK into their regular work routine of catching cases. This meant that they were restricted to working on the Wallace/Pergamint cases in between the newly reported complaints. Performing a day tour, Sheridan received a call from Greasy Jake.

"Detective Sheridan, it's me Jake, your favorite hot dog man."

"Hey Jake, what's up?"

"That cross-eyed guy you want, could he have one leg?"

"Is the guy with one leg tall?"

144

"Oh, I forgot that you want big. Forget about it, this guy is a shrimp."

"Thanks anyway, keep digging for me."

"Don't worry, the word is out," Jake assured him. "We all have our eyes open."

"Thanks Jake, you're the best. Say hello to Benny Leonard for me," he said before hanging up, referring to the old-time lightweight champion.

As Sheridan hung up the phone Detective DeCesare came rushing over to his desk with big news: Jeanette Pergamint spotted the person who tried to kill her on the street. Sheridan leaped from behind his desk to join DeCesare, who already had the car key in his hand. The two detectives ran out the door to meet Jeanette, who they found standing in a doorway across the street from a drugstore.

"He's inside that drugstore," advised Jeanette, who was filled with excitement. She called the squad only after realizing she didn't have it in her to stab someone in the back.

"What's he wearing?" asked DeCesare.

"He's wearing a black suit, a black tie, and carrying a briefcase. He's has gray hair. Look in the aisle where the razor blades are."

DeCesare advised Sheridan that he'd go inside the pharmacy to get an eyeball on their suspect. Returning shortly, he advised that the suspect was still standing by the shaving supplies. Sheridan called for a car to transport Jeanette to the precinct, where she would await the arrival of the detectives with their prisoner.

"We'll see you at the precinct, Jeanette," advised DeCesare. "Go with the officers when they get here."

"If he puts up a fight, don't take any chances. Use the bullets," she urged.

Sheridan was amused by the remark. "We'll know how to neutralize him."

"Don't underestimate him, keep your guns handy," she said as the police car pulled up. Having regained her lost nerve, she regretted not sticking her attacker with the knife she had tucked away in her bag.

DeCesare and Sheridan determined that their best option was to apprehend their man inside the pharmacy. The narrow aisles would work to their advantage should the suspect put up a fight or make a run for it. Producing his .38 caliber detective special, Sheridan led the way into the pharmacy.

"There he is at the register," said DeCesare, swiftly moving in on his man. "You cover him." Sheridan drew down, prepared to shoot if necessary.

Flashing his tin, DeCesare grabbed the suspect by the back of his collar. The man in the suit was shocked at the way he was being manhandled. DeCesare forced his man's torso over the counter. "Put your hands behind your back," ordered the detective, hollering into the man's ear.

Sheridan stepped forward to push the suspect's head downward onto the countertop with his gun barrel. He placed his upper weight on the suspect's back while DeCesare put hand cuffs on his man. Cognizant of the cold steel pressed into the back of his head, the suspect went along without resistance.

"What have you got in the valise?" asked Sheridan.

"Just some business material, go ahead and look."

"I will," replied Sheridan, opening the brown valise.

The detective was disappointed to find that the suspect was being truthful. The man in custody demanded an explanation at this point. He addressed Sheridan, who was obviously the senior detective.

"What is this all about?" The handcuffed man turned to face the cashier, looking for some support. None came.

"We'll explain in the car, let's go," replied DeCesare, taking his prisoner by the arm.

The suspect complied until they reached the street, at which point he stopped walking. He turned to address Sheridan. "I demand to know what this is all about!"

Seeing his man in the light of day, the detective could plainly see that he had perfectly aligned brown eyes. This opened Sheridan to the possibility that Jeanette may have made a mistake.

"How about we just get in the car and go to the precinct where we can hash this out," said Sheridan, using a mellower tone than previously.

"*I will not*! We'll hash it out here!"

DeCesare's rush of adrenaline was still in full force. "Look asshole, you were fingered in a crime by a complainant, now get in the car."

"What crime? What complainant?"

"Do I have to knock you on your fat ass first? Just get in the back seat."

Sheridan weighed in to help convince the suspect to go quietly. "Sir, listen and come along. If there is some mistake, we'll void the arrest and let you go," explained the detective. "If you don't get in the car, well, you'll be leaving us no choice other than to use necessary force."

DeCesare looked at his partner with surprise, wondering why he was treating the suspect with kid gloves.

"So I'm arrested then?"

"You are wearing bracelets, aren't you?" asked DeCesare sarcastically. "Now get in!"

With no alternative, the suspect agreed to enter the unmarked car, but not before making a statement. "My name is J. Hanley Delmont, I'm the president of Woodrow-Brown International Lines, and I *don't* commit crimes," he declared. "What am I suspected of doing?"

DeCesare never heard a word of what he said. "Cut the shit and get in the frigging car," ordered the impatient detective.

"We shall see about this," said the peeved Delmont, before entering the vehicle. He was a man not accustomed to such disrespect.

On the trip to the precinct Sheridan explained to Delmont what caused them to single him out in the pharmacy. After being apprised of Jeanette's identification and of the seriousness of the crimes under investigation, the law-abiding Delmont felt some satisfaction in at least knowing why he was taken into custody. Once inside the precinct DeCesare posed a question to his partner.

"Sherry, do you think we need a line up?"

"No. The complainant already picked him out in a public venue, so let's just do a show up to make certain that Jeanette identified the right man."

"What precisely is a show up?" asked Delmont, who was listening to their conversation.

"A show up is when the victim sees you up close," explained Sheridan. "It's the quickest way for or us to get you out of here if you're not the man we want."

"Well by all means then, let's get on with this unbridled foolishness," said Delmont.

Sheridan, after hearing this remark, felt pretty sure that Jeanette fingered the wrong man. He placed the prisoner inside an office where he was asked to face a mirror contained within the door that led into the room. DeCesare fetched Jeanette, positioning her on the other side of the door's one way glass to view the suspect.

"Is that him?" asked DeCesare.

Studying the suspect closely, Jeanette answered the detective's question with a certainty that left no room for doubt. "That's not him. I made a mistake."

"Are you sure? Do you want us to bring him closer to the glass so you can see him better?" asked DeCesare.

"No, that's not necessary. I'm telling you he's not the man."

"Would you like to hear him speak?"

"*No*...I said it *isn't* him! How many times do I need to say it?" Her sharp tone unmasked her embarrassment over having made such an error.

"Alright, cool down Jeanette," advised DeCesare. "Remember, I'm on your side."

After DeCesare escorted his complainant off the floor, he returned to the room where Sheridan and Delmont were. After he learned of the results of the show up, Sheridan quickly left the room, leaving his partner alone with Delmont. DeCesare took the handcuffs off. "I'll void the arrest, sir."

"I told you, but *you* refused to listen to reason," lectured Delmont, as if talking to a child. DeCesare took his tongue lashing without complaint.

"*You* simply didn't want to hear it, now did you?" The former prisoner scolded, making the most of his exoneration. "You can rest assured that there will be a price to pay. Do you *always* leap before you look, officer?" asked the wrongly accused, before correcting himself. "Oh, I forgot you *are* supposed to be a detective, aren't you?"

Wrong man or not, DeCesare was fast approaching the end of his rope. "The victim made the mistake, not me. What can I tell you?"

The conversation was interrupted when Sheridan returned to the room. He was carrying a case folder in his hand.

"Mr. Delmont, we owe you an apology," announced Sheridan. I am so sorry for the inconvenience we put you through."

Delmont remained cool. "Yes, I'm sure you are...*now*. Are you also sorry for placing a gun to my head as well?"

"I most certainly am, sir." Undaunted, Sheridan continued his attempt to mitigate the damage. "The complainant feels absolutely awful that she made such a blunder, putting us all in such a situation. She's still a wreck from what happened to her. Did I tell you that she was garroted? Her throat is still bruised by the strangulation. Take a look at these, just to give you an idea...their ghastly."

Sheridan removed the crime scene photos from the folder. "These pictures were taken after the incident. Check out the ligature marks on this poor woman's neck. And here are the crime scene photos of the handyman who was murdered. The blood that poured out of him was enough to swab a deck."

Delmont's eyes squinted as he looked open mouthed at the gruesome photographs. Sheridan was glad to see the pained expression come over Delmont's face while viewing the disturbing pictures. The detective figured right: Delmont didn't have the stomach for it. Visibly shaken after seeing what happened to Jeanette and the handyman, the businessman realized his ordeal paled in comparison. Seeing Delmont's outrage deflated, Sheridan played his hand for all it was worth.

"She was lucky to survive the attack alright, Mr. Delmont. Four other women were not so lucky—they were all strangled by this maniac. Want to hear something else, sir?"

Delmont nodded slowly, not sure if he really did want to know more.

"After this madman strangled this poor woman, he urinated on her. Can you imagine doing something like that to a breast cancer survivor? You want to know something else?" the detective asked, not waiting for a reply. "She's a former Peace Corps volunteer to boot...a heart of gold."

"I wasn't aware of any of this."

"There is more."

"Really...I've heard enough. This is terrible."

"Terrible?" asked Sheridan. "I'll tell you what's terrible...that poor handyman was a real decent guy who didn't have two nickels to rub together. He left a wife and four kids, one blind. Mr. Delmont, I ask you, where's the justice in this world?"

Delmont gulped at hearing the fictionalized biographies presented by Sheridan. "Oh, my God," were the only words he could think to say.

"And that's not even the worst of it. After the louse did this, he...ahh, forget it, the details are too gruesome for me to even repeat. Anyway, the victim was a little mixed up. She really wants to get this fiend off the street, as you can imagine."

"My God, I should hope so."

"Look, like I said, the victim feels awful about this. Do you want me to get her in here to apologize to you? She offered to do so."

The wrongly accused had a change of heart. He was no longer bitter about his own inconvenience. "Err ... no. I don't think that would serve any useful purpose."

"That's very decent of you Mr. Delmont," said Sheridan. "Again, my partner and I both apologize for your inconvenience. No hard feelings, sir?"

"Under the circumstances, knowing what I now know, there are no hard feelings." The exonerated man willingly took Sheridan's extended hand—a display that made it clear all was forgiven.

"Thank you again for understanding. Can we give you a lift any place, sir?"

"That's alright, forget it, misunderstandings occur. Just do your best to get this fiend! I'm way behind schedule. I have to get uptown now for an appointment."

"Let us take you. We'll put the siren on and get you up there in a jiffy. Matter of fact, you can sit up front."

"Really?" asked Delmont, thrilled at the prospect of riding in a police car with the siren going.

"Certainly. You can work the siren."

"No handcuffs, I hope?" asked Delmont, showing a lighter side.

"No handcuffs, Mr. Delmont. We're on the same team now," smiled Sheridan.

Before they left the precinct, DeCesare went to see Jeanette, who was seated at a desk in the squad room.

"I'm sorry detective. When I saw him on the street I really thought it was him."

"No problem, Jeanette. I'm glad it happened, because it indicates to us that you really do know exactly who you are looking for," replied DeCesare. "Is your neck healing?"

"Yes, it's getting better."

"I'll get you a lift home."

"No, I want to walk back. I'm still hoping to see that bastard someday on the street!"

DeCesare couldn't help but smile at the crime victim. "What a woman you are."

Returning to his partner DeCesare marveled at how well Sheridan and Delmont were now getting along, He found Sheridan's craftiness admirable in the way he turned a sure civilian complaint into a pat on the back. He couldn't help but think that maybe it was Sheridan who belonged in acting class.

17

The Feathered Fink

"The guy who did this was some kind of a nut. Did you check to see if anyone busted out of the crazy house?"

-Gussie Cursio

GUSSIE FACED EACH DAY with little enthusiasm now that Thelma was gone. The nonagenarian, with a net worth of five million dollars, was slipping into a state of depression. His daughter had been his primary connection to the dwindling generation. that shared his point of view. Thelma had been around her father long enough to speak his language. She knew what *Ballin' the Jack* meant and that Eddie Cantor coined the term *"March of Dimes."* Thelma, like Gussie, saw the humor in the antics of prankster jazz violinist Joe Venuti, who sent the one armed trumpet player Wingy Manone a single cufflink for Christmas. Now, what did it all matter? He couldn't even boast of having once danced with actress Alice Faye in a nightclub. Who was around that heard of her anymore? Cash buried in the backyard, property, rental incomes, social security and money generated from the candy store all began to fade in importance. Even getting up in the morning was now overrated.

The candy store owner, depressed or not, still adhered to a daily stretching routine that was effective in keeping him relatively limber. After rising in the morning Gussie went downstairs to open the store. The first thing he did was to clean Edna's cage. The African Grey had been acting peculiar as of late. For some inexplicable reason Edna's early morning habit was to cower in the corner of her cage. "Could it be that she too missed Thelma?" Gussie asked himself. After awhile the bird came around to resume her chatterbox ways. Once Edna uttered, *"Thelma, you're getting too fat,"* Gussie knew that all was well. After the cleaning he covered Edna's cage with a thin white sheet. It was something he did when he wanted his pet silenced. The arrangement seemed acceptable to Edna. It was probably a big improvement from the morning squirts that had been Thelma's pleasure.

After muting Edna, Gussie took in the deliveries of newspapers, magazines, bagels, and rolls. He then put on a pot of coffee and assumed Thelma's old post behind the register. Straightening out behind the counter, he came across Edna's black water pistol. Looking at the squirt gun, Gussie wondered why it was there. He turned to open the Bible that was inconspicuously positioned on a shelf behind the counter. Seeing the loaded pistol housed inside the hollowed out holy book made him curious as to why his daughter didn't go for the good book when attacked. He questioned his decision not to keep a shotgun under the counter like Thelma wanted. Gussie had been beating himself up with such guilt-ridden thoughts ever since Thelma's death.

Gussie's morose state was interrupted by the son of a tenant. Hector was an upbeat youth of fifteen. Gussie liked the boy, who he'd known from birth. He was a polite, bright eyed, respectful youth who was never without a pleasant smile.

"How you doing, Mr. Curcio?" asked Hector, who was carrying a quart size glass jar.

"Hello kid," answered Gussie. "How are your people doing?"

"Everybody's fine, thanks. Do you need anything from outside?"

"No, I'm good, kid. What's that you got in the jar there, a quart of beer?"

"Nah, something better than beer for you, Mr. Curcio," Hector laughed. "My moms wants you to have some of her special sopa de pollo. Everybody is worried about you." On the spot, the old man made up his mind to do something for the boy: he intended to amend his will, leaving Hector sufficient funds to finance whatever education he desired, including medical school. In order to avoid any hoopla, Gussie wouldn't mention his decision to the boy or his family. When the time came, if he was gone, his lawyer would explain the origin of the endowment. Pondering the future gave Gussie something he desperately needed: a reason to go on.

"There was that guy who died a few years back at one-hundred-seven years old," Gussie said, thinking out loud about the producer George Abbott. "He was still working at one-hundred-four!"

"Who is that, Mr. Curcio?"

"Forget about it kid, I was just thinking about something I need to do. Tell me, do you like school?"

"Yeah, I like it a lot."

The old man was pleased to hear that. "Good. Make sure you get all the education you can, maybe even shoot to be a doctor or a lawyer. What do you think?"

"That costs a lot of money," said the boy.

"Yeah, well save your money. You want to work in the store part time? Make a few bucks?"

"I definitely would."

"Alright kid, make sure it's okay with your folks. If you get the green light let me know when you're available. We'll work around school. I can teach you a few tricks."

"That sounds great!" said the boy enthusiastically.

"Now give me the soup and be sure to thank your mother for me. How is your father, anyway?"

"He works hard on the truck."

"It's no picnic working with your back. That's why you got to go to school."

"Did you go to school?"

The old man just laughed. "Grab a couple of those movie magazines for your mother. Bring them back when she's done reading them. And do me a favor; make sure nobody draws mustaches on the pictures like last time."

"Thanks Mr. Curcio. Remember, if you need anything just call, we're right upstairs.

After the youth left the store Gussie began to wipe the dust away from the shelves. As he did this, he was startled by a disruptive noise coming from the front door.

"Whoa...take it easy over there!" the business owner yelled over to his friend. "Where the hell are you going with that tank?"

This door weighs a ton, Gus," said the friend, as he struggled to enter the store with his bicycle.

"What are ya looking to do, bust up the place Patsy, or what?"

At eighty-one-years-old, Gussie's friend was a good deal younger than he was. Despite the age disparity, the two shared commonalities. Both were widowed, served in the army and were raised in East Harlem.

"How's it going today, Gus?"

"Okay, until you came in with that paddleboat."

"Come again?"

"I SAID YOU SHOULD LEAVE THAT WHEELCHAIR OUTSIDE," repeated Gussie, raising his voice to accommodate his hard of hearing friend.

"Maybe I'll switch to a wheelchair. This bike *is* getting a little tough for me to handle."

Gussie looked at the green Huffy Radio bike with its fenders, white wall tires, attached radio and battery box. It was something from the mid-fifties.

"That thing's older than me for Christ's sake! It must weigh a ton," commented Gussie. "Go get yourself a new one, an English Racer or whatever the hell they got now."

"What's that you said?"

"YOU NEED A NEW BIKE!"

"Why? This still works," said the friend. "So what's doing?"

Gussie shrugged his shoulders as if to ask what could be doing. The friend, a clean-shaven man with a mole on the tip of his nose, could tell that Gussie was still grieving over Thelma.

"Hey Gussie, it's just a rough patch. You gotta keep moving in life." The store owner's friend got into a low crouch. Pretending to be boxing, he began to slowly bob and weave while throwing punches in the air.

"You're nuts," said Gussie, chuckling. Gussie jabbed his thumb toward his mouth three times. It was his way of offering a beverage. "YOU WANT A MANHATTAN SPECIAL?" he shouted.

"No thanks, Gus," replied the friend, waving him off. "Seriously pal, you gotta snap out of it. You got up this morning didn't you? You don't need a wheelchair, a walker or even a cane. You got all your marbles and everything probably still works, right?"

"Yeah, last time I checked," replied Gussie, nodding his agreement.

"You go regular and you don't pee the bed, so what the hell else do you want? Remember, we're from East Harlem, baby! We don't cry in our beer over here."

Having an epiphany, Gussie looked at his half deaf friend. There he was, living alone in a basement apartment on a small pension and social security. Yet, he was all about living. Feeling ashamed, Gussie straightened up and walked over to Edna's cage and removed the covering he used to shut the bird out.

"HUNGRY?" Gussie asked his friend, with a new found energy.

154

"No, let's eat later. How about we get a couple of Whoppers for dinner? We can play a little rummy, a quarter a game. What do you say?"

"Yeah, I'd like that, a quarter a game. You fly and I'll buy the Whoppers. I'll even throw in a couple of beers!"

"You're gonna have to talk louder."

"YOU NEED AN EAR TRUMPET."

"What are you talking about...ear trumpet? You better get up to date, pal. Want me to bring over a couple of live ones later?" teased the friend, behaving like an aged imp.

"You want a blond or brunette?"

That brought a smile to Gussie's face. "C'MON, WHO YA KIDDING? JUST BRING THE WHOPPERS. AND YOUR QUARTERS."

"Okay, Gus. I'll see ya later."

Gussie was glad Hector and his fellow vet came around. They turned out to be the right medicine.

ARRIVING AT THE EAST HARLEM PRECINCT, Markie and Von Hess stopped at the front desk before going up to the squad. Identifying yourself and stating your business was the old school way—a gesture that recognized the authority of the ranking officer responsible for holding down the station house during a particular shift.

After receiving the blessing of the desk, the investigators proceeded up to the squad where they introduced themselves to Detective Ozzie Perez. Perez was engaged with a local resident who was reporting the disappearance of her husband.

"I'm afraid there isn't anything I can really do," said the detective.

"But he hasn't been home in two days. He could be dead someplace."

"He's an adult, he's not mentally challenged, and there aren't indications of foul play. *Bad news* travels fast, so if he were in a hospital, the victim of a crime or whatever, you would have been notified," Perez advised. "He probably isn't ready to come home yet."

"Are you telling me that nothing can be done?" asked the worried wife.

"I'm afraid for now, that's about the size of it," replied the detective. "He's only gone a couple of days. Let's give it some time before we start worrying."

Once the woman left Detective Perez approached his visitors. "Her old man went out drinking and forgot to go home. You know how that can go. He's probably sleeping it off someplace or shacked up."

"People don't like to hear the truth sometimes," said Markie.

"You think?" asked the squad detective. "She'd rather believe her husband was abducted by aliens."

After introducing himself to the investigator, Markie steered the conversation to what he was there for. "The strangulation of that woman in the candy store, what does it look like?"

"In terms of evidence, there isn't much to work with, sarge. The victim lived with her elderly father above their candy store. The perp attacked her inside the store a short time after she opened up. There is nothing to suggest that this was a robbery.

"Were there witnesses?"

"None, no one was around to see anything."

"Is there anything that needs to be done on the case?" asked Markie.

"To be honest with you, I'm at a dead end," replied Perez. "The victim was a homebody. She never went any place and had no outside interests."

"What about the father?"

"He's ninety... just an old man hanging in there," replied Perez. "That's not saying he was too feeble to do it. I just doubt that he did."

"Mind if we take a look through the case folder?"

"Sure thing," responded Perez. "I'll go pull out the file for you."

Coming back with the case folder, Perez handed it over to Von Hess. Once their review was completed, Markie and Von Hess had a short conference, after which Von Hess returned the file to Detective Perez.

"It looks like you covered the bases pretty well. Nice job," complimented Von Hess.

"I think we are going to stop by the candy store to talk to the old man," said Markie. "Interested in joining us?"

"Definitely I'm interested. After all, it *is* my case," answered Perez. "I was intending to talk to Gussie again anyway."

When the three law enforcement officers arrived at the candy store, they found Gussie behind the counter, reading a newspaper.

"Hello, Mr. Curcio, how are you doing today?" greeted Perez.

Looking up, Gussie immediately recognized Perez. "I'm still here anyway. Did you find out anything?"

"Not yet sir, we're still working on it," the detective replied, "that's why we came by."

"Good, you want something to drink?"

"No thank you, sir," said Perez. "This is Sergeant Markie and Detective Von Hess. They're working on the investigation with me. They have a few questions for you."

"Okay, go ahead."

"Mr. Curcio, did your daughter have any disagreements with anyone?" asked Von Hess.

"No, I already told you guys that. My daughter was the stay at home type. She was with me all the time. There were no strangers coming around here either," he added.

"Did Thelma gamble? Was she ever short on money or anything like that?"

Gussie scoffed at the thought. "No, she hardly ever left the house, for Christ's sake. She'd say her prayers every night."

"Do you suspect anyone at all? Could be for any reason, regardless how farfetched you might think it is. A boyfriend, maybe?" asked Markie.

"You're way off base." The old man shook his head in disbelief. "Look sergeant, my daughter wasn't a young woman. The guy who did this was some kind of a nut. Did you check to see if anyone busted out of the crazy house?"

Von Hess smiled. "There are no more crazy houses," said the detective. "Not that we couldn't use a few institutions like that."

"What about your vendors?" queried Markie? "Have you had any issues with them?"

"I'm with the same vendors for years," he said. "I'm telling you, this was the work of some nut. Who else would do something like this without robbing them?"

"That's a valid point. Did you happen to notice any new customers hanging around the store?" Before Gussie could answer Edna weighed in, letting her presence be known.

"That's a valid point."

"I'll buy the whoppers."

"Thelma, you're getting too fat."

"Poor, poor Mrs. Trapani."

"Give me one without the thumb."

"Thelma, you're getting too fat."

The investigators abruptly turned to where the voice was coming from. They gazed at the cage containing the African Grey, after which the detectives then looked at each other. All three law enforcement officers had the same thought. Markie posed the question. "What the heck kind of a bird *is* that?"

"That's my company, Edna. She's an African Grey," advised the old man. "She repeats what she hears. Cost me a bundle, that bird."

"This bird stays in the store all the time?" asked Von Hess.

"Yeah, she stays here always."

"Do you know where she picked up those phrases from?"

"What do you mean?" Gussie did not understand the question.

"The phrase 'Give me one without the thumb,' do you know where that came from?"

"Yeah, of course I know. Edna heard some kid say that. The kid thought Thelma put her thumb in his ice cream."

"I see," said Von Hess.

"You know, Thelma chased that kid out of the store. You think he could have come back?" asked Gussie. "He was just a kid."

"I don't know," replied Von Hess. "How big a kid was he?"

"Not too big, he was about fourteen or so."

"What about the reference about Thelma getting too fat, do you know who it was that said that?"

"That's an old one from me. I said that just once and it stuck with Edna ever since."

"Who is Mrs. Trapani?

"That's a new one Edna picked up. I don't know where it came from."

"When did the bird first start saying that?"

After reflecting a moment, Gussie answered. "You know, I heard Edna say that for the first time *after* Thelma die"

"Are you sure of that?" asked Markie.

"I know that for sure because Thelma and I would always talk about the new phrases Edna repeated." After thinking about the words, the old man posed a question to the detectives. "So you don't think it could be the kid with the ice cream?"

Shrugging his shoulders, Markie answered. "It's not likely. Does Edna ever get to move around? I mean, does she ever leave this store?"

"No, she never leaves the store. Edna stays right here 24 hours a day."

"Let's go back for a minute to Mrs. Trapani," injected Perez. "I want to get something straight. You don't know anyone named Mrs. Trapani?"

"I never met anyone by that name."

"Did Thelma ever mention the name?"

"Never," said the old man.

"How could you be so sure of that?"

"Edna never repeated anything Thelma ever said. The bird is quirky that way,"

Perez glanced at Markie and Von Hess before commenting. "So the name Mrs. Trapani could have been heard *during or at some point after* the attack."

"I don't know where the hell Edna's picked up the name from," advised Gussie. "All I know is that if the bird said it before Thelma died, we would've talked about it, that's for sure."

"She might not have lived to tell you," pointed out Von Hess. "After Thelma died, is it possible that someone could have come into this store without you being here?"

"No chance of that."

When the detectives finished speaking to the old man, they thanked him and left the store. Once outside, they conferred among themselves.

"You know, I think we stumbled onto something," said Markie. "This bird really could have heard the name mentioned during the commission of the crime."

"The bird could have picked it up from the radio," said Von Hess;

"I never heard a radio playing any time I ever went into the store," said Perez. "Do you suppose this Mrs. Trapani fits in someplace?"

"That's the question," replied Markie. "How about we do this: Ollie, you research the name and see where that takes us," Then turning to Perez he said, "How about you canvass your precinct to see if the name Trapani rings a bell with anyone?"

"No problem sarge. I'll keep you posted if I get anything. You'll let me know if something develops on your end?" asked Perez.

"You bet," replied Markie.

Markie took the keys to the car and dropped Von Hess and Perez off at the precinct where they began their research. "Ollie, I'll be available on my cell phone, call me if you need me. I'll be back in about an hour and a half."

No problem boss, I got plenty to do. I'll be here."

Von Hess located hundreds of people with the name Trapani living in the United States. With a cup of coffee in one hand and a pen in the other, he began to drill down. He started making calls to the local people named Trapani.

MARKIE WALKED THROUGH THE door of Fitzie's with the good intention of patching things up with Alley. Things changed when he saw Alley Cat being overly chummy with a customer. The sergeant proceeded to the back of the bar without looking at Alley as he passed her. He sat on a stool brooding, waiting for her to extricate herself from the hangman game she was engaged in with a sheet metal worker. Markie had little use for the tin knocker, a rough sort who he suspected of having amorous designs on his girl. Seeing a peeved look on Markie's face, she joined the sergeant at the end of the bar.

"I wasn't expecting you."

"Obviously," he replied tersely. "Give me the usual, *when* you have the time."

"Are you pissed off at me?" she asked. "If so, I think it should be the other way around."

"Look, do I get the drink or do I go elsewhere?"

Before she could answer, the tin knocker called out to her. "Hey Alley, where are you?" It's your turn," he said, referring to the game they were playing.

"I'll be right there," she yelled over, flashing a false smile.

Markie rose from his stool and walked out of the bar. Alley Cat was baffled. It was the first time she had been exposed to the sergeant's jealous side.

"Screw you!" she said to the man who was no longer there.

"Hey Alley, do you want to finish this game or what? It's your move sweetheart," yelled out the tin knocker.

"You win," she answered. It was another one of those times that Alley took the pledge against all things male.

18

Ambition Abounds

"I can't have women getting bumped off in Manhattan! We aren't talking about a shithole outer borough where a few bodies more or less won't mean much."

-Chief of Detectives John Randolph

CHIEF OF DETECTIVES JOHN RANDOLPH ruled supreme over his investigators. His office was one of the most coveted pieces of real estate inside police headquarters. In a city that hosted many sensational cases, it was not unusual for the chief to be in the public eye. When things went well, he was a hero. When they didn't, his underlings paid the price.

Randolph was an educated man who earned his business management degree by attending night school. The chief was a results-oriented executive of great confidence. He was also a man capable of wearing many hats. Perhaps his greatest ability was rooted in his being a social chameleon. He was no stranger to rolling up his sleeves and guzzling a few beers in some poker game with his cronies. On these occasions he'd talk tough. It was typical for him to lay down a winning hand of three queens and announce, "Read-em and weep, I got three whores." Conversely, when mingling with the toffee-nosed set, he'd gently sip his martini as he casually referenced the poem "*A Word to Husbands*" by Ogden Nash when looking to impress. This particular work was his standby whenever the topic of marriage arose.

The chief was in line for appointment to the post of police commissioner. All he needed to do was breathe...*and* continue to dodge political embarrassment. The current commissioner's ill health made it just a matter of time. Such close proximity to the job he desired made Randolph sensitive to any risk that could potentially derail his career. With this concern he summoned his old friend, Inspector Harry McCoy, to his office. McCoy coveted Randolph's job with the same chop-licking hunger that the chief held for the commissioner's post. The man behind the big desk motioned the inspector to close the door. Noting the serious look on the chief's face, McCoy eased into a seat on the subordinate side of the desk.

"Harry, we got a problem," began Randolph. "I can't continue to play with dynamite. I'm too close to the blue-ribbon to start taking chances now."

"You're talking about the strangulation murders, chief?"

"Certainly, I'm talking about the strangulations! I can't have women getting bumped off in *Manhattan*! We aren't talking about a shithole outer borough where a few bodies more or less won't mean much."

"I'm on the case chief, I..." McCoy's alibi was abruptly silenced.

"Do yourself a favor Harry, just listen." McCoy complied, holding his tongue. "How much longer do you think these strangulations can go unnoticed?"

"John, trust me, I'm working to get my arms around this."

"That doesn't guarantee my protection," snapped the chief. "We have a serial killer on the loose who needs to be stopped pronto! I've given you the support you asked for, didn't I?"

The inspector nodded. "The problem here is that we haven't caught a real break on any of these homicides. We're dealing with a slick customer who knows how to cover his tracks."

The chief sneered at the excuse. "Is that what you expect me to tell people?"

"But it's the truth, John. I could explain to the commissioner..."

"The poor prick is on his last legs. He's riddled with cancer," said Randolph, in a raised voice. "The next thing he'll be hearing are bagpipes!"

"What can I say, John?"

"Let me say it, Harry. I have to take some kind of action before somebody important dies." The definiteness in the chief's voice was intimidating.

"I hear you," acknowledged the inspector. Sucking it up like a good soldier he was prepared to take his hit.

"You do?" asked Randolph, who reached for his economy size bottle of Tums. "So what do you propose to do about it?"

"We got a nibble with the last case, the one in the Village—at the bakery. With that one, we finally may have a witness."

"Yeah, sure," said the chief, tired of hearing the same old-same old. "Look, you got a witness who describes a perp with a friggin fly taking a dump on his nose!"

"John, that's not ..."

"Harry, we go back since our rookie days, so let me make it clear t you. I'm *not* getting embarrassed for you or anyone else."

"I don't expect you to."

"The weight has to fall on you," warned the chief. "*You're* the one who'll be taking the hit, not me. To be blunt, if this caper isn't solved soon, y*ou* will be gone!"

"I got it."

The chief exhaled loudly—it was the first sign that he was settling down. "Harry, don't you realize that I'm on the cusp of being the next PC? *You'll* be sitting in my seat right here if you don't screw this up."

"I know."

"Yeah...you know. You know everything," said the chief with disgust. "It's what you *don't know* that concerns me, like who in hell is knocking off all these skirts. I'm giving you two weeks to get this cleaned up, or else I'm going to have to pull the rug out from under you. I don't want to, you know that...but I need to protect myself by taking steps that show I'm on top of things. I'm going to have to begin shaking the tree."

"I understand."

Inspector McCoy left the office a rattled man. Facing banishment to a dead end slot in the basement of a building someplace was a terrible thought. Or worse, he could be demoted a rank. For McCoy, such a humiliation would be unbearable. He'd have to retire, an awful fate for someone not yet ready to pack it in. The inspector needed to figure a way to save himself. Picking his own brain for solutions proved fruitless—he was too upset to think straight. His only hope rested in Markie.

MARKIE PARKED AROUND THE corner from a small gin mill called Rita's Roost. A karaoke platform stood to the right of the entrance. The sergeant found himself an isolated spot at the bar away from the other patrons. The bartender, who was in his early twenties, was a tall, slender man in a white short sleeved shirt. He approached with a friendly smile.

"Jack Daniels straight up and a glass of Budweiser," ordered Markie, trying to figure out what the full length tattoo on the bartender's forearm was supposed to be.

"You don't want the Jack, you want the Bud instead?" asked the bartender.

"No, I want both."

The bartender returned with a Jack Daniels on the rocks with a bottle of Budweiser. Markie could live without a glass for his beer, but not watering down the whiskey. "I asked for the shot straight up, and I need a glass for the beer."

"Oh, okay. No problem," answered the bartender, tugging at the earlobe with the stud.

Markie watched him use a spoon to hold down the ice as he drained the Jack Daniels into a new glass. "Here you go, sorry for the mix up," the bartender announced, picking Markie's money off the bar.

First it was Alley Cat and the tin knocker, now this. Saying nothing, Markie drank the bourbon, took a sip of beer, gathered his money and left without leaving a tip.

VON HESS IDENTIFIED SIXTY-THREE families named Trapani currently residing within the five boroughs of New York City. He went down the list of names, contacting those with available telephone numbers. He thought he hit pay dirt with Blossom Trapani.

"Hello?" barked the husky masculine voice, sounding as if he were put out.

"Can I please speak to Ms. Blossom Trapani?"

"*Who* is this?" the voice asked in a demanding way.

"I'm Detective Von Hess from the Police Department. Does Blossom Trapani still use this number?"

"I'm her husband, what's this all about?" Once Von Hess explained why he was calling, the man summoned his wife to the phone.

"Hello, this is Blossom," said the female voice. She spoke slow, almost sounding sleepy.

"Hello Mrs. Trapani, thank you for taking my call. I'm sort of looking for a needle in the haystack," related Von Hess. "I'm calling all of the people named Trapani in New York. I'm trying to identify a *particular* Trapani who we need to speak with. So, I'd like to ask you a couple of questions, just to see if you are that person."

"You're looking for Blossom Trapani?"

"I'm not even sure of the first name, Mrs. Trapani. Actually, we don't know anything about the person we're looking for. That's why I need to ask you a couple of questions."

"Well go ahead, ask me your questions."

"Do you know Thelma Curcio? She worked in a candy store in East Harem."

"No."

"Do you know anyone named Thelma?"

"No."

"Do you know *anyone*, man or woman, who is cross-eyed or has some type of eye impairment?"

The woman was taken by surprise at the question. "Are you really a detective?"

"Yes, I am. If you like, you could call the precinct and ask for Detective Von Hess to verify who I am."

After thinking a moment, the woman responded to the question. "No, that's alright. The only person who had that kind of problem was my uncle Jimmy."

"Had? Did he have his eyes corrected?"

"No."

"What color are his eyes?"

"I don't know, I guess sort of a bluish gray."

"Bluish gray...tell me something, is Jimmy a big man?"

"Pretty big, about six feet I suppose."

The information excited Von Hess. "Tell me, where does your uncle live?"

"Where does he live now?"

"Yes, Mrs. Trapani, now. Where is your uncle now?" By this point Von Hess knew he wasn't conversing with a superior intellect.

"He's in Cypress Hills," she answered. "He fell in a cement mixer at work five years ago."

Von Hess felt deflated. "I see. Well, thanks for your time. I'm sorry to have bothered you."

The detective scratched Blossom Trapani off his list. He looked over the rest of the Trapani names to call. Feeling overwhelmed, he decided to take a break. He called his wife to tell her about his conversation with Blossom.

❖

UNABLE TO BEAR THE ANTICIPATION of waiting for the phone to ring, Inspector McCoy decided to go visit the West Village squad and see for himself how things were progressing. Entering the precinct, he immediately recognized the desk lieutenant: it was a woman who he hadn't seen in years. Time may have taken its toll perhaps, but there was no mistaking who she was.

"Lieutenant," McCoy said with a distinct reverence. "Remember me?"

Feeling awkward for not recognizing the man before her, the lieutenant put on her glasses for a clearer look. Finally, after recognizing McCoy, a half smile came to her face. "Harry McCoy! Or should I say, *Inspector* McCoy?"

"Ahh, come on, we go back way too far for any of that formality."

"It's been a long time, Harry."

"It certainly has. You haven't changed a bit," he fibbed.

Knowing that he was shoveling it, she was nevertheless pleased. "I always knew you'd rise up through the ranks. You were one of the good ones who deserved to get ahead."

"You didn't do too badly yourself."

"Me? I'm content. I messed up on the last captain's test, but I had a good run."

"They'll be another one."

"Not for me Harry, in a couple of months I hit the age limit. It'll be out the door for me. I'll have to retire."

"Good Lord...she's sixty-three!" The realization of the lieutenant's age was an eye-opener for McCoy. "You'll be packing it in with a lot of good years ahead of you, a great pension and lots of time for fun in the sun!" said McCoy, trying to put a positive spin on things.

"What fun in the sun? I have small grandchildren that need keeping an eye on."

"How wonderful, you must be very proud of them." McCoy's smile was contrary to what he was thinking..."Jumping Jesus, she's got grandchildren no less!"

"Did you ever marry?" she asked, wondering if McCoy ever did.

"No, I'm still a bachelor." The inspector let it go at that. "Well, I have to go up to the squad. I'll catch up with you later."

The desk lieutenant watched McCoy walk off. The history they shared was their little secret. Back in the day her being married prevented any crossing of the line. It was

167

strictly a matter of a young buck infatuated with a woman a little older who enjoyed the attention.

MCCOY ENTERED THE SQUAD COMMANDER'S office quietly. Markie was seated at the desk doodling on a piece of scrap paper. The sergeant found it a worthy exercise that helped him think. It would be something hard to explain to the inspector.

"Hi, inspector, I was getting ready to call you in a little while. I was just thinking out the next move."

"Really?" asked the skeptical inspector. "Do you always do your thinking while drawing cartoons?

"Don't worry inspector, I'm not sleeping on you. This helps me think."

"Do you have any news for me, sarge?"

"We may be at a place in the tunnel where there's some light," replied Markie.

"Jeanette identified somebody on the street as the perp. After an up-close look at the guy she realized she made a mistake. At least she knows *who* it is she's looking for.

McCoy was disappointed. "You'll have to do better than that—the chief just gave me the business."

"There's some more. The East Harlem candy store homicide had a talking bird. We believe the bird was likely present during the commission of the crime."

McCoy stared at Markie incredulously. "Don't tell me that the bird is supposed to be some kind of an eyeball witness!"

"No inspector, not a witness. An African Grey *is* known to repeat what it hears. The bird was in the store when the victim bought it. The bird repeated the name...Trapani."

"So?"

"The victim lived and worked with her father. The old man never heard the bird mention the name before. We have reason to suspect that the name came up during the commission of the murder."

"So who is this Trapani then?"

"Von Hess is running that down, inspector. We still have things to do on the other cases as well," added Markie.

"Look, I've been given two weeks to wrap this thing up or else it's the ballgame for me."

"Two weeks?"

The inspector looked at the sergeant very seriously. "I know it's not much time, but I need you to pull a rabbit out of a hat. Work through the night if you must. As far as I'm concerned, money is no object. At this point in the game its sink or swim for me. I'm counting on you to throw me a lifeline."

"I hear you inspector. I'll do my best," replied Markie.

"I'm counting on it that you will."

19

All You Need Is Love

"Yeah, he went out all by himself. Like I said, he looked like he had a good time. You know, worn out."

-Paul Armand Belvedario

DETECTIVE EDDIE ST. CLAIR LOVED where he worked. There were few commands better suited for a young single detective. For those out for a good time, as St. Clair was, his precinct afforded lots of bars and restaurants, a friendly community, and a light caseload. The only downside was the pricey toll connected to his commute to Manhattan from Staten Island. Looking to cut expenses, the dark-haired investigator with the Elvis sideburns sought to reduce his traveling cost by staying over with someone residing close to the precinct. St. Clair reached out to an old complainant who had been the victim of domestic violence. The woman was surprised to hear from the detective who arrested her live-in boyfriend the month prior.

"Everything has been fine, detective," the former complainant advised.

"I'm glad Ms. Croft. I just wanted to check in to make sure that Tex wasn't coming around to bother you. You didn't take him back did you?"

"No, I'm done with him," she advised. "I heard that he went back to El Paso."

"Well, that's good. Again, I was just concerned, so I reached out to you."

"Thank you so much for following up, that's very sweet of you."

Satisfied that he had planted a seed, St. Clair looked to conclude their conversation.

"Okay then, Donna...oh, excuse me, I mean Ms. Croft."

"That's okay, you can call me Donna."

"And you can call me Eddie. I like to stay in touch with my complainants from time to time to make sure things remain copasetic. You don't mind my checking in on you, do you...Donna?"

"I don't mind at all," she replied, now beginning to suspect that St. Clair had more than a professional interest in her.

"Cool. When I'm back from New Orleans I'll reach out."

"New Orleans? What's happening there?" she asked. Her curiosity was now raised.

"I have some interests there," he lied, intentionally being vague. "Bye, Donna. I've got to go now, but I'll talk to you again."

After hanging up the telephone, St. Clair turned his attention to his female partner who was seated at the desk directly in front of his. She had been trying to ignore his conversation as she typed a report. The close-cropped haircut and formidable features of the sixteen year veteran gave her a no-nonsense appearance. With little tolerance for her partner's telephonic trumpery, the mother of three bristled when St. Clair addressed her.

"Does Eddie Boy have that magic touch or what?" he asked.

"Eddie Boy is a regular Casanova," she replied sourly, without turning around.

"Did you hear how I set the stage?" asked St. Clair, speaking to the back of his partner's head. "It's all in the ingredients. A quarter cup of interest at first, add a pinch of mystery and then let it settle long enough to get them wondering if you'll ever call again. When you do...well, let's just say the nectar is ripe for consumption. Have I got a mind for seduction or what?"

"Simply diabolical," she answered caustically.

"C'mon, you know you love me," he challenged.

Before she could respond the detectives from the Strangler Task Force arrived. Their presence caused the squad detectives to wonder who they were and what their business was. The general concern was that they were from internal affairs.

"Is Detective St. Clair around?" asked the older man. "I'm Detective Von Hess and this is Sergeant Markie."

With trepidation, St. Clair nodded, acknowledging that he was the man they were looking for. Looking over to the office of the squad commander, the detective felt some inner relief in knowing that his boss was just a few feet away.

"I'm St. Clair."

"We're from STF, the new Strangler Task Force. We're here to assist in the Johnson homicide."

"Oh, well...let's go and see the lieutenant," said St. Clair, relieved that he wasn't caught up in some internal probe.

"What's up?" asked the lieutenant. The squad commander was sitting behind his desk hard at work. With an inspection team due in to evaluate the state of his command, he was up consumed with righting clerical deficiencies. Squad audits were implemented to ensure that the procedures of the bureau were being adhered to.

"We have a sergeant and a detective here saying they're going to work on the Johnson homicide, boss," apprised St. Clair, who then turned around to leave the office.

"I'm Sergeant Markie, boss. We're from the new task force."

The squad commander rose from his chair to greet Markie. "I received a telephone call from the borough saying something about a new special task force."

After just a few minutes of conversation, the lieutenant called St. Clair back into the office. "Cooperate with the sergeant. He's doing us a favor by helping us solve your case."

St. Clair had no choice but to go along. "I'll pull the case file for you guys."

St. Clair's female partner snickered quietly as she continued on with her work. She was happy to see her partner's cockiness wilt. As Von Hess began to look through the case folder, Markie queried St. Clair concerning the homicide of Laura Johnson, the third strangulation in the series of murders committed by Everett Skidmore.

"So what's the story on this case?"

"The victim was a real estate broker who did very well for herself," advised St. Clair. "She was a knockout, could have passed for a model. Take a look at those photos in the white envelope. She kept vacation shots of herself on display in her apartment."

"It was a straight strangulation?" asked Markie, looking through the photographs.

"That's right."

"Was she dealing with any new clients around the time she was murdered?"

"Not that I'm aware of," answered St. Clair, not sure one way or the other.

"What about her personal relationships?"

"She wasn't seeing anybody steady and she was never married."

"There isn't an ex-boyfriend in the picture?"

"There is no one turning up that we know of."

"Do you have any suspects?" asked Markie.

"We just have a description. It looks like she just ran into some bad luck by taking home the wrong guy that night."

"So this woman lived alone?"

"She did."

"Anything noteworthy in her apartment, like a diary or something?" asked Von Hess.

"Not that I saw."

"Did anyone see her with the guy she took home?"

"The man holding down the lobby desk," St. Clair answered. "He saw her come in with an older man he never saw before. He gave us a description: big male white, gray hair and wearing a dark suit. He looked at a ton of pictures, but no luck with an ID."

Von Hess nodded. "Do you think he *could* identify the man if he saw him again?"

"I think he probably could."

"Did this witness notice anything unusual about the guy, specifically something pertaining to his eyes?"

"He never mentioned anything."

"Any evidence recovered?" asked Markie.

"Not a lick. The apartment was wiped clean of prints."

"I see. Let us finish looking through the case folder," said Markie.

Von Hess zipped through the thin homicide folder quickly. Once he was finished, he briefed Markie privately. After their conversation, Markie advised St. Clair that he and Von Hess were going into the field to do a little nosing around. As a courtesy, he asked the squad detective if he cared to accompany them. Having no desire to do so, St. Clair begged off. His excuse was that he had a complainant coming into the office concerning another case he was working on. Markie and Von Hess made their way back to their unmarked car and proceeded to where Laura Johnson had resided.

"Remind me Ollie, that if I ever have to kill somebody, to do it in this precinct when *that* empty suit is working," declared Markie.

Von Hess laughed. "I hear you. You should have read his reports...forget about it."

"Did you get a whiff of the cologne that guy was wearing? He smelled like he took a bath in Canoe!"

Von Hess did a double take. "That stink was coming from him? I thought it was coming from the female detective!"

❖

LAURA JOHNSON LIVED IN AN UPSCALE APARTMENT BUILDING. Entering the glass door to the main entrance, the detectives proceeded to the front desk, where a ruddy complexioned man in his seventies was seated. The man was attired in a light blue short-sleeve shirt, dark blue tie and gray slacks. His thin forearms revealed two bluish tattoos that were mostly illegible due to smudging caused by aging skin. Hanging off the back of his chair was the standard blue blazer worn by the building concierges. Von Hess flashed his badge at the landlord's representative.

"Detectives," announced Von Hess,

"I know who you are," said the man behind the desk, instantly recognizing fellow members of the law enforcement fraternity. "I have one of those." He then produced his own gold shield, which was a duplicate of the one he returned to the police department many years prior when he retired. "I'm Teddy De George. I'm retired from the job. What can I do for you men?"

Von Hess was always glad to meet retired detectives. "Where did you work, Teddy?"

"I retired out of intelligence," he answered.

"How long are you out?"

"I'm off the job twenty-five-years already," answered the former investigator.

Markie was impressed. "That's a long time to collect. I guess you got your money back."

"You bet." The retired detective then smiled mischievously. "I beat them good. I've been collecting forever, and they'll be paying my pension for a lot more years too!"

"Way to go, Teddy," encouraged Markie. "We're part of a task force looking into the homicide of the Johnson girl," informed the sergeant. "Can you tell us anything about her?"

"What a shame with her. She was a real nice kid, respectful...nothing snooty about her at all. She was always good for an envelope around the holidays or even a bottle once in awhile if we did something extra for her," answered De George.

"Ever see her with any guys?"

"She was a hot number, so I don't think finding company was ever a problem for her. But there was nothing promiscuous about her. She didn't run people in and out of here, like some we got. I don't think there was anyone steady in the picture at all."

"But she did bring a pick-up home, didn't she?"

"She was human," answered De George. "Hey, everybody gets lonely once in awhile."

"Did you ever see her with a big gray-haired guy?" questioned Von Hess. "Or anyone cross-eyed, man or woman?"

"Not me. You guys have to talk to Paulie."

"Who is Paulie again?"

"Paulie is the evening guy who worked the desk that night, he relieves me."

"We definitely would like to talk to him," said Von Hess. "Is he in tonight?"

"Yeah, he'll be in later. Why don't you guys go and grab a bite to eat. By the time you finish, Paulie will be here."

Markie nodded. "Good idea. Anyplace around here good?"

"Go out the door and make a right. When you hit the corner you'll see Piper's Place. You can grab a burger and a beer in there. Let them know who you are," advised the old shamus. "Tell them your friends with Teddy, the retired bull," he added with a wink.

Markie smiled, asking one final question before he left the lobby. "Did Laura Johnson hang out at Piper's Place?"

"Nah, she hung out at another dump, Danny Dimes. Danny's joint is a little too snooty for guys like us, if you know what I mean," replied De George.

"Thanks Teddy. You've been a big help, we'll be back to see Paulie," said Markie.

Von Hess ascertained the address of Danny Dimes. The location was within walking distance. When they got there they noticed a thin woman in her forties seated alone at the bar reading a newspaper. Her eyeglasses rested on the tip of her nose. An undisturbed glass of white wine sat on a napkin in front of her. Also at the bar was a middle-aged man conversing with a young woman. Both were dressed in business attire. There were two bartenders stationed behind the long bar. The older of the two held down the front of the bar. He was a strapping, middle aged man with large jowls.

"What can I get you gentlemen?" he asked. Von Hess flashed his gold badge. "Is there any problem, detective?"

"No problem, we just need to ask a few questions," replied Von Hess. "Have you been working here a long time?"

"Pretty long, I'm here about twenty-two-years."

"Do you know a woman named Laura Johnson? We're told she hung out in here?"

The bartender hesitated briefly before answering. "I don't get personal with the customers that come in here."

Markie didn't buy it. "Look, how about you just answer the question. Do you know her? She's a real estate broker who lives in the neighborhood."

The bartender remained cautious. "What did she do to bring the law looking for her?"

"Let us ask the questions. Do you know her or what?" asked Von Hess. He was beginning to lose his patience. "We're here because of what was done to *her*."

The bartender snapped to attention. "Something happened to Laura?"

176

"So you *do* know her then."

"Well, if it's who I'm thinking of, I do. But she hasn't been here lately."

The sergeant was tired of the games. "She was strangled by someone she took home one night," Markie related bluntly. "She's cold as a mackerel...so that's the story."

"Oh, Jesus!" blurted the bartender. "This is terrible!"

"You want to see a picture?"

"No, I know her," confessed the bartender. "There's only one Laura Johnson that hangs out in here that worked in real estate...a sweetheart of a woman."

At this point Von Hess wanted to establish for certain that they were talking about the same person. He produced a vacation photo of the victim that he had removed from the homicide folder.

"Yeah, that's her," exclaimed the anguished bartender. He reached for a bottle of bourbon. He placed three shot glasses on top of the bar, pushing two of the glasses toward the detectives. "On the house," he said, as he poured.

"When was the last time you saw her?"

"She was here the night of her birthday. She got stood up, that's why I remember that night," he explained. "She ended up leaving with another dude."

"Can you describe the guy she left with?" Von Hess asked.

"He was a lot older than she was, maybe even older than me, and I'm 50. He was a big solid looking guy with gray hair, the athletic type."

"Did you know him?"

"No, that was the first and only time I ever saw him."

"Was anything unusual about his eyes? Or even his manner of dress?"

"No, there was nothing unusual about him. He was clean cut, dressed like a businessman. You know...suit and tie."

"Are you sure that there wasn't anything unusual about his eyes?" questioned Markie.

"No, nothing about his eyes stood out to me."

"Can you describe him in a little more detail?"

"Well, he looked rugged, but he spoke like a gentleman. You know, like an educated man. Even so, I could tell that he was a knock-around guy by the way he carried himself."

"Do you remember anything else?"

"I overheard something about playing basketball in a schoolyard up in Harlem. That caught my ear."

"Did he say where in Harlem?"

"Nah, they were just bullshitting about kids and basketball. I was pretty busy, so I heard things in drips and drabs."

"But you are certain they left the bar together?" asked Von Hess.

"I definitely saw them shove off together. They ate and then left. He left me a decent tip so I wouldn't forget that."

"Could you think of anything else that might be of value to us?"

"No, just that she was really a nice lady."

Markie had one question that needed asking. "Have you ever seen a big red-headed cross-dressing dude come into this joint?"

The bartender didn't know if he should take the sergeant seriously. "Are you putting me on?"

"No put on, square business."

"Then the answer is not that I know of. When people come in here, I don't ask them to lift their dress for me. That's for shit sure."

Markie nodded his head understandingly. "What about the guy who stood her up, you know anything about him?"

"If I have the right guy, they were acting pretty chummy the last time she was in here with him. The guy had an odd name, hold on a minute." The bartender signaled for the other bartender to join them. "These men are detectives. Who is that foreign guy with the accent that just started coming in? The guy that always hits on the women."

"Do you mean Ivan, the Russian guy?"

"No, I don't mean Ivan. You know the guy I'm talking about, he wears the beret."

"I'm not sure who you mean."

The older bartender became frustrated. "You definitely know him. He had a cleft in his chin like Kirk Douglas. Was his name...Audie, Augie, Organ?"

"Oh, now I know who you you're talking about. You mean Aubin, the Frenchman."

"Yeah, that's the guy!"

Von Hess put a halt to the conversation between the bartenders by asking a single question. "Exactly how big is this Frenchman?"

Once the investigators learned that Aubin wasn't close to the size of the man they were hunting, they thanked the bartenders and left Danny Dimes.

The detectives stopped for a quick bite at Piper's Place before returning to the lobby of the building where Laura Johnson lived. The man behind the lobby desk was fast to recognize the detectives.

"I'm Paulie, are you the detectives?"

"Yes, answered Von Hess. "Do you know why we're here?"

"Yeah, I got the story from Teddy."

"What's your full name, Paulie?" asked Von Hess.

"Paul Armand Belvedario."

"Where do you live?"

"I live in Brooklyn."

Markie looked at Paulie with unusual interest. "What section in Brooklyn?"

"I'm originally from Vanderbilt Avenue. You know Brooklyn?

"Yeah, we both know Brooklyn," said Markie. "The guy Laura Johnson took home the night she got killed, you saw him?"

"Yeah, I did."

"Tell us about it."

"Not much to tell. They came in together lovey-dovey—like, you know, their arms locked."

"What time was that?"

"It was around ten or eleven o'clock. He stayed less than an hour and left."

"What was their condition?"

"They were happy. You know, smiling and happy."

"Was there anything weird about him?" asked Von Hess.

"Not as far as I could see. He was dressed up in a suit and tie. I figured he came down after having a good time."

"What makes you say that?"

"He left *without* the tie on."

"Do you remember the color of the tie?"

"I think it was red."

"Can you describe him?"

"He was a big guy, over six feet and broad shouldered. He had to be in his late forties to early fifties, judging by his gray hair.

"He walked out of the building alone, right?"

"Yeah, he went out all by himself. Like I said, he looked like he had a good time. You know, kind of worn out."

The detectives nodded that they understood. "Did you notice his eyes?"

"He had on sunglasses when he left. I thought that was nuts because it was dark out."

"Could you recognize him again if you saw him?"

"Definitely, I'd know him, no problem. He's an easy guy to remember."

"Thanks Paulie, you've been a big help. Did you look at pictures in the precinct?" asked Von Hess, preparing to leave.

"I did. He wasn't in the bunch of pictures I looked at."

"Alright, thanks again, we won't tie you up any longer."

"Hold it a second, Ollie," said Markie. He then turned to Paulie. "Are you any relation to Bingo Belvedario?"

"You know Bingo?"

"I don't exactly know him. He did me a favor once."

"What favor was that?"

"I got into a beef with a wise guy's nephew many years ago when I took my first apartment. My landlord knew somebody, so there was a sit-down chaired by Bingo. He heard both sides of the story and ruled. It cost me three yards."

Paulie chuckled. "Bingo's my uncle. That was his favorite number back in the day for taxing bullshit, three hundred bucks. It could fix anything!"

"Is he still alive? I know he must be up there now."

"Yeah, he's alive. He's eighty-six."

"Tell him Tommy West's cop tenant said hello."

"Forget it, I can't tell him I talk to the law."

Markie nodded once it registered. "I see your point."

20

A Friend In Need

"YES! This is what friends do! Don't you think it's time you started walking erect?"

-Karen Markie

EVERETT WAS RELAXING IN HIS APARTMENT. He was reading the newspaper when he heard from his mother. *"That's the phone, dear,"* said the good voice of Adele.

"I hear it," answered Everett.

When he picked up the telephone he was surprised to find Stanley Addington on the other end of the line. Stan's voice gave the impression that he was stressed out. This concerned Everett because it caused him to wonder if there was a problem regarding his naughty behavior with Doris at the party.

"Everett, I need to talk to you. Got a minute?"

Everett braced himself for an uncomfortable discussion. "Sure Stan, what's up?"

"Did you have a good time at the house?"

Expecting bad news, Everett responded cautiously. "Yes, everything went off well I thought...right?"

"Everyone had a *great* time, especially Doris. She absolutely loves you. Actually, my wife said Doris is anxious to see you again."

Everett was relieved to know there were no repercussions as a result of his dalliance with Doris. "I'm glad to hear that, Stan. Doris is a wonderful woman. We hit it off nicely."

It soon became clear that Addington was the one with a problem. "You know Everett, I feel awkward mentioning this to you but I need your advice on something."

"Talk to me, Stan. What's wrong?"

"It's my Science 101 class. No matter what I do, I can't control the students."

Without hearing more, Everett knew that the root of Stan's problem was his weak image. "Freshmen are the worst. Something happens to kids around thirteen and fourteen, especially boys. They have this need to prove something. But don't worry, they'll settle down some by the time they come back in September."

"I understand that, but my problem is what is happening *now*."

"What are they doing exactly?"

"They're disruptive in class. It's all spitballs, shouting out and paper airplanes. Last week they began to throwing chalk whenever I turned around to face the board. Every day it's something new with these little bastards."

"He shouldn't be referring to the students so callously, dear. Why didn't he put his foot down in the first place?" asked the good voice. Everett raised a finger to the side of his face and waved it, signaling his mother not to interfere. "Did you try to do anything about it, Stan?" Everett asked.

"Of course I tried," he replied, becoming defensive. "I spoke to them nicely, trying to appeal to their better nature. But clearly, my kindness was construed as weakness. When I doubled up with the homework it didn't even faze them. Half the time they don't do their homework. I've even tried threatening to fail them."

"It should never come to that," commented Everett.

"I know," concurred Stan. "I brought in a television and started showing the class videos of course-related material, just in the hope that it would keep the noise level down."

"How did that go?"

"It was a disaster! The first time I left the room they put on reruns of *The Gong Show*.

Everett had to laugh. "So what's happened that brings all this to a head?"

"It's not funny! I had to break up a fist fight in class. Two of the boys actually traded blows."

"What were they fighting over?"

"Who the hell knows? They like to bust chops. Then come the threats and next thing fists start flying."

"That's not good, Stan. What did you do?"

"What could I do? I broke it up. I'm worried that if this continues, it's going to draw attention to my classroom. How is it going to look that I can't control my class?" he asked, not expecting an answer. "What happens if someone really gets hurt, maybe even stabbed one day? Their parents will sue me personally for not keeping their little monsters safe!"

"What about the girls in the class? How are they behaving?"

"The girls," said Stan, "are witches who are as bad as the boys!"

"C'mon, Stan...you know you don't really mean that."

"I know. I don't really mean what I say. But it's so frustrating some time."

"You might want to take this up with the administration just to cover yourself. There are liability concerns that do exist, Stan."

Stan knew Everett was right. He envied his co-worker for his confidence, his assertiveness and physical dominance. "I really hate to do that."

Everett kicked the situation around in his head. Suddenly, an alternative solution came to him. "You ever play any basketball, Stanley?"

"Sure, I used to play when I was young."

"Were you any good?"

"Sure, I think so."

"How about we show your class another side of you? Let's do this, starting next week we're going to play..." Everett laid out a strategy that called for challenging the unruly students to a basketball game after school. "Don't worry Stan, it'll all work out...*and* as an added bonus it'll keep you in shape."

"You think that playing ball with them will actually make a difference?"

"Trust me, Stan." Everett intended to whip the youths into line once he got them under the boards.

Addington was amenable to giving it a try. He then changed the subject. "So what do you want to do about Doris?"

"What did she say?"

"To me, she said nothing. But she stayed up talking to my wife long after I went to bed. Iris told me Doris wanted to know every detail about you. She asked if you were ever married, your age, if you were seeing anyone and so on. You definitely made a hit."

Everett liked hearing that. "Perhaps I should give her a call before she goes home..."

❖

MARKIE TOOK A SWING by Flo's place. His children lived with his ex-wife and her parents in a four-story brownstone off Fort Greene Park. The high value property was in Flo's family for generations. Every time Markie visited he couldn't help but think of how great a future he could have had. With his ex-wife being an only child, Markie would have eventually attained security beyond his wildest expectation. The sergeant, who maintained a good relationship with Flo's father, was hoping that he'd be around so that he could say hello. The genuine fondness that existed between the men eliminated any concern of awkwardness. The primary purpose behind Markie's visit was to check on his youngest son. In the aftermath of the boy's love letter, the sergeant wanted to see for himself how the little guy was doing. As Markie drove around looking for a spot his cell phone went off. It was Inspector McCoy returning his call.

"Hi boss, I'm in the car. Thanks for calling back."

"So, what's up?"

"We're moving along. In the Laura Johnson case we have two witnesses who can identify the perp. Laura is the woman who worked in real estate."

Inspector McCoy listened attentively as Markie updated him. "What's she doing in a bar on a week night? Didn't she have to go to work the next day?"

"What can I tell you, inspector? It looks like it was a one-night-stand gone sour."

"Unreal," commented McCoy, who could be a real jerk at times. "Another *Looking for Mr. Goodbar*," he added, referring to the movie that came out a dozen years earlier.

"There is only one way in and out of her building, sarge?"

"Correct. A concierge is posted at the lobby desk. He sees her coming in with her company. He then sees the guy leave alone about a little later. The description given by the bartender *and* the concierge match perfectly: gray hair, dark suit and red tie."

"Was there any sexual attack involved in this?"

"No. According to the guy on the lobby desk the suspect just came downstairs looking, you know...spent. But get this, the guy was wearing *sunglasses* when he walked out, and this all goes down at night."

185

"Couldn't somebody have entered her apartment from elsewhere in the building after he left? Like from another apartment?"

"Well, I guess that's possible. There were no signs of a forced entry. I suppose somebody could have been invited in by the victim after our guy left."

"And that *is* possible," reminded McCoy. "Did you check to see if she was friendly with anyone in the building? Maybe even dating someone who lived there..."

Markie was fairly certain that the inspector was drifting off in the wrong direction, yet he had to humor his boss. "We didn't go that route boss. We're zeroing in on the guy who we *know* went in the apartment, more than who *might* have gone into the apartment."

McCoy let it go. "Nothing recovered from the crime scene, correct?"

"Correct."

"Any cameras stationed on the floor or in the building?"

"None, boss."

"By any chance, is anybody saying that the guy she took home is cross-eyed?"

"That's the only fly in the ointment. No one stated that the guy was cross-eyed," Markie answered. "But he did leave wearing sunglasses...*at night.*"

"Okay, I got that. Any talk about a big red-headed woman?"

"Negative, we asked about that as well."

"You got anything else?"

"The bartender overheard the suspected perp talking to the victim about playing basketball in a Harlem schoolyard," advised Markie. "There can't be many oversized, gray haired, white guys in Harlem playing round ball."

"Wasn't one of the homicides in East Harlem?"

"That's right, boss."

The inspector was still not feeling great about things. "Are we going to be able to solve this in the short window we have? Tell me the truth."

Markie went out on a limb. "I honestly think we have a good shot."

"You plan on heading up to Harlem?"

"Yeah, boss. We're gonna canvass Harlem. Then I want to look into the fourth homicide, the usherette case in Midtown."

"Okay, keep at it." McCoy was struggling to be optimistic. He felt a little better now that he had something to tell Chief Randolph if queried.

Once off the line with the inspector, Markie called Von Hess. "Ollie, are you still working on the name Trapani?"

"Yeah boss, I've been working a few hours each night on it. There are a million Trapani's to dig into."

"Okay, knock off when you want, but be ready to saddle up tomorrow morning, we're heading out to Harlem, baby."

"Which part of Harlem?"

"Where ever they play schoolyard basketball. I'll get a list together of some courts up that way," advised the sergeant. "Let's drive into the city together in the morning. Figure on picking me up at eight o'clock. Let me go, I see a spot."

Markie parked his car two blocks away from the Brooklyn brownstone. As he approached the house, he could see Flo's father with a hose in his hand washing down the front stoop. A self-employed electrician, he spent his career working out of a van. Now semi-retired, he only worked a couple of days a week on small jobs.

An eight foot gaslight was positioned behind the front iron gate and the first floor windows of the building. It stood about six or seven feet to the side of the front stoop and provided ample illumination during the hours of darkness. The lighting made the stoop a convenient haven for people to hang out after dark. Those comfortable with trespassing used the steps as a venue to eat, drink, talk and sometimes nap. Markie's former father-in-law could often be seen hosing down the steps. Soggy pants were always good deterrent.

Markie looked up at the cornice of the well maintained brownstone. "Hey, the cups are still working," he said to Flo's father with a smile. He was referring to the dangling plastic cups that hung from the roof. Their blowing in the wind was a cost-effective way to stop the birds from congregating and soiling the building with their droppings.

"Hey Al, I'm glad to see you! What brings you around?" Flo's father was genuinely happy to see his former son-in-law. "How about having something to eat?"

"No, I'm good thanks. I just wanted to check up on the little guy. Flo called me about the incident at the school. I guess you probably heard about it."

The grandfather shook his head disapprovingly. "Can you imagine that school making such a big stinking deal over such kid bullshit?" Part of the reason why Markie got on well with the electrician was because they thought alike. It was their similarities that drew Florence to the sergeant in the first place.

"Can I go in?" Markie asked humbly.

"Of course, go ahead. Flo's not around, though—she went to get her hair quaffed. Her mother's in the yard pulling weeds. The little guy and his sister are inside. The big guy is...well, I don't know where that bronco is."

"Thanks," replied Markie as he headed into the house. "I'll see you before I leave."

Markie found his 16-year-old daughter sitting upright on the living room couch watching television. Stretched out with his head on her lap was an 18-year-old boy that she worked with at a neighborhood day camp. The sockless six-foot teenager had a leg over his bent knee. Not hearing her dad come in, the sergeant's daughter continued to circle her finger in her friend's hair as she spoke.

"I wish I had hair like Jennifer Aniston," she mused. "Don't you just love her hair?"

Markie chaffed at what he was witnessing. The sight of the lanky boy in shorts splayed on the couch with his head on the lap of his daughter was upsetting, but seeing his long toes casually wiggle in the air was what really irked him.

"What brings you around, dad?" asked Karen, finally noticing her father.

When no effort was made to modify their positioning, Markie bristled at what he viewed as disrespect. He expected them to jump to their feet at the sight of his walking in on them. "Don't get up," he announced sarcastically. "I'm here to see the little guy. Where is he?"

"He's in his room," answered the daughter, picking up on her father's attitude.

Markie couldn't leave without saying something to his daughter's friend. "Are you comfortable?"

A look of uncertainty came over the face of the guest. There was only one way to take the question. "I'm fine, thank you," answered the boy, who was now ill at ease.

Without another word, Markie spun around and left. He stepped heavily as he took the stairs to the second floor to see his young son. Within ten minutes of talking to the little guy, the sergeant was satisfied that his son was experiencing no ill effects of what transpired at the school. In fact, Markie was pleasantly surprised to see how well the boy held up. With that matter under control, he returned downstairs to the living room where the other drama continued to unfold. Karen, sitting alone with her arms folded and her legs tightly crossed, was juggling the flip-flop she wore. Her body language made it exceedingly clear that she was unhappy.

"Where's the boyfriend?"

"He's not my boyfriend! And, thanks to *you,* he left."

"Me? What did I do?" Markie asked, feigning bewilderment.

"You know *exactly* what you did...and you did it on purpose!" accused Karen.

"Wait a minute, back up. Let's get something straight," responded Markie. "First off, that kid was too comfortable. He didn't even have socks on his feet for Christ's sake. I come in the room and Huckleberry Finn doesn't budge? He has his head on *your* lap and he doesn't so much as blink an eye when he sees *me?* You know what that tells me?"

"His name happens to be Jason, not Huckleberry Finn."

"Whatever. The point is this, where is the respect in this *swain* of yours? He's fearless!"

"Oh, *come* on! We're just friends! Ask mom, she can tell you."

"Oh, so you two are just friends?" asked Markie, sounding innocent in tone.

"YES! This *is* what friends do! Don't you think it's time you started walking erect?

"Ohhh, I see. What's wrong with me?" Markie was speaking with false sincerity.

"You're a Neanderthal...that's what's wrong with you!" barked the daughter.

"Tell you what, how about we do this. What's the name of this boyfriend again?"

"None of your business, and we are just FRIENDS!" answered Karen harshly.

"Why don't you have Huck's parents over for coffee and cake one night so that we can all sit down, chat and make nice. After I fatten his mother up with a strawberry short cake, we'll sit on the couch. Then I'll lie down and rest my melon on mama's lap. How about we do that?"

"I can't talk to you anymore!" declared the daughter, disgusted at her father's ridiculousness.

"What's the problem? Huck's father won't mind. If he says anything, *I'll* tell him that me and his old lady are just... *friends!*"

The teenager rose from the couch looking straight into the face of her father. "We *can't* do that, because YOU don't live here anymore," she declared, intending to cut deep.

"Ouch!" Markie said in a low voice, as his daughter walked off. "It looks like she's got me there."

❖

INSPECTOR MCCOY PICKED UP Chief Randolph's call on the first ring. He'd been expecting a call back from his boss.

"You called?" asked Randolph.

"Yes, chief."

"Talk to me."

"We now have three witnesses that can identify the perpetrator instead of one."

McCoy paused, waiting for a reaction from the chief. When none was forthcoming, he continued. "We picked up another piece to the puzzle. Our perp plays basketball uptown in Harlem. We're closing in on this bastard, John," said McCoy, "I feel it in my bones."

"The clock is ticking, Harry."

"I know John. But this perp is unique: he's a fiftyish, gray haired white guy shooting hoops in Harlem. He's got to stick out like a sore thumb!"

"Get it done, Harry," said Randolph curtly before hanging up. McCoy knew that an arrest was the only news his boss wanted to hear.

###

VON HESS STOPPED TO GET some coffee during their ride uptown. Once alone in the car, Markie dialed Alley. Unwilling to apologize for his jealous behavior, he concocted a scheme to make amends.

"Why are you pissed off at me?" she asked. Her question was cautiously posed, as if she were treading on unsecure ground.

Markie capitalized on Alley's state of mind. "It's okay, you sent me a message and I received it loud and clear."

"What are you talking about? What message?" she asked, taking it up a notch.

"You declared yourself an independent contractor. And that's alright, I'm okay with it."

"Declared myself?" Alley Cat was perplexed.

"Let me ask you something, did the fleet go back out to sea?" he asked, deliberately provoking her.

The cruel remark hit home, getting the results he was after. The barb surfaced Alley's own dark side. "How about I declare this...*you* go to the waterfront, find yourself a short pier and take a flying Brody!" she said harshly, before slamming down the phone in anger. Alley's reference to Steve Brody—a man who claimed to have survived jumping off the Brooklyn Bridge—was a tidbit she learned from her employer Fitzie.

Markie was satisfied in how things worked out. He had been purposely rude in order to lay the groundwork for a future apology that he found more comfortable in making. Since he couldn't bring himself to cop to jealousy, he created a substitute. Rude and nasty was doable as something that he could easily apologize for. He could cite a host of reasons why he acted the way he did under that heading. Admitting to jealousy was another matter. To do so would be giving Alley too much power. Truth be told, he missed her terribly.

21

Beginning Of The End

"What are you doing over here, pal? Halloween ain't until October."

-Sergeant Wes Fulton

ABOVE ALL ELSE CAPTAIN LOWELL STEEL wanted to be promoted to deputy inspector. The heavyset sixty-year-old was considered by those assigned to his Brooklyn precinct as the commanding officer from hell. At six-feet-five he was shaped along the lines of a baseball diamond. The crooked sneer under his potato-like nose was his normal expression. Subordinates likened him to Wolf Larsen, after Jack London's fictional captain in *The Sea-Wolf*. Like the sadistic Wolf, Steel ruled by fear.

The captain found the precinct complaint reports disturbing. The documents reflected two robbery patterns that could potentially derail his promotion. To offset any negative perception of his ability to fight crime, Steel fell back on a time tested solution that called for lots of robbery arrests regardless of circumstances. Numerous arrests for robbery would showcase his aggressiveness in combating the condition and offset unflattering statistics. To achieve this goal meant turning up the heat on those assigned to his command. Sergeant Wes Fulton, the precinct's plainclothes anti-crime supervisor, was the first to be called on the carpet. At forty, the bearded sergeant was considered a tad eccentric by police standards. He favored wearing a gold earring in one lobe and rode to work on a Harley. When he wore his black leather vest he did so without wearing anything underneath the vest. When bare-chested, a tattoo of three tiny blood-teardrops could be seen dripping from the nipple of his right boob.

"Sit down sergeant," the captain said gruffly, "and shut that door behind you."

"Yes sir," answered Fulton, wondering what the problem was this time.

"I assume that you like working in plainclothes and looking like a pirate?"

"Yes cap, actually I do."

"What's the mission of anti-crime, sarge?" Steel sat back with his arms folded, resting them atop his ample belly.

"Our mission is to make arrests for in progress crimes."

"What kind of crimes?"

"Assaults, burglaries, robberies..." Fulton wasn't permitted to finish his sentence.

"ROBBERIES!" yelled out the commanding officer forcefully.

The sergeant jumped at Steel's sudden vocal eruption. The word came bursting out with force enough to shake loose the captain's wobbly bridge. Once he adjusted his teeth, he resumed. "We have two robbery patterns in this command that must be stopped!"

The sergeant didn't require a diagram to be drawn for him to understand. "We're out there, Cap, let me tell you—"

"No, let *me* tell *you*...I want robbery arrests, and you better damn well start giving them to me! I don't care if it's a kid taking a lollypop out of a baby's hand while he's sucking on his mama's boobs. I want to see cuffs on the little bastard! I need numbers that will knock down these robbery stats!"

"Got it, Cap," replied Fulton.

"Now either you go out there and get me those arrests or dust off your uniform!"

After Fulton left the office the captain summoned his patrol supervisors. He wanted them to make sure that every officer who prepared complaint reports knew to downgrade a robbery complaint into a larceny and how to upgrade a larceny into a robbery when there was a perpetrator present for arrest.

THE ANTI-CRIME SERGEANT got down to business as soon as he was dismissed from the captain's office. He started with an analysis of the robbery patterns. After reviewing the complaint reports it was clear to him that he was looking for two different perpetrators working independently of each other. After recording the descriptions and clothing worn by the perpetrators, Fulton pinpointed the time, day of the week and location where each robbery occurred. Once his intelligence gathering was completed, he assembled the three anti-crime officers who were working.

"From now on we're taking any ground ball robbery collars we can get," announced Fulton.

"Even kiddie collars?" asked Officer Lino Luzzi, the senior anti-crime officer.

"Yeah, that's the final word until we put an end to these two pattern robberies. Your team will be working nights, covering the Smith and Ninth Street subway station. I'm scheduling the other team to work early mornings around the Smith and Bergen train station.

"What are our tours, boss?" asked Luzzi.

"Six o'clock at night to two in the morning," advised the sergeant. "Your target is a real cutie pie: after he robs his victim he takes their identification and announces that he knows where they live. It's an old gimmick, but still very effective."

"Armed with a gun, right sarge?" asked Officer Kevin Moran.

"Yeah, your man is packing a black handgun. He's a short male white, thirties, beige waist-length jacket. He wears a Mets baseball cap, has a black mustache and is wiry looking. He's picking them off on West 9th Street just east or west of Smith Street. Are there any questions? Blanchard?"

"I got it, sarge," said Officer Nilsa Blanchard, who was only assigned to the unit for a week.

"Okay then, that's the story. Let's get the old man off our neck and get out there and make some robbery arrests. Remember, there is a thin line between larceny and robbery, so make it work for us."

EVERETT SAT ALONE IN HIS APARTMENT wrestling with a personal decision. He was torn between asking Doris out and fulfilling his desire to cross-dress. With Adele no longer physically present in his life, her influence in preventing him from acting on the impulse to dress as a woman was limited, but not totally non-existent.

"What are you thinking, dear?" asked the good voice.

"It's just something that I like to do once in awhile," he answered.

"Ridiculous!"

"Why do you keep saying that?"

"Oh, stop it!" scolded the good voice.

"I'm sorry, but you'll not talk me out of it again! I'm not dong anyone any harm."

"Do what you want, but don't expect my approval of *such nonsense!"*

"What's the big problem?" asked Everett. When he received no answer he knew their conversation was over until his mother cooled off.

Everett removed a celery green pants suit from the bedroom closet. He slowly rubbed the pants material between his fingers. After putting on the outfit, he double laced his low white sneakers. Once he finished preparing himself the science teacher was out the door.

Everett boarded a Brooklyn-bound F train to explore courts that existed in the outer borough. Aware that Carroll Gardens was known to be evolving into a progressive neighborhood, he ventured there. He knew of courts just a short walking distance from the Smith and Ninth Street train station. When he got there a half-court game was underway. The players, all boys, were fifth and sixth graders. The only spectator, Everett watched as the kids fought for rebounds, took shots, and attempted the moves that they'd seen the pros pull off on television. The teacher was impressed by the diminutive players—they were doing very well for their age. Everett became so engrossed in the game that the thought never entered his mind to leave before seeing the outcome.

As Everett watched the game, Sergeant Fulton's anti-crime officers rolled out of the precinct to begin their hunt. The team proceeded directly to West Ninth and Smith Streets to conduct surveillance. The attention of the officers was diverted before they were able to set up on the assigned location.

"Hey look, there's Jerry the Bop!" declared Officer Moran. "What's he doing all the way over here? He lives over in the Hook, on Van Brunt Street."

They called him Jerry the Bop because of the way he walked. His habit of stepping high off the toe of one foot caused him to rise up and down every other step, giving a bop to his walk.

195

"You know what…Jerry's about the right size of the guy we're looking for," commented Officer Blanchard, who was seated in the back of the car. "He's even got the mustache."

"Yeah, but he's no robber, Nilsa," stated Officer Luzzi with pessimism. "He's a junkie burglar. He doesn't have the balls for a stick up. Besides look how he dresses. It's all wrong. No baseball cap, no jacket."

"Maybe he graduated. Junkie's have been known to rob people too," pointed out Moran.

The senior officer conceded the point made. "I suppose. What do you want to do?" Moran made the call. "Why take a chance, let's stick with him and see what he does. If he takes off on us, then we'll know he's dirty."

The officers watched Jerry bop his way over to a waiting late-model Cadillac that was pulled over to the curb on Hamilton Avenue. Swiveling his neck around to see if anyone was watching, the drug addict paused before reluctantly entering the passenger side of the waiting vehicle. Jerry's hesitation made it apparent to the cops that he recognized their undercover vehicle. Having been busted on prior occasions by the anti-crime unit, their dark blue sedan was the one vehicle Jerry knew on sight. Within seconds Jerry emerged from the vehicle. He began to cross Hamilton Avenue, in the direction of where he lived as the Caddy drove off.

"Something is definitely up here," said Luzzi. "We could get Jerry anytime. Let's see who the other guy is. Put up the light Kevin."

Moran removed the red portable turret light from the glove compartment. "Let's rock and roll," he said, after affixing it to the top of the vehicle.

As the Cadillac was being directed to pull over, Blanchard silently wondered to herself what her partners were thinking. They were tasked specifically with finding robbers, not hunting down suspected drug dealers. Being new to the unit, she feared that if she spoke up she'd be labeled a poor fit for anti-crime work by her male counterparts. For this reason she kept her silence.

The driver of the Caddy looked in his rear-view mirror when he heard the siren. Locking eyes with those of Luzzi, he decided to make a run for it. With a burst of speed he took off, weaving in and out of traffic as he sped along Hamilton Avenue.

"He running, Lino!" exclaimed Moran.

"This sucker has got to be dirty," declared Luzzi. "Hold on to your hat."

"There goes West Ninth Street," commented Blanchard, unable to resist reminding her partners of their assignment.

"Ahh, the hell with it, we're committed now," said Luzzi, commencing the chase.

"He who hesitates is lost," chimed in Moran. "Besides, this could be something related to the stick-ups, for all we know."

196

Moran put out a description of the Cadillac over the radio, alerting the other police in the division that the anti-crime unit was in pursuit of a fleeing vehicle. The Cadillac entered onto a highway where it continued to maneuver in and out of traffic recklessly at a high rate of speed.

"This maniac is going to kill somebody!" yelled Blanchard, who was hunched forward in the back seat. "Look! He's emptying bags of white powder out the window!"

The adrenaline pumped through all three officers, as they observed the driver dust the ground with bags of white powder as he drove. The fleeing Cadillac managed to gain highway distance on the more cautiously operated police vehicle. From afar, the drug trafficker was seen zooming toward an exit ramp. When the police caught up all to be seen was the now unoccupied Cadillac crashed into a pole on a small island at the foot of the exit ramp. The cracked windshield indicated that the driver had to have sustained injuries.

The anti-crime cops emerged from their vehicle unsure of suspect's whereabouts. They were guided by pedestrians standing on the sidewalk across from the island, who all pointed to the direction of flight. Moran, the fleetest of foot among the trio, ran in the direction indicated. He cornered his prey behind a truck parked in a gas station. The suspect's last-ditch effort to avoid capture was thwarted by the cop's flying tackle. Once their man was apprehended, the officers removed their prisoner to the precinct. They were received at the stationhouse steps by a visibly perturbed Sergeant Fulton.

"What the hell is this?" asked Fulton, who heard the chase over the division radio.

The anti-crime members were reprimanded by Fulton for being misguided in their judgment. The only one of the three not surprised at the sergeant's reaction was Officer Blanchard.

"You guys are supposed to be catching stick-up men, not chasing a stolen car or a drug dealer or whatever the fuck it was!" exclaimed the annoyed sergeant. "So who's got this mess?" he asked, now noticing that the prisoner was in need of stitches.

The officers hesitated in answering, not having previously discussed among themselves who was to be the arresting officer. Finally, Blanchard stepped up. "I'll take it sarge," she volunteered, wanting to show that she was a team player.

"Ok, Nilsa. You take the collar." The sergeant then pointed to the gash across the prisoner's hairline. "Have a radio car take you to the hospital with the prisoner. The guy needs to get patched up."

"Charge him with reckless driving, sarge?"

"Yeah, that and reckless endangerment. Be sure to go through his car to see if there are any drugs or weapons. If you come up with anything, even if it's only drug residue or paraphernalia, voucher it and add it to the charges."

"Okay."

Addressing the two male officers, the sergeant tossed his head in the direction of the door. "Let's get out there and do what we're supposed to be doing. I'm going with you."

❖

EVERETT WAS THOROUGHLY ENJOYING himself watching the half-court game. Without a preference as to the outcome, he was thrilled in general at the closeness of the competition. It amused the science teacher to see the boys deny blatant fouls and toss around profanities. Everett could tell by the way the youngsters played, that they knew how to think on their feet. The boys weren't above bending the rules in order to snatch a victory. Everett was okay with that: he was a grape that had grown from the same vine. Professionally, the teacher felt it his duty to taut the value of fair play and the need to follow rules. But he condoned sharp elbows when it came to gaining an advantage on the court. His belief was that some rules needed occasional breaking.

In the end, the upper grade whipped the lower grade in what turned out to be a close game. Considering the disparity in age, the game was extremely competitive. The losers demanded a rematch— a game Everett wasn't going to miss. During the break between games, the boys drank water to cool off. They noticed Everett on the other side of the chain-link fence, not knowing what to make of him. When the lady with the red hair asked if it was alright to take a couple of jump shots during the intermission, the youths were taken aback. Collectively the boys felt safe, so they agreed to toss Everett the ball. Dribbling skillfully to loosen up, the teacher then sank a couple of long ones that got the respect of the youths. Everett's appearance suddenly became secondary. The general consensus was that Everett was just another one of the newcomers that had been infiltrating the neighborhood...and could this newcomer play ball!

Before the onset of the second game, the name of one of the youths was shouted by an older man who was seated behind the wheel of a Mitsubishi parked at the sidewalk.

"Hey Butchie...who won?" croaked the man loudly, addressing his grandson. Sounding thuggish, it was his way of making his presence known to Everett.

"They did, 21 to 18. There is gonna be another game," shouted the boy to his grandfather.

The man in the car looked at his watch. Seeing that it was still early, he nodded approvingly to his grandson. "Alright, go on, finish up. I'll be sitting *right here watching* from the car." He then glared at Everett, making it clear that he was keeping an eye out.

Everett got the message loud and clear. He looked over at the older man, who after making eye contact, had returned to reading his newspaper. Based on the newsboy cap he was wearing, Everett could see that the man in the car was an old school Brooklyn type. He respected that the grandfather was keeping an eye out for his grandson, and didn't take the message he was sent it personally. Sensitive when it came to youngsters, Everett considered himself something of an authority on what it was like to be a victimized child.

The second game was a nail biter, with the younger team snatching the win by the skin of their teeth. There was no way Everett was leaving Smith Street without seeing who was going to take the rubber match. By this time the players had gotten accustomed to his presence. His enthusiastic encouragement from the sidelines was appreciated by both teams, even though they were a little spooked by their fan's masculine voice.

Realizing that the noise ceased in the schoolyard, the grandfather in the car looked up from his paper. "Ooooo...is it all over or what? What happened?" he shouted, directing his questions to his grandson.

"It's even-steven," the youth yelled back. "We got one more game to play. It's the best two out of three."

"Well hurry it up already, will-ya Butchie. Put it to bed. It's getting near time to eat. Your grandmother's waiting."

"It's the last game..."

"Alright, get movin' then," said the grandfather, now anxious to get home.

Everett was getting tired of standing. With the strap of his bag slung over his shoulder, he raised both of his arms upward to grip onto the chain-link fence for support. This position pronounced his broad back, powerful hands and developed shoulders. It was something that didn't escape the attention of the anti-crime team working the area.

OFFICER LUZZI SLOWED DOWN the car to take an extended look. He didn't like what he was seeing. Feeling that something might be amiss he apprised the others accordingly.

"Hey, look at that shit over there," said Luzzi, pointing toward Everett.

"Where?" asked Officer Moran.

"By the basketball courts, near those kids."

As the officers were eyeballing Everett, one of the sixth graders grabbed a rebound, took the ball out to the foul line, quickly pivoted and took a lunging shot at the basket to score. This was met with a grand reaction by Everett who let out an enthusiastic and very masculine cheer.

"What the hell was that? Did you hear that? "asked Luzzi.

"That's no woman!" declared Moran.

199

"Looks to me like somebody is just watching the game," answered the sergeant, trying to downplay things.

"C'mon, Wes, those are kids," said Luzzi. "What about it, can we go check it out?"

The boss knew Luzzi was right, especially since minors were involved. "Jesus, Mary, and Joseph, we're never gonna get around to catching any damn robbers!" voiced the exasperated sergeant. "You win Lino, let's go check this asshole out."

The unmarked car pulled up to where Everett was standing with his back toward the street. The officers, led by their sergeant, approached the teacher.

"What are you doing over here, pal?" Fulton asked, in a huffy voice. "Halloween ain't until October."

Everett turned around to the voice. "Who are you?" he asked.

"Police," replied Moran, producing his shield. "Let's see some identification."

Being approached by the three cops embarrassed Everett. His feeling of awkwardness was magnified when, after fumbling through his handbag, he realized that he left his identification home. The science teacher attempted to explain himself. As he did, his nervous demeanor became evident by the twitching of his lips.

"I'm sorry officer, but I'm afraid that I left my wallet home. I reside in Manhattan, here are my apartment keys."

"That's all you have on you?"

"No, I also have money with me." Everett reached into his bag for the couple of hundred dollars in cash he had.

"Take your hand out of that bag nice and easy," ordered Luzzi.

"Here, see for yourself," he said, holding out his bag. He tried to hand the sergeant both the bag and the cash that was held together by a rubber band.

The teacher was met with blank stares. The sergeant considered the overture an attempt at bribery. "Put your money away pal, that won't help you with us," said Sergeant Fulton.

Everett grew resistant. "Help with what? I've broken no laws. What's this all about?"

"It's *about,* what you are doing here with these kids."

Everett now understood. He resented that the police would think such a thing of him. He was glad that the good voice was not a party to this exchange. He was in no mood to hear his mother lecture him about his cross-dressing.

"How can you jump to the conclusion that I..."

The sergeant wasn't about to let Everett give him an argument. In response, he went on the offensive. "Okay pal, c'mon ...lets go. Get in the car," he ordered, figuring if push came to shove he had Everett for attempted bribery.

"In the car?" asked Everett, stunned. "What for, watching a basketball game?"

"Get in."

"I'm not in violation of *any* laws," said the astonished Everett.

"We need to verify your identity. Then there is the matter of you pushing money at us."

"I never did any such thing!" Everett protested loudly.

The anti-crime sergeant grabbed Everett by the hair, pulling off the manufactured hairpiece. Fulton looked at the wig that he now held in his hand. He tossed it to Luzzi as if it were a hot potato. Several of the youths who were looking at the action through the fence were heard shouting, "Ohhhhh, shit!"

Everett was outraged at his treatment. "Just who exactly do you think you are?" he demanded to know.

"There's no thinking about it, we're the guys locking you up!" answered Luzzi."

The basketball game came to an abrupt halt as the young players remained fixated on Everett's interaction with the law. By the time the grandfather emerged from his car, Everett was in the back seat of the police vehicle. The old man watched along with the youths as the police pulled away from the curb, merging into the oncoming Smith Street traffic.

Once at the precinct the tension leveled off. Everett gave the authorities his full name, date of birth and address. In his handbag, along with his sunglasses, was the magazine he read during the train ride to Brooklyn. After examining the magazine, which Everett subscribed to, the sergeant was able to verify his identity to some degree by the name and home address reflected on the mailing label. The science teacher was home free after Luzzi called the owner of Everett's building. The landlady provided the authorities with Everett's description, right down to the red wig he occasionally wore.

"He comes back clean all around, sarge. He had no arrest record and no warrants on him," advised Moran.

The robbery pattern remained central on Fulton's mind. The sergeant didn't want to lose another officer due to an arrest. He decided to give Everett the benefit of the doubt concerning the suspected bribery attempt.

"Okay...write him a summons and get him the hell out of here," ordered Fulton. "We have other fish to fry in the street."

"What for?" asked Moran, seeking a charge.

"Charge him with disorderly conduct."

"That's it, sarge?"

"Yeah, wouldn't you say he created an offensive condition that served no legitimate purpose?" asked the sergeant.

"But just disorderly conduct?" repeated Moran, thinking they were better off tacking on the attempted bribery charge. "Why don't I just take him for the bribery?"

"Because I need you to make robbery collars...remember?"

Moran conceded the point. "So I'll just write him a tag for disorderly conduct then."

"Yeah, that's what I said didn't I? One look at this guy on a dark night would scare the shit out of Jack the Ripper. I'd say that's enough to cause public alarm."

"Right boss," said Moran, who went along even though he thought otherwise. He wrote Everett the summons.

"What's this summons for?" questioned the science teacher.

"Disorderly conduct, you'll pay a small fine and it'll go away."

"How can you charge me with disorderly conduct? I didn't…" Officer Luzzi stopped Everett in his tracks.

"Hey fuck-o, you're a city employee, a teacher you said. The book says we're supposed to make notifications about this shit. We didn't even ask you what school you work at. Consider yourself ahead of the game."

"Yes, but—"

"Another thing, genius," interrupted Moran, "you have no identification on you. Technically, we're supposed to print you and put you in the system if we can't establish for certain your identity. It'll mean you sitting in a cell until your prints come back from Albany, *before* you get to go in front of a judge. *That*, my friend, is a process that can take time."

At this point Luzzi reentered the conversation. "Let's make it even clearer. Dressed like you are, the bullpen is not a good place, even for a big guy like you. Do you understand this? If you don't, in another minute we'll be tacking on a bribery charge."

"No, that won't be necessary." Everett accepted his situation quietly. His stone face and grim expression resulted from his thinking of how unpleasant things could be.

"So, any more questions about disorderly conduct?" asked Moran.

"No."

"You live alone or are you married?" questioned Luzzi.

"I'm single. I haven't been fortunate enough to meet the right woman yet, if that's what you're wondering," answered Everett, with a not so slight trace of attitude.

"You probably always lived in Manhattan, right?"

"Wrong. I'm originally from Brooklyn."

"Where in Brooklyn do you come from?"

"Bedford Stuyvesant, a small block called Yarrow Street."

"That's where the peanut factory is," noted Moran, as he wrote the summons.

"Yes, officer, that's correct. May I leave now?" Everett was in no mood for further conversation.

"You bet, go ahead," said Moran, handing him the citation. "But do yourself a favor, stay away from that basketball court."

"Yeah, it's probably best to stay out of this neighborhood altogether," added the senior officer.

Everett walked away without responding. His anger remained bottled up.

Moran whispered to his partner as Everett was leaving the precinct. "You think he'd know that blonds have more fun."

Everett never heard the last remark. It didn't matter. He already had a good idea of where they were coming from.

22

Sizzling Shades

"They called him Sizzling Shades during the game. The dude was playing with sunglasses hanging from his neck."

-Dondi Ross

EVERETT COULDN'T GET AWAY from the house of handcuffs fast enough. In his urgency he lost focus on where he was. He stopped to ask for directions from a man sitting on a stoop. He was gripping the red wig so tightly that the blue veins on the back of his hand bulged.

"Where is the best place to find a cab around here?" he asked. The unconventional appearance of Everett caused the man to stare before answering. After a few seconds he provided directions to a nearby car service.

As he was being driven along the darkened streets of South Brooklyn; Everett stared blankly out the window rehashing the entire ordeal he'd been through. He questioned whether his thrill was worth all the grief, which included the alienation of his mother. Confused, the pendulum was swinging as to whether he should or shouldn't discontinue his cross-dressing. The sound of the driver's voice returned him to his present surroundings.

"So, what's it going to be?" asked the driver, as he looked through the rear view mirror.

"What was it you asked me?"

"Do you want me to go over the bridge or through the tunnel?"

"Whatever's fastest," Everett answered.

"The tunnel is the fastest way," suggested the driver.

"Anything, just get me home," said Everett tartly, not looking for further conversation.

Resting his head back, Everett closed his eyes. His greatest anguish rested in the concern that his mother might be ashamed of him. Would she ever come back and talk to him? Using the litmus of Adele's day, his dressing up was something beyond comprehension in terms of acceptability. Police involvement incorporated a new wrinkle that compounded matters. Adele would most certainly view the situation as a reflection of her ability to raise a masculine child.

By the time he arrived at his apartment Everett was well into a downward spiral. The first thing he did was to take a good look in the bathroom mirror. With a hand on each side of the sink, he leaned forward to gaze deeply into the glass. He took notice of every facial imperfection. His brow lines seemed more pronounced and the small bags under his eyes were puffier. An overall troubled look caused his face to sag, aging him. "Is this what I've come to?" he asked himself mournfully.

Everett's despair sparked an extreme reaction. Holding his wig in hand, he suddenly began to wipe his mouth vigorously with the red topping in an effort to expunge all remnants of lipstick. He then stormed into the living room where he filled a water glass with brandy. Draining the glass with several long guzzles caused the alcohol to race to his head. Disrobing, he entered the shower for a full cleansing. The brandy he consumed was potent enough to dull the sting of the hot pellets that flowed from the overhead spray. Everett began to roughly scrub himself with a soapy washcloth. His enthusiasm in sanding away the shame reddened his skin, causing a very noticeable rawness. When done punishing himself, the teacher donned his white terrycloth bathrobe. Falling into his easy chair he poured himself a second drink, this one equally as large as the first. After consuming the second stimulant, everything became a lot easier in terms of what to do.

"Where are you, bitch?" he thundered. Wheeling around he challenging Granny to appear. There was no response from the evil voice. The teacher was too far gone for it to matter anyway.

After a few minutes Everett rose to gather up every stitch of feminine apparel in the apartment, including all accessories. Now unsteady, he stumbling along managing to stuff the items into green commercial garbage bags. He stacked the bags along a wall, intending to put them out for the next collection. Everett poured himself yet another drink of jumbo proportion. He drank standing until he fell heavily into the easy chair. With slurred words he solemnly pledged to never cross-dress again.

"That's more like it, dear," said the good voice soothingly. *"Now don't you feel better, dear?"* His mother's voice was the last thing the teacher heard before passing out.

MARKIE AND VON HESS set out to Harlem with the weather on their side. Their intention was to visit the outdoor basketball courts. Since they felt optimistic, they looked forward to this leg of their investigation.

"Where do you want to start, sarge?"

"Anyplace is fine, as long as it's up north."

"We got a good day," said Von Hess. "There should be lots of activity on the basketball courts."

The first court they visited had a list of names neatly painted on a nearby wall. The roll call consisted of notables who played on the court at one time or another.

"It would be hot stuff if our guy had his name up there," commented Markie.

"It wouldn't surprise me, stranger things have happened. You know it's very historical up here," pointed out Von Hess, making conversation. "There were several colonial forts in this area years ago. Fort Washington was here."

"I knew about Fort Washington, but I didn't realize there were others. You have an interest in that kind of stuff, Ollie?"

"Me? I don't have *any* interest," replied Von Hess. "I just remembered it from helping my kid do a paper when she was in school."

"Yeah, I remember doing the same thing with my older two. Whenever a paper was due, if I wasn't working, I'd sit with them. That's what made me an expert on The Borgo Pass."

Von Hess turned off the engine after parking and then turned to face Markie. *"The Borgo Pass?"* he asked.

"It's a road in the Romanian Mountains that links Transylvania with *Buk-o-vina,* Mol-davvv-ia," explained the sergeant, dragging out the words to pronounce them as Bela Lugosi's Dracula would.

The investigators joined an audience of about forty people who were watching an intense basketball game. The arrival of the law didn't escape the attention of those in attendance. Word soon spread that the DTs—a common street name for detectives—were in the area.

The investigators zeroed in on a young man in his early 20's. He was standing alone off to the sidelines, a short distance from the court. Based on his attire, they assumed he worked in the area. The young man watched the two detectives as they approached him. They walked with the confidence that spelled cop.

"You work around here, my friend?" asked Von Hess, flashing his tin.

"Not far from here. Is there a problem, detective?" The young man gazed warily at the two plainclothesmen, wondering if he was being targeted as a suspect in a crime.

The detectives were not surprised by the man's leeriness. "Relax, you got no problem. We're just looking for some help and want to ask you a question or two. Have your ever see an old white dude playing basketball over here on this court?"

The young man displayed a surprised look. "Over here?"

"Not just here, any place where there is a basketball court. We're looking for a big white guy, broad shoulders with gray hair?"

"I never saw anybody like that."

"What about a big red-headed white woman, who looks like a man?"

"No, never," answered the man. The very idea caused him to pucker his lips and puff out a short breath. He thought the police might be playing with his head.

"You come here a lot?" questioned Markie.

"Whenever I'm on a break, I work for the Housing Authority."

"Doing what?"

"I work in maintenance."

"Oh, housing is a good job," noted Von Hess. "How long you been working around here?"

"Couple of years, but I never saw anybody like the people you described," stated the maintenance man.

"I have one last question," said Markie. "Ever see a cross-eyed white person around here?"

208

"Nah, c'mon man." His response was accompanied by a skeptical expression and a smile.

Von Hess looked over to Markie after seeing the man's response. The sergeant lifted his chin, indicating that the two should move on. "Thanks, man," he said before walking off.

After receiving similar results in conversations with several others, Markie and Von Hess returned to their vehicle to visit the next location. They met with negative results at the Harlem Lane Playground, St. Nicholas Park and Marcus Garvey Park. Undaunted, they continued to plug along with their canvassing until late afternoon. It was at Morningside Park where they finally gained some traction. It came when they engaged two local youths in their mid-teens who were watching a game. Once again, the situation was such that no introductions were necessary. Von Hess was first to approach the boys.

"You two ever see an old white dude with gray hair coming around here?"

"Nah," answered the glib, short haired teen who was wearing black glasses with a black elastic band attached.

"Are there any old white men coming here just to *watch* the games?"

The youth wearing glasses suddenly perked up. "Ohhhh...yeah, I know who you mean," he said. "You're talking about that big white dude with the gray hair."

"What's that?" asked the second teen, who'd stopped paying attention shortly after the conversation began.

"C'mon man, you remember that time when Leroy Kinnebrew made that crazy ass hook shot?"

Reference to the hook shot refreshed the memory of the second youth. "Oh yeah, I remember that, it was just a lucky shot."

"Right, now do you remember the old white dude who was clapping like he was at the circus or some shit? You remember, we were laughing at his ass."

"Are you talking about that big dude in the suit?"

"How many other suckers you know coming up here looking like him?"

"Yeah, I remember him."

"Do you know his name?" asked Von Hess.

"What?" Markie began to wonder about the teen's allotment of gray matter.

"He's talking about the old white dude, dummy!" said the boy wearing the glasses.

"Nah, I don't know his name."

"Well, that sounds like the guy we want," stated Markie.

"You're talking about the teacher right?" the second youth asked.

"Yeah, that's right the teacher," injected Von Hess, anxiously. "What do you know about him? How do you know he's a teacher?"

"I forgot that," chimed in the first youth. "The dude *was* a teacher."

"Talk to me, how do you guys know that?"

"Dondi said he was a teacher."

"Wait a minute, back up. You lost me." said Markie. "*Dondi* said he was a teacher?"

"That's right," answered the teen with the glasses.

"So who the hell is Dondi?"

"What's Dondi's last name?" asked the glibber of the two youths, turning to his friend.

"Ross."

"Do you know where Dondi Ross lives?" Von Hess asked.

"He lives in the projects, I know that. He usually hangs around here most days," said the first teen. "Where's his crib at?" he asked his friend.

"You're talking about Dondi?"

"Now do you see what I have to deal with?" The first youth said, addressing the detectives. "Who do you think I'm talking about? I'm talking about *Dondi,* fool!"

"Who are you calling a fool?"

"We're talking about Dondi, man. Where does he live?"

"How am I supposed to know where he lives," barked the second teen. "Get your ass over there and go ask *him!*"

"Where's he at?"

"Over there by the water fountain, *fool!*" said the second teen with satisfaction.

"Oh, shit!" said the teenager wearing the glasses, as he placed a hand across his mouth to conceal his smile. "There he is, man, the dude wearing the black baseball hat."

Dondi was tall youth of around the same age as the other boys. He was standing about one-hundred yards away from the investigators.

Markie removed a ten-dollar bill from his wallet. "Here, whack this up between you," he said, handing over the money to the teen who was wearing glasses.

The youth examined the bill closely before passing it to his friend. Taking the money, the second youth had a surprised look on his face.

"That clown must be on the take," commented the youth wearing the glasses. Both boys then shook their head knowingly. They were in total agreement.

Dondi had been watching the whole discussion take place, so there was no surprise when the detectives made their way over to him. He knew he had been pointed out by the other boys. Having done nothing wrong, he waited with indifference.

After the detectives explained their purpose, they began to receive answers to their questions.

"I don't know his real name," Dondi told them, "but that old dude could play some basketball. I've seen him make lots of long jump shots. He plays with his students, man—the dude is cool. He's a teacher."

"You saw him play on this court?" asked Von Hess.

"I never saw him play *here*. I've seen him play in East Harlem."

Von Hess pressed for a name. "Think hard for a minute, Dondi: what did they call him when he was playing? Did they call him coach or anything like that?"

"No, they never called him coach. But those dudes he played with, they *were* calling him something."

"Try and remember what they called him. This is important."

"It was some kind of nickname that they called him when he'd be getting hot."

"What do you mean by hot?"

"You know, scoring points. It started with an S."

Markie began to rattle off names. "Sam, Sal, Sean, Sol, Stan, Sid? Or was it maybe a nickname, like Scooter, Shooter, Slick, Skip, Speed, Spike."

Dondi nodded as the name started to come to him. "It was two names. Skizzle or...no, wait a minute. I got it, it was *Sizzle*! They called him *Sizzling Shades* during the game," announced Dondi triumphantly. "The dude was playing with sunglasses hanging from his neck."

Markie glanced at Von Hess before speaking. "That's the way to do it, Dondi. Now come on, try and think about the school they came from. Do you know which one it was?"

"I'm pretty sure that they came from East Harlem somewhere. I'm not sure what the name of the school was though," answered Dondi, "but I know the schoolyard."

After receiving the information the detectives thanked Dondi. "You're a good man." said Von Hess, peeling off a five to give him.

"Nah, that's alright, you don't have to give me anything," said the youth.

Taking the five dollars off Von Hess, Markie added his own five dollar bill. He then forced the ten bucks into Dondi's pocket. "Nothing is for nothing kid. If somebody's offering, *wanting* to give it...and you earned it legit, take it," advised the sergeant.

"Thanks," said the youth, accepting the money.

Markie and Von Hess both took a liking to Dondi. "Are you still in school?"

"Yeah...I'm a junior."

"You intend to go to college?"

"Yeah, I'm going to go to John Jay. I want to be a cop."

The sergeant was surprised at hearing his. "You want to be a cop? Why do you want to be a cop?"

"My father was a cop."

"No kidding, where'd he work?" asked Von Hess, with sincere interest.

"Transit, but he's dead now."

"Oh, I'm sorry to hear that, kid," said Von Hess.

"Listen to me, kid," advised Markie. "You stick to school, keep your nose clean and you'll be wearing the blue uniform one day."

"Remember not to get caught up with the wrong friends," warned Von Hess. "They could bring you down."

"That's right," concurred the sergeant. "The wrong crowd will trip you up every time. All you need is a little beef and it could prevent you from getting on the job."

Both investigators handed Dondi a business card. "Give a call when you're ready to take the test. Good luck kid," said Von Hess.

Markie and von Hess returned to their unmarked car without speaking. Once they were rolling their conversation resumed.

"That Dondi turned out to be a nice kid," said Markie.

"Yeah," agreed Von Hess. "He'll probably make a decent cop."

23

Wanted, Dead Or Alive

"If we grab this motherless heathen before you do, you could tell the judge to take the day off and go fishing. They'll be no need for an arraignment.

-Archie "Two Fingers" O'Sullivan

THE TASK FORCE DETECTIVES CONTINUED to move from case to case. They next delved into the strangulation of Martha O'Sullivan, the senior citizen who worked in the theater district. A pipe smoking precinct detective named Grover Rhodes was assigned to the investigation. Rhodes was polished investigator who fancied himself as a sleuth of high intelligence, something along the lines of a Sherlock Holmes minus the violin.

"Now that you've read the file, what are your conclusions, gentlemen?" asked the soft-spoken Rhodes.

"Just like the other cases, there isn't a lot to go on," answered Von Hess.

"But we do have something. In this homicide we recovered red particles of material from the victim's neck area. This physical evidence will likely prove valuable down the road."

"What do you know about the victim, Grover?" asked the sergeant.

"She was an exemplary widow who purported herself impeccably. By all accounts, she was a staunch proponent of God, church and family"

"Do you have any theory as to why she was clipped?"

"Unfortunately, no. However, there must be a motive behind this senselessness. I find it interesting that when we removed her body from the dumpster she still had her jewelry and pocketbook. There was cash remaining the purse—it wasn't even unzipped. So clearly, robbery wasn't the intent of the killer."

Von Hess nodded in agreement. "No signs of a sexual assault, right?"

"None," replied Rhodes."

Von Hess turned to Markie. "It might be good to get a visual of the crime scene."

Markie checked his watch. "Good idea. It's around the estimated time of the homicide, so let's go see what's out there. Care to come along, Grover?"

"I only recently revisited the crime scene. You'll find that they've removed the dumpster from the lot," advised Rhodes. "Naturally, I've diligently continued to beat the bushes, only to learn that this killing has most definitely unsettled many of the local citizenry, far beyond the norm."

"Are you saying you're getting pressured?" asked Markie.

"In so many words, yes. Both sides of the fence have expressed interest as to my progress."

Markie got the detectives' drift. "Well, let's try and dig up something to give them."

"Good show. If you need anything on my end, just call. I'll be at my desk toiling over a new case. It's an interesting forgery." Markie and Von Hess looked at each other.

"I'd have to say he is one odd duck," commented Von Hess, once they were in the car.

"He is a bit of a windbag," replied Markie. "Did you notice how he raises his chin up every time he opens his yap? It's like he's giving a lecture."

"Yeah, he reminds me of a smug politician who loves to pontificate on how great he's doing.

"But I'd have to say one thing to his credit, he seems like a worker," concluded Markie.

MARKIE'S FIELD INVESTIGATION BEGAN at the Bigelow Theater. From there, he and Von Hess traced what they believed to be the likely path the murder victim traveled to get home. They drove through the streets slowly, stopping at the beginning of the block where the usherette met her end. After parking, they each took a side of the street to walk down. With flashlights in hand the men began searching for clues.

Von Hess passed three shabbily clad men sitting up against the exterior wall of the Averyton Iron Works. The entity was but one of several commercial buildings on the block. The most functional of the indigents was swilling down what was left of a cheap bottle of whiskey. Von Hess passed them by unnoticed. The thick odor of drink in the air made it obvious to the detective that the men were inebriated.

"There's a crew of boozehounds who set up house on my side," said Von Hess, regrouping with Markie at the end of the street.

"What are they doing?"

"Two were totally out of it, but one guy looked like he was still drinking."

"Let's go take a look at the crime scene before we talk to them—they're not going anyplace soon."

The detectives approached the lot where the victim's body had been discovered. They found the location unsecured and vacant.

"Rhodes was right, the dumpster is gone. This lot looks like it just got a makeover, it's all cleaned up," noted Von Hess. "It looks nothing like the crime scene photos."

"The ground is newly paved," said Markie, "and the curb is cut. It looks like they're preparing to make a parking lot out of it."

The oversized windows in the surrounding factories were all dark, with some being blackened. It was obvious that there was no business being conducted at this hour of the evening. The investigators moved to the center of the lot. Markie looked up and down at the high brick walls covering the three sides of the opening. As he was doing this, Von Hess walked along the interior building line of the property examining the ground. After squaring the lot, Von Hess rejoined the sergeant.

"There is nothing here, boss, just flat ground and brick walls."

"Somebody must have told them to take the dumpster away and clean up the place," conjectured Markie. "I'm surprised they didn't put a fence up to restrict entry."

"Want to talk to those rum pots, sarge? They look like they could be regulars around here."

"*Lay on McDuff*," said Markie, with a bit of theatrics.

Von Hess stopped in his tracks. "You mean *lead* on, don't you, boss?"

"No, it's *lay* on. Shakespeare's Macbeth, Act 5, Scene 8," corrected Markie, tapping his index finger against his temple as if he were an authority on the subject.

Von Hess shook his head. "So where did you pull that one out of?"

The sergeant came clean. "DeCesare smartened me up. He takes acting classes."

The two investigators approached the three men sitting against the building. The air was polluted with the stench of cheap booze. Three shopping carts containing their belongings were connected to each other by a common rope. The carts formed a three-sided corral that restricted interior access. Within this protected zone were two large cardboard boxes used to shelter the men from inclement weather. Contained inside the boxes were sleeping bags and some old blankets.

The water dripping from the uncapped fire hydrant on the opposite side of the street led Markie to assume that there was a wrench secreted somewhere among their belongings. Access to the water enabled the men to drink and wash themselves. The sergeant's mind was quickly changed after he noticed the wire, rags and two sticks inside one of the carts. No, there was no wrench, Markie concluded. These were odds and ends used to open a fire hydrant in lieu of a wrench. Markie remembered how he'd done the very same thing as a youngster. He and his small friends would collectively shoulder the sticks of the make-shift wrench to generate enough power to turn the square nut that freed the water.

The detectives gave each of the sitting vagrants a careful scrutiny. One of the men, in his mid-thirties, was leaning back against the building in a daze. His thick, brown hair looked dirty. Open mouthed, unshaven and clammy faced, his eyes were drooped as he stared blankly ahead. Although haggard, one could see that if he were cleaned up and in the right clothes, he'd be quite presentable. Nestled alongside him was a slightly built man of about forty who was contently smiling. The neatest of the three, his face was hairless. The red waves in his hair were neatly combed back. He had a tiny nose and pinkish complexion. Part of his tongue could be seen pushing against the interior wall of his lower lip. With closed eyes, the happy man rested his head peacefully upon on the younger man's shoulder. A closer inspection by Markie revealed that he had his right hand deep down into the front pants of his friend.

Markie nudged Von Hess. "Hey Ollie, take a look at this...this one has a grip on his pals bowl of fruit," whispered the sergeant. Von Hess looked, shrugged, and said nothing.

The only somewhat alert person among the three was a greasy looking man pushing seventy. He was stocky, mostly bald, with long stringy hair covering his ears and collar. His green, long-sleeved buttoned-down shirt was in desperate need of cleaning.

Von Hess was the first to address him. "How you doing?" asked the detective, flashing his badge. Although he didn't hear the question, seeing the badge and suits registered with the man. No stranger to a rousting, he responded with excessive politeness.

"I'm Daniel Bibbinger, sir," he said in a gravelly voice, trying not to sound drunk.

"Are you here every night, Daniel?"

The drunkard immediately became defensive. "We ain't bothering anyone here officer, we're gone by the time the businesses open up. We don't come back until after everyone's gone home. We ain't causing problems."

"What time do you get here at night Daniel?"

"We only come here after everybody goes home."

"What time is that?"

"That's usually when it gets dark out."

"How long has this been going on?"

"We've been here for months, never a problem."

"What makes this place so special?"

"It's better than those damn shelters. You got too many crazies over there."

Von Hess nodded. "Are there any other people out here at night besides you three?"

"No sir, I found this little oasis," he answered with pride. "It's been our little secret."

"Where are you from Daniel?" asked Markie, picking up on his non-New York accent.

"Cut and Shoot, Texas, sir. It's a small town forty miles north of Houston."

"You're a long way from the ranch aren't you cowboy?"

"I am, and I travel with a long story. Are we going to lose our little ranch here, sir?"

"It's still your little ranch if you try to help us out," said Von Hess. "We're looking for a cross-eyed guy with gray hair. Ever see anyone like that around here Daniel?"

Daniel became pensive. He then cleared his throat as he tried to rise, but quickly slid back down.

"That's alright Daniel; you don't have to get up." Markie felt a little sorry for the derelict.

"Are you looking for Billy One-Eye? If so, you can find that vicious louse at the shelter on East 2nd Street. He wears a black eye patch. Be careful, he's a dangerous man."

"Is he a big man?" Markie asked.

Bibbinger threw his neck back before answering. "No, he's not very big. He's scrawny, but he'd slice you in a second."

"That's not our boy," answered Markie. "Are there any violent *big* gray-haired guys with bad eyes around here that you know of, about fifty years old or so?"

"There's nobody violent over here officer, that's why we're here. Those bastards at the shelter would eat him alive," said Daniel, pointing to the man with the warm hand.

"One last question, is there a large redheaded women who comes around here?"

"Are you kidding?"

218

The detectives laughed at the way Daniel responded. "Yeah, we're just kidding," said Von Hess.

"Well that was a waste," commented Markie on their way back to the car. "How about we head over to the Bigelow? Let's see what we can sniff out over there."

❖

The detectives entered the Bigelow after the final performance. Once the theater crowd passed through the exit doors, the investigators made their way inside. After explaining their business to the manager, they were introduced to an elderly usherette who worked the night Martha was murdered. The two women had been friends.

"Thanks for taking a moment to talk to us, ma'am," said Markie.

"You are very welcome. This is about poor Martha, I suppose?" she asked, as she removed her cap and ran her fingers through her snow white hair. Her bright red nails greatly contrasted the back of her aged pale hands.

"Yes, it is. To the best of your knowledge did Martha have enemies or any problems with anyone?"

"No, Martha was very well liked by everyone."

"What kind of person was she?"

"Martha was fun, very positive. She never missed a good time."

"A partier?" asked Von Hess.

"Oh no, don't get the wrong idea. She went to church regularly, was kind-hearted and very charitable. For years Martha sent money every month to poor children overseas."

"I see," said the detective. "Can you think of anything to tell us about Martha's last night that might be of interest? Did anything out of the ordinary occur?"

The usherette hesitated before finally answering. "Well, to be truthful, she wasn't in the best form her last night here."

"How is that?" asked Von Hess with a raised eyebrow.

"This is confidential, right?" she asked. "I wouldn't want it said that I was talking badly."

"You have our word, it goes no further than here," assured Markie.

"Well, Martha had a couple of nips before coming into work," she confided.

"Understand I'm not saying that she wasn't able to do her job of course, but *this* particular evening she came in feeling...*exceptional*, let's just say."

"Did she have a drinking problem?" asked Von Hess.

"No, no, no. Martha was a social drinker, like most of us girls. If anything, she was a woman with a wooden leg who could hold her drink! I only happened to take notice that night because I thought there was going to be trouble."

"What kind of trouble?"

"She collided into one of the theatergoers or maybe he bumped into her. I'm not sure. Either way, the man ended up spilling his drink," the senior explained. "Now you know how some people can make a federal case over the smallest things."

"You witnessed this?"

"I didn't exactly see them bump into each other, but I was near enough to see afterward."

"Was there an argument as a result of spilling the drink?"

"Not an argument. I will say, at the time I thought there might be words exchanged."

"Ma'am, are you saying they had *no* words?"

"Not a peep, *but*...you should've seen the look that man gave her! Let me tell you, it was far from friendly!"

Both Markie and Von Hess sensed they might have hit upon a lead. "Could you please expand on exactly the type of look he gave her, was it a dirty look?"

"It wasn't a plain everyday dirty look. It was more of a *weird* look I'd say."

"Weird?"

"Well, he looked at Martha like, I don't know. There was just something about his look that just didn't seem right...it was a *peculiar* look."

"Did you see his eyes?" asked Markie.

"No, I was too far away for that, if you're asking me for their color."

"How far away were you from him?"

"I was about nine or ten rows away, perhaps."

Von Hess cleared his voice. "Excuse me ma'am, but could you describe the man physically for us."

"I think so," she replied. "He was a bigger man than either of you two gentlemen, taller and wider at the shoulders. Compared to me he was the size of a refrigerator," she added for emphasis. "I'd think most would consider him nice looking. He was clean cut and well dressed. Judging by his gray hair, he couldn't be all that young."

"Did you ever see him before?"

"Yes, I've seen him at the theater several times over the years."

"You did?" said Von Hess, in a surprised tone. "Are you sure of that?"

"I'm certain of it. He always came in well dressed and with an older woman. It's really her that I remember best."

"Why is that?"

"She was a very large woman, almost as big as he was. She stood out."

"Did you ever speak to her?" asked Markie.

"Speak to her? Never, she'd stroll down the aisle like she was the Queen of Sheba and he was part of her caravan. It seemed to me like she could have been his mother."

"Was the older woman with him when he ran into Martha?"

"No, that night was the first time I ever saw him alone. Anyway, if she was with him I didn't see her."

"Do you know the man's name or where he comes from perhaps?"

"No, I only know that he's been here to see shows."

"After the drink was spilled, what happened next?"

"Well after that, he did something very odd. He put on a pair of dark sunglasses."

"What did he do next?"

"He stormed out of the theater in a huff. He never looked back—just kept his head down at the floor all the way out. You know, he never did get to see the performance."

"Do you know where he went?"

"At first I thought he ran off looking to complain or ask for a refund. But he didn't do any of that. He just left the theater altogether."

"Do you think you could recognize this man if you saw him again?" asked Markie.

"I could."

"Do you know if Martha drank at home?"

"I doubt Martha ever drank at home. She used to say drinking alone is a bad habit."

"I see. Have you any idea where she'd go if she felt like having a drink?"

"McAvoy's on 11th Avenue, of course. She lived upstairs so it was a convenient arrangement for her. Her habit was one drink a night at McAvoy's, unless of course there was an occasion. Everyone knew that about Martha. I think she may have had some family connection in there, but I don't know that for sure."

"Have you ever seen a big, cross-eyed woman with red hair around?"

"Good heavens, no," she said chuckling. "I'd surely remember seeing anyone like that."

The detectives thanked the usherette before setting out to McAvoy's.

THEY DROVE AROUND UNTIL they found a parking spot a block away from the saloon. They had to wait to speak to the bartender because he was busy with a customer. When he was finished he worked his way down the bar to where Markie and Von Hess were waiting. Cautiously he approached the detectives. Von Hess flashed his shield before asking questions.

"You guys new in the precinct?" asked the bartender.

"No, we're on a special assignment. Are you the regular evening bartender?"

"I'm McAvoy, I own the joint. What do you need?" he asked, sounding far from friendly.

"It's about Martha O'Sullivan, the woman who lived upstairs," stated Von Hess.

McAvoy's face turned serious. "What about her?"

"Were you here the night she was murdered?"

"I was."

"Was she in here that night?"

"She was."

"What was she like that night? Anything unusual happen?"

McAvoy shrugged. "She came in for a blast, like every night."

"Can you tell us anything about her?" asked Markie.

"She paid her rent on time," replied the bar owner.

"What kind of shape was she in when she left here?"

"Same as when she came in."

Von Hess wasn't happy having to pull teeth to get an answer. "Was she in here alone?"

"She was having a drink with an old friend of her dead husband."

"Who might that be?"

McAvoy didn't want to give up the name. "I forget, I get a lot of customers in here."

"Look pal, how about you cut the shit? An old lady got murdered and unless you did it, why in hell would you be evasive?" asked Von Hess, clearly annoyed..

McAvoy begrudgingly conceded the point. "Mike Cahill," he finally uttered, nastily.

"They left together?"

"No."

"So what about this Mike Cahill, did he leave after Martha?"

"I don't remember."

"What's Cahill's business?"

"Retired...I think."

"I see. Did Martha ever stop in here for a drink *after* she finished work? Or, did she ever leave the bar with a stranger when she was drinking?"

"Look, she was a nice old lady, for Christ's sake. Every morning you could have found her in a pew someplace praying." McAvoy had grown tired of their questions.

"We have to ask, pal." Von Hess said with an edge to his voice. "Did she have any family problems that you know of?"

"Tell you what, hold on. You're talking to the wrong guy. I'll be right back."

McAvoy walked to the rear of the bar and disappeared into a back room. After a couple of minutes he reemerged, returning to his position behind the bar. "Go to the back and knock on the door before you go in. You'll find somebody in there to talk to."

"Who are we looking for?"

"Let him tell you."

The detectives proceeded to the back. Inside the room there was a table, some chairs, and a television set. A man and a woman sat at the table, splitting a pitcher of beer. The man also had an empty shot glass alongside his beer.

"I'm Archie O'Sullivan," he announced. "Martha O'Sullivan was my aunt."

Archie Two-Fingers was a thin lipped, hard-looking man with high cheekbones. Of average size, he was in his early fifties. Deep lines could be seen etched in his chiseled face, with pronounced crow's feet at the outside corners of his blue eyes. From afar, his stylishly combed blond hair and thin frame gave him the appearance of a younger man. The woman sitting with him was ten or fifteen years his junior. Her figure was slim, her long fingernails finely manicured. The open-toe shoes she wore revealed thin ankles, thin toes, and a perfect pedicure. She sat silently with the right side of her body against the edge of the table. Her lower limbs were exposed, thanks to the loose dress she wore that was hiked up high.

"I'm Sergeant Markie, this is Detective Von Hess."

"Are you working on my aunt's case?" asked Two Fingers.

Markie and Von Hess quickly sized up O'Sullivan as a hood. "We are. I'm sorry for your loss," said Markie. "Is there anything we should know?" he asked, cutting to the chase.

"Like what?"

"Like anything that can be useful in getting to the bottom of this." Markie then leveled with O'Sullivan concerning the task force and its mission. "So, now you know that there is a lot more riding on this than you might have thought. Believe me," said the sergeant, "we want to nail this sucker to the wall as much as you."

O'Sullivan's eyes widened at the remark. The sergeant was talking his language. The vibes he received made the thug more comfortable than he'd normally be with the police. It led him to put some of his own cards on the table.

"It's a close-knit neighborhood that we have here. We take care of our own," advised Two Fingers. "I'll clue you in on one thing. *Whoever* did this isn't anybody *known* around here. I turned this neighborhood upside down before I came to *that* conclusion!"

"Got it," answered the sergeant. "You got any suggestions?

"One thing, and I'm not suggesting," said Martha's nephew.

"What?"

"If we grab this motherless heathen before you do, you could tell the judge to take the day off and go fishing. They'll be no need for an arraignment."

The detectives didn't flinch. "He doesn't deserve any better," Markie said grimly. "No tears will be shed on this end." Markie was trying to give the impression that a possible alliance could be formed.

Two Fingers seemed to be receptive. "Do you have any ideas as to who did it?"

"Not yet," answered he sergeant. "We're still digging, but we'll get there."

Markie's confidence got a rise out of the gang leader. "Well, if you do find out...now, I'm talking to you guys man to man... correct?"

"Say what you need to say," assured Markie. "We're not altar boys."

"I didn't think so. Figure on a bounty going to the man who brings him to me. I'll pay five-grand dead and ten if he's hand delivered to me breathing."

"That's good to know," answered the stone-faced Markie, pretending as if he held an interest in delivering a man to his doom.

Their conversation concluded with a nod that conveyed a mutual understanding. On the way out the detectives stopped to speak one last time to McAvoy before they departed.

"One final thing," Von Hess said. "How do we get in touch with Mr. Cahill?"

"Why ask me?"

"Thanks." Von Hess handed McAvoy a business card. "I'm sure Archie will appreciate your help. If you see Cahill have him call me."

"Brooklyn Homicide...what's this?" asked Knucks, after reading the card.

"Like we said, we're here on a special assignment."

Knucks thought about an angry Archie Two Fingers. He called out to the departing detectives. "Hey, talk to Detective Rhodes. He knows the guy you want to talk to."

Markie nodded. "Let's take a swing by the command, Ollie."

"Let me call up Rhodes, it'll save some time if we can get the information over the phone."

Von Hess explained the situation to the precinct detective. As it turned out Rhodes was a man with many neighborhood contacts. The detective advised that he knew Michael Cahill to be a onetime union rep for the stagehands. After making a call to a third party Rhodes was able to provide Von Hess with Cahill's home phone number and address.

"Think it might be too late to call Cahill?" asked Von Hess.

Markie thought about it before answering. "Nah...what the hell, let's give him a call."

Von Hess dialed Cahill's number. After telephonically interviewing him he was satisfied that Martha's friend was unable to contribute anything that would further the investigation. After checking the time, Markie dialed the number for Inspector McCoy to fill him in on where they stood with the investigation.

"What did McCoy say, boss?" asked Von Hess, who was privy to only one side of the conversation.

"There is never enough you could do to please these guys."

"What's the next step?"

The Doctor Culbrenner homicide is next on the list. If our boy is that close to his momma, maybe he takes her to a doctor."

24

Frieda's Finish

"Wrong? Why no, on the contrary, his eyes were beautiful, the kind you or I would kill for. They were an absolutely beautiful sky blue."

-Lois Royster

FRIEDA WAS AN ELDERLY WIDOW who hardly ever slept. Day or night, she'd rush to the front window at the sound of footsteps coming down the stairs of her Tenth Avenue building. If street activity interested her, she'd pop out with a broom to sweep the sidewalk. Acutely aware of this, Everett held no expectation of disposing of his garbage unnoticed.

On the evening before collection day Everett put out the commercial trash bags for pick up. After doing so he immediately returned to his apartment. He shut off the lights and assumed a position a couple of feet away from the front window. The brightness of the streetlight allowed Frieda to examine the bags Everett placed at the curb.

"Look at this," Frieda muttered. "Sanitation won't take these bags if their too heavy."

Frieda lifted each bag to make sure they were acceptable. Since she was already handling the bags, she decided to satisfy her curiosity and see what exactly was being put out for collection. She stopped pawing through an open bag after finding a lengthy vibrator in the mix. The astonishing discovery caused the old woman to cross herself. She then began tapping her fist against her forehead. "Crazy!" she said in a huff, as she shook her head with disapproval. Having seen enough, the property owner hurriedly secured the bags and returned to her apartment.

The landlady's fist tapping met the shaking fist criteria that detonated Everett. The crossing of his eyes and the evil voice came simultaneously. The science teacher rubbed his eyes in an attempt to see clearer. No, there was no mistake—the landlady had become Granny Trapani.

"*Eh, what-a-you- look?*" weighed in the evil voice.

"I see *you*," answered the teacher sternly. "Don't you worry one bit about that."

Everett stared down at the unsuspecting Frieda as she reentered her building. Confident that the other tenants would soon be turning in for the night, he patiently waited. When the time was right he put on his sunglasses and selected one of his red ties from the closet before heading downstairs to Frieda's apartment.

FRIEDA WAS HAVING A CUP OF TEA as she mulled over her discovery. Unearthing the sexual stimulator caused the old woman to wonder who the nine-inch joy toy actually belonged to. The whole idea of a mechanical substitute for the real thing was foreign to Frieda. After awhile she let it go, opting to clip food coupons out of the newspaper. When she recognized the pattern of Everett's footsteps coming down the stairs she went to the front window. She was surprised when she heard the unexpected knock on her door. Leaving her window post, she opened her apartment door to find her hulking tenant standing before her.

"Is everything alright?" she asked, worried that an emergency repair might be necessary.

"Everything is just fine...*Granny Trapani*!" Everett declared in an *"aha!"* moment.

"What?" Frieda asked, now wondering why he was wearing sunglasses.

Everett uncorked a two-handed shove that was forceful enough to knock the senior citizen back onto her living room floor. The shooting pain coming from Frieda's hip signaled that something was broken. Oblivious to the landlady's groans, the teacher entered the apartment. Everett quickly looped his tie around Frieda's neck and garroted her. Once she was gone, he rose to his feet to straddle the lifeless torso of the woman he saw as Granny Trapani.

"I'm no longer powerless," he declared. I'll dispose of *all* of your guises!"

Everett checked the entire apartment just to be sure no one else was there. When done, he sat at the kitchen table. After a few minutes of collecting himself he grew hungry.

"See what's in the refrigerator, dear. Whatever is in there will only go bad if it's not eaten," said the good voice.

"I suppose there is no harm in doing that," he answered.

Everett opened the refrigerator to see what was available. When he saw the Bratwurst he couldn't resist making a meal of the veal sausage. He washed it down with a cold bottle of Spaten beer. Granny slaying was a business that worked up an appetite.

MARKIE LOOKED THROUGH HIS NOTES regarding the homicide of Doctor Culbrenner. Finally he found the contact information for the doctor's office manager. "Here we go. Ollie, do me a favor and pull over a minute. Call this woman Royster and see if we could go see her."

After getting Royster on her cell phone Von Hess explained his purpose for calling. The former office manager was amenable to meeting with the detectives when she got home from her new job. When he got off the phone Von Hess stopped to purchase two containers of coffee.

"Finally, you missed one," said Markie after a few minutes of driving.

"What's that, sarge?" asked Von Hess, after taking a sip from his container of coffee.

"I got the coffee all over me. You've been hitting every pothole in the city, Ollie."

Von Hess pulled over at the first opportunity so that they could finish their coffee without further incident.

VON HESS PULLED INTO THE DRIVEWAY of the private house. The red brick building was a semi-attached two family. The entrance to the garden apartment was located to the side of the exterior stairs that led to the owner's unit on the second floor. Lois, hearing the car pull up to the front, opened the door before the detectives had a chance to ring the bell.

Wearing white flip-flops, Lois was dressed casually in faded jeans and a pink t-shirt bearing the face of Albert Einstein sticking his tongue out at the world.

"Please come in," Lois said, after verifying the identity of the detectives.

"Thank you," answered Markie respectfully.

Von Hess followed behind the sergeant as they entered the apartment. Markie turned to face the detective, looking for his reaction to the Einstein t-shirt. The somber expression of Von Hess revealed little. Markie raised his eyebrows and continued on.

"We won't take up too much time, Ms. Royster," said Markie, entering the kitchen.

Seated at the kitchen table was Eugene, her husband. Attired in a short sleeve black polo shirt and jeans, Eugene studied the two investigators. After being introduced, the construction worker nodded his hello.

"I still can't believe that this happened to the doctor," said Lois, with a sad look on her face. "Would you gentlemen like something to drink...coffee?"

"No, nothing, thank you," replied Markie, "we're fine."

Lois turned to Von Hess. "Are you sure that *you* wouldn't like something to drink? I also have tea or soda..."

"No thanks," answered Von Hess, anxious to address the business at hand. "To the best of your knowledge, did the doctor have any enemies or problems?"

"What kind of problems?"

"Something of a financial, drug or alcohol related nature? Or even some possible romantic discord."

"No, there wasn't anything like that going on, as far as I know." She then turned to her husband, attempting to be inclusive. "Right, Eugene?"

Eugene concurred. "The doctor was focused. She was not one prone to distractions."

"Eugene and the doctor are first cousins," Lois explained. "They've known each other since they were children."

"I see," Markie said. "So there was no drama going on in her life that either of you were aware of?"

"Nothing as far as I know," replied Lois. "The doctor was a workaholic, and a woman very devoted to her husband. It was all about work and home for both of them." After saying this Lois again turned to her husband. "Wouldn't you say so, Eugene?" Lacking his wife's enthusiasm, Eugene simply nodded.

"What about her patients, any issues with them?"

"I don't think so. Doctor Culbrenner was a great doctor."

"There were never *any* issues with her patients?"

"Well, I suppose at times her bedside manner could've used some improvement."

"Please explain."

Lois was hesitant. She turned to look at Eugene, whose facial gesture encouraged her to speak up. "Sometimes the doctor expressed herself in a way that seemed, I don't know, distant I suppose would be the correct term."

"Could you give us an example," asked Markie.

"She wasn't big on showing emotion. Know what I mean?"

"Did this ever lead to her having words with anyone?"

"Oh no, there were never any harsh words," explained Lois. "But some people did make remarks to me about her."

"What kind of remarks?"

"Oh, I don't know...little stuff, like she could have been more personable, things like that. I think she had a hard time letting her guard down. She rarely smiled."

"That was just her way," injected Eugene. "She didn't even smile on her wedding day."

"I see," said Von Hess.

"I always said that instead of kissing, she shook hands," added Eugene, attempting to be humorous.

"The funny part is that she was not really anything like what she projected. She was actually a *very* nice person," said Lois.

"Ms. Royster, do you know who the doctor's most recent patients were? Any issues of *any* kind with any of them?" asked Von Hess.

Looking at the detective she shook her head in the negative. "There were never any problems. She took everybody's insurance and everything ran smoothly."

"Who were her most recent patients?"

"I kept my own appointment book that has all the patients and their telephone number, just in case I ever had to call them. Give me a minute, I still have it." Returning with the book, Lois handed it to the detectives for their review.

Von Hess scanned the book in search of a familiar name. "These last names reflect her most recent patients?" he asked.

"Yes."

"Do you recall any negative experiences with any of these patients, or perhaps people close to them?"

"No, none," answered Lois.

"Everyone is a satisfied customer then?"

"Yes."

"Any of these people suffer a lot or die unexpectedly?" asked Markie.

Lois took the book back. After looking through it, she replied. "Only two people, one died at home and the other one in the hospital," she answered.

"Which names?"

"Bernardini and Skidmore."

"What was the story with those two?" Von Hess asked.

Lois responded without having to think. "Mr. Bernardini was sick a long time. He died at home with his family around him. I think they were relieved when he went. That's usually the case when people linger for a long time."

"What about the other one?"

"Mrs. Skidmore, unfortunately, was more of a surprise. She expired unexpectedly—all of a sudden she went downhill."

"What about her family? They were ok with everything?"

"Well, Adele Skidmore's death went hard with her son. He was her only child."

"How old is he?" asked Markie.

"He's a middle-aged man who lived with his mother. He was extremely devoted to her. I would have to honestly say he was devastated at her passing."

Markie leaned in closer to the table for his next question. "Did the doctor *say* anything that would give you the idea that the son took it hard?"

"Well, not really. I just know he was devastated; I used to talk to him during his mother's office visits. That was before she got bad."

"What kind of guy was he?" asked Von Hess.

"He was a nice guy. I was always surprised he never married."

"Why is that?" asked Eugene, who stirred in his seat. His suspicious nature tickled, he was curious as to why his wife was so attuned to Everett.

"At work I chat with all the patients," answered Lois defensively, unaware that she may have activated her husband's distrusting side. "Everett was a caring man. He was also a very handsome man, tall, well-built, and quite a gentleman. I have to say that he was really a pleasant person to talk to."

"What makes you say he took it unusually hard?" broke in Von Hess, interrupting what he feared had the makings of a domestic squabble.

"I just know he did," answered Lois. "Mrs. Skidmore's son always took her to the office for her appointments. It was really touching to see how he stepped up to meet the needs of his mom."

This glowing assessment caused Eugene to slowly stew. He intended to wait until the investigators left before initiating his own questioning of Lois. The detectives both picked up on the rising tension. Von Hess tried to hurry things along.

"Can you provide us with a description of the son?"

"Like I said, he was a handsome man. He was well over six feet, solid, broad shoulders, clean shaven and quite rugged, but not in a roughneck way."

"What about his hair?"

"He had a full head of gray hair."

"What would you put his age at?"

"That is very hard to tell, because he was built like a young guy. His posture was erect, stomach flat like an athlete. He carried himself better than half the young men." Eugene really began shifting in his seat after taking a look at his own pouch.

"Was his mother a big woman?"

"Yes, Adele was very big. She was almost the size of her son."

The two detectives glanced at each other. Markie stepped in with the next question.

"Was there anything at all *wrong* with his eyes?"

"Wrong? Why no, on the contrary, his eyes were beautiful. He has the kind of eyes you or I would kill for. They were an absolutely dreamy sky blue."

The flowery description of Everett's eyes accelerated Eugene's discomfort. The more Lois spoke favorably of Everett, the deeper the hole she was digging herself into with her husband. Eugene took out a cigarette and held it in his mouth unlit. He then nervously began to tap the non-filtered end on the kitchen table.

"Don't you want to smoke that outside, honey?" asked Lois.

Eugene replied snippily. "If I wanted to smoke *outside*, I'd be outside smoking."

Von Hess stepped between them with another question. "What's the son's name?"

"His name is Everett Skidmore."

"Do you happen to have his address?"

"No, I don't have anything other than what I have in my book," informed Lois.

"No idea where he lives?"

"The mother and son definitely lived together in Manhattan someplace, that I remember. I just don't know where exactly."

"Do you know what he does for a living?"

"Yes, I asked him once. He expressed so much interest when it came to things medical that I was curious. He was well enlightened in that area."

"What did he say that he did?" Markie asked.

"He told me that he was a science teacher."

"Did he say what school?"

"No, the conversation didn't get that far," she replied. "Do you suspect *him* of anything?"

"Not really," Von Hess answered. "We just want to learn as much as possible."

"I'm glad to hear that. He was really sweet. I feel for him now that he's alone," Lois expressed, unintentionally sticking it to Eugene a little deeper.

The former office manager did herself no favor at home with her last comments. Eugene possessed an imagination whose thoughts were far out-running reality. Markie posed the next question.

"How did the son usually dress?"

"He was always professionally dressed, coming to the office in a suit and tie. I seem to remember him favoring bright colored ties."

"Do you still keep in touch with him?" Von Hess knew that he was treading on dangerous ground with Eugene in the room, but it was a question he needed to ask.

Lois immediately shot a look over at her husband, who was waiting anxiously to hear her response. She pondered the question before replying honestly. "No, but I *was* actually thinking of calling him," she answered. "I feel so sorry for him."

Von Hess looked down at his pad while Markie stared at the ceiling. Any doubt that the former office manager had put her foot in her mouth was put to rest after Eugene abruptly stormed out of the room. Trouble was now definitely in the air. Markie felt obligated to say something to Lois.

"How about you put any calls to Everett Skidmore on the back burner for awhile, Lois," he advised. "Give us a chance to unravel this mystery first, ok? You never know."

"Yeah, but…" Markie silenced her by pointing to the empty seat at the table. Lois finally realized how much she pissed off Eugene. "Alright," she answered timidly.

The detectives were outside on the street no more than thirty seconds before they could hear the shouting emanating from inside the apartment.

"What do you think boss, should we go in and break up the donnybrook before the riot squad is called in?"

"What are you kidding? We're not getting in the middle of *that* beef, Ollie. I don't think I could take Eugene if I went up against him with a blackjack."

Von Hess thought about it before commenting. "I think you may be right," he said, as he got behind the wheel of the car. "It would take bullets."

25

Conflict Resolution

"We learned a long time ago that there is no upside to being an afterthought. Make the most of your chance when you get it."

-Detective Frank E. Fogel

WHILE THE BROOKLYN ANTI-CRIME SERGEANT didn't *think* that Everett was a pedophile, experience taught him never to rule out any possibility. Preoccupied with catching robbers, he neglected to do something about Everett in a timely fashion. When he finally got to it, he phoned the appropriate office in headquarters.

"Sergeant Asbrook, how may I help you?"

"This is Sergeant Wes Fulton, Seven-Six Anti-Crime."

"What can I do for you, sarge?" asked the female supervisor.

"I'm not really sure if I have anything worthwhile, but I thought it best to pass along some information to be on the safe side."

"What have you got?" she asked, picking up the pen off her desk.

"We grabbed a guy the other day dressed in drag. He was hanging around a schoolyard watching some pre-teen kids play basketball, so we figured him for a possible chicken hawk."

"What was he doing, trying to lure one of the kids to go with him?"

"No, it wasn't anything as cut-and-dried as that. At first, we thought that might be the case," explained Fulton. "Are you guys working on anything where a cross dresser comes into play? This character is a big sucker who wears a red wig."

"Not that I'm aware of. Does he have roots to the area?"

"No connection to this neighborhood at all. He's a Manhattan guy who came over here, *according to him*, to watch schoolyard basketball games."

"We have plenty of schoolyards here in Manhattan, why Brooklyn?"

"Who knows, maybe Manhattan became too hot for him. That's why I'm calling you."

"Did you book him for anything?"

"We wrote him a summons for disorderly conduct."

The sergeant was curious as to why Fulton waited so long in reaching out. "How come you waited until now to call us?"

Since she wasn't his superior, Fulton didn't like the idea of her questioning him. "Look sarge, do you want the information or what?" he asked tartly.

"Okay, okay don't get excited. I was just wondering. Let me have his information. I'll have someone over here check it out."

"Everett Skidmore, his date of birth is 6-26-47,"

"Give me his home address and let me have a detailed description." After receiving the requested information Asbrook commented dryly, "He must cut quite a figure."

"Yeah, and under the red wig he's got a full head of close-cropped gray hair," said Fulton.

"Is there anything unusual about him?"

"Isn't that enough?"

"I guess it is," she replied.

Another thought then suddenly popped into Fulton's mind. "No, wait a minute, there is one other thing…he's a teacher someplace in Manhattan."

"Now, isn't that just grand. Did he tell you he likes to watch young boys at play?"

"No, he *never said* anything like that," replied the anti-crime sergeant.

"You didn't happen to take a picture of him by any chance did you?"

"You bet, we don't dick around over here. I got photos with and without the wig."

"Oh, that's great. Can you make a copy and send it over through department mail?"

"Sure thing, I'll do it once I hang up with you," said Fulton.

"Thanks."

After hanging up the phone, the female sergeant walked over to the desk of the senior detective in her office. "Frankie, take a look at this information that just came in. I got it from an anti- crime sergeant in Brooklyn. See if it fits with anything we've got going."

"Will do sarge," said Detective Fogel, taking the slip of paper from his boss. After viewing the details, he declared enthusiastically, "Holy shit! This is a cross dresser!"

"We have something?"

"We may, boss. The squad in the West Village is looking for somebody fitting this script in a homicide."

The sergeant was surprised to hear this. "Run with it if you have something. Just keep me in the loop so I know what's going on."

"Did they say anything about having a picture of this character, sarge?"

"Yeah, the anti-crime sergeant is sending us a photo. His precinct is just over the bridge."

"It is?"

"Yeah, so why don't you go and pick up the photo. It'll save time and maybe even a life."

"I'll call the squad and let the case detective pick up his own picture…"

"Let's stay in the middle of it, Frankie. If it pans out, this office will get some credit."

After taking a second to think about it, Fogel agreed. "Okay, after I get the picture, I'll take it to the squad that caught the case."

"Just remember, I can't justify overtime for this. Look for the anti-crime sergeant when you get to Brooklyn, he's working now."

"No problem, I'm on it, boss. I'll find him."

Speeding over the Brooklyn Bridge, Fogel arrived at the precinct in short order. The detective went directly to the anti-crime office on the second floor. Looking through the open door, Fogel saw a bearded man, attired in jeans and a cut off sweatshirt, seated behind a small desk.

"Excuse me, I'm looking for the anti-crime sergeant," he announced.

"You're looking at him, Detective Fogel."

"Oh...do we know each other, sarge? Have we met?"

"Your boss called. Here are the pictures you want."

"Beautiful."

"No problem," answered the sergeant. "In case this turns into something, be sure to let the right people know where the ball first started to bounce," reminded the sergeant. "We could use a little positivity. I got a certain captain climbing up my ass."

"I hear you sarge, we have the same tunnel diggers in Manhattan. If anything pans out, I'll see to it that you guys get your due."

Once back in his unmarked car, Fogel looked at the photos. He immediately telephoned his old friend Detective Sheridan.

"Sherry boy, I might have something for you regarding the big redhead with the Adams apple that you're looking for."

"You do! No shit, what have you got?" asked Sheridan excitedly.

"We identified somebody fitting the script you gave me."

"You got a picture?"

"Don't ask silly questions, it's in my pocket as we speak," answered Fogel smugly. "I got a picture of him as both Dr. Jekyll *and* Mrs. Hyde."

"Terrific! Do you want me to come over and pick it up, Frankie?"

"Hell no, you ain't getting off that easy. I'm in the car on my way to you. How about we meet at Biff's Burger in half an hour? I'm simply *famished* after all this work."

"Okay, Frankie...you got it coming." Sheridan cupped the phone before turning to DeCesare, who was seated at the desk alongside his. "Looks like we're gonna have to feed this guy."

"What was that you said?" asked Fogel.

"Nothing," replied Sheridan. "I'm talking to my partner. We'll see you over there."

"You didn't think I was gonna let you off the hook easy did you?"

Sheridan ignored the question. "Frankie, before you go, the guy in the picture...what about his eyes? Are they crossed?"

"I am afraid not, Sherry. What the hell do you want for a burger?"

"Okay, just don't expect any dessert."

Sheridan turned his attention to Detective DeCesare, who was going through the latest mug shots of eye damaged perps he received from out of state agencies. "Is there anything good in that batch?"

Holding the pictures in his hands, DeCesare looked toward his partner. "I got two pictures in this mailing...one male and one female. Both have screwed up eyes."

"How many does that make now?"

"With these, we're up to sixteen."

"How many has Jeanette already looked at?"

"All but these I have in my hand. I'm about to call her up to see if she's available."

238

"Hold off on that call," said Sheridan. "We have an appointment in fifteen minutes to see a man about a guy who could be our perp."

"Really," said DeCesare anxiously. "What have you got?"

"Don't pop a nut just yet, this guy isn't cross-eyed. C'mon, let's get going."

BY THE TIME DETECTIVE FOGEL arrived at the restaurant, Sheridan and DeCesare were already seated. Wasting no time, Fogel went straight to their booth and tossed an envelope containing Everett's photos and pedigree information on the table.

"I got this from an anti-crime sergeant in South Brooklyn," he said. "Make sure you guys include him in your report if this goes anyplace. They picked up this clown in front of a schoolyard where some kids were playing round ball. They figured him to be up to no good, so they rousted him."

Sheridan opened the envelope and removed the photos. He then passed the envelope to DeCesare, who removed a sheet of paper containing Everett's information. "He lives in Manhattan," noted DeCesare.

"Just take a look at these pictures, it'll be hot shit if this really is our boy," said Sheridan.

DeCesare looked at the photos. "There is nothing wrong with his eyes. Here, take a look at this note with his information."

Sheridan took the paper from his partner. "It says here that he's a city worker. He's a school teacher. Can you believe it?"

"I'll notify Sergeant Markie about this."

Sheridan balked at DeCesare's suggestion. "No, no, no, hold off on that. Wait until our last day tour and we'll show Jeanette a photo array," said the senior detective. "This way, if we get a hit, we can work into our days off."

DeCesare didn't like the idea of procrastinating. "Wait for what?"

"Relax, partner. Trust me on this," said Sheridan. "On our last tour we'll shoot for the identification from Jeanette. If we get a hit, we'll go find the perp, do a line up, the works. We might as well make some overtime on this."

DeCesare wasn't thrilled with Sheridan's motives, but he remained silent. As a new man in the squad, he felt it best—begrudgingly—to acquiesce. The senior detective could see by the look on his partner's face that he was unhappy.

"Don't worry," assured Sheridan. "There will be plenty of time to call Markie once we got the perp all wrapped up with a bow on his head." He turned to his old friend Fogel for support. After giving Fogel a wink he said, "Help me convince him, Frankie."

"Sherry is talking good sense, kid," said Fogel in a fatherly fashion. "Sometimes, too many cooks spoil the broth. Never allow yourself to get lost in the shuffle. Do it Sherry's way. If things work out, then everybody knows it was *you* who cracked the case, and *you* did everybody else a favor by calling them in to share in the pat on the back *you* earned. Plus, you'll make a few bucks. The other way, with you tipping the task force off first, *they* take charge, *they* grab the perp and *they* get the glory."

"And sometimes the promotion to boot," added Sheridan. "Don't forget that."

"Right," agreed Fogel. "We learned a long time ago that there is no upside to being an afterthought. Make the most of your chances when you get them."

As DeCesare was digesting this advice, a waitress came over to take their order.

"What'll it be gentlemen?"

"You call it, Sherry Boy." Fogel said, smiling at his old friend.

"Three cokes and three burgers," said Sheridan, with a pained look in his face. Then, turning to his partner DeCesare he said, "We're splitting this bill, we have to treat Detective Fogel here for doing his job."

"You haven't changed a bit, you old piker!" said an elated Fogel.

Before the waitress could jot down their order, everyone's attention was drawn to a table a short distance away. A scuffle had broken out between two young men in wheelchairs. Both were swinging wildly, trying to land blows. A woman at their table, also in a wheelchair, screamed at the dark haired man, who was by far the more aggressive combatant.

"STOP IT JOE!" she shouted frantically. "WHAT ARE YOU DOING?"

The blond man, his wheels now turning away from his adversary, was getting the worse of the exchange. The detectives rose to their feet to quell the ruckus. Fogel removed the blond battler to the front of the eatery, while DeCesare took charge of Joe.

As the two combatants were cooling off, Sheridan took the opportunity to speak to the woman who had been at the center of the dispute. It soon became evident to the detective that the twenty-seven-year-old was not just well spoken, but also appealing. Her long light brown hair was stylishly cut, her eyebrows just so. Judging by the gold adornments that decorated her neck and ears, a degree of affluence was apparent. The low-cut lavender top she wore was filled out nicely.

"So what started this *Thrilla in Manila*?" asked Sheridan.

"Ohh, it's a long story," she replied.

"Go on, I'm listening," said the detective.

"This all started last night with Joey, he's the dark haired one."

"And you are?"

"I'm Marlene."

"Go on, Marlene"

"Jeremy, the blond boy, came in from California to visit me yesterday. He's a friend I went to college with. Last night, he was at my place. We were sitting on my waterbed, *just talking*, when Joey came in unexpectedly."

"He broke in?"

"He's got a key."

"I see, so you *gave* Joey the key to your apartment? He didn't clip it from you?"

"No, I gave it to him years ago. He's my boyfriend."

"Oh, boy," commented Sheridan, seeing where things were going.

"Exactly," she said with a slight laugh. "Oh boy is right! Joey is the *extremely* jealous type. You can't imagine how he can get."

"I think I can. He seems to have an antiquated perspective," said Sheridan sardonically.

"You think?" asked Marlene with a chuckle.

"So once Joey sees you and Jeremy a-sea on the love boat, the bell for round one goes off. Then what happened?"

"It was no love boat," she corrected. "We were just talking."

"It really makes no difference," said Sheridan, "it's all about perception. Please continue."

"Joey started screaming at the top of his lungs. It was a big scene, with people from the building coming in to intervene. I live in this high rise where things have to be just so."

"So how does this spill over into today, Marlene?"

"We were supposed to all meet, the three of us, and straighten things out. Well, things flared up when Jeremy jokingly said that he only kissed the hollow of my elbow. When Joey heard that he went off. You saw the rest for yourself."

Amused by the story, Sheridan shook his head. "Are you going to keep Joey around?"

"I don't know, he has such a temper," she replied lazily. "I'm not quite sure anymore."

"So take your key back and tell him that you don't want him to call you anymore," suggested the detective.

"But I want him to call me," she admitted shyly.

"Well, do you like the other guy, what's his name again...Jeremy? You like him too?"

"I do, but I consider Jeremy more of a friend," she confided.

"So you *still* care for Joey then?"

"Yes, I really do."

"I'm just curious, why Joey over Jeremy?"

"He makes me feel special, and he's fun. I never know what he's going to do next."

Sheridan understood. "I get it. I guess starting a riot would remove any lulls."

"What do you think I should do?" she asked.

The detective cut to the chase. "Does your family like Joey?"

"Oh yes, they like Joey a lot."

"He works?"

"Of course he works, he does very well. He's a cartoonist."

"Does he get violent with you or anything like that?"

"Oh no, he never gets crazy with me."

"Okay, so he's never abusive to you?"

"No. He's always very good with me. If anything, he's *over* protective."

"Alright, then show a little respect for Joey and ship the other guy back to California."

Her eyes opened wide. "What can I tell Jeremy?"

"Tell him next time to mail you a letter," advised Sheridan. "Just be upfront and let him know he's out and Joey's in."

Things calmed down once Jeremy was sent on his way. Marlene and Joey returned to their table alone to sort out their problems quietly. Sheridan looked over at them every once in awhile to see how the couple were progressing. He watched with satisfaction as they continued on with their meal as if nothing occurred, amorously engaging in smitten behavior between bites of hamburger. The manager of the eatery took a moment to stop by the table to say thanks.

"This check is on the house," declared the manager. "Come over and take this order," he said, after signaling the waitress.

"Burgers?" she asked.

Sheridan spoke up quickly. "Give us three Dewar's on the rocks and three hanger steaks with all the trimmings." He was happy as a lark once he knew the cost of the meal was going to be on the arm.

26

Horse Play

"Slurp"

-Aging Gray Horse

EVERETT'S KILLING OF HIS LANDLADY, which came on the heels of the Pergamint Bakery attack, was to be his most complex assassination of all. By the time the teacher finished eating Frieda's leftovers he had devised a plan of action. Leaving Frieda to be discovered in her apartment would bring the law too close for comfort. With so few tenants, he was bound to be questioned. With that there would be risk of the law discovering the summons he received in Brooklyn, a red flag that that might lead to further scrutiny. Frieda needed to do a Houdini, regardless of the labor involved.

"*Do a good job cleaning up, dear,*" reminded the good voice.

"Don't worry, I know what I have to do," Everett assured his mother.

Everett remembered seeing a vintage Westinghouse Coca-Cola cooler in the cellar. It was a massive chest, one large enough to serve as a temporary coffin. He retrieved the landlady's key ring from a hook on the kitchen wall and locked the apartment. He tiptoed up the stairs to the other apartments and placed an ear to each door. Once satisfied that everyone was tucked in for the night, Everett returned downstairs and slid the deadbolt on the front door to restrict access into the building. He then ventured to the cellar where he found the electric cooler still on hand. After plugging it in, he was relieved to hear it humming.

Everett perused the cellar to identify other useful items. A wooden work desk and an abundance of old tools were on hand. Several heavy-duty hand saws, all showing signs of rust, hung off large nails that were imbedded into the stone wall above the desk. There was a six-foot cast-iron trough sink against the rear wall of the cellar. The teacher turned on the faucet to test if the water would flow smoothly down the drain of the deep sink. It did. Everything the teacher needed to dispose of Frieda he had at his disposal.

Everett returned to his own apartment to retrieve a box of heavy-duty commercial trash bags from the storage area beneath the kitchen sink. Several plastic drop cloths were on hand as well as general purpose tape. After depositing these items in the cellar, he returned to the apartment of his victim. Steadying his legs, Everett hoisted the body of his landlady onto his shoulder in a fireman's carry. He took his victim down to the basement. Lifting the top off the cooler, he gently lowered Frieda into it. The landlady was tiny enough for him to close the lid. Before leaving, Everett secured the cellar door using another key on the ring he'd confiscated. Before returning to his apartment, he slid open the deadbolt on the front door, again allowing access into the building. As far as Everett knew, the widowed landlady had no family. This allowed him to assume it would be a long time before anyone noticed her missing.

Once back in his own apartment Everett opened a bottle of seltzer. He sat in front of the television catnapping until it was time to call in sick for work.

NOW ARMED WITH THE NAME EVERETT SKIDMORE, Markie and Inspector McCoy agreed that a meeting of all the investigators involved in the strangulation murders was in order. The first person notified was Detective DeCesare.

"DeCesare...it's me, Sergeant Markie.

"Yeah sarge, what's up?"

"It looks like we finally got a break on these serial killings."

"You did?"

"Yeah, it looks like we may have your boy in the bakery case identified."

DeCesare's mouth dropped. "Really?" he asked with some hesitation. "Who is he?"

"Some teacher named Skidmore. You guys are working tomorrow, right?

"Yeah, we're doing a day tour."

"Okay, I want you to plan of staying late tomorrow for an all hands on deck meeting at your squad. I'll get authorization for the overtime. I'll see you tomorrow at the squad at about 7:00 p.m."

"No problem, boss. I'll be here waiting."

"It'll be all hands on deck. I'm ordering in every squad detective who caught one of these homicides to be there. Reach out to your complainant. I want to have her available for an ID when we take this guy down."

"Okay, boss. What about Sheridan? You want him there also?"

Markie thought about it for a moment before answering. "Alright, might as well invite him to the party."

Shortly after hanging up the phone DeCesare heard his stomach begin to make odd noises. He was fretting over what was going to happen once Markie learned that he and Sheridan had been withholding information. DeCesare turned to where his partner was working. "Sherry, the task force feels they identified the perpetrator in the bakery case."

"You have to be kidding me?" said a stunned Sheridan.

"No, I'm not kidding you."

"Who do they think did it?"

"Who do *you* think?"

"Don't tell me...Skidmore?"

"Correct answer."

Sheridan immediately regretted the decision he'd made to hold back the information they received from Detective Fogel. "What are the freaking odds of that happening?" It was all the detective could think of saying.

VON HESS WAS IN THE HABIT of driving with the window down. He did this in order to be able to hear a citizen cry for help. His elbow rested casually on the window ledge as he engaged Markie in conversation. Stopped at a light, the detective turned to the sergeant to clarify a point being made by his boss.

"What was that you said, sarge?"

"I don't see a rosy future for this department," repeated Markie. "Did you see the number of retirements this month?"

"Yeah and It's a real shame," replied Sheridan. "We were once the most sought after job in the city. Nobody ever looked to retire."

"I'm sorry to say that ship sailed."

"I can't understand what these politicians are thinking. We're the only thing holding the bad guys at bay."

Markie let out a deep breath. "I guess it's a lesson to be learned the hard way. When the tiger is rendered toothless, I'm afraid to even think of what will happen."

As they were complaining over the state of affairs, a carriage pulled by an aging gray horse crept up alongside their car. The curious horse began shaking its head, expressing an interest in the unmarked police vehicle. Von Hess, who was now talking, had his back to the animal. Markie kept an eye on the horse, while at the same time, listening. The size of the nag's head seemed tremendous in comparison to the window opening. The sergeant, seeing what was coming, was unable to warn Von Hess in time. He could only watch as the horse stuck its long snout into the window to nuzzle Von Hess. Startled, Von Hess quickly spun around in his seat. As he faced the horse the detective was greeted with a wet slurp. Von Hess felt the warm moisture from the animal's floppy pink tongue as it made its way into his mouth and nostrils.

"WHAT THE..." yelled the startled Von Hess, throwing himself to Markie's side of the vehicle.

Somehow from his awkward position, the detective managed to maneuver the car away from the huge animal. The visibly shaken nvestigator rolled up the window as he drove off, getting far away from the carriage horse. Markie laughed hysterically, but it took several blocks of travel before Von Hess himself saw the humor in the incident.

❖

BACK AT POLICE HEADQUARTERS, Detective Silverlake walked into Inspector McCoy's office with several papers requiring his signature. "These are for your John Hancock, boss."

"Anything doing?" asked the inspector.

"Sergeant Markie called for you."

"Why didn't he call me direct on my cell?"

Silverlake hunched his shoulders. "Search me, boss."

The inspector reached out to Markie with a frown on his face. After their conversation a delighted McCoy emerged from his office a very different man. It had been awhile since the last time Silverlake saw this side of his boss.

"Detective Silverlake," announced the inspector officially, "go get us two big cups of black coffee," he instructed.

While tempted to update the chief of detectives with the news he received from Markie, McCoy decided to wait. He felt it wise to postpone his victory whoop until after the task force had someone in cuffs. For now it was safer to celebrate with a healthy blast of Irish coffee with Silverlake.

27

Coming Together...And Apart

"BINGO!"

-Inspector Harry McCoy

EVERETT LEFT HIS APARTMENT very early in the morning. Dressed in his oldest casual clothes, he took an uptown train to the Bronx where he rented a U-Haul van. He felt renting the vehicle from a location where he wasn't known to have any ties, would be a prudent thing to do. While in the Bronx, he pulled the van over to purchase a dozen newspapers. Upon returning to Manhattan, the teacher parked at a meter close to his building. He'd have to feed the money gobbler of course, but paying for metered parking was the least of his concerns.

After ascertaining that the other tenants had gone off to work, Everett marked time for an additional thirty minutes, just in case someone happened to return home for some unforeseen reason. The science teacher then proceeded to the basement, where he spread a plastic drop cloth along the cement floor near the sink. Everett next selected the tools he needed, placing them neatly atop the work desk. He put on work gloves before lifting the lid to the cooler that contained the body of his landlady. The teacher scooped out the cold body and transferred the corpse into the spacious trough sink. Everett placed an old towel over Frieda's face, to avoid looking at her.

Through trial and error, Everett identified the proper implements to use for the dismemberment. As the tap water flowed, he soon realized the task at hand was more complicated than he'd imagined. To complicate future identification of his victim, Everett snipped off each of the landlady's ten fingers with a bolt cutter. Unscrewing the heavy iron cap that sealed the hole that accessed the sewer, Everett dropped the digits in, along with the victim's wedding band. He then screwed the cap back on, satisfied that the insects who populated the sewer would do their part. Everett went on to encase each detached body part within newspaper, as if he were wrapping fish. After securing the paper by taping, the teacher placed the wrapped parts inside doubled up green industrial garbage bags. Everett was careful to keep the bags light in order to prevent their breaking. Completed bags were placed in a line against a corner wall, where they would remain until it was time for transporting to the waiting van. After hours of work, all that remained was the landlady's head, which Everett put into a five-gallon plastic bucket he'd found in the cellar. Affixing the lid to the bucket symbolized a form of closure for the mentally ill teacher, who then placed the bucket into its own independent bag. Everett took pains to be thorough in the clean up process. When he finished he returned to his apartment.

After showering, Everett put on a comfortable purple track suit. Famished, he put on a pot of coffee to have with the fried egg sandwich he prepared for himself. After eating he proceeded to jockey the trash bags from the cellar to the parked van. Once loaded, he took a slow drive to the Pine Barrens in New Jersey where he dumped the heavy-duty commercial trash bags. By the time he returned the van to the Bronx and got back home, Everett made up his mind to take another sick day. He needed the rest.

"*You earned a holiday, dear,*" chimed in the good voice of Adele.

With the ordeal behind him, Everett turned his thoughts to a more pleasant activity to pursue. He was thinking in terms of enjoying the company of a woman. His first thought was of Doris, but he soon dismissed her as an option. The combination of Doris, Stan and his wife Iris amounted to expectations to high for this particular time. The murdering teacher wasn't in the market for heavy lifting. Instead he was out for a quick release, a sure thing just to take the edge off. *In and out*, that was the ticket. He drew upon an old flame that he considered more suited for what he had in mind. The teacher picked up the small leather book he kept on the end table next to the phone. Taking a seat on the couch, he leafed through the pages in search of her number.

"Here we go," he said, picking up the phone.

After making his selection he soon heard the discouraging voice of his mother. "Oh, please, Everett! Not that one! She's absolutely impossible that girl!"

"She isn't so bad once you get to know her."

"Then do what you want!" snapped Adele abruptly, ending her end of their mental communication.

Everett rolled his eyes in frustration as the phone began ringing. "Hello, Trudy?"

"Who is this?" asked the woman on the other end of the line.

"It's me, Everett Skidmore. How are things, baby? It's been much too long."

Trudy was flabbergasted at receiving a call from a man she last heard from eight months prior. "Now isn't this a surprise! To what do I deserve *this* great honor?"

"I know it's been awhile, but I've had lots going on with my mother being sick and all."

"Oh, so how is *she* doing?"

"Fine...uh," said Everett catching himself. "I mean, actually she isn't. She passed away not long ago."

Without the slightest trace of sympathy, Trudy expressed herself bluntly. "Oh...so she's dead."

Everett never realized the depth of the animosity that existed between the two women. "Yes, she passed away recently," he said sadly. "I'm calling you because I really miss you. I'm hoping that you could join me for dinner. How does tomorrow look?"

"Thank you, but I have prior plans."

"No problem, I understand that this is short notice. When are you available?"

"After *all* this time...I don't hear a word from you? *Now,* I'm supposed to drop everything and have dinner with you?"

"You have no idea; I've had a lot on my plate."

"Goodbye, Everett. I'll talk to you again when somebody else dies and you need a shoulder to cry on." Trudy's hang up was abrupt and definite.

Everett was of the opinion that Trudy must have lost her mind. "Something must have happened to disturb her psychologically," he said, addressing Adele. He scratched Trudy's name out of his book.

"Good riddance to bad rubbish!" commented Adele. "That's all I can say."

❖

DECESARE AND SHERIDAN WERE trying to figure a way out of the predicament they were in. "The only chance we got is to make it seem like we just received the information from Fogel," said the scheming Sheridan.

DeCesare was annoyed at the suggestion. "You really think compounding this with a lie is the best way to go?"

"What else can we do? We can't get away with showing Jeanette the photo array now." DeCesare offered no response. Sheridan got the message and dropped it.

The meeting with Markie was still a long time off. Sheridan began reading over a new complaint report concerning a past assault when the office phone rang.

"Detective Sheridan, how may I help you?"

"Sheridan...it's me Jake."

"Hey Jake, what can I do for you."

"Listen. I think I got a line on that guy."

"You do...the cross-eyed guy?"

"I don't know for sure about that part, but I got word there is a guy comes around by the basketball court near the West 4th Street subway. He's supposed to be a big man who dresses like a woman."

"You know the guy?" asked Sheridan.

"I never seen him, but Mohammed has his stand there...he sees him. Mohammed said the guy watches the games once in a while."

"Mohammed? That's the hot dog man with the long beard, right?"

"You got the right guy, but he sells falafels, I sell the hot dogs."

"Same shit. He's out there now?"

Jake wasn't too happy about Sheridan's comparison. "My hot dogs are the best you can get. The company that produces my hot dogs has the finest reputation in the industry. You can't get better..."

"I know that Jake, you carry the best. But tell me, is Mohammed out there now?"

"Mohammed's not there now because of the rain. He's only out there when the weather is nice," advised Jake.

"Thanks Jake, I owe you one."

"Say Sheridan, do you think I can get a detective card for my wife?"

"You got it, Jake—I'll stop by with one later in the week."

"Beautiful!"

Sheridan hung up. "That was Greasy Jake," he told his partner. "He said our wig-wearing friend might be a guy who hangs out at the basketball court on Avenue of the Americas."

"That fits. Jake saw him there?" asked DeCesare.

"No, Mohammed the falafel guy did."

"I guess we should go talk to Mohammed."

"Yeah, but he's not out there now. He's only there in fair weather."

DeCesare looked out the window. "You know what, Sherry, it looks like its clearing up. Let's go look and see for ourselves. I'm going crazy just sitting around here waiting."

"Yeah, I hear ya. I could use some air too," agreed Sheridan.

The detectives arrived at the court expecting it to be empty. They weren't disappointed. A few people were briskly walking along the street, mostly entering or exiting the subway. There was no sign of Mohammed. Rubbing his chin, Sheridan realized that he could use a shave. If he was going to have to face the music, he figured he might as well look good for the concert.

"Take a drive by the barbershop over on West 3rd Street. I want to see if I can grab a quick shave," said Sheridan.

The detectives parked the squad car and entered the barbershop. The proprietor was seated in one of the barber chairs reading a newspaper. At eighty-five, he was still giving trims and shaving a few of the old timers in the area. The shop looked pretty much the same as it had sixty years earlier. To the left of the front door was a vintage motorized horse that could still offer a ride to anyone with a coin that fit into the slot.

"How are you doing?" announced Sheridan loudly, startling the old barber.

Recognizing the detective, the business owner responded. "What happened?"

"Nothing happened. How about letting me jump the line for a shave?"

"What...you want to start a riot with this crowd?" the barber asked, making light of his lack of customers. "C'mon, sit in the chair," he said. "I'll clean you up nice."

"You feeling good?" asked the detective.

"I'm still here, ain't I? Where's Gallo been?"

"Gallo retired," replied Sheridan, referring to a former partner.

"Retired? He can't be retired, he's too young!"

"He got tired of working,"

The barber applied a crisp white covering over his only customer of the day. He then adjusted the barber's chair low, and then far back, elevating the detective's feet until they were almost higher than his head. DeCesare watched the process with some degree of interest. The younger man never received a shave from a barber with a straight edge razor.

With a hot towel placed over his face, Sheridan closed his eyes and tried to think relaxing thoughts. "You of know any cross-eyed people around here?" asked the detective.

"Yeah, Ben Turpin," answered the barber, naming the silent era comedian.

DeCesare watched the barber apply shaving cream to Sheridan's face. It was then that he noticed his trembling fingers. "Well how about this! This old buzzard has the shakes," thought the young detective.

DeCesare looked on with trepidation as he saw the barber's quivering hand hold the straight edge razor up to his eyeglasses. After his examination of the instrument, the hair cutter slowly brought down the razor and began scraping. Amazingly, he never drew blood. DeCesare thought Sheridan was lucky to get away with his nose.

The barber nonchalantly re-lathered the Detective's face for a second go-round. When the risky business was concluded, Sheridan felt refreshed thanks to the coolness of the after-shave application. Touching his now smooth chin, the detective was satisfied.

"Nice job. What's the damage my friend?" asked Sheridan.

The barber waved his hand dismissively. "Give me what you want."

"Thanks," said the detective, not giving the old barber anything. It was only after Sheridan saw the barber strike a match to light his cigarette, did he realize how far the Parkinson's progressed.

Once back inside the unmarked car, DeCesare was unable to resist mentioning to his partner how close a shave he actually received. "You are a lucky man, Sherry," advised DeCesare. "The old man has the shakes. His hand was jumping like crazy."

"Yeah, I know. The poor bastard's been like that for a while. Parkinson Disease, it gets progressively worse. But you can't beat his prices. That's one thing that doesn't change."

MARKIE STOOD AT THE HEAD of a long rectangular table inside a small conference room. Von Hess, DeCesare, Sheridan, Billings, Perez, St. Clair and Rhodes were all present. The only one yet to arrive was Inspector McCoy. The room was without amenities: no overhead screen, no beverages, no pads, pencils or pens. Just gray armless metal chairs around a gray metal table. The detectives sat quietly enveloped in their own thoughts as they awaited the inspector's arrival.

Detective Billings was confident that there would be no surprises in the Doctor Culbrenner case. She felt her time was being wasted. For Detective Perez, he saw success in the Thelma Curcio candy store murder as a potential path into the homicide squad. Detective St. Clair wondered why such a fuss was being made over some real estate bimbo who was foolish enough to go with the wrong guy. Detective Rhodes was eager to discover the common thread that linked Martha O'Sullivan to the other victims. What was the motive? The causation factor both fascinated and challenged him. DeCesare and Sheridan were beyond thought as they sat glumly in their seats awaiting a possible unpleasant fate.

When Inspector McCoy arrived, he stood at the back of the room. With his arms folded across his chest he waited for silence. When it came he signaled Markie to start the meeting. For the sergeant it was payback time.

"We're all here because we're close to wrapping this up. Let's briefly run through the cases one at a time so that we're all on the same page. Ollie, you take some notes."

"No problem, Sarge," Von Hess said.

"Okay. Let's start with the first strangulation. Detective Billings, talk to us about the Doctor Culbrenner case."

Detective Billings shifted in her seat. She wasn't comfortable being called on first. Fearing that she might be sandbagged by Markie, she tried to pin him down. "Do you want to hear anything specific or just a general overview?" she asked.

"Just give us a nutshell version of the homicide." His answer provided little guidance.

"The crime was committed during the evening hours when the doctor was alone in her office. There was no indication of a robbery, no forced entry. The perp could have pushed his way in, been let in, conned his way in, or snuck in unnoticed during business hours. The victim was beaten before being strangled. No witnesses, no evidence, no motives and no leads."

Markie's opportunity to embarrass Billings had finally arrived. He simply nodded after she gave her summary. "Ollie, fill us in on what slipped through the net."

Von Hess didn't particularly enjoy this payback aspect of his job. "We re-interviewed the doctor's office manager. She said that the doctor was having no problems of any kind, personal or professional. According to her there was no history of disputes, no money issues, no substance abuse problems and no marital heartaches."

Billings exhaled loudly. "I already established that," she interrupted. "I told you when you came to the squad, that I already interviewed the woman."

Markie looked directly at the detective, savoring the moment. She reacted as he knew she would. The sergeant was happy that the detective had now drawn further attention to herself.

"Lois may have neglected to mention a couple of things to you," said the sergeant, displaying the same gloat she had once given him. "Go on Ollie, let's have the rest."

Von Hess continued. "The doctor supposedly didn't have the greatest bedside manner. So, we took a look at her appointments."

"Oh, shit," thought Billings to herself. She could almost feel the egg on her face.

The people in the room stirred as Von Hess revealed the information he and Markie gathered concerning Adele and Everett Skidmore.

Inspector McCoy asked Von Hess the most obvious question. "Are his eyes crossed?"

"No inspector, Everett Skidmore has perfect eyes, according to the office manager."

Detective Billings sat at the table doodling with a stern look on her face. Her ego now jarred, there was no denying that she wasn't a happy camper. Markie felt that he now settled the score with the detective. He was now prepared to move forward with Billings as if nothing happened. Markie was the sort who needed to avenge any slight or insult…regardless how trivial. Once this was accomplished, then all was back to normal.

"Do you have any address on Skidmore? Anything else to run with?" asked McCoy

"No exact address yet, Inspector, replied Von Hess. "However, the office manager felt sure that he lives someplace in Manhattan. He works as a science teacher. We got a tentative address from DMV."

Sheridan and DeCesare looked at each other briefly, not saying a word. Markie moved on to the Thelma Curcio candy store homicide.

"Detective Perez, talk to us."

Perez was eager to participate. "The victim is an older woman who was accosted in her East Harlem candy store. She was temporarily blinded with some kind of spray before being dragged to the rear of the store and strangled. No witnesses, no apparent motives. We have no physical evidence other than spray samples taken off the store counter. The lab people believe the killer likely concocted the mixture himself."

"Don't forget Edna," reminded Markie.

"That's right, sarge. Edna is a bird that repeats a lot of what she hears. The bird was in the store when the victim was attacked. We heard the bird, firsthand, repeat things that we suspect the killer said when with his victim."

"The bird was an African Grey," injected Markie.

"How did you arrive at the conclusion that the bird spoke the words of the killer?" asked the inspector.

"According to the victim's father, the bird never said certain words before. Since the victim's death, this bird had no opportunity to hear anyone speak without the old man being around. We suspect that the bird learned these *new* words *during* the commission of the homicide," explained Perez.

"What exactly are these new words?" asked McCoy.

"Specifically of interest is the name *Mrs. Trapani*. We've been looking into that name. I checked around the precinct to see if anyone knew the name and came up dry. The name never made it into any police report either. Detective Von Hess identified all the female Trapani's in New York City. We're still in the process of reaching out, but as of yet, no headway has been made. Right, Ollie?" Von Hess nodded in the affirmative.

"Thanks, Perez. OK, murder three, the real estate woman. Detective St. Clair?"

St. Clair, who had displayed no prior interest in the task force or their work, was now visibly nervous due to the lack of effort he'd put into his own case. He addressed the room as someone with limited knowledge. "The victim was a young woman who was strangled in her apartment after she took some guy home. The scene was wiped clean of prints. That's about the size of it. We got no suspects, no nothing." The detective secretly hoped that the results of the task force's work wouldn't be any more informative.

Markie turned to Von Hess. "Ollie, update us."

"We identified the bar where the Johnson girl was drinking. The victim got stood up on the night she was killed. According to the bartender, she ends up licking her wounds with another guy, who she winds up taking home. The relief pitcher leaves the victim's apartment a relatively short time after he gets there. It's nighttime, and the man holding down the lobby desk sees him without a tie on and wearing sunglasses when going out the door. The victim is later found strangled in her apartment."

"Could the first guy be involved...a jealousy thing?" asked McCoy.

"Nothing indicates that boss," answered Markie. "Ollie, give us the rest."

Detective St. Clair shrunk further into his seat as Von Hess continued. "We got two people who actually saw the suspect. The bartender who served drinks was one, and then later, the concierge in the building where the victim lived. They both describe the guy the same way, well dressed in a suit, gray hair, over six feet and in his 50s. This pretty much matches the script of the dead patient's son in the Doctor Culbrenner homicide."

"Did anyone say anything about the eyes?" queried Inspector McCoy.

"We got nothing concerning the eyes, up and down the line," answered Von Hess.

McCoy was disappointed at that. "Any other information gathered?"

"Yeah, boss . . . the bartender remembered the victim's pick up as being a well-spoken man. He overheard him talking about playing basketball in Harlem."

"I have something to add," said Markie. "We conducted a canvass of the schoolyards. There's a teacher in East Harlem who plays basketball with his students. This guy fits the script of our subject. Supposedly he always plays ball with sunglasses hanging from his neck, so they call him Sizzling Shades."

"Continue, sergeant," said McCoy.

"Homicide four was Mrs. O'Sullivan, the usherette. Detective Rhodes, you got the floor."

The detective read off his note pad. "The homicide occurred outdoors, during the evening hours in Midtown. She was a senior citizen found inside a dumpster in a vacant lot. Tiny red particles of red material were removed from the neck of the victim. Her nephew is a local gang leader who did his own homework. According to him, the perp isn't a known entity from the neighborhood. The task force gathered additional information. Do you want to talk about it, Ollie?"

"No, you can do it—you know the story."

"No problem," answered Rhodes, who was glad to have the floor. "The deceased was an usherette at the Bigelow. A woman who worked with her observed a man who matches the description of the suspect we've been talking about. He was at the theater the night of the homicide. The usherette said the man and the victim collided into each other inside the theater, causing his drink to spill. After giving the victim a dirty look, he abruptly leaves the theater in a huff, looking down at the floor as he scoots out. He made his exit wearing dark sunglasses."

"Do we know what kind of drink he was having?" asked the inspector.

"No inspector, we don't," injected Von Hess. "But the witness remembered seeing the guy in the past at the theater accompanied by a woman believed to be his mother. It couldn't fit better with what we already have."

"Okay, sarge, let's get to the last homicide," said Inspector McCoy.

Markie resumed. "The last time the perpetrator struck there were two attacks that both occurred in a West Village bakery. Detective DeCesare, take it from there."

DeCesare was clearly nervous. "One incident was attempted murder by strangulation of a woman at her business and the second was the shooting death of a handyman in a makeshift studio apartment located in the back of the store. The perp left the woman for dead, urinating on her before he made his getaway. The surviving victim believes she previously was attacked and groped on the street by the same person, when the perpetrator was dressed in drag."

McCoy looked at DeCesare. "What's the evidence?"

"The perp wore gloves so all we have are body fluids." replied DeCesare. Regarding the handyman, we have ballistics."

"Any bites with the sketch? Is there anything coming from Sex Crimes?"

"There were no bites regarding the sketch, inspector. The description provided is consistent with the other cases, with a couple of twists. This surviving victim insists that the perpetrator is severely cross eyed," said DeCesare, "*and* a cross-dresser."

"You buy that?" questioned McCoy. "Could she be mistaken? Or could there be a second perp?"

"I don't think she's mistaken, Inspector—she is pretty adamant on who she saw."

"What about there being a second perp?" McCoy was looking at Von Hess, but Von Hess turned to Markie for an answer.

"It doesn't seem likely, inspector," replied Markie. The sergeant then turned to Sheridan, "Anything else?"

Sheridan sighed deeply: the moment he was dreading had arrived. "We just got this in from my friend over in sex crimes, sarge. An anti-crime team in Brooklyn South stopped a guy who was dressed in drag. He matches our suspect. This character was watching kids playing basketball in Brooklyn." Sheridan swallowed hard before continuing. "They took him into custody thinking he might be some kind of pedophile."

"How did all this come out, again?" asked the sergeant.

"The Brooklyn anti-crime sergeant notified sex crimes, who notified us."

"When was this?"

Skipping over the question, Sheridan offered an alternative answer. "We got two photos of the guy, sarge. One is of the suspect as a man and the other of him dressed as a red-headed woman."

The pictures were a potent distraction, enough to draw the attention away from *when* the detective gained this information. Sheridan passed them to Markie. "Here, look at these, boss."

After looking the pictures over the Sergeant gave them to Von Hess to pass around the table. "So they arrested this guy?" asked Markie.

"They gave him a summons for disorderly conduct," said Sheridan.

"Who exactly did all this?"

"An anti-crime team in Brooklyn snatched him after seeing him around kids playing basketball."

"So he's a pedophile?" asked McCoy.

Sheridan shrugged. "That may or may not be the case, inspector. That's what the cops originally thought, but they ended up giving him just a summons. Luckily for us, they were smart enough to take the pictures and then call sex crimes."

"I want you to get me the names of the anti-crime people, Sheridan," said the inspector. "They need to be officially recognized if this pans out."

"So who exactly *is* this guy in the picture?" asked Markie.

"Everett Skidmore," said Sheridan sheepishly. "He lives in an apartment above a liquor store on Tenth Avenue here in the city. He was born on June 26, 1947, has no prior's *and* he's a schoolteacher in the city someplace."

Inspector McCoy jumped up from his seat shouting, "BINGO!"

"So exactly when was it that you came up with all this information, Detective Sheridan?" asked Markie coldly.

"Not too long ago sarge, we were waiting for the next meeting to tell everyone."

"Precisely how long is 'not too long'?"

Sheridan began to stir in his seat, stalling. The sergeant looked over to McCoy. The inspector shook his head in a way that indicated that Markie should let it go. Since Sheridan was not technically one of his men, Markie didn't argue about overlooking the detective's selfish play.

As it turned out Sheridan was surprised to see that there were no repercussions.

What he didn't know was that with Markie, there would be another day down the road for squaring their account.

"Inspector, it looks like we have our man. Do you want me to run with the ball or leave it to the individual squads?" asked Markie.

"See it through," answered McCoy. Then, he tersely addressed Sheridan and DeCesare. "If you like where you work, I suggest from here on out you operate as a team."

"Yes sir," answered Sheridan sheepishly. His response was echoed by DeCesare.

McCoy turned to Markie. "Take it home—let's grab this son-of-a-bitch and get it done now. I'll be sleeping over in my office waiting to hear something from you." McCoy departed the room happy as a pig in slop.

"Okay, we all heard the man," said Markie. "It's our time to play some basketball of our own. Let's start with a full-court press. Ollie, you and I will hit the street to talk to those anti-crime folks. Maybe there is more of a story connected to that—if there is, I want to know about it."

"Righto, boss," answered Von Hess.

"DeCesare and Sheridan, you two take these photos and make copies of them to distribute to everyone working the case. Then make up a photo array with this character, *as a man*, and show it to Jeanette Pergamint for the identification."

"You got it," acknowledged both detectives.

"Remember this, call me *immediately* after she sees that photo array. I'll give you further instructions once that's done." Markie turned to Detectives Perez and Rhodes. "You two sit on the perp's apartment over the liquor store. If Skidmore comes out, I want you to stay with him. If you see him going into the house, let him go. I prefer not to grab him until we have a positive identification. Call me every hour, even if you don't see anything."

"Got it," said Rhodes.

"Okay, let the games begin! We have to try and wrap this baby up before this lunatic hurts somebody else." declared the sergeant.

Detectives St. Claire and Billings had been written out of the script. The two detectives felt as if they were placed in the corner of the room, facing the wall while wearing a dunce cap. They watched in silence as everyone left to carry out their assignments. Now frozen out, they had no choice other than to return to their respective squads wishing things could have been different.

28

Heading For Home

"THAT'S HIM! NUMBER FOUR, YOU FOUND THE
BASTARD!"

-Jeanette Pergamint

EVERETT NOTICED THE POOR CONDITION of the ties hanging in his closet. All were red, with the exception of the sole black one he wore for somber occasions. It occurred to him that the ties he used in his strangulations could be incriminating evidence. He took the red ties to the kitchen, where he removed a scissors from a shelf over the sink. The teacher went on to cut up the weathered fabrics into small pieces. He then divided the scraps of cloth into three plastic bags, mixing them in with leftover food waste. After doing this, Everett, who was casually dressed in athletic wear, headed out for the long walk to a midtown clothing store. He disposed of the plastic bags one at a time, making deposits into public trash baskets every few blocks.

Arriving at the clothing store, Everett quickly selected three new red ties. Two were made of silk and one of wool for the winter months. With the ties in hand, he proceeded to browse the store. His attention was soon drawn to where the dress shirts were on display. A canary yellow three button had caught his eye. Although he favored traditional whites, he took a moment to examine the garment. It was the only color reduced in price.

"Hmmmm, there must be a reason for this," he muttered to himself, "probably not selling well this year."

"*That isn't for you, dear,*" said the good voice, "*it's way too loud. I think it best that you stick to white or a light blue.*"

"Just looking," he whispered in response.

Everett noticed that a salesperson was looking at him. She was a dignified-looking woman with a polite smile. She walked toward him taking smooth, even strides. Everett found her attractive in the navy blue suit she wore. The outfit seemed a little snug on her, pronouncing her figure. Her dark straight hair was neatly combed back. It was cut short, with some graying visible at the sides.

"May I be of service to you, sir?" she asked. "I'm not sure if you noticed, we have some wonderful short sleeve shirts that are on sale. We have them in several lovely colors."

"No thank you, I'm just looking."

"Why of course, sir. I'll be by the counter if you need assistance," she advised pleasantly.

"Would you ring these things up now, please."

"Certainly, please follow me," she said in a cheerful, sing-song voice. "Would you like the ties gift wrapped?"

"No, thank you. Excuse me, I hope you don't mind my saying so, but the outfit you have on is very becoming."

"*Everett, she is way too old for you!*" scolded the good voice. Adele was unhappy about his sending out a feeler.

The saleswoman was flattered that Everett noticed. Over the years, she experienced more than her share of retail Romeos, but it had been a long time between compliments."

"Why thank you, sir!" she answered, smiling broadly as she rang up the transaction.

"Here are your ties, receipt and change. Please *do* come again...I'm Cecelia."

"Cecilia, now that's a lovely name." Everett began whistling a melody of a long forgotten song by that name.

"Oh, no!" she said laughingly. "How could you possibly know that song?" she asked. "It was my mother's favorite song."

Everett smiled. "I may be back for that shirt. In the meantime have a wonderful day."

"You can't be serious about that woman, dear!" voiced Adele.

"I was just being nice," the teacher replied to his mother as he headed for the door.

Cecilia came from behind the counter to watch Everett leave. She couldn't help but wonder if he'd really be back. She was hoping he would.

The day had become iffy in terms of the weather. Everett decided to take a leisurely stroll downtown along Avenue of the Americas anyway. When he reached the schoolyard in the West Village he wasn't surprised to see that there wasn't a basketball game underway. He stopped to treat himself to takeout from a Chinese restaurant before heading home. Once there he fell into the recliner in front of the television. He eventually dozed off after eating a container of pork fried rice, two eggrolls and a soda. It turned out to be an early night for him.

DETECTIVES PEREZ AND RHODES DRANK coffee as they staked out the residence of Everett Skidmore. Armed with a picture of their target, the team locked themselves in for what figured to be a long night. Due to the hour, the chances were high that their prey was already inside his apartment for the night.

"Why can't we just knock on this guy's door and see if he's home?" asked Perez.

"Markie wants the identification made before we take him into custody," replied Rhodes. "I concur that your way would probably expedite matters considerably. A line up at the squad could easily be conducted once we have him in handcuffs. However, there *is* one benefit to doing it Markie's way."

"What's that?"

Rhodes smiled at Perez. "We'll earn a substantial amount of overtime."

Perez considered this. "You know what, maybe that's probably *why* Markie wants it this way," he said.

Rhodes looked at Perez and smiled. It amused him that Perez spoke as if he just unraveled some complex enigma.

❖

DECESARE RIFLED THROUGH DOZENS of old arrest photos before he came across five acceptable blue-eyed men in their 50's with gray hair. These, along with the photo of Everett, made six—the desired number for the photo array he was preparing.

"Hey Sherry, are you ready to take a ride over to the bakery?" asked DeCesare.

"Let's go," answered Sheridan. "You know, the more I think about it, we really got off easy at that meeting, kid. I'm sorry for making the wrong play."

"Forget it. It turned out to be no big deal anyway. It's not like the perp's in the wind someplace."

"No, I messed up on this one," admitted Sheridan. "I never thought the task force would come up with anything. I figured we could've wrapped up the case on our own."

"Let's just hope we get the identification."

"This ID should be a lock, with or without the eyes. I'd bet the ranch on it."

Just as the two detectives were preparing to leave the squad the telephone on Sheridan's desk began to ring. The detective picked up the phone. "Detective Sheridan, how may I help you?"

It was the precinct desk lieutenant, advising that a man named Falcon was in the lobby asking for him. "You could send him up," said Sheridan, recognizing the name.

The lieutenant looked down from his perch at the neatly dressed man "Take the stairs up one flight. You'll see the sign for the detectives. What business is it you said you were in?"

"I own Falconetti's Pasta House."

"You *own* Falconetti's?" asked the lieutenant, quite impressed. "That's the best restaurant in the precinct."

"Thank you, we think so. You should come by sometime. You people are always welcome."

"I may just do that. Look, if you need anything, and I mean *anything*, don't hesitate to let me know," said the lieutenant handing him a business card.

"Thank you."

Sheridan greeted his visitor as soon as he entered the squad room. "Hey Falcon, how the hell are you my friend?" asked Sheridan, with great animation.

"I'm good." The visitor, noticing that DeCesare was in close proximity, lowered his voice while talking to Sheridan. "Can we talk a minute privately?"

266

"Sure thing, hang on a second." Sheridan called over to his partner. "Gary, I'll meet you downstairs as soon as I'm through here."

"No problem, I'll be outside waiting," answered DeCesare.

Once they were alone, Sheridan devoted his full attention to Falcon. "What brings you here, my friend?"

"It's like this. I found a couple of hand grenades stashed in my restaurant."

"Hand grenades!" said the astonished Sheridan. "What the hell are you doing with those?"

"I'm having some renovations done in the upstairs room and one of the workers found a tin box in a drop ceiling. When I opened it up I found the grenades. I was hoping it was money."

Sheridan didn't balk. "No problem, let me just ask you a couple of things. "Did the grenades belong to someone in the family or a friend?"

"I got no idea. It's the first time I've ever seen them. They were probably kept by my father as a memento from the war."

"What was he in, World War Two?"

"It wasn't exactly that kind of war," answered Falcon sheepishly.

Sheridan thought it best to cease with the questions. "Let's keep it simple by distancing you from the grenades altogether. I'll take care of it," assured Sheridan.

"What are you going to do?"

"I'll toss them in the drink. I'm in the middle of something right now, so hang onto the grenades until I come by one day next week. I'll dump them in the East River for you."

"That's it? I could do that myself," said Falcon.

"No, if you get caught doing that you'll have a headache. Leave it to me."

Grateful, the restaurant owner nodded his appreciation. "Come by the restaurant one night and bring your wife. I got a nice Veal Osso Buco waiting for you."

"What I really go for is your pasta fazool," said Sheridan.

"Pasta fazool? That's peasant food, I got veal for you!"

"Whatever...just don't worry about anything. Leave it me to take care of this problem for you."

Once the restaurant owner was sent on his way, Sheridan joined DeCesare in the unmarked car. "What did that guy want?" asked a curious DeCesare.

"He wanted a reference for a cousin of his who wants to come on the job."

"Are you going to do it?"

"Certainly not, I told him I'd like to, but I just can't. It wouldn't be right without me actually knowing the kid," said Sheridan.

"How did he take it?"

"I don't think we'll be eating in Falconetti's anytime soon," said Sheridan with a straight face. "You got the photo array, right?"

"Yeah, I got it," said DeCesare, who then took a slow drive over to bakery to see Jeanette Pergamint.

JEANETTE PERGAMINT WAS IN A SURLY MOOD. Forrest's observations regarding the emerging pattern of large wholesale stores offering bakery product was not something she wanted to hear. This set the stage for bickering over their American Express bill.

"How many more holes in our belt do you think I can honestly punch?" asked Forrest, responding to his wife's suggestion that he tighten up on expenses.

"Well, you're supposed to be the genius—you tell me what else we can do?"

"What more can we possibly do, Jeanette?" he asked. "We already extended the hours we're open. We can't work around the clock can we?"

"Cut down on your expenses," she suggested, not having a better answer.

"*Cut my* expenses? Are you joking, I'm using the same razor blade for a month!"

"So grow a beard!"

Since Jeanette's assault story was now old news, business again suffered. Without relief, her only option in order to make rent was to go along with the sexual demands of Rudy the Hunch. Tapping her fingers on top of the store counter, she cast a frosty glare at Forrest as he began to re-straighten items that were already straight. At this moment the pressure she was under caused her to only see imperfections in her husband, the most critical being his inability to pull them out of their financial bind. The tension didn't escape Forrest, who turned to a broom and dustpan for relief.

"I'm going out to sweep the front sidewalk," he announced.

Jeanette remained silent. "Look at this loser, all he can think to do is sweep up. What am I doing swimming with a jellyfish in shark filled waters?" she asked herself.

As the shine on Forrest continued to dim, Jeanette was finding herself drawn to things macho, as opposed to intellectual. She begrudgingly admitted that her military father might have been right all along in his low opinion of Forrest. Even Rudy, who she might have to accommodate, was seen as having more substance to him.

As Forrest swept the front he considered divorcing his wife. When he looked up to see where the shadows on the sidewalk were coming from, he was surprised to see Sheridan and DeCesare standing in front of him.

"Hello Mr. Pergamint, you guys are open pretty late," said Sheridan.

"Yeah," answered Forest in a subdued tone. "The way business has been going, pretty soon we'll be advertising buy one, get one free discounts."

"Has it been that bad?"

"Worse than bad, Detective Sheridan, it's been worse than bad."

268

The wheels began turning in Sheridan's head. "You know, I have some friends in the restaurant businesses around here. I might be able to get your desserts in some places."

"That would be absolutely terrific, detective," said Forrest, jumping at the opportunity to energize his business.

"We'll work something out once this case is behind us."

"Definitely," replied Forrest.

"Is your wife around?" asked Decesare.

"She's inside. It's kind of late for you guys, is everything alright?"

"Everything is just fine. You may want to join us for this," suggested Sheridan.

The greeting the detectives received from Jeanette was one laced in cynicism. "Don't tell me you have more pictures of the wrong person for me to look at."

"I won't comment just yet, Jeanette. I just want you to look at this one photo array I have for you," stated DeCesare.

Jeanette sensed that DeCesare was onto something. He was too serious for this to be just another routine viewing of photos. After viewing the array Jeanette's reaction could be heard in the street.

"THAT'S HIM! NUMBER FOUR, YOU FOUND THE BASTARD!" she shouted, her heart racing as she grasped DeCesare's arm in a vice-like grip.

"Are you sure Jeanette?" asked the detective.

"Am I sure? A thousand percent I'm sure!"

"But Jeanette, look at his eyes. They aren't crossed," pointed out Forrest.

Jeanette turned on her husband viciously, releasing all the hostility that was bottled up inside her. "His eyes are *blue,* aren't they?" she shouted in a flash of anger. "Cross-eye or Pop-eye, I'm telling you that number four is *definitely* him!"

"I'm just saying—"

"Will you please stop it, Forrest? Did you ever think that the bastard could have had his eyes corrected?"

"That's good enough for us, Jeanette," said Sheridan.

"So what happens now?"

"Just sit tight and be patient a little longer. Go get yourself some sleep. We're going to need you later. We'll come around to pick you up about five or five-thirty, and don't worry, we'll grab him in the morning as soon as he shows his face."

"Okay, I'll be waiting."

"Keep your cell phone on just in case we need you before then," instructed Sheridan.

"Don't you worry about that, I'll be right here waiting for the phone to ring!"

After the two detectives left the bakery, Jeanette was in a more positive frame of mind. Their assurances of an arrest overshadowed all of the other negativity. It even put into check her current low opinion of her husband.

269

MARKIE COULDN'T GET ALLEY CAT out of his mind. His not hearing from her was beginning to concern him. He was worried that he might have overplayed his hand. Concerned that he might lose her, he decided it was time to dial her number.

"Alley?" he asked softly.

There was a hesitation on her end of the line. After several seconds, she responded with a testy "WHAT?" In truth, she was actually relieved. She'd been hoping he would call.

The sergeant came at her in an unexpected way. His intention was to catch her off balance. "You got your bags packed?" he asked.

She was perplexed by the question. "Packed for what?"

"For the trip we're taking."

"I'm not going on any trip with *you*," she replied, her voice losing a little of its bite.

Markie could sense the thaw. "Look...ok, I'll admit it. I was dead wrong. What can I tell you?"

"How about starting with how sorry you are."

"I'm sorry for the nasty crack. I'm *very, very* sorry. Do you still want me to walk off a pier?"

She ignored his question. "Why would you say such an awful thing like that to me?" she asked. "It was really hurtful."

"Let me make it up to you. What do you say to us taking an overnight trip to Atlantic City?" Alley loved to gamble—Markie was baiting her with the one temptation he knew she would find hard to resist.

"Atlantic City?" she asked, then adding skeptically, "With what?"

"My overtime check comes in next week! Think about it, multiple-handed video poker! We'll play the machines, craps or whatever. It'll be fun, fun, fun!"

Alley was a sucker for his silliness. Besides, her loneliness ran concurrent with her desire to gamble. The combination made forgiving him easy.

"When do you want to go?"

"As soon as I wrap up the case I'm working on, which should be very soon."

"I can only go on a Sunday and Monday." she said.

"That's fine, figure on our heading out Sunday. Are you around tomorrow?"

"I might be."

"If you are, can I come by?"

Alley took several seconds before replying. "I suppose so. Does Chinese food work?"

"I'll bring it over with me. General T's for you?"

"That's good. Don't forget the egg roll and Won Ton soup."

"You got it, see you tomorrow."

"Okay, see you tomorrow."

"Hey Alley…"

"Yeah?"

"You know, I really…uh, never mind I talk to you tomorrow."

After hanging up the phone Alley Cat decided to coat her fingernails and toes bright red. It was Markie's favorite color. His hesitation in revealing what was in his heart spoke volumes. Now, for the first time, she realized that she had the elusive sergeant hooked. It would just be a matter of time.

29

Sina The Cat

"She said Everett told her that her grandmother's cats were her evil soldiers. Adele and I thought that was just hysterical, you know, coming from such a little boy and all."

-Joan Adeline Trapani

MARKIE WAS ANXIOUS TO HEAR how DeCesare and Sheridan made out with the photo identification. While confident that the results would likely be positive, a shred of concern nevertheless existed. When the phone finally rang he couldn't pick up the call quick enough.

"We got a positive hit on the photo ID, sarge," advised DeCesare.

"Beautiful." Markie felt that a weight had been lifted from his shoulders. "Hang on a second." He turned to Von Hess, who was driving. "We got a hit, Ollie."

"I figured we would," replied the detective.

Markie returned to his conversation with DeCesare. "Tell the complainant that you and Sherry will be back to pick her up at 5:30 A.M."

"It's already done."

"Good...after you pick her up, I want you to set up in the vicinity of where Skidmore lives on 10th Avenue," directed Markie.

"See if he wants us to go knock on Skidmore's door later if he stays inside. DeCesare relayed the message to Markie as told.

"No, no, no. I want an eyeball identification made on the street. Just wait for Skidmore to come out of the house and have Jeanette make the identification when he's walking along the avenue on his way to work or wherever," directed the sergeant. If he fails to make an appearance we'll figure out what to do later. Remember, when he does come out just wait for Jeanette to let you know she spotted him. I don't want a tainted ID."

"DeCesare was put off a bit at the explicitness of the sergeant's instructions—he didn't like being treated like a rookie. "What do we do until it's time to pick up the complainant?"

"Whack it up with Perez and Rhodes. You guys take the first break and then give the other team a blow while you hold down the fort at the house. I want all hands on deck with the complainant by 5:45 a.m."

"What if the perp leaves for work before the witness gets here?" asked DeCesare.

"That's not likely. This is a weekday, so he's probably working normal school hours. But, in the event of that happening, we'll have no other choice but to take him into custody," instructed the sergeant.

After hanging up with DeCesare, Markie telephoned Inspector McCoy to advise him that things were moving along nicely. McCoy indicated that he would remain in his office all night awaiting further good news.

"McCoy's a happy camper, Ollie."

Von Hess shook his head. "Since we're looking at an all-nighter I better call the wife."

"Good idea."

It was moments like this that Markie reflected on days past when he had someone to call with such news. He was on the fence as to whether or not he missed being compelled to check in with a wife. Sure, he had Alley and she certainly cared, but by his way of thinking their relationship fell short in comparison to the obligation that came along with marriage.

❖

INSPECTOR MCCOY CLOSED THE DOOR FOR PRIVACY. As was his custom, he used his private office as his man cave for the night. Optimistic that a successful conclusion was just hours away, he turned on the radio. He was in the mood for some easy listening music. He kept the sound level just audible enough to hear. He was hoping to hear the soothing voice of the crooner Perry Como. He always managed to put McCoy to sleep. After stripping down, he slipped into the cotton pajamas he removed from the footlocker he maintained in his office. He also removed a beat-up pair of terrycloth hospital-socks, a small pillow and two blue bed sheets. Sandwiched between the sheets he made himself comfortable on the office couch. The inspector curled up with a rare first edition he picked up in a secondhand bookstore the week prior: the 1927 novel *Patrol* by Phillip MacDonald. It was a story about a party of cavalrymen fighting snipers in the Mesopotamian Desert.

The inspector had some difficulty concentrating. After every page, his mind returned to the pleasure he intended to reap after informing Chief Randolph of his investigative triumph. No longer were there concerns about banishment to some roach-infested basement in a remote part of the city—or even worse, facing a forced retirement. After a while, the book slipped down onto his chest, with McCoy gradually succumbing to the relaxing sounds emanating from the radio. With slumber came a tale of heroics, as he dreamt of his evening the score with enemies that had been picking off members of his platoon in the desert.

❖

WHILE THE DETECTIVES STAKED OUT Everett's residence, Von Hess and Markie met with Sergeant Fulton, the anti-crime supervisor in Brooklyn. Fulton, who was working evenings, willingly fielded Markie's questions.

"Did you notice anything unusual about Skidmore's eyes?"

"Like what for instance?"

"Were his lamps crossed in any way? Did he have some kind of visual disability?"

"His eyes were fine," replied Fulton.

The answer disappointed Markie. "In talking to Skidmore, was there any other information that you learned about him? Like where he worked, his interests, stuff like that."

"He mentioned that he originally came from Yarrow Street in Bedford Stuyvesant."

Von Hess suddenly came alive. "Wait a minute! I remember seeing that street on my Trapani list. Let me take a quick look at something." Von Hess opened his notebook, where he kept a folded printout of people named Trapani stapled to the inside of the back cover. "Here it is sarge...118 Yarrow Street. It's the home address of a woman named Joan Adeline Trapani," said Von Hess.

Markie looked at his watch to check the time. "It's getting kind of late. How far is Yarrow Street from here?"

"If you a make some noise with the siren you can get there in probably ten or fifteen minutes, maybe less," replied the anti-crime sergeant.

"Let's saddle up, Ollie." Markie then turned to Fulton, "Inspector McCoy said he's going to write an attaboy letter for you guys."

"Be sure that he sends it to our captain, we could use it."

Taking the red lights, Markie and Von Hess made it to Yarrow Street in less time than expected. The block was dark, desolate and depressed. A flashlight was used to make out the faded address numbers on the stoops. The address in question was one of just a handful of residential homes on the block. It was clear that the three-story building had been long neglected. Most of the steps on the stoop were chipped. The front iron entrance gate, the exterior fence, and the first-floor window bars all showed signs of peeling and rusting. Several window screens were torn from past hailstorms. The wooden cellar board was crumbling.

Von Hess rang the bell, hoping it was in working order. "They may be in bed already, sarge."

"Talk about a dump," commented Markie.

"Yeah, it is pretty crappy here."

"This block is like a ghost town in a B-western. I'll bet coyote's run around at night."

"On two legs," quipped Von Hess.

"Try banging on the window, Ollie."

"I did hear the bell ring, so I know that it's working."

Inside the house sitting at her kitchen table was the eighty-four-year-old Joan Trapani. Living in a high-crime neighborhood taught the senior citizen to always be on her guard—especially since the death of her husband years prior. Living in the building alone, her greatest fear was of an overnight break-in. As a result she long altered her sleeping habits. Joan would go to bed at daybreak for a few hours, then nap on and off as necessary in an easy chair throughout the rest of the day. Wide awake, the senior citizen was scanning the obituaries, looking to see if anyone she knew died. She was having coffee and eating a small bowl of cornflakes when she thought she heard the doorbell ring. She rose from the table to see if there was anyone out front. As she moved toward the front door, she placed her hand on the loaded revolver she kept in the pocket of her cooking apron. The handgun had been in the family for years, originally belonging to her father-in-law. The weapon later became the property of her late husband Tom without the complication of any legal formality. Once Tom was gone, she naturally assumed custody of the revolver, viewing it as *an* equalizer when facing those out to victimize her.

When Von Hess saw a figure at the window he held up his badge announcing his authority. Seeing two men in suits, the old woman went to the front door inclined to believe they were the law. Bringing her face to the iron door, she peeked through the spaces with her finger firmly on the trigger of the secreted revolver.

"Yes?" she asked through the door holes.

"We're looking for Joan Adeline Trapani."

"I'm Joan Trapani, what do you want with me?"

"Do you know anyone named Skidmore?"

"What was that name you mentioned?"

"SKIDMORE," repeated Von Hess in a louder voice.

"Oh, Skidmore, I didn't hear you. Of course, I know that family. They lived across the street years ago. What happened? Did Adele die?"

"Could we come in to talk to you, or could you come outside so we could explain to you why we're here?" asked Markie.

"You could come in. Just let me see your badge."

Von Hess placed his shield and ID card against the hole in the gate. Through squinting eyes she satisfied herself that she was talking to the police. She opened the gate for the detectives and led them into the living room. After inviting them to sit down, she offered them something to drink. Markie took a seat on the couch while Von Hess sat in the chair that was once the favorite of Joan's late father-in-law.

"You sure you don't want something to drink? How about a soda? I have some nice beer…Miller High Life." Starved for company, Joan was only too glad to entertain the investigators now that she felt safe.

"No thank you, Mrs. Trapani. You're in this house a long time, aren't you?"

"Oh yes, since I first got married to my husband He was a good man my Tom, it's hard to believe he's been gone so long." Shaking her head, she sadly added, "Now I live here alone."

"Tell me, did you know Everett Skidmore?" asked Markie.

"Oh dear, yes, of course I know Everett. His mother and I were *very* good friends. They lived just across the street from here. I was sick when they moved away. Their house is an empty lot now—they knocked the building down. I don't know why, it was a perfectly good house."

"Did you stay in contact with them after they moved?" Markie asked.

"Only a little bit at the beginning, by phone. They moved far, all the way over in New York someplace. I hope you aren't going to tell me that Adele died."

Von Hess put a serious face on. "Yes, I'm afraid Adele did pass away, a little while back."

"Oh, I'm so sorry to hear that. I didn't see any death notice in the paper. She was such a good woman, and how she doted on her son! That boy was all she had, you know."

"So you knew Everett then?"

"Of course I knew Everett. He used to play with my daughter Leslie when they were children. You know, Adele was a very attractive woman. Even though she was a very big woman, she could have remarried anytime she wanted to. A lot of men like large women, you know."

"So it was just the mother and son?" asked Markie.

"Just the two of them," she confirmed. "She had her opportunities, Adele did. Even the grocer wanted to marry her. But she never married because she didn't want anything to get between her and her son. Everett was illegitimate you know. Adele once told me that his father was some merchant marine who came and went."

Markie tried to get a word in. "I see, what about—"

"My Leslie moved to New Jersey—to Toms River—with her husband. She's got her own family now."

"I see. So, can I ask—"

Joan again interrupted. Continuing to drift, she steered the conversation in other directions. "I have two grandchildren, a boy and a girl. Leslie has been after me to move to Jersey, but I don't know. It's not always a good idea to live with in-laws."

"Did Everett have eye problems?" asked Von Hess, trying to get back on point.

"Everett? No, I never heard of him needing glasses, if that's what you mean. But he was crazy for sunglasses though. I remember him always wearing dark glasses, even as a little boy."

"Did *you* ever have a problem with Everett?"

"Me? Oh, no never," she replied. "Is he in trouble?"

Von Hess shot a glance at Markie. "Was he a bad boy or a good one?"

"I always thought he was a good boy, although my Leslie told me how all the kids in the neighborhood were afraid of him."

"That's interesting. We had heard that he might have had a problem with a Mrs. Trapani," advised Von Hess.

She paused to think a moment. "Oh, wait a minute. You must mean my mother-in-law."

278

"Her name was Trapani also?"

"Yes, of course, Alfonsina Trapani. Everybody called her Sina for short. She's been dead for many, many years."

"What was the problem between Everett and Sina?"

"My God, that story is so old—older than dirt, even," she said. "Leslie and Everett were about four or five at the time. They were playing outside in the backyard here. Sina was very peculiar and a very old-fashioned thinker."

"I see...." said Von Hess.

"It took Sina a long time to warm up to me, but her husband was very gracious right from the beginning. The Trapani side of Tom's family was much easier to get on with."

The detectives realized that she was again drifting. "Tell us more about Sina's problem with Everett."

"Sina just didn't like the idea of boys and girls playing together period, so she scared Everett off one morning in the yard."

"How did she accomplish that?"

"All it took was for her to give him one dirty look, if I remember right," laughed Joan, recalling the incident. "She might have even said something nasty; I'm not too sure what exactly happened. But I do know Sina never hit him or anything like that."

"And?" asked Markie.

"Like I said, that's all it took. Everett flew out of this house as if his pants were on fire! That kid was terrified of Sina. You know, he never would come back into this house."

"No kidding."

"My husband was very annoyed at his mother over that, and he was a man who never went against his mother. Sina always felt guilty about what she did. She tried her best to make amends with that boy, but Everett wouldn't hear of it."

"What did Everett's mother have to say about all this?" asked Markie.

"What was there to say? We all felt terrible over it—we were good friends remember. But I do recall Adele telling me that Everett thought Sina was a witch or a crone or something like that. Adele and I had a good laugh over that because we joked that the child was probably right."

"Did Leslie ever say anything else about Everett?"

"Well, now that you mention it, yes. You know what Leslie told me?"

"What?"

"She said Everett told her that her grandmother's cats were her evil soldiers. Adele and I thought that was just hysterical, you know, coming from such a little boy and all. What an imagination." Von Hess and Markie exchanged looks as the old woman continued. "And you know something else...I have to be honest," Joan let out a small laugh. "Sina *did* love her cats and she *could be* a miserable old lady at times."

"Was Everett ever violent, to the best of your knowledge?" asked Markie.

279

"Well . . . he might have killed a cat once. He was about eleven or twelve by then."

"Tell us about that."

"You sure you don't want something to drink? I'll put on a pot of coffee…" Joan was so enjoying the company of the investigators that she was looking to extend their visit.

"No thank you, we're sort of pressed for time and it is getting late. We don't want to keep you up. Please continue about the cat."

"Keep *me* up? Don't you worry about that, I'm up all night."

"What was that about the dead cat?"

"Dead cat?" she asked, forgetting for a second. "Oh, yes, Adele's landlord was an old man from the other side. He was the one who told me that he saw Everett around the corner on Park Avenue, standing alone in one of the empty lots. He said he called Everett from the sidewalk to make sure he was okay."

"What was wrong with being in a lot?" asked Markie.

"Well, around here you always had to look after each other, especially where kids were concerned. It's always been that kind of a neighborhood."

"I understand, but tell us about the lot. What was Everett up to?"

"Oh, yes. Well, Adele's landlord went into the lot to see what Everett was doing. He said that Everett was standing over a dead cat that had been cut open. He said Everett had a bloody knife in his hand."

"Did the landlord say anything else?"

"He told me he asked Everett what happened. He said that Everett told him that the cat was Sina, or it was her cat or something like that. I don't exactly remember."

"You don't remember what he said exactly?"

"The old man was sometimes hard to understand, his English wasn't the greatest."

"I suppose he's no longer alive . . . ."

"Do you know how old he would be now? He was 40 years older than me for God's sake. He ended up going back to Italy to die. He had a wife over there."

"Did anyone else know about this story?"

"No, I never said anything to anyone because I wasn't even sure if it was true. The old man was a little off, so I didn't know if he was just trying to be funny. I never mentioned it to Adele or even my husband. I didn't want to hurt Sina's feelings, or cause any trouble, so I just let it go."

"Did the landlord tell Adele?"

"I don't know, but I doubt it. Adele would have probably told me if he did."

"So you think the landlord was just trying to be funny?" asked Markie curiously.

"Maybe he was. You know after that, every time I saw that old man, he'd ask me if I counted all the cats. He had an odd sense of humor, that one," she recalled.

"Thank you for your time, Mrs. Trapani," said Markie. "You've been very helpful."

"You are very welcome. Come by whenever you are around here. I don't get too much company. People are afraid to come visit me."

"You know Toms River is a beautiful place to live Mrs. Trapani," said the sergeant in parting.

"That's what Leslie keeps telling me. It's not for me; there are too many bugs in the sticks."

Markie nodded. He hated bugs as well. When the investigators returned to their car Markie was the first to speak. "That cinches it, this Skidmore is a psycho."

"He must be," agreed Von Hess. "The cat, the grandmother . . . the whole thing is nuts."

"Yeah, but one thing still puzzles me—the eyes. With the eyes unexplained, there may remain a speck of doubt in the mind of some people. That piece to the puzzle is missing, unless of course this Jeanette is totally off base in saying that the perp is cross-eyed."

"I don't know boss—maybe she did make a mistake. Maybe he just *seemed* that way to her, or in the heat of battle his eyes shifted for a second."

Markie took a deep breath. "Yeah, I suppose that could be, but the accounts of the perp wearing sunglasses lends credibility to Jeanette's claim that the guy has eye issues. I'd like to tie up the loose ends, and that means getting to the bottom of the eye business."

"Know what worries me about this, sarge?"

"What?"

"That this psycho might figure he's got to keep going until he reaches nine."

"Nine?"

"A cat has nine lives."

30

Game Time

"I've got Everett Skidmore in a cell in the West Village. It all went off without a hitch."

-Detective Sergeant Al Markie

FORREST COULD SEE THAT his wife's impatience was getting to her...and to him. "Jeanette, try and relax, you have plenty of time." His advice went unheeded. In fact, Jeanette never even heard him.

Clutching a light windbreaker to her chest, Jeanette stood by the window of the bakery as she awaited her pickup. When the unmarked police car pulled up she rushed to join the detectives without saying goodbye to her husband. The thoughtlessness of her departure was hurtful to Forrest. Treated as if he were a nonentity, he stood at the window glass watching. Forrest finally reached a point where such slights were no longer tolerable.

"Here she comes," said Sheridan to his partner, as they watched Jeanette hurry to the car. "She's raring to go."

"Yeah, she's loaded for bear," answered DeCesare. He exited the vehicle to open the rear door for the complainant. Jeannette quickly slipped into the back seat.

"Good morning Jeanette," greeted Sheridan.

"Good morning. You guys couldn't get here fast enough for me."

DeCesare just nodded. "Well, it won't be long now. We're just gonna take a little drive. All you need to do is keep looking out that right window. If at some point you recognize anyone, you just let us know."

Jeanette was confused. "I thought you said you *knew* who he is."

"We suspect who it is, but we need *you* to make a positive identification. We don't want to influence you or be suggestive in any way."

The drive over to the residence of Everett Skidmore was made in silence. Jeanette knew what was expected of her, so there was no need for further conversation. Sheridan pulled up alongside the vehicle occupied by Detectives Perez and Rhodes. They were parked in front of a fire hydrant not far from Everett's residence. DeCesare exited the unmarked car to coordinate with the other team.

"Is there anything happening?"

"Nothing dong here," said Perez. "We checked the bells—his named is listed so he definitely lives here."

"I guess I should have done that first thing," admitted DeCesare. "Do me a favor, let's switch spots. I want the complainant to have an unobstructed view of the sidewalk."

Sheridan parked by the fire hydrant while Perez found another spot. Jeanette was instructed to concentrate on any people walking by on the street. The detectives were careful not to draw attention to exactly where Everett lived or the direction he would be coming from. Before long, people on their way to work began populating the avenue. When Everett finally exited his building, he appeared to be an average businessman on his way to work. Attired in a charcoal suit and signature red tie, he quickly blended into those already walking along the sidewalk. Detective DeCesare was the first to see the teacher. The others in the car, Jeanette and Sheridan, missed seeing him. DeCesare said nothing to alert the others, but kept his eyes fixed on the big man with the head of gray hair.

"Let's take a slow drive along the avenue, Sherry," said DeCesare.

Sheridan quickly realized that he must have missed his man. The detective pulled out and began creeping along the avenue. When he finally spotted Everett, he slowed up a bit.

At last, Jeanette noticed Everett's gray-haired head standing out above the other people walking along on the sidewalk. "LOOK...OVER THERE," Jeanette shouted, pointing to Everett. "I THINK THAT'S THE BASTARD!" She nervously began tapping the top of the front car seat in her excitement.

"Are you sure that's him?" asked DeCesare

Her adrenaline pumping, she yelled, "PULL UP FURTHER! HURRY, GET IN FRONT OF HIM, I WANT TO GET A BETTER LOOK AT HIS FACE!"

Sheridan pulled slowly ahead of Everett. Now, with a clear view of the killer's face, Jeanette made a positive identification. "THAT'S DEFINITELY HIM!" she declared, as Everett continued strolling along unaware that he was under observation.

DeCesare radioed the other team. "Subject heading northbound on the eastside of the avenue. He's got gray hair, a dark suit, and red tie. I'll be coming up behind him on foot. You guys bring your car over to where we were parked and pick up the complainant. Somebody take her home."

"On the way," replied Rhodes.

With DeCesare now on foot pursuing his man, Sheridan deposited Jeanette on the sidewalk, advising her to wait for her ride. "Nice job, Jeanette," said Sheridan. "The other team is coming to take you home."

The dismissal caught her by surprise. "That's it?"

"For now," said Sheridan, talking through the car window. Don't worry; we'll be reaching out to you later today. You'll see the DA and all that good stuff," he explained. "Here is your ride now," he added, seeing the other unmarked car pull up to his rear. After Jeanette got in the other vehicle Sheridan sped off.

"Detective Perez will take you home," announced Rhodes anxiously, before racing on foot to catch up with DeCesare."

Sheridan drove past Everett and pulled over about four-hundred-feet in front of his man. Double parking, the senior detective emerged from his vehicle and walked back toward Everett. He could clearly see DeCesare to the rear of Everett and Rhodes a little further back. With the killer now boxed in, the detectives moved to take down their man. Sheridan walked directly up to Everett, stopping about fifteen feet in front of him with his weapon drawn. Taking a police combat stance with both hands on his gun, the detective aimed the barrel directly at the chest of the startled schoolteacher. Using his most commanding voice, he loudly shouted, "POLICE! DON'T MOVE!"

Facing the barrel of a gun, Everett was sensible enough to comply. He stood motionless, waiting for further instructions.

"GET YOUR HANDS UP ON TOP OF YOUR HEAD...SLOW!" bellowed Sheridan, issuing his next order."

Everett lifted his hands gradually, careful to keep them in clear view. Just as he was placing his hands on top of his head, the teacher received an unexpected rush from the rear by DeCesare and Rhodes. The momentum of the detectives was force enough to propel Everett up against a parked car. Rhodes, who took hold of Everett's bicep, was surprised to see how solidly put together the teacher was.

"PUT YOUR HANDS BEHIND YOU!" directed DeCesare loudly, struggling to get one of Everett's now stiffened arms behind his back. Rhodes clamped a side headlock on Everett, using his full upper body weight to bend the schoolteacher's neck sideways. The pressure applied created enough leverage to bring Everett to the ground on one knee. Everett let his arms go limp, permitting the detectives to rear cuff him. After being patted down for a weapon, Everett was placed in the rear seat of Sheridan's police vehicle. DeCesare, as the arresting Officer, assumed a seat alongside his prisoner. On the drive to the precinct, DeCesare read Everett his rights. The prisoner remained silent throughout. The detectives were surprised that Everett didn't ask what he was arrested for.

Rhodes dialed up Markie from the car. "We got our man in handcuffs, sarge—the complainant came through like a champion. We're bringing him in now."

"Beautiful!" Markie immediately relayed Von Hess the good news."They picked him up, Ollie."

"Did he give them any trouble?"

"Apparently not, they're on the way into the station house and not the hospital."

"I'll put on a pot of coffee," said Von Hess.

Within minutes of the notification, the prisoner arrived at the squad. Everett was perp-walked to the squad while cushioned between DeCesare, Sheridan and Rhodes. Still rear cuffed, Everett was taken to a room where he was searched and relieved of his property. Markie and Von Hess remained on the sidelines during this process. Afterward, the prisoner was placed in the squad holding cell. With Everett now behind bars, Markie called DeCesare, Rhodes, and Sheridan into the squad commander's office, leaving Von Hess to keep an eye on the jailed prisoner.

"So is this guy all there or what?" asked Markie.

"I'm not really sure, sarge. He hasn't said a word since we pinched him," answered Sheridan.

"Where's the complainant?"

"Perez took her home after she made the identification," advised DeCesare. "She'll be available whenever we need her."

"Did you read him his rights?"

"I gave him his rights in the car," said DeCesare.

"Did he say anything?"

"Not a peep came out of him, sarge. He just nodded that he understood his rights."

"What about his eyes?"

"They're normal," said DeCesare. Markie looked at Sheridan and then Rhodes, who both concurred.

"Okay, let's try and get a statement out of him," directed Markie. "DeCesare, I want you to hook up with Von Hess to see what you can do with him. Rhodes, when Perez gets back, I want you both to go pick up your homicide folders and come back. The DA is going to want to talk to you guys about your cases."

"You want me to notify the duty captain on this, sarge?" Sheridan asked, looking to be useful.

"Not yet, let me talk to Inspector McCoy first. Why don't you see what you can do about getting the ball rolling for a warrant of the perp's house?"

"You got it, sarge."

Everett was taken out of the cell and removed to a private office where he was cuffed to a chair. Von Hess began the questioning. "Listen, you have serious charges against you. You must have known this was coming, right?" Everett remained mum.

"Don't say anything to them, dear," warned the good voice. *"Call a lawyer."*

"Do you know why you're here?" asked the detective.

Everett finally broke his silence. "In all due respect, I have nothing to say to you. I've done nothing to be ashamed of. I'd like to exercise my entitlements under the law. I'm permitted a phone call and an attorney...is that not true?" He sounded like a man well attuned to his rights.

"That's correct, but I'd like to—"

"Then I'd like my attorney to represent me immediately," demanded Everett. "Please let it be understood that I will not speak *until* I'm represented. I haven't done anything to be ashamed of."

It was crystal clear to Von Hess that Everett wasn't budging. "Alright, pal, you can have it your own way. Tell me, who is representing you?"

"Tobias Prescott."

"What firm?"

"The firm is Robin, Robin and Prescott."

"Never heard of them," DeCesare commented.

"Are you going to allow me my phone call?"

Von Hess pushed the desk phone toward Everett. "Knock yourself out, call whoever you like."

"I don't have the number," said Everett.

"Where is he located?"

"The firm is on Court Street in Brooklyn."

Von Hess secured the telephone number to the law office and gave it to the prisoner, who promptly dialed the firm. Since it was still too early in the morning for anyone to be working in the office, Everett left a message on the lawyer's answering machine.

Acknowledging defeat, Von Hess and DeCesare had no other option other than to return Everett to the cell. They went to the squad commander's office to fill in Markie.

"He clammed up on us, sarge," advised Von Hess. "He wants his attorney."

"No wiggle room with him?" Markie asked.

"Not this guy—he was adamant. Trust me, he's immoveable."

"Well that's the ballgame as far as a confession or a statement."

"Not quite, said Von Hess. "He did blurt out one thing. He said, and I quote, "I've done nothing to be ashamed of.""

Markie instructed DeCesare to make an entry in his report to reflect the statement.

"Be sure to include the date, time, location and the fact that the words were said after Miranda," reminded the sergeant. "Who knows, maybe those words will help the prosecution somehow."

"No problem."

"Sheridan is seeing about getting you a search warrant for his residence."

"Okay, boss."

Ollie, you reach out to the squad commanders where Billings and St. Clair work. Let them know what we have over here. They'll have to get their homicide case folders dusted off for the district attorney. Let's try to arrange this mess as orderly as possible."

"No problem, sarge, will do."

"One other thing—when Rhodes and Perez get back, I want them to canvass the eye doctors in the city. I want to see if this guy has had any corrective surgery. Also, send them out on a food run. Make mine a bacon and egg on a roll."

"Righto, do you want to feed the prisoner too?"

"Yeah, might as well see if he wants something to eat."

Once the office was cleared, Markie picked up the telephone to brief Inspector McCoy. The inspector was still in his pajamas. He had just finished giving his face a buzz with his electric shaver when his phone rang.

"McCoy," answered the inspector.

"It's me, Markie."

"I've been waiting to hear from you. What gives?"

"I've got Everett Skidmore in a cell in the West Village. It all went off without a hitch."

"Outstanding!"

"He called for legal representation right off the bat, so unfortunately we weren't able to get a statement out of him."

"Makes no difference, we got the identification and we got him. That's the key thing. So tell me, are his eyes crossed?" inquired McCoy.

"No Inspector, that's the one damn thing that doesn't seem to fit"

"Whatever. We got the identification. It's the DA's job to prove cases in court. What have you got going on now?"

"I'm getting all the paperwork together on all the cases for the district attorney. I'm also trying to get a warrant for the perp's apartment."

"Good show—keep at it and keep me informed." McCoy felt like breaking into a little dance before he dressed.

The inspector went to the office of Chief Randolph to convey the good news. Surprised at the early morning visit, Randolph looked at McCoy's happy face and knew he would be hearing good news.

"You solved it?" asked the chief.

"Johnny Boy—oops, I mean *chief*. Chief, I'm glad to report that the matter that had my skinny neck in the ringer can now be entered into the annals of the NYPD history books...case closed with arrest!"

"Excellent!" exclaimed the chief, glad to hear of the positive results. Without asking for further details, Randolph emerged from his chair with a wide grin. He stepped around from behind his desk with his arms stretched wide apart. The chief converged on McCoy with an embrace that could not have been any warmer. "I want you to know that I had no doubts about you coming through the storm, Harry!"

"You called for it and I got it done, John. It took some doing, but I got it done. I wasn't just talking."

"I can see that, Harry. But it took you to the damn eleventh hour to do it! Sit down my friend, *now* it's time for us to make some real plans."

This was what McCoy hoped would happen. "Thanks, chief."

"First off, I'll call the commissioner and tell him about how we kept things in the shade to avoid causing any unnecessary public alarm. He'll like that. Then, we'll plan to have a press conference. That'll be after the DA draws up the papers. Maybe it will be a joint press conference. We'll break the news to the public together, just so everybody gets a taste of positive exposure. It'll be the commissioner who decides that, though. Who knows, maybe even the mayor might want to get his own finger in the pie."

"Slick thinking John, real smart," said McCoy.

"You have to max out on these things when they come along, Harry," lectured Randolph. "Always be sure to offer the big guys a chance to share in the glory. That's something they'll always remember."

"I hear you on that, chief. How about we grab some lunch today?"

"Good idea...say noon?"

"Perfect."

"I'm going to let you in on a little secret Harry, something hot off the presses."

"What is it?"

"The commissioner announced to the mayor that he's stepping down at the end of the month. He's pulling the pin because he wants to spend whatever time he has left with his family. Do you know what that means for *us,* Harry?"

"I hope it's what I'm thinking."

"I got word from City Hall that I'm the mayor's choice for the PC's replacement. I've been asked if I had an interest. Can you imagine their asking me if I had an interest?"

McCoy smiled broadly. "Congratulations, John!"

"Thanks, Harry. Oh, and one more thing. Get ready to start packing. You'll be moving into this office."

A wry smile crossed McCoy's face. "Wonderful," he answered, as he tenderly rubbed the shamrock tattooed on his forearm.

31

LAWYERING UP

"I understand Toby. I still got some of the money we made as *partners.* You remember that arrangement, right?"

-Everett Skidmore

EVERETT WAS ALONE IN THE SQUAD holding cell. DeCesare had stripped him clean, relieving the teacher of everything except his clothing. Without sunglasses he would have to keep his eyes closed should he hear from Granny Trapani. The prisoner stretched out on the wooden bench inside the cell. He passed time by counting the number of off-white cinder block squares that made up the walls of his confined area. When finished, he inventoried the number of iron bars. His attention was diverted after hearing the voice of Detective Sheridan talking to his wife on the telephone. Everett looked between the bars and saw the detective banging away at a keyboard preparing a report while on the phone. He was speaking loudly into the device that was lodged between his neck and shoulder. The prisoner's eyes suddenly turned to a uniformed cop entering the squad with an elderly woman in handcuffs.

"I gotta go," said the detective, quickly ending the call. "What's all this?" he asked the officer.

"Felonious assault," announced the officer.

"Who the hell did she assault?"

"Her husband, she clocked him one upside the head with a frying pan."

Sheridan dropped his jaw and looked over his reading glasses at the officer. "How bad is the damage?"

The officer shrugged. "He's eighty-six and in critical."

"Do you think he's going out of the picture?"

"He might."

Sheridan exhaled deeply. The arrest meant more work for him. He now had to interview the prisoner and review the officer's arrest in order to tighten up the case against the old woman. "Put her in a chair and cuff her to the cell bar. I'll get to her in a minute."

Everett watched as the new prisoner was positioned with her back just outside his cell. The teacher pitied her for her age, her white hair, old housedress, battered pink slippers and the white socks that covered her feet. Everett nevertheless found her presence uplifting. The new prisoner reduced his feeling of isolation.

When Sheridan got around to questioning the woman he moved her next to his desk. Everett was attentive to the situation because it temporarily took his mind off his own problems. He was surprised to learn the female prisoner called the police on herself. Curious as to the specifics, Everett placed his ear against the bars, straining to hear more. As far as he could gather the prisoner was home cooking when fumes caused by burning fat consumed her kitchen, activating a smoke detector. Everett heard her explain to Sheridan that the ear shattering wailing of the alarm irked her husband. "He got all nasty with me," the prisoner could be heard stating. "He said I couldn't cook poop without setting off the damn alarm. Just like that, he said it. He's got no right talking to me like that and I told him so."

"I see," said Sheridan. "Then what happened?"

"He kicked me in my butt!" she replied with her eyes bulging. She lifted her chin in defiance as she conveyed the rest of the story. "That kick landed me on my fanny...and my tailbone is *still* hurting me."

"You need to go to the hospital?"

"No, but I just know it's gonna hurt when I have to go."

"I suppose it might. What happened next?"

"When he sat down I went behind him and gave him a good one with the frying pan. That's all there is to it. He won't be doing that again!"

"Everett winced as he imagined the pain. He felt for the woman—the very thought of striking a female repulsed him. He considered it unmanly behavior.

MARKIE SAT ALONE IN THE squad commander's office. Staring at the telephone there was little else to do other than pine for Alley. Since they recently spoke, he couldn't reach out to her again so soon without seeming like a pest—or even worse, needy. He had to settle for memories. As for the future, Atlantic City was on the horizon. That was something.

"GOOD MORNING MR. PRESCOTT," greeted the lawyer's secretary. In her late thirties, she was a neatly dressed brunette.

"Good morning," the lawyer replied, quickly stepping into his private office.

After a few minutes, the secretary entered the room with Tobias Prescott's usual breakfast of coffee with skim milk and a lightly buttered pumpernickel bagel.

"Any messages?" asked Prescott, who was now seated behind his desk.

"Yes, there were two on the machine. The first was from your friend in the garment district. Murray wants to know how his father's appeal is going."

Prescott frowned. "Who was it that left the other message?"

"Someone named Everett Skidmore."

"No kidding," said the surprised attorney. "Did Everett say what he wanted?"

"All he said was that he was arrested this morning by detectives in the West Village. He mentioned in his message that he needed you."

They were classmates. Their relationship began as teens who shared a mutual love of sports. Together Everett and Toby watched the Knicks from the rafters in Madison Square Garden and the Yankees from the bleachers. Their association developed into a business partnership. They spent their college years selling marijuana to fellow students. It was a way to help defray the cost of their education.

"So, you know him," said the secretary.

"Yes, of course I know Everett. He was a dear friend and classmate of mine back in my school days. He was handsome, strong as a bull and quite the athlete. We used to hang out together all the time," he said, reflecting back. "The girls went for him in a big way."

"Oh, he was another lady killer."

A slight smile formed on Prescott's face. "Let's just say I did alright with his spillage."

Prescott turned serious once it dawned on him that revealing their history could potentially damage his professional reputation. After law school Prescott began his career as a former Assistant District Attorney in Kings County. While there he established a solid reputation thanks to several high-profile convictions. Defense attorneys marveled at his ability to sway those in the jury box to his way of thinking. When courted by a firm in need of a capable trial attorney he jumped at the opportunity. From a financial perspective, it was the smartest decision the lawyer ever made. After achieving the status as the firm's biggest revenue producer, he negotiated a new deal which included a name partnership. Prescott knew that he had a lot to lose should his past be made public.

"It's been years since I've seen Everett. Do we know what he's being charged with?"

"No, he didn't mention the charges."

"I wonder if he's still a teacher. I can still picture him in those dark sunglasses he always wore."

"Do you want to hear the recording?"

"No, that's not necessary. Give me the number to the precinct. I'll call over there. Let's just hope he has some money."

The attorney, a short, long haired man with glasses, took out a pad and pen as he placed the call to the precinct. He stirred his coffee as the phone rang. Reaching the precinct telephone switchboard operator, he identified himself as the attorney for Everett Skidmore.

"What was the name of the prisoner again, counselor?" asked the officer.

"Skidmore, Everett Skidmore," repeated Prescott.

"Hold on a minute." The officer turned to the day tour lieutenant on the desk.

"Loo, do we have prisoners in the cells?"

"No, the cells are empty down here. But they have a woman for assault upstairs."

"Is there a guy named Skidmore in the command log? I have his lawyer on the phone."

"Let me take a look." After reviewing the book the lieutenant informed the officer that no prisoner named Skidmore was booked at the precinct.

"You got the wrong precinct, counselor. We don't have your client down here."

Hearing the words "down here" reminded Prescott that Everett had been arrested by detectives. He was aware that sometimes the squad bypassed the formality of stopping at the front desk to be logged in with their prisoner.

"Did you check with the detectives? They were the ones who arrested him."

"Why didn't you say that in the first place? I'll transfer you to the squad."

"Detective Sheridan, how can I help you?"

"I'm Tobias Prescott, the attorney representing Everett Skidmore. You do have Mr. Skidmore under arrest at your precinct, correct?"

"Yes counselor, we have him here."

"I do not want him questioned, detective. Is that understood?"

"No problem. Do you want to speak to him?"

"Yes, please. Thank you."

"Hang on." Sheridan called over to DeCesare, who was seated at his desk filling out arrest papers.

"Yeah, Sherry, what's up?"

"It's the lawyer for your prisoner. Okay if they talk?"

"Okay."

Sheridan stretched out the cord and carried the phone over to the cell so that Everett could consult with his lawyer.

"Hello?" said Everett into the phone.

"Everett! It's me Toby. Jesus, what the hell happened?" asked the attorney.

"These detectives arrested me at gunpoint a block from my house. I was going to work."

"They took you at gunpoint? What did you do?"

"I don't know what the charges are. I haven't opened my mouth. I only asked for permission to call you."

"That was smart, Everett. Was there a line-up? Was there an altercation?"

"I wasn't in any line up and there was no altercation. Can you come down here?"

"Sit tight, Everett, I'm on the way. Remember, say nothing."

"Okay, Toby, try to hurry."

"I will. Let me talk to the detective."

Everett signaled Sheridan at his desk to come back to the cell. When he got there the teacher handed him the phone. "My lawyer wants to talk to you."

Sheridan took the phone from the prisoner. "Hello..."

"Detective, what is my client being charged with?"

"He is booked for homicide on one case and attempted murder on the other."

Prescott couldn't believe what he was hearing. "There are *two* cases?"

"That's right, I *this* precinct alone."

"Are you saying there are *other* cases elsewhere?"

Sheridan glanced at Everett. The science teacher's head was bowed like a man pronounced guilty. Turning his back to the cell, the detective spoke to the attorney in a low voice as he walked back to his desk with the phone.

"Let me put it this way, counselor: it's complicated. You got yourself a job. You're likely facing multiple homicides."

The phone went silent for a second as the attorney digested the information. "I'm coming to the precinct—he's going to be there for awhile, right?"

"We're gonna be here for quite a while."

"Good enough, I'm on the way. Can I just talk to my client for another minute?" The detective again walked the phone back to Everett.

"Everett, this sounds serious. We are going to have to mount a defense. Are you still a teacher?"

"Yes, for years now."

"You work for the city, right?"

"Yes, I teach science."

"Good, that'll show stability. How are you fixed for money?"

"I'm alright, I've always worked, I never married, and I have no children or debt...so I have a decent nest egg."

"I have to be honest; this is going to come to a significant amount of money. I'll do what I can to keep the costs down of course, but we have a battle on our hands. You have to be prepared take a haircut."

Everett didn't appreciate the talk of money. "I understand, Toby. I still got some of the money *we* made as *partners*. You remember *that* arrangement, right?"

Prescott got the message. "Let's not talk on the phone. Don't worry about the money, Everett. You can count on me to substantially discount the fee."

Everett responded confidently. "Thanks, Toby. Just do whatever you have to do. I know I'm up against it and that you'll do the right thing by me."

"Alright Everett, no more talk. I just wanted you to be aware that there will be *some* cost. I'll be there within the hour. Keep your lip buttoned until I get there." Prior to leaving his office Prescott issued instructions to his secretary. "Reach out to my private investigator and tell him not to get lost, I'm going to be in need of him."

"Do you want him to meet you at the precinct?"

"No, I'll call over to his office later today, once I wrap my arms around this thing. One other thing, order me that new desk and chair set I liked...the expensive one."

DECESARE MET WITH THE DISTRICT ATTORNEY'S OFFICE to secure the appropriate papers for a warrant to search Everett's apartment. Afterward he met with a judge in his chambers for his signature. The justice, a former prosecutor, was old school. He wore his hair slicked back, in a style that pronounced his widow peak hairline. As he reviewed the warrant, he did so with a stern face. When done, he signed the document and casually lit up a smoke. Never asking a question, he returned the papers to DeCesare and said, "Good hunting."

Once the investigator left the courthouse, he telephoned Markie. "Hi sarge, it's me DeCesare."

"How did you make out?"

"No problem, it was a piece of cake. The judge just signed off on the warrant."

"Nice. Head over to the Skidmore apartment, we'll meet you over there."

Markie stepped out of the office and into the squad room where Von Hess and the other detectives were. "Okay boys, we're going out to execute the search warrant. Ollie, you and Rhodes come with me."

Perez rose from his desk to talk to Markie. "What do you want me to do?"

"You stay back with Sheridan and babysit our boy in the pen."

The search warrant of Everett's apartment netted the plastic spray containing the mace-like substance used on Thelma Curcio. Other evidence included gloves, red neckties, and several pairs of dark sunglasses. There was no evidence discovered in the apartment that suggested the prisoner had a firearm. Markie knew that lots of people have dark suits, but he retrieved those as well, to support the description provided by witnesses.

AFTER MAKING NUMEROUS CALLS Rhodes and Perez had come up empty concerning their canvass of eye doctors. After being apprised of their lack of success Markie remained undaunted. The sergeant was still determined to get to the bottom of the eye controversy. He felt an answer must be within reach. He fully intended to do whatever he could to gain more information in order to ensure success in the Pergamint/Wallace cases. At this point it was a personal challenge. His only problem was that he drew a blank in coming up with a way to explain how a man with seemingly perfectly normal eyes was cross-eyed.

Markie sat at his desk tin the squad commander's office thinking hard. He picked up the pencil off the desk and stated doodling feverously on a yellow legal pad. He was hoping that this would help him come up with some ideas.

32

Reckoning Day For Everett

"Trust me on this, Everett: no matter how real it may or may not be. If you want to get your ass out of here, none of that shit happened."

-Tobias Prescott, Esquire

HIS BEING WELL AWARE THAT Toby Prescott was a man totally devoid of ethics made it somewhat easier for Everett to confide in his attorney. What remained a secret to the prisoner was the extent of Prescott's crookedness. In his current position Prescott regularly engaged in padding client invoices, double billing and whenever possible, bribing judges. It was not uncommon for him to receive cash fees under the table in return for his legal services. When the shady lawyer arrived at the squad room he was met by DeCesare, the arresting officer.

Everett was relocated to a corner desk where he could converse with his attorney in private. Cuffed to the arm of a metal chair on wheels, he was in full view of the detective at all times.

"Everett, roll your chair around closer to me. I want your back to the detective."

"Thanks for coming right over, Toby."

"Keep your voice down," said Prescott, leaning closer his client. "Now look, you have to come clean with me and tell me nothing but the truth. We're talking about your neck here, so we can't afford to slip up and have any unforeseen surprises jump up and bite us in the ass later."

"Confide in him Everett, Toby was always a nice young man," urged the good voice.

"I'll tell everything," Everett replied to his mother.

Prescott believed his client was responding to him. "Good, Everett. So tell me, what the hell is going on here?"

"You want to hear it from the beginning?"

"Absolutely, start from the very beginning and give it to me straight."

"It all started from when I was a kid, Toby…"

While Prescott anticipated hearing of some foolish choices that led to violence, he never expected to be privy to the narrative he received. The lawyer listened in amazement as Everett unfolded the tale that began with his Yarrow Street childhood. Everett detailed his victimization at the hands of Granny and spoke of how she appeared to him in the form of insects, cats and later, random women. The evil voice in his head, his eye issues and the circumstances surrounding each murder all made it to the table. Aside from neglecting to mention the good voice of Adele and the homicide of his landlady Frieda, Everett was forthcoming. He felt it prudent not to compound matters by introducing a killing in which, to the best of his knowledge, remained in the shadows. As far as discussing his mother, the prisoner found it too personal to go there.

The jaw-dropping account left Toby Prescott astonished. There was no denying it, the kid he used to sell pot with turned out to be a very sick puppy. But addressing Everett's mental illness would have to come later, after the acquittals . . . *if* he were fortunate enough to gain them. What the attorney found truly unbelievable was not the fact that Everett was able to function all these years in an unbalanced state undetected—he knew plenty of psychologically challenged people out there functioning among the masses just fine. What was mind boggling to Toby was how he himself missed the red flags. But all that was for another day. Presently, the lawyer was tasked with figuring out a defense strategy for a homicidal maniac that he had a history with.

"Look Everett, as it stands right now, I can only see two paths for us. We stick with this story you told me or…"

"This is no bullshit story!" interrupted the prisoner gruffly. Seeing the emergence of Everett's other-side, Prescott backed off. The last thing he needed was a powerful psychopath turn angry when only an arm's length away from him. Prescott's lips tightened to form a tolerating smile.

"Everett, you have to understand something. *Sometimes* in this business we need to massage things."

"You don't believe me, do you?"

"It's not a question of what you or I believe, or even the truth for that matter," said the attorney patiently. "It's all about getting a jury to have doubts about the case being presented by the prosecution. To accomplish this, you need to do exactly what I tell you."

"Listen to Toby, dear. He knows best," advised the good voice.

Everett nodded. "I hear you both. I'm with you, Toby" said Everett.

"Both?" asked Prescott.

Everett didn't respond, so his attorney simply moved on. "Look Everett, trust me: I'd never steer you wrong. What do you do when you need a two pointer in order to win and there's only seconds left on the clock? You get that shot off, right? Well, my job is to create the opening for that shot…which in this case is doubt."

"I understand, Tobias."

"Okay then. Right now there are too many uncertainties. I don't know which way to go. It'll all depend on the evidence they throw at us. Whichever road we opt for, we need to get a few things straight right out of the gate.

"Do you intentionally cross your eyes?

"No."

"Could you stop it from happening?"

"Of course I can't stop it from happening! I have no control over this damn curse," answered Everett with a bite.

"Okay, easy. It comes and goes then?"

"Yes, whenever Granny Trapani rears her ugly head."

"I see," replied Prescott, clearing his voice. "Who alive has seen you cross-eyed?" asked the attorney, assuming for a moment that Everett's eyes actually did cross.

"The only person living is the woman in the bakery. Granny moved on to another body before I could get back to her."

"What do you mean…another body?"

Everett realized he slipped up. Not looking to complicate matters further by bringing in Frieda the landlady, he quickly covered his tracks. "I meant to say she *probably* moved on to another body."

"So no one else alive saw your eyes crossed other than the woman in the bakery?"

"She's the only one."

"Are you sure?"

"Yes, for sure," answered Everett. "My eye condition is something I've learned to hide well."

Prescott could attest to that himself firsthand. "Alright, we're talking just one person then...and that is a good thing. You got nothing wrong with your eyes from what I can see, and this is a big card for us to play. Do you have any history with an eye doctor?

"Not really."

"Have you had any problems with your eyes that ever required treatment or medication of any kind?"

"No, I don't even wear prescription glasses. But I did have my eyes checked out once.

The statement got a rise out of Prescott. "You did? When was that?"

"That was years ago, when I was a little kid."

"Do you remember who the doctor was?"

"No, all I can recall is that he was really old. He had an office in the neighborhood.

"Ok, that's nothing to worry about then. He's got to be long dead by now. Just remember that the visit never happened. One other thing...get it in your head that there is absolutely nothing wrong with your eyes and there never was...period!"

"I got it."

"Now don't get offended, but I have to ask. Did you ever undergo any psychiatric treatment?"

"No."

"Never met with a shrink...*ever*?" asked Prescott with some doubt in his voice.

"I said, never."

"Okay, that's good. Now, get these bullet points straight:

- Number one, you are never, *ever* again to mention a word to anyone about hearing voices.
- Number two, Granny Trapani never assumes the body of others.
- Number three, there was no curse put on you or any other off-the-wall shit like that...*ever*!

Trust me on this, Everett: no matter how real it may or may not be. If you want to get your ass out of here, none of that shit happened."

"Alright, Toby, I understand. I lived my whole life carrying this secret, it's been my cross. I know you're right: my own mother wouldn't believe me when she was alive."

Prescott nodded his acknowledgment before changing the subject. "Now, as far as the dressing up goes, since the cops are aware of it, we can't deny it. I think that we may be able to work that angle to our advantage. I'll use it to mix up the jury. When I'm done, they'll think it plausible that the witness *could* have been confused—you know, mistaken in her identification. When I'm through with her she won't know herself."

"Let's hope," said Everett.

"Now look, Everett: right now we're in the dark as to their evidence. So, we're going to have to hit the ball as the pitches are thrown. Our strategy may have to change as we travel down the road, but for now, those are the ground rules. Okay?"

"I got it."

"One last thing, Everett: like I told you on the phone, this defense is going to cost you some money. You have to be prepared to take...a *small* haircut."

"I understand, Toby. I can live with a *small* haircut."

Everett adhered to Prescott's instructions. The teacher remained silent, only answering questions for the purpose of arrest processing. As far as anyone could see, the science teacher seemed to be of sound mind and competent to stand trial.

PRESCOTT LEARNED THAT THE PROSECUTORS intended to proceed with the bakery case first. Faced with mounting a defense, Prescott wasn't discouraged. The urine evidence recovered at the scene turned out to be problematic because Jeanette's urine-soiled clothing was improperly handled by DeCesare. This made DNA identification iffy. Since urine is not considered the ideal source for DNA anyway, it meant that Jeanette's identification of Everett was paramount. Another positive for the defense was the issue of the eyes. It was something that the prosecution would have difficulty navigating around. If Prescott could discredit Jeanette it would mean that there would be no Carson Wallace homicide to fear.

Thanks to his private investigator, Everett's lawyer gathered information pertaining to evidence in the other cases. Prescott learned that the analysis and comparison of Everett's ties to the material recovered from the neck of one of the victims, proved to be inconclusive. A decision regarding the mace-like spray in the candy store murder still hadn't been rendered. Prescott snickered at the notion of defending his client against a talking bird. The lawyer's second meeting with Everett was optimistic.

"We may be in decent shape on these cases, Everett."

"You think so, Toby?"

"Yes, I really do. But for right now, forget all the other cases. We're going to bat on the bakery cases, so those two are the ones we need to focus on."

"Okay."

❖

WITH THE APPREHENSION OF EVERETT, orders were cut that disbanded the task force. For Markie and Von Hess, this meant going back to their job at Brooklyn homicide. Once Everett's trial date neared, the two detectives were notified to report to the Manhattan District Attorney's Office to meet with Zoe Taylor Wiggins, the daughter of a judge and the ADA assigned to the bakery cases.

The thirty-two-year-old Wiggins grew up in the Riverdale section of the Bronx. From an early age, her father tutored his daughter on his own life lessons. His words continued to resonate with her.

"It's always best to get on with people," was a favorite line of his. "When waters are rough, never be wishy-washy. People will follow strength and most will remember who got them through the storm," was another. Perhaps his most often imparted advice came once she started working as an ADA, "When it comes to controversy, keep your nose out of it. Let the others take their stand…and the arrows that go with it. Stick to this credo and with a little hard work, you'll get ahead."

When Markie and Von Hess presented themselves at her office, Wiggins immediately rose from her desk to greet them. The fair skinned ADA walked with her shoulders pulled back. She extended her hand cordially, taking Markie's hand in hers.

"Nice meeting you," she said.

Already seated in Wiggins's office were Detective DeCesare and Jeanette Pergamint. As the case officer, DeCesare was responsible for escorting Jeanette to and from her appearances. It was a basic precaution: the prosecution needed to be sure that their complainant would show up. In Jeanette's case, there was nothing to worry about. She was chomping at the bit to see justice served. At the conclusion of the trial prep, all involved departed the office comfortable in the knowledge that they had a common goal.

The ADA had discussions with Toby Prescott about cutting an early deal, but the talks went nowhere: the defense attorney made it clear that the terms offered were totally unacceptable. Relying on Jeanette's conflicting descriptions, Prescott felt confident that he could create enough confusion for at least one juror to question the reliability of Jeanette's testimony.

The prosecution and defense combed through the potential jury pool, with each weeding out those who they felt could potentially jeopardize their interest. Eventually an agreement was reached that resulted in a diversified jury comprised of six men and six women of various ages and ethnicities. Once the trial was underway, the proceedings moved along swiftly, with both sides scoring points. As expected, Jeanette's pointing out Everett in open court was the most damaging evidence presented by the prosecution. However, under cross-examination, the defense was able to weaken her identification with continual references to Everett not being cross-eyed.

Prescott:	"Didn't you testify that your attacker was unquestionably cross-eyed?"
Jeanette:	"Yes."
Prescott:	"Look at Mr. Skidmore, Ms. Pergamint. Clearly he *isn't* cross-eyed, is he? I ask you now, is he cross-eyed?"
Jeanette:	"No, not now."
Prescott:	"You testified that Mr. Skidmore accosted you on the street on a prior occasion. Is that correct, Ms. Pergamint?"
Jeanette:	"Yes."
Prescott:	"This is a copy of that police report. Does it not reflect that you told the police you were accosted by a *woman*?"
Jeanette:	"Yes, but—"
Prescott:	"Thank you Ms. Pergamint, you've answered the question."

When Prescott produced a copy of the police sketch that displayed a fly on the nose of a cross-eyed suspect, he knew that he got some of the jurors thinking. The sketch came as a surprise to ADA Wiggins, who had no knowledge that a prankster had been going around undermining the artistry of Detective Wu. Prescott's private investigator, a retired police detective, had been able to secure a copy of the altered sketch through one of his police contacts.

Prescott got Jeannette to admit that she previously saw the sketch with the fly posted in the precinct. He further got her to admit that she never took steps to contest its depiction, leaving the jury to wonder if the witness concurred with the sketch as portrayed. Jeanette flustered when not allowed to clarify this point.

Prescott ramped up the pressure with a blistering series of questions designed to lead Jeanette into a state of wild agitation. The crime victim did not disappoint. At one point she lashed out at the defense attorney, going so far as to incorporate offensive language in her testimony. This outburst was not exactly according to script. After allowing her emotions to get the better of her, Jeanette soon regretted her foolish choice of words. Even she realized that her remarks probably alienated some of the twelve on the jury. Feeling empowered, Prescott pushed on. He continued to drill down on ambiguities with a battery of questions.

"You really don't know if your attacker was a *male or female*, now do you?"

"You told the police that you couldn't identify your street attacker. Now you can?"

"Wasn't it a *tattooed* fly on your attacker's nose that you actually saw?

"Do you see a tattooed fly on Mr. Skidmore's nose?"

And so it went. Prescott hammered Jeanette, claiming that she had to have been too traumatized to remember anything with accuracy. He even asked her if she was guessing at what her attacker looked like.

"Look at the sketch, Mrs. Pergamint!" Prescott shouted. "Who looks like this? Certainly not Mr. Skidmore, just look at him yourself." Turning to the jury box the defense attorney asked, "What if it was a member of *your* family being accused under such flimsiness?"

As Jeanette testified on the stand, Everett wondered why he no longer saw her as the evil Granny. He could only attribute this phenomenon to Granny having moved on to Frieda, his landlady. It caused the teacher to wonder where Granny was hiding presently. Everett sat quietly in open court with his baby blues perfectly aligned. *"Isn't he doing a marvelous job for you, dear?"* asked the good voice. Everett just nodded, saying nothing. His fingers were crossed, hoping that the evil voice would continue to remain elsewhere.

With the trial going well, there was no reason for Prescott to put Everett on the stand. That would be a last resort, a strategy to be used in the event Prescott needed to convince the jury that his client was insane. When the judge recessed for lunch, Markie and Von Hess escorted ADA Wiggins back to her office.

"The guy is guilty as sin," commented the sergeant as they walked..

The ADA didn't agree or disagree. She simply said, "I think we're screwed. It seems impossible to get around the eye situation."

"You think so?"

"I'm afraid so," she answered. "I know that Jeanette was extremely adamant in her claim that her attacker was cross-eyed...yet, as you can see for yourself, the defendant shows no sign of such a condition. His appearance directly contradicts her testimony."

It was clear to Markie that Wiggins was having her own doubts. "This is incredible," commented Markie.

Wiggins stopped walking. She turned to face Markie as she spoke. "Incredible? How did his eyes look to you in that courtroom?" she asked.

Markie pondered the question before answering. "Now that you mention it, I can't answer that question."

"What do you mean?"

"I mean this. When I was on that stand, every time I looked at Skidmore he looked down or had his eyes closed. He never looked up once or directly at me. I'm thinking that he intentionally avoided eye contact with me."

The ADA turned to Von Hess. "Did he do that with you?"

"It was the same thing with me."

"How was he when you had him in the precinct?" asked the prosecutor

"When we booked him his eyes were fine," admitted Markie. "All I'm saying is, in that court, he never looked at me. Could his eyes only cross when he gets nervous?"

"I don't know, sergeant."

"Can we somehow pressure him to find out? Maybe get him to look at us in court?"

Wiggins slowly nodded as the wheels turned in her head. "I can ask the court to order him to look at us."

"You can?"

"Yes...and I can ask for more than that. I can ask to have him stand up and face the jury, eye to eye!" The prosecutor sounded newly energized by the thought of introducing a theatrical element into the prosecution.

"Even if his eyes are just a little off, the jury will take note of it. That should help," encouraged Von Hess.

"I'm doing it!" declared the ADA.

After lunch, the time of reckoning soon arrived. Over the emphatic objections of Toby Prescott, the judge gave the prosecution the green light to proceed with their experiment. The court ordered that Everett stand directly in front of the jurors seated in the jury box. Everett was nervous, fearing that the voice of Granny Trapani wouldn't remain dormant. Escorted to the front of the jury box by two court officers, he looked at the jurors with his head up. The defendant's prayers had been answered. The evil voice in the strangler's mind remained asleep.

Prescott smirked, feeling that he'd won. But his glee was short-lived. On his way back to his chair, Everett glanced at Wiggins. In her disappointment the prosecutor balled her fist and nervously shook it before dropping her arm to her side. The gesture was sufficient enough for Everett to see Granny Trapani manifested in the form of ADA Wiggins.

"You-gonna-like-a-jail," taunted the evil voice in his head. "Lots-a-fun, inna-the-jail."

That did it. The rubber band holding Everett's sanity together finally snapped. He whirled around with eyes that were blatantly crossed, screaming at Wiggins.

"You! I should have known you wouldn't be far away, you old witch!" The deranged teacher then lunged at the prosecutor.

Luckily for the ADA, Everett's rush was body-blocked by a fleet footed court officer. After a violent struggle with the officers the teacher was subdued and carted off to the holding pen behind the courtroom; he could be heard having a profanity-riddled argument with his imaginary tormentor.

A deflated Toby Prescott sank into his seat. The defense attorney resigned himself to the fact that there was no longer hope for his client...the cross-eyed strangler.

❖

MARKIE INVITED ADA WIGGINS to join the detectives for a celebratory drink at Forlini's, a nearby lower Manhattan bar restaurant. As a rule, this type of invitation was rarely extended to an ADA. But due to the unusual circumstances of the case, Markie felt that there was reason for an exception, especially for someone as easy to work with as Wiggins. Everyone contributed by bucking up until there was a sufficient amount of money on the bar to cover drinks. The ADA was the only one who took a seat at the bar. After receiving her drink, the prosecutor spun around in her seat to face the investigators who formed a semi-circle around her. Feeling like the queen of the senior prom, she took a hardy gulp of her cosmopolitan before speaking.

"My God, he was an absolute madman...he so scared the living shit out me, I'm still shaking! If it weren't for the court officers being so alert, he would have killed me."

"Skidmore is flat-out nuts," added DeCesare. "Did you see that judge boogey out of there?"

Wiggins was the first to answer. "She flew off that bench like she had wings! I couldn't believe how fast she moved."

"And she isn't exactly what you would call a spring chicken," noted DeCesare.

"No, she isn't young by any measure! She must be in her late seventies," said the lawyer, laughing with great gusto.

"At least this ended well, a little dramatic maybe, but well," observed Markie.

"This was certainly one for the books, sarge," said the prosecutor, who then emptied her glass. "I think I can truly understand how poor Jeanette Pergamint must have felt."

"Jeanette's very strong, don't you worry about her," observed Markie.

"That's for sure," added DeCesare.

"I thought Jeanette's husband was a pretty decent guy," commented Sheridan, who hadn't forgotten the business arrangement he was cooking up.

Markie ordered another round of drinks. The conversation eventually drifted from the case to general criminal justice topics. In time the talk embodied the drivel one enters into when drinking. The revelers concluded their discussion with the pros and cons of polygamy. By the time the party broke up everyone was toasted.

33

Jersey Guacamole

"Say, what did you eat this morning? Besides, forty dollars and you're looking for a matinee?"

-Alley Cat

ALLEY SAT BY HER TELEPHONE WAITING. When it came to doing the things she liked she tended to be quite excitable. When the call finally came, she picked up so enthusiastically that she dropped the phone.

"Are you still there?" she asked.

"I'm a couple of blocks away," advised Markie. "I'll beep when I'm outside."

Alley checked the stove, shut the lights and put her travel bag by the apartment door. As soon as she heard the two rapid-fire automobile toots coming from the street she was out the door. The beautiful weather was a pot sweetener for their Atlantic City overnighter.

While Markie waited out front his phone rang. Seeing it was his ex-wife, he hesitated to answer. Ultimately he took the call, fearing that it could be something serious. Florence got right to the point. "Can you make yourself available tonight?"

"What is tonight?"

"I bought an ice cream cake for my father's birthday. It's going to be a small surprise party for him. He still thinks you walk on water, so I know he'll love seeing you there."

"It's tonight?"

"Yes, today is his birthday. Between work and the kids I got so caught up that I forgot to call you sooner."

"I would love to go, but unfortunately I'll be in Atlantic City with my girlfriend."

Markie immediately bit into his lip, regretting having mentioned the word girlfriend. However unintentional, it was cruel thing to do. He knew there was never anyone else, with him having been the only man in her life. Even though they were officially divorced, he knew that any reference to a paramour would come with a sting to Florence. His involvement elsewhere was the one thing he wanted to keep from his family. Making his relationship with Alley known to his family would only complicate matters.

"Never mind," said Florence stiffly. "I understand," she added before hanging up.

Markie looked into the dead phone wondering how he could have been so stupid. This was one of those delusional moments in his life that he thought Florence was too fragile to ever go on without having him nearby. He called Flo back looking to undo the damage, but as expected, the call went unanswered. He sighed, figuring that he terribly upset her. She was upset, but not for the reasons he thought. Florence had planned to spring a surprise not just for the benefit of her father.

Markie's regret had a short shelf life. Once Alley came bouncing out of her building wearing a tank top, Florence became an afterthought. The sergeant stretched across the front seat to roll down the passenger window. "You ready, Freddy?"

"Yep, and feeling lucky, ducky!" she replied, tossing her bag in the back seat. Once Alley was inside Markie's car, the sergeant leaned over to give her a passionate kiss. "Down boy," she said, taken by surprise at his friskiness.

314

Alley pressed down the button to lock the car door. Securing the door in this fashion was a reminder that Markie's car was a relic. With well over one-hundred-thousand miles recorded on the odometer, it was a wonder how the car was still on the road.

"Can we put on the air conditioning?" she asked.

"It's on the blink."

"Oh, no, it's not working! Why didn't you get it fixed?"

"It was either I fix that or the brakes. I went with the brakes."

Alley gazed down at her feet; her flip-flops were resting on a square piece of mat-sized plywood. "What happened to the floor?"

"You remember that rust spot I had there for years—it finally corroded through."

"How big a hole is it?"

"It's nothing to worry about. It's not big enough for you to fall through."

"Now isn't *that* a lovely thought," she answered, shaking her head. "So all you're going to do is cover the hole with a piece of *wood*?"

"Yeah, what do you expect, Italian marble?"

"I think the floor isn't the only place where there's a hole!" she answered, shaking her head. "Have you ever thought that it may be time for another car?"

Markie looked to change the subject. "Do you want to stop at Mickey D's?"

"Let's just get coffee to drink on the road. We can eat something once we get down here."

"Okay, boss." Alley liked being called *boss*. It made her feel more like they were in a committed relationship.

The couple made it down to Atlantic City without incident. After checking into the casino hotel they went for something light to eat. Sitting across from each other over breakfast they discussed their upcoming gaming activity.

"What are you going to play?" he asked.

"I'll be on the penny machines, unless you want me to tag along with you," she said, hoping he would want that.

"How about we shoot some dice? We'll go partners, you toss the dice and I'll make the bets. Does that work?"

"Great! Let's do it!"

"Okay...give me a hundred bucks."

"A hundred bucks...what for?" Alley asked, putting down her fork.

"You wanted to go partners. So, we'll each invest a hundred. Are you in or what?"

"Forget it! I'm not giving you my money to lose shooting craps."

Her response amused the sergeant. "Okay, don't get your bra twisted. We'll use my money and you can still throw the dice. Better?"

"Yes," she answered, quite pleased with the final outcome. "And I'm not wearing a bra, in case you haven't noticed."

"Don't worry about that, I noticed."

After eating they proceeded directly to the casino. Markie took Alley Cat's hand and led her to a crap table were the action seemed to be hot. As the dice passed from shooter to shooter, they held their own. When the two cubes reached a man at the far end of the table, Markie bet with him because he had the look of a winner. The stranger began shaking the dice. In her anticipation Alley leaned over the table with her arms folded under her chest.

"Number seven! It's a winner!"

Alley Cat jumped up and down with delight, much to the glee of everyone at the table who also placed a win bet. After the payout the stickman pushed the dice to the same shooter for another go.

"Nice going!" said Markie. "C'mon now, do it again, one more time!" he encouraged, increasing his wager on the pass line.

The point was six, which meant a six was needed to be thrown before a seven.

"Come on, you can do it again." called out Markie to the stranger. "Do it one more time."

After taking a hard look at the shooter, Markie threw caution to the wind. He placed one hundred dollars on the hard six, which would pay off with nice odds only if the man rolled two threes. The shooter, noticing the wager, threw the dice with extra oomph. One cube hit a stack of chips and flew high in the air landing down the front of Alley Cat's tank top as she continued to lean over the table.

"I'll get it!" volunteered someone. The remark caused everyone at the table to laugh out loud.

By the time they were through playing Markie was ahead by a few hundred dollars. "Here is your end," Markie said, handing Alley Cat forty dollars In chips. Feeling shortchanged, she protested.

"I thought you said we were partners?"

"You could've been my partner, but you chose to be an *employee* on salary." Alley Cat accepted the payout with mixed emotions over the uneven split. "I'm going over to the circular bar to have a nice quiet drink," said the sergeant. "I'm looking to pace myself and walk out of here with their money for a change."

"Good idea. I'll meet you there in a little while," said Alley. Later we'll take a walk along the boardwalk."

"Whatever you want to do is fine with me."

Forty minutes later Markie's solitude was disrupted. Alley Cat came bursting onto the scene with her purse filled with money. "I hit for eighteen-hundred dollars!" she shouted gleefully.

"Wonderful!" answered Markie, genuinely glad to see her so happy. "What are you drinking?"

"Nothing!" she replied. "We're going for that walk on the boardwalk and then have ourselves a big dinner. It'll be my treat!"

"I thought you wanted to play."

"I'm done gambling. I'm going shopping with my winnings," she declared.

The alcohol the sergeant consumed fueled his carnal desires. "How about we go to the party first?" he suggested hopefully.

"What party?"

"The one we're gonna have up in our room."

Alley Cat smiled. "Say, what did you eat this morning? Besides, forty dollars and you're looking for a matinee?"

"What? No good?"

"No, it's okay. But later, *if* you're good

THE SERGEANT AND ALLEY STROLLED along the boardwalk with the breeze at their back. Markie picked up a cigar to smoke as they walked.

"So what do you feel like eating?"

"Let's go to a seafood place," Alley suggested. "I know you like salmon."

"I like Italian better." he answered.

"Since when don't you like salmon? You always get salmon."

"What are you talking about? I only eat it when I'm with you," said Markie.

Alley Cat stopped in her tracks. "Wait, you're the one who always wants to go to the House of Fish, luv...not me."

Markie looked at her like she was crazy. "You think I'd suggest that joint for my pleasure? I only suggest that place for *your* pleasure, because I know how *you* like lobster!"

"Me?"

The two stood face to face on the boardwalk debating the issue. Alley commenced to detail all the times that Markie ordered salmon. It was as if she had a photographic memory. As she was citing instance after instance, they stood there, oblivious to the seagulls that were soaring overhead. One of the airborne sharpshooters dropped a package that landed on Markie's lower lip as he emphasized his preference for Italian food. Alley nearly fell over laughing at the sergeant's misfortune. Markie shook his head as he searched his pockets for something to wipe his mouth with.

317

"You have to laugh at this shit," he said, as Alley Cat wiped his lips dry with a tissue she retrieved from her handbag. "Tastes like guacamole," he quipped. "So should we go have that matinee now?" he asked.

"Ugh...forget about it!" Came her immediate reply.

34

Happy Days

"Attica isn't that bad, Toby. Once you find your niche."

-Everett Skidmore

AFTER GOING BESERK IN COURT, Everett was removed to a psychiatric ward. According to the staff reports, he reacted well in this environment. Against all advice, Everett refused to consider a plea of guilt due to insanity because he felt he wasn't insane. Instead he confessed his crimes and received a life sentence. He was sent to a correctional facility for psychiatric and physical evaluation. This particular period of confinement lasted a six months. Once a battery of doctors identified an effective medication to put Everett's delusions of Granny Trapani in check, they claimed success and shipped him out to Attica where he went on to function within the parameters of incarcerated normalcy.

Serving his time in the upstate prison, he became just another number added to the general population of inmates. Inside the walls Everett no longer heard from the evil voice or had to deal with Granny appearances. However, as a precaution he continued to have sunglasses handy just in case.

Life behind bars was an environment that Everett adapted to. He still had Adele to talk to and his athleticism helped facilitate his social integration. What really gave him prominence among those incarcerated was the special basketball trick shot he could perform. Everett, with his back to the basket, was able to sink a ball from half court. He did this with relative consistency, while never sharing how he was able to perform this feat. No one seemed to realize that on a full court, once you had the distance down, all it took was to line the ball up with the basket the shooter was facing. Another thing that Everett had working for him was his teaching expertise. He displayed an unselfish willingness to help fellow inmates. He taught those lacking the basics how to read, write, and do math. He clarified the sequence of history and demystified science so that it made sense. Sometimes, he'd help with inmate appeals. His popularity soared when he began to delve into more questionable instruction, such as how to conjure up a poison and prepare a basic bomb. Within the jail community, these were skills that were deemed worth learning. Everett took a *special* interest in those he favored.

"Hey Everett, you gonna help me fill out those papers later?" asked a fellow inmate.

Everett looked at him a second or two before answering. He was an averagely built young man of twenty-seven. His having short hair and being clean shaven, gave him a well-maintained look. "Sure, as soon as I finish what I'm doing. I think we can get together," he advised.

Perhaps Everett's acclimation to incarceration was best expressed in a letter to his attorney. "Attica isn't all that bad, Toby, once you find your niche."

❖

AFTER THE POLICE COMMISSIONER DIED, John Randolph was appointed to the post he so coveted. As planned, the new commissioner appointed his friend Harry McCoy to succeed him as the chief of detectives. Markie was another among those chosen for promotion. He was now going to receive the pay of a lieutenant. A ceremony was scheduled at police headquarters to make it official.

The weekday ceremony was held in a large auditorium. Those being promoted filled the front rows looking sharp in their crisply pressed dress uniforms. The audience was comprised of family members, well-wishing co-workers, and representatives of the media. A high point of the ceremony was the George M. Cohan medley played by the department band. Von Hess, who was one of the well wishers, snapped to attention at hearing The Marine's Hymn during the musical salute to the armed services.

Markie sat quietly awaiting his turn to be called to the stage to shake hands with the new police commissioner. This was the fourth time he had been called onto the big stage during his career. The first time was when he graduated from the academy as a Police Officer. His wife Florence attended that one. Then, when he made detective, Flo and her parents turned out for the big day. When upped to Sergeant, the kids were added to the list of family coming out for him. Now, as a man living apart from his family, there was no one to impress...not even Alley. Markie never even mentioned to her that he was getting promoted. The jaded sergeant intended to take her for a fancy dinner without telling her there was an occasion to celebrate.

After the ceremony Markie was met at the back of the auditorium by Lieutenant Wright, Von Hess and a few others from homicide. While Markie appreciated their taking the time, he would have been perfectly fine going it alone. His outlook at this point was rather grim: he knew the next ceremony would be his final one. It would be the big sendoff, that tearful brouhaha in which you don't even get to smell your own flowers. Legacies held no meaning for the sergeant. Such was the stuff for people who fooled themselves into believing they'd be around to hear the praise.

After the glad-handing was concluded Lieutenant Wright, Markie's commanding officer at homicide, had a message. "Chief McCoy just went upstairs. He wants us to meet him in his new office once we're through down here."

"Should we go up now?"

"Yeah, might as well."

McCoy was at his desk reading over the list of those promoted when he noticed the three men standing at his office door. They humbly waited to be invited in before entering. The new chief of detectives was the picture of contentment. Seated between the arms of his throne, he immediately waved them in.

"Come in gentlemen," McCoy declared warmly. "Take a seat."

"Congratulations chief, everyone in Brooklyn was glad to see you take over," said Wright, assuming the role of spokesman for the three.

"Appreciate that. How long have you had homicide, lieutenant?"

"Eight years, chief."

"That is a long run. Are you happy over there in Brooklyn?"

"Yes, sir, I live in Maspeth, so my commute from Queens is a good one. I found a home there…I think," said Wright, revealing his uncertainty as to what the meeting was about.

The chief smiled. "Relax, this is all good." He turned his attention to Markie. "How is the travel for you, sarge?"

"It's fine for me, chief. I live in Brooklyn so it's very convenient."

"And you, detective?" he asked, looking at Von Hess.

"Anywhere works for me, chief."

McCoy nodded approvingly. "You're already a first grader, right Von Hess?"

"Yes, I am."

"Lieutenant, you *don't* have captain's money correct?"

"Correct," Wright said with a smile. "I don't have the money."

"Gentlemen, I want you to know that the commissioner and I were *very* satisfied with the results of the Skidmore case. Once again, you men proved your value. We don't want to see our resources wasted, so let me explain the proposition. I'm inheriting a lieutenant from internal affairs who comes with big pull. As a result, I have to see that she hangs her hat someplace nice. She'll be taking your slot in Brooklyn, lieutenant. That'll more than satisfy her."

Wright's mouth dropped open, stunned by what the chief was proposing. "What happens to me, chief?"

"You'll be assigned to my office right here, in charge of a new squad." The three visitors sat up in their seats, their attention fully focused. "You will report directly to me. This is a money slot—captain's pay for you if things work out. How does that sound?"

Wright was delighted. "I am flattered that you'd even consider me."

"The new squad will cover the entire city. You'll make your own hours as *you* see fit. All I ask is that you make every effort to bring your assignments to a satisfactory conclusion in a timely fashion."

"What kind of cases will we be working on, homicides?"

"Not exclusively. You three will be sort of a trouble squad, called in to handle sensitive cases."

"It will just be us three?"

"For now, it's you, Markie, and Von Hess. In terms of additional support, you'll get whatever you need on a case to case basis."

"I see."

"Now understand something, Wright: your job is to protect *me*. You must prevent embarrassment to me, this office, and the department by staying ahead of the curve on any investigation your squad undertakes."

"Understood," said Wright.

"Let Markie run the cases, while you serve in an administrative capacity. You'll post me accordingly and upon completion of an assignment, turn in a report summary."

"No problem."

"Those reports need to include recommendations concerning areas that require improvement. I want you to recommend who needs to be transferred. I want to know what squads are being poorly run and so on. Rest assured that I'll tighten the screws accordingly to attain efficiency in my squads."

"No problem."

"Anyone *not* want to sign on?" The chief's question was met with silence. "Excellent. I'll send out a telephone message concerning your transfers first thing in the morning. Meanwhile I'll set you men up with an office and some lockers."

With the meeting concluded, Wright lagged behind for a word with McCoy. "Chief, can I ask you a question?"

"Go ahead."

"Honestly, why am I here? I've done nothing special."

"I selected you for very good reasons. You have the highest homicide clearance rate out of all five boroughs, so performance wise, you stand out. Markie is the street man, I know that. But his accomplishments have come under your supervision. That's something not to be undervalued, but rather, something to capitalize on. You have the right technique with him and I intend to preserve a proven formula. I want everybody happy...and I'm happy with things this way."

Lieutenant Wright left the chief's office knowing that his promotion depended on keeping the chief *and* Markie happy. As a result, his first official act was to honor the sergeant's vacation request.

35

Myrtle Beach
Merriment

"You see that guy? All he does is walk the floor, day and night. Every time he passes this door, he wakes me up by saying hello Walter. I swear to Christ I'm going to put a pillow over him one night!"

-Retired Detective Walter Conroy

BEING INVITED TO GO ON vacation in Myrtle Beach with Markie caused Alley to think that her ship was finally coming in. Should she now row out to meet it or wait until it came to her? Opting to lay back, she put off broaching the subject of marriage. Even though making things official had been on her mind for awhile, she knew that a divorced man might tend to be squeamish in taking another plunge. With this in mind she decided to bide her time.

"C'mon baby, shake a leg. It's time to rock and roll."

"What took you so long?" she asked. "It's after midnight already."

"I waited to the last minute to pack," answered Markie through the passenger side window. "Did you bring the moonshine?"

"Yes, of course. Give me a hand with this suitcase."

Markie quickly exited the car to get her grip. "Fitzi had no problem giving a bottle to you?"

"No, he was great," she answered. "He actually made a present of it."

"Nice," he commented. Markie was surprised at how heavy her suitcase was. "What have you got a body in here?" he asked, as he lifted the luggage into the car trunk.

Within a minute the couple were heading south on their way to Myrtle Beach. After listening to the news they switched to a country western station. When Alley Cat began to sing *Emotion* along with Brenda Lee, Markie turned to stare at her. She half-smiled in response to his peculiar look.

"What?" she asked, curious as to what the look was supposed to mean.

"The last time I heard a voice like that was when the cat fell in the bathtub," he teased.

"Aren't you the funny one."

When it got light out Alley Cat noticed that the back seat contained a case of bottled water and a beat-up canvass gym bag with a leather grip. "Don't tell me that gym bag is all you took with you..."

"Yeah, that's it. We're only going to be gone a week."

"Do you think you might have over packed?" she asked sarcastically.

"Think so?"

Feeling the vibration at her feet, Alley looked down at the floor. The square piece of plywood reminded her of what separated her feet from the pavement. "I hope we make it to Myrtle Beach in this jalopy," she stated with pessimism. .

"I got the mechanic's blessing. This car can get down there and back on its reputation."

"Let's hope so."

"When we get there, let's look up my friend first thing," said Markie.

"Who is that again?"

"A guy I used to work with. Johnny Nine-Ball is the old-timer who broke me in as a rookie detective. He showed me the ropes and I owe him a lot."

"Johnny Nine-Ball? What kind of name is that?"

"We used to shoot pool in the precinct where we worked. No one could beat him at nine-ball, so that's how he ended up with the name."

"You know more characters..."

Markie nodded. "Well, let me warn you now. You better buckle up because this guy is a trip." Markie began to laugh as he thought about some of his friend's antics.

"What's so funny?"

"I was just thinking of the time the chief of detectives was on the stage handing out training certificates. When Johnny went up to receive his, he dropped to his knees and kissed the chief's ring. Everybody cracked up."

"He sounds like a nut."

"I suppose so," said Markie sighing.

"Do you think you'd like to live down south someday?" Alley asked, hopeful he would.

"I've thought about it."

Alley Cat decided the time was right to drop a hint. "I think Florida would be a great place to live someday. You know, when you retire. You can't beat the weather."

"Yeah, Florida is nice."

"So you *are* thinking about it?"

Markie became defensive, wanting to avoid any suggestion of commitment to a life with Alley far away from his children. "How can I go to Florida? My kids are in New York."

"Do you think you'd *ever* want to make the move down here?"

Markie quickly changed the subject. "I'm really looking forward to seeing Johnny." Alley took the hint and dropped it.

MARKIE AND ALLEY STEPPED UP to the front entrance of The Nine Ball Inn. Several unoccupied rocking chairs were visible on the porch. The building was old, but well maintained.

"This is some place he has here," said Markie, who was impressed.

A woman of about sixty stood behind the registration desk that was off to the right of the entrance. Her stiff haystack-like white hair sat high atop her head.

"Welcome...how can I help you?" she asked, speaking with a slight drawl.

"Is Johnny around?" asked Markie.

"Are you a bill collector or a friend?" she asked.

The first thing Markie noticed was the wide space between her two front teeth. "A friend, we used to work together."

"You must be one of his New York detective buddies?" said the woman after noticing the detective ring on Markie's pinky.

"That's right."

"What's your name, honey?"

"Tell him it's Alfie."

"It's nice to meet you, Alfie. I'm June, Johnny's wife. Let me go get him, he's in the office. He's always loves it when you boys come by."

"*Alfie?*" asked Alley, the moment June walked off.

"That's what Johnny always calls me," explained Markie. "Every time I see this guy, he's got a new wife."

"Alfie?" she repeated, in a more pronounced way.

"At least it's better than Alley Cat."

"He was married before?" asked Alley, preferring not go there.

"This one is number four that I know of."

"ALFIE BOY!" thundered the familiar voice of Johnny. "How the hell are you, kiddo?"

Other than walking with a slight limp due to a corn on his toe, the sergeant's former partner seemed to be as robust as ever. With good skin and most of his hair still dark, he deceivingly appeared to be much younger than his years.

"Johnny Nine-Ball!" said Markie loudly, opening his arms to embrace his friend warmly. "I'm doing great, Johnny. You haven't lost a step. Say hello to Alley."

Johnny performed a quick visual evaluation of Alley from head to foot. Once he determined that she passed muster he nodded to Markie approvingly and said, "You did real good, kiddo!"

Alley, whose skin was thickened by working for years in Fitzie's place, was no stranger to such behavior. "At least he didn't kick the tires and ask for a test drive," she quipped to Markie, who was a bit embarrassed by what she said.

Alley's remark caused Johnny to howl with laughter. "You're alright, Alley!" he announced happily. "C'mon, let's all go over to the bar for a cocktail."

About a dozen men, all in golf attire, were scattered around the bar having drinks. Serving drinks was a young woman in her early-twenties, attired in a top that was meant to draw customers. A waitress, similarly clad, serviced several small tables.

"What'll it be, Alley?"

"I think I'll have a gin and tonic."

"Give Alley here a gin and tonic and a couple of shots for me and the boy."

"Let's do Irish," suggested Markie.

"You got it, Alphie. Make it Old Bush and two short beers on the side, Ivy." said Johnny, addressing the bartender.

"So how's business, Johnny?"

"Knock wood, pretty good. I always seem to have most of the rooms rented, the kitchen hold's its own and the bar business is steady. It's a nice gig."

"I would think this is an expensive place to maintain," said Markie.

"You have to keep the overhead low. This being a big golf community with lots of strip clubs, I have to appeal to the guys. My workers are hot-looking girls, they draw the guys in," explained Johnny. "In here they get to look, maybe even hook up with a local if they get lucky and all without pissing away the rent money. A guy could have a lot of fun down here, kiddo."

"When he's single he could," Injected Alley, not missing anything.

"Yeah, well...I might be doing something about my current status when it comes to that department," the host confided in a voice low enough that his wife wouldn't hear.

"You're too much," said Markie, shaking his head. "You know, Alley tends bar in Brooklyn."

Johnny was surprised. "No kidding."

Alley smiled. "It's just a small dive."

"Every saloon is a dive," said Johnny. "I wouldn't care if it was in the fanciest hotel...to an owner; every joint operates with the same goal."

"I suppose."

"Alphie, you know I even host card games once in awhile."

"I never knew you to gamble," commented Markie.

"It's no gamble. I just deal and get a piece of each hand."

"What are the stakes?"

"It depends." A knowing look then crossed Johnny's face. "When people are short on funds, they know they can come to me," he added sheepishly with a crooked smile.

Markie exchanged smiles with Alley Cat. It wasn't hard to picture his friend as an occasional shylock.

"Let's move our drinks to my table. I want you two to order something to eat. We serve nothing fancy here, but the burgers are pretty good."

"Thanks, Johnny."

"Where are you two staying?"

"Well, we've not really decided."

"Then stay here. I got a clean room for you on the second floor and it won't cost you a dime. All you have to do is take care of the tips."

"No, we couldn't impose like that," said Markie.

"What *impose*? I'm telling you this is on the arm, since when does on the arm get a *no*? What are they feeding you guys back in New York?"

330

"We don't want to take advantage, Johnny."

"C'mon, you'd be doing me a favor. It's all settled. For me, this is a treat that breaks the monotony."

Markie nodded okay, agreeing to stay. "Oh, before I forget, I got something for you in the car."

Markie went to his car to retrieve the gift they brought down from New York. Returning to the bar he handed his friend a bag. Johnny pulled out a quart bottle containing a clear liquid. He removed the cork for a whiff.

"Potcheen!" Johnny declared with delight. "It looks like we are going to have a time tonight! Drink up what we have; we'll put a dent in this baby right now!"

With the lodging addressed, the three went to work on the bottle of moonshine. After several drinks the two former partners went down memory lane, as Alley listened.

"Say Al, you know who is in the hospital down here?"

"Who is that?"

"Walter Conroy. Do you remember him? He worked in night watch?"

"Sure I do. That name is a real blast from the past. What's wrong with him?"

"He's been down here a couple of years already. I ran into him one day in a store and we kept in touch ever since. He sold his house in Queens after his wife died. They never had kids, so he settled down here to be near his sister and her family."

"What's the matter with him?" Markie repeated.

"It has something to do with his ticker. They're checking him out."

"Is he still big?"

"Still a big boy, but I suppose they'll put him on a strict diet after this. Say, why don't we go say hello to him in the hospital tomorrow?"

"Yeah, let's do that. I'd love to see him again," answered Markie.

Alley Cat remained expressionless. Visiting some old man in the hospital wasn't exactly her idea of fun.

"Done, we'll sneak him in a taste."

IT WAS EARLY AFTERNOON the following day when they arrived at the hospital. After stopping at the reception desk, they made their way up to the floor where the patient was. The visitors peeked into rooms until they came upon their friend.

"So how's the old man?" asked Johnny boisterously, as he led the trio into the private room.

"Hey Johnny," replied the surprised Conroy, who was sitting up in his bed, reading a magazine. "What are you doing here?"

"Out for a little fun," said Johnny, pulling his sport jacket apart by the lapels. Conroy and Markie let out a howl after seeing that Johnny had pinned a dozen condoms to the inside lining, six on each side. Allie was mortified.

"Oh, you are too much!" said the patient.

"What do you want? I'm here to cheer you up, Walter. You remember my old partner, Alfie?"

"Sure I do. How are ya, kid? How are you doing?"

"I'm fine Walt. I'm sorry to hear about your loss."

The patient tossed his head to one side, indicating that there was nothing to say about the matter.

"We got a little get-well present for you," said Johnny, changing the subject.

"Oh, no kidding, what did you get me?" asked Walter.

Johnny closed the door to the room and returned to his friend's bedside. He removed four shot glasses from the side pockets of his jacket and a flask from the breast pocket. He then poured out four shots.

"What the hell is all this?" asked the patient.

"We got you some medicine. It comes straight from the witch doctor in the old country."

The four downed their shot. The drink was potent enough to redden the cheeks of the patient. "Better take the glasses, put away the drink and open that door now," said Walter. "I don't want to hear it from these people."

"Ahhh...relax, it'll be no problem," Johnny assured. "Let's do one more." After the second shot he returned the glasses and flask to his pockets and reopened the door to the room.

"Hello Walter..." came the faint sounding voice from the hall. Everyone looked toward the open door where there was a frail male patient slowly passing by with the help of a walker.

"Hello numb nuts," said Walter, in a low voice as he flashed a false smile and waved hello to the man who continued walking.

Johnny and Markie laughed at hearing Walter's greeting. "Who the hell is that?" asked Johnny.

"You see that guy? All he does is walk the floor, day and night. Every time he passes this door, he wakes me up by saying hello Walter. I swear to Christ I'm going to put a pillow over him one night!"

Late that night in bed Markie had thoughts of his visit to the hospital. Seeing Walter reminded him of the wayward detective Fishnet Milligan. No one would have thought that Fishnet could recover from the bullet he took from the gun of Red Harris. But if the reports were accurate, his health was miraculously improving. "Go figure," said Markie, "just leave it to a prick like that to beat the odds." He then turned over and went to sleep.

36

The Miracle Man

"As soon as I could move I'm gonna run the wheels of this chair over those fat little sausages she calls toes."

-Bruce "Fishnet" Milligan

SINCE THE WEATHER WAS FAVORABLE, Hope decided to wheel the patient into the yard area of the Staten Island facility. "Let's go outside for some nice sunshine *Mr. Fish-Hook*?" said the nurse's assistant. She spoke loudly with a tendency of shouting her words. "If you don't want to go outside, just blink once for Hope."

Fishnet Milligan disliked Hope. Aside from her tone and clipped manner of speech, he hated the way she bastardized his name. For her comeuppance the former detective banished her to a not so nice section of his fantasy world. He had Hope toiling over burgers on a greasy commercial grill in a windowless kitchen on a boiling summer day. After factoring in a malfunctioning cooling system, Fishnet could be seen smiling as he imagined the salty beads of sweat slide off Hope's brow and mix into the burger juice. The patient might have been physically distressed, but his imagination remained at peak performance.

Hope adjusted the cotton sheet that covered the paralyzed detective's lap. After wheeling Fishnet outside she stopped to have a chat with a grounds keeper, leaving Fishnet exposed to the direct rays of the sun. Unable to speak, he silently seethed as he listened to their piffle.

"Did you hear about what happened to Herman?" Hope asked her friend.

"No, what happened to him?"

"Will you just listen to these two," Fishnet bemoaned internally. "I'm left sitting here in the sun to fry and they're shooting the shit like they're on an air-conditioned bus heading to Saratoga for the races!"

Eventually Hope remembered Fishnet. "Now *Mr. Fish-Hook*, you give me a wink with one eye when you want to go back inside....and no funny business with you blinking both eyes all fast like. It's not nice to confuse Hope—I'm here to help you," she said in her rat-a-tat-tat shouting style. Hope then resumed her conversation with her friend.

"What did I ever do to deserve this bullshit?" he asked himself. "I'll even the score with this one if it's the last thing I do. I'll give her Mr. *Fish-Hook!*"

Since the shootout with Red Harris, Fishnet regained the ability to move several of his fingers and toes. Having made some progress, he no longer doubted that one day he would regain his prior form. His being left facing the sun so perturbed Fishnet that he managed to mutter something. While the words came out more like a slurring gurgle, it nevertheless was a major breakthrough. He had been trying to call Hope a voodoo-worshiping whore. The sound coming from the patient was not inaudible to Hope.

"*MR. FISH-HOOK!*" Hope exclaimed. "Did you just say something?" she asked, genuinely thrilled at the prospect of having heard him speak. "Blink once if you did!" Come on *Fish-Hook* ...blink...blink...I said, BLINK!"

Hope moved close enough to his face that Fishnet thought she just might give him a smack to bring him around. Noting that she was wearing flip-flops instead of her usual white shoes gave him ideas.

"As soon as I could move I'm gonna run the wheels of this chair over those fat little sausages she calls toes," thought Fishnet.

Once it was clear to Hope that she wasn't getting anything out of Fishnet, she wheeled him back to his room. Left alone he calmed down to a point where he was able to once again have pleasant thoughts, like how great the fireflies had it. Wouldn't it be wonderful to cut to the chase by lighting up your nose to signal others that you were looking to get a little?

37

Saddle Up

"We got a line on what really happened to that soldier and it isn't pretty."

Lieutenant Wright

MARKIE AND ALLEY WERE ALMOST home when the sergeant's phone went off. It was Lieutenant Wright calling.

"What's your ETA, Al?"

"I'm a couple of hours out, maybe. It all depends on traffic. What's doing?"

"I need you to debrief a snitch Brooklyn. Can you come in to work?"

"No problem, have Ollie meet me at my apartment in two hours. It'll save time."

"That'll work. Did you ever hear of a guy named Cornell Mathis?"

"Wasn't that the soldier who never came home from a National Guard drill?"

"Yep, that's right. We got a line on what really happened to that soldier and it isn't pretty"

After hanging up, Markie turned to Alley to explain the situation. "I have to go in."

"I gathered as much," she answered.

Markie stepped on the gas. He couldn't wait to get started on his next adventure.

THE END

www.ingramcontent.com/pod-product-compliance
Lightning Source LLC
Chambersburg PA
CBHW072053020726
47501CB00003B/572